"YOU EXPECT ME TO DEPART ON YOUR QUEST. I DO NOT INTEND TO DO SO."

Luc took a step closer and Brianna, remarkably, backed away, her retreat fueling his suspicions. "Why are you so eager to see me gone, my lady?"

"I am not!" she protested, her guilt more than clear.

"Then what difference does it make whether I linger here or not?" Luc asked. "Tell me what you are scheming."

"I simply want you to go on my quest." Brianna looked away, then glanced up at Luc. "Because I like you best," she said, her cheeks flaming.

'Twas so obviously a lie that Luc laughed aloud. "Aye? Then, if you favor me so very much, why not grant me a token of your esteem?"

Brianna blinked. "What kind of token?"

"Your kiss," he said, and then waited for her consent.

A sparkle danced in the emerald depths of her gaze. "One kiss," she whispered breathlessly.

This, he resolved, would be a kiss worth remembering.

PRAISE FOR THE PRINCESS

"Reading *The Princess* is like sipping vintage wine—delectable."

—*Rendezvous*

"Ms. Delacroix conjures up a marvelously beautiful tale of love. Exquisite!"

—*Bell, Book and Candle*

The Princess

Claire Delacroix

A Dell Book

Published by
Dell Publishing
a division of
Bantam Doubleday Dell Publishing Group, Inc.
1540 Broadway
New York, New York 10036

ISBN: 0-440-22603-1

Printed in the United States of America

Published simultaneously in Canada

September 1998

10 9 8 7 6 5 4 3 2 1

OPM

For Angela Catalano,
with thanks.
Again.

Prologue

ULLYMULLAGH COULD NOT BE LOST!

Brianna ran down the corridor, blind to the intricate tapestries hanging on every wall and indifferent to the wondrously fitted stones of her sire's creation. She tripped over her full skirts, cursed with a vehemence that would have made her father scowl, then gathered her embroidered hems by the fistful and ran on.

A deadly silence permeated the keep, a marked contrast to the rumbling of men's voices and clunk of pottery that usually echoed from below.

Brianna's heart began to pound with foreboding. There were men in the hall despite the quiet, she knew it. The smell of wet wool and leather assaulted her nostrils, mixed with the pungency of many mens' scents. There had to be an entire army below.

Yet they stood mute and still.

Tullymullagh had been surrounded these last two weeks, a foreign and unfamiliar banner riding high above the numerous troops. Brianna's father, King Connor of Tullymullagh, had refused to surrender. None had been able to guess why the attackers waited to take the keep, but it had been clear enough their unknown leader waited for something.

Or someone.

Until this very morn. The battle for the gates had been brief but brutal, then silence had claimed the keep. Trepidation could not keep Brianna from needing to see the truth with her own eyes. She took a deep breath and plunged down the stairs to the great hall.

She halted halfway down, stunned by the sea of armored men that filled the hall. They stood shoulder to shoulder, their broad backs confronting her, each and every one oblivious to her arrival. Their gazes were fixed on the dais.

There, Brianna's proud father knelt before a stranger, his silver mane falling forward to obscure his expression. His voice carried clearly, though, his solemn tone making a hard lump of dismay rise in Brianna's throat. She could hear her sire's heartbreak echo in his very words.

The tale that had carried to her rooms *was* true.

"I, Connor of Tullymullagh, concede my ancestral holding of Tullymullagh and its environs, including Castle Tullymullagh, its gardens and fields, village and mill, as well as the Priory of Endlist, to—"

"Nay!" Brianna cried. "Father, you cannot do this!"

The trio of unfamiliar men on the dais turned as one to face her, but Brianna had eyes only for her father. When he lifted his head, she was horrified to see how severely he had aged on this day.

Brianna knew Tullymullagh was everything to him, and she could not let him cast it aside—for any price. A king in his own right, Connor of Tullymullagh had reigned over his ancestral holding with pride for twenty long and prosperous years, his sire even longer before him. And Connor had built the very keep they stood within.

'Twas doubly his by right.

"Father, do not surrender! Promise *anything,* but, I beg of you, do not abandon Tullymullagh!"

The other men, the ranks of unfamiliar mercenaries and knights who filled her father's hall, turned to seek the source of the interruption. Brianna's cheeks burned with awareness of their appraisal, well aware that the golden mane that was her pride hung loose like a sunlit cloud.

Her father had oft said those very locks would snare a man in desire and indeed, he forbade Brianna to leave her chambers with it unbound. Too late, she realized that her fitted emerald surcoat showed her slender curves to an advantage, and one that was unwise given the circumstances. Indeed, the wide embroidered belt that slung over her hips might draw a man's eye too quickly to Brianna's narrow waist.

Only now did Brianna perceive the luxury found within the walls of a secure household. Only now, when that protection was gone, did she see the merit of what she had long taken for granted.

These men were soldiers of war, well used to partaking of the spoils of battle. She saw the truth in their hardened faces, saw a glimmer within the eye of more than one that made her shiver.

But Brianna was not one to cower before a challenge. She lifted her chin, determined to let no one see her newfound fear.

Connor's lips twisted ruefully at her plea. "I have no choice, child," he said quietly, though the resonance of his words carried easily to Brianna's ears. "We have been soundly defeated by the king's own vassal."

King.

Brianna looked belatedly to the trio of men on the dais with her sire. The man whom her father knelt before wore a simple gold circlet over his fair hair. The rings on his fingers and the splendor of his mail revealed his noble status. The telling Plantagenet insignia on the banner hoisted above the high table, those three golden lions of Anjou, made his identity most clear.

Connor granted Tullymullagh to the very hand of King Henry II of England.

His vassal. Brianna's gaze danced over the pair of men who stood alongside Henry. She guessed that one or both of them had been responsible for the seige upon her home. The dark-haired man to the king's left looked every inch the jaded Norman knight. The older man beside the knight was clearly a roughened mercenary of common origins.

The mercenary, Brianna noted with annoyance, was looking about the hall with a decidedly avaricious gleam in his eye. His heavy face was tanned and lined, the mark of countless years both in the sun and the alehouse. His armor was sturdy and well-used, the leather of his gloves slick with age. His eyes were small and shone greedily, his lips drawn so tight as to have disappeared.

Aye, this was a mercenary whose allegiance was bought and sold—for a hefty price.

A mercenary who had been sent to win Tullymullagh for the English king. This could only be the man whose alien banner had fluttered in the breeze while he awaited his overlord.

An overlord who would steal all Brianna's father held dear.

Brianna would have her say first. "But you cannot surrender Tullymullagh!"

Connor shook his head. "We fought valiantly, child, but lost. There is naught else to be done." His eyes flashed a warning that Brianna did not miss. " 'Tis beyond fair that this righteous king does not see us all dead for greeting his vassal with swords."

Brianna eyed the army within the hall and understood. Submit or die had been her sire's choice. 'Twas unfair!

"And who," Henry demanded with a coy quirk of his brow, "might this vision of loveliness be?"

Brianna bridled, but bit her tongue, valiantly trying to keep her silence. Men who composed flattery easily were seldom sincere.

Holding her tongue, however, was not a talent that came readily to Brianna. She struggled against the urge to tell this king precisely what she thought of him and his vassal.

"This is my daughter, Brianna," her father said proudly, his introduction one more suited to the leisure of a social gathering. "My *only* daughter," he added, no doubt also seeing the gleam that brightened the king's eye.

Brianna glared back at the king. Aye, Henry was known to have an appreciation for women. Indeed, none other than the legendary beauty Eleanor of Aquitaine warmed his own bed.

Though the English king was seldom found within it.

"And a beauty she is," Henry conceded. He smiled, but Brianna stood stiffly and did not respond. "I had heard that the Rose of Tullymullagh was beyond fair, but never guessed such beauty could truly exist."

Connor straightened and inhaled sharply. "She is *not* a spoil of battle," he declared with new steel in his tone.

Henry turned to Brianna's father with feigned surprise. "Connor! You surprise me with your mistrust!"

But Connor's eyes burned with anger and his voice throbbed low. "Should any man be fool enough to despoil my daughter, I shall hunt him down and see he has naught with which to repeat the deed."

A murmur of uneasiness slid through the assembly of men at that declaration. The king looked at Brianna, who folded her arms across her chest.

"Provided his weapon survives the deed itself," she added, putting enough emphasis on the word "weapon" to make the men fidget anew. Brianna had never been one to stand by and let the fates decide any matter for her—and she would not begin now.

Whether the conquering king approved or not.

Henry cleared his throat. The men near her sidled away from the base of the stairs, granting her slightly more room. Henry watched their move, then summoned a smile that did not fool Brianna.

Henry had a scheme, she would wager, and 'twas not one that either she or her father would like.

"You must think my men base curs to even make such a charge," he said smoothly.

Neither Brianna nor her father argued the point.

A frown momentarily marred the king's brow, then he waved a hand dismissively. "But, I cannot take a man to task for holding his only child so dear. On the other hand, I see no reason not to use any available asset to ensure the stability we now need."

The king gestured impatiently for Connor to rise. "Consider yourself divested of Castle Tullymullagh and its properties," he said curtly. "I will accept your pledge of allegiance with all the others."

Brianna bit back her gasp of outrage, but Henry waved smoothly to the older mercenary. "And you, Gavin Fitzgerald, as a result of your loyal service to both me and my family, shall have this prize keep to call your own."

This was the man who would be granted her stolen home? *This* was the man who would reign in her sire's stead? 'Twas unacceptable! What could this man know of good governance? The mercenary grinned outright, revealing at least one missing tooth, as Brianna simmered.

"I thank you, my lord, for this token of your generosity," he muttered and bowed awkwardly. His left leg stuck out stiffly, as though he had been lamed.

But then the king pivoted to face Brianna, his bright gaze

seeming to read her rebellious thoughts and cared little for them.

What plan did Henry have in store for her?

"And fear not, Connor. Your wish shall be fulfilled," he declared with a decisiveness that made Brianna dread what he might say. "Your lovely daughter will not be *wasted* in all of this."

The mercenary grinned. Brianna's heart skipped a beat and a horrible suspicion rose in her mind.

Before any could ask, Henry continued. "Brianna's hand in marriage will seal together old and new, by my dictate."

Marriage? To that mercenary? Not so long as Brianna drew breath!

"You cannot wed me to that old goat! You cannot bend me to your will in this!" The words were out before Brianna could consider the wisdom of uttering them. She crossed the room with furious steps, the men in the hall parting before her anger, and halted before both dais and king.

She jabbed her finger toward a king who looked decidedly displeased. "I will *not* wed this man and you cannot make me!"

The fighting men chuckled at her obvious distaste, but the king did not smile.

"On the contrary," Henry agreed too easily for Brianna's comfort. "I suspect Margaux de Montvieux would not take kindly to her husband accepting another bride." He arched a brow. "And Margaux is not a woman whose spite I would think it wise to cultivate."

Gavin flushed at Henry's comment, but Brianna had no interest in whatever marital troubles he—or the king—might have.

Indeed, it appeared that she would soon have some of her own.

"Then, who will you force me to wed?" Brianna demanded when the king did not continue quickly enough for her taste. She hoped against hope that her fear did not show in her voice.

"Gavin's son." Henry smiled coldly. "Of course."

And in that very moment, Brianna guessed the ebony-haired knight's claim to a position on the dais.

When she turned to look at him, that man bowed low with a grace alien to his sire. "Chevalier Burke de Montvieux, at your service," he said in a voice that might have been pleasant enough under other circumstances.

Not only did Brianna have very definite ideas about marriage, but this scheme did not fit with them at all. She had decided long ago to follow her parents' example and wed for love alone.

Time 'twas to make her feelings clear.

Brianna squared her shoulders and looked the king dead in the eye. "I cannot wed a stranger! I will not wed this man, simply because of your dictate."

"You have little choice," the king retorted, his lips thinning with impatience.

"Father?" Brianna appealed, well aware that her father had never before denied her anything she had requested.

To her horror, Connor shook his head. "I can do naught in this, child. The king's will must be the way."

Brianna was not prepared to make that concession. Her thoughts flew like quicksilver as she sought some escape from this quandary.

The king had said that she had little choice, but Brianna would make as much of it as she could. She looked at this Gavin and knew instinctively that he was a man to deny himself naught, whether he was wed to a virago or not.

Aye, Brianna suspected his seed was spread far and wide.

'Twas a remote chance but the best one she had. Brianna took a deep breath, crossed her fingers, and hoped her suspicion proved right. She turned to the hardened mercenary and summoned every grace she had ever learned.

"I mean no offense, sir, but is this man your *only* son?"

"Brianna!" Her father chided her rudeness, but to Brianna's delight, Gavin shuffled his feet and did not respond. A dull red rose over his ears and his lips thinned. Gavin glanced at the knight beside him, thence to the king, his mood clearly less than prime.

"Surely," Henry commented drily, "you have not forgotten the number of your own progeny, Gavin?"

The mercenary fired a glance of loathing at Brianna. "My lord, I truly believe that this match is one best made by Burke—"

The king interrupted crisply. "But I choose to indulge the lady. She has, after all, a certain charm."

Brianna ignored the fleeting smile the king sent in her direction.

"But, my lord," Gavin stepped forward with obvious consternation. "Rowan travels with my lady wife and I know not where they are these days."

"Then you shall find them," the king retorted. "Immediately."

"My wife may protest. She is quite attached to Rowan."

Henry straightened and his tone was chilling. "Rest assured, Gavin Fitzgerald, that if Margaux de Montvieux has an argument with this arrangement, she may pursue the matter with me." Henry arched a regal brow. "Am I understood?"

"Yes, my lord. Of course, my lord. 'Twill be done immediately, my lord. Rowan shall be summoned at your dictate, my lord." And Gavin bowed not once but twice to show his obeisance.

Fawning cur.

"And?" the king asked archly.

Gavin failed to contrive an innocent expression. *"And,* my lord?"

Henry's smile faded as he eyed his vassal. "Are you not forgetting someone else?" he asked sharply.

Once more, Gavin colored deeply. "I truly do not believe, my lord, that 'twould be appropriate—"

"The lady has requested a choice—" Henry's tone was harsh "—and she shall have the choice of all *three* of your sons, regardless of your beliefs about the matter."

Three?

"You have *three* sons?" Connor asked quietly.

"Aye," Gavin conceded with evident reluctance. "There is also the eldest, Luc."

"The eldest?" Connor echoed and drew himself up at this affront. Indeed, he once again looked the proud warrior Brianna knew and her heart danced at the sight. Connor fixed Gavin with the cold eye for which he was reputed far and wide. "There is an *elder* son than these two?"

Gavin nodded unwillingly. "But—"

"But *naught!"* Connor turned that glare upon Henry in turn. "You would dishonor my daughter by not wedding her to the eldest son, to the heir? What travesty is this? What mockery do you make of me in my defeat?"

"It matters little, in truth," Gavin protested with unexpected fervor. "Burke is my heir."

Why would the second son be heir? Brianna was curious despite herself. Why did Gavin prefer to forget this eldest son?

Was he bastard-born?

"Connor," Henry interjected, evidently intending to be the voice of reason. "In truth, Burke is the greater heir, though he is indeed the second son. His mother's holding of Montvieux in Normandy is a wealthy one and is destined to pass to him."

"Normandy?" Brianna echoed with horror. "But what about Tullymullagh?"

"Dare I hope that your generosity should provide for my son to inherit Tullymullagh after me, my lord?" Gavin inquired of the king with a deep bow.

Brianna barely kept her lip from curling. She had never seen a man grovel like a dog awaiting scraps from the table—indeed, she would not have tolerated such behavior even from Tullymullagh's hounds!

"Of course," Henry agreed. He flicked a small smile to Brianna. "However, I see no harm in letting the lady choose between all of your sons." His gaze was openly assessing and Brianna's ire rose that he spoke of her as though she were not present. "She appears to be one more easily managed when occasionally given her way."

Brianna felt her cheeks flush scarlet at this assessment. Oh, she would see that her acquiescence was not easily won!

"Then, I shall send word to both sons." Gavin made another painful bow.

The king turned his piercing glance upon Brianna with an abruptness that made her fear he had heard her thoughts. "Think well how you will choose between these men, Brianna of Tullymullagh," he counselled sternly, "for you will know none of them any better than you do now. I have indulged you, as doubtless your father has done many times before me, but do not mistake kindness for weakness."

Brianna straightened as she stared proudly back at the king. She was not a slow-witted child to be lectured by some foreign king bent on humiliating her father.

"And I would suggest, my lord," she countered with all the sweetness of fresh honey, "that you not mistake concession for submission."

Her father inhaled sharply, but Henry's lips quirked with reluctant amusement. He eyed her for a long moment, then turned away. " 'Tis with regret that I must abandon matters here just as they become interesting, but duty summons me on to Cashel."

"We shall miss your august presence, my lord," Gavin declared.

The king slanted the older man a wry glance. "Do not fear for your prize, Gavin. I shall invest you with Tullymullagh this very day." He turned to Brianna. "Lady Brianna? Will you grace these ceremonies with your presence?"

How dare he ask her to watch her father's defeat?

"I will not bear witness to such injustice," Brianna snapped, then spun on her heel and stalked back up the stairs. The king's mocking laughter taunted her, and she loathed how quickly Gavin echoed his sovereign's mirth.

They would not steal Tullymullagh away from her sire, Brianna resolved as she stormed down the corridor. Somehow, in some way, Brianna would thwart their plans. She would wed *none* of Gavin's sons.

Brianna stopped short, suddenly recalling the king's words. He had called this a contest for her hand.

A *contest*.

Could she truly ensure there was no victor in this contest? Aye! If Brianna set terms upon the resolution, the brothers would have to meet them. 'Twould be just like a bard's tale, the princess demanding that a trio of suitors compete to earn her favor.

And, indeed, if she could think of a challenge that was fiendishly difficult, it might well be that none of the sons would complete it.

The very idea made Brianna smile for the first time that day. She must devise some test of valor, some ordeal of great proportions that would ensure she did not have to make this loveless match in the end.

Indeed, if the quest were demanding enough, that old mercenary could draw his last breath before all was resolved. 'Twas true that Gavin did not look to have many years left in his sorry hide.

And if all three brothers failed, the rulership of Tullymullagh could revert to her sire. Aye, 'twould only be sensible, if the conqueror died and Connor had pledged fealty to England's king.

Perfect.

Brianna's maid burst from her chambers in that moment. Fenella was the dark-haired daughter of a distant cousin, sent to Tullymullagh a year past to learn matters of a household. She was perhaps overly inclined to giggle, and one to give too much credit to news gleaned in the kitchens.

But now, her dark eyes were wide with uncertainty, her expression distraught. "My lady, is it true?"

"Aye, Fenella," Brianna admitted, slipping an arm over the girl's shoulders when they sagged with defeat. She felt a surge of confidence in her fledgling plan and gave the maid's shoulders a minute squeeze.

"Do not fret, Fenella," she declared. "They may have claimed Tullymullagh, but we are not defeated yet."

The hope that dawned in the maid's expression was all the encouragement Brianna needed. She would win her way in this—for her father and all those who looked at him for protection.

'Twould only be right.

Chapter One

November 1171

*L*UC FITZGAVIN CAME TO TULLYMULLAGH UNDER protest, his displeasure with that fact rising with every mile of the road that passed beneath him.

'Twas true that Gavin not only knew the perfect bait to lure his eldest son, but only the manipulative old mercenary had had the audacity to use it. The Welsh barony of Llanvelyn hung in the balance.

Again.

Indeed, Luc told himself that he would not have left Llanvelyn for any lesser price. He refused to consider either how his restlessness had grown in recent years or how much he had enjoyed the long voyage to Ireland.

Luc had pledged, after all, to live a simple life at Llanvelyn for the rest of his days. He was quite certain he only answered his father's bidding to set matters to rights. And this time, Luc intended to see the seal of Llanvelyn safe within his own hand before he returned to his chosen home.

On principle alone, Luc was prepared to dislike everything about Tullymullagh, no less its spoiled princess. But the first sight of Tullymullagh's high square tower awakened an unexpected admiration within Luc.

'Twas a feeling he would have preferred to be without, and it did naught to improve his mood.

But Tullymullagh—oblivious to Luc's desires—remained perfectly nestled in the green hills of the valley. A river wrapped around its curtain wall, as though the keep were one with the land and had always been there. The tall tower stretched to the sky as though it would etch the clouds with the cross on its summit. The mist was rising from the river, wreathing the walls in gossamer, and the sunlight, piercing through the mist like a spear, painted rainbows in the air.

Luc could not help but be impressed. He had seen many keeps in his days, he had called many his home, but he had never glimpsed the like of Tullymullagh.

As he eyed the majesty of the keep, Luc became aware of the simplicity of his own garb, his lack of retinue, the humbleness of his steed. Luc had no sword, no mail, no fine tabard upon his back.

For the first time in eleven years, Luc felt the absence of all he had cast aside.

But that was nonsense! He had made a choice and he would live with it! Luc scowled and dug his heels into his palfrey, refusing to think about the spurs that no longer adorned his heels.

This Tullymullagh would show its weakness soon enough. Was its princess not a woman who could see no further than her own entertainment? Aye! What manner of woman would summon all to do her bidding on a matter of such ridiculous whimsy as *marriage?*

Luc snorted. Marriage, after all, was at the root of all of his father's troubles. Three sons borne by three different women, all manner of difficulties throughout the years. Far too much trouble for a sensible man. Women were a delight, but Luc had seen enough to know that marriage was for fools.

Fools like Gavin Fitzgerald.

Nay, the sooner Luc found his misguided sire and obtained Llanvelyn's seal, the sooner he could return to the simple life he knew he craved.

• • •

TIME DID NOT reveal the flaws Luc was certain Tullymullagh must hide. The high vaulted hall was simple, yet gracious; the richly embroidered tapestries hanging on the walls were beyond elegant. The stone fireplaces at either end of the hall were carved with marvelous skill, the linen adorning the dais table was rich.

Indeed, this tangible reminder of all he had abandoned made simple, charming Llanvelyn seem a paltry prize. Luc cursed his own traitorous thoughts and scanned the contents of the hall with disapproval.

There had to be some slight he could dislike.

Certainly, the lines of knights, even their squires and pages, were outfitted in fine fashion. Their armor gleamed, and their tabards were lavishly embroidered. Luc supposed they were all pledged to his sire's hand, regardless of what loyalty they felt within their hearts. His sire, however foolish with women, was not one to be remiss in matters of such tactical import.

Just the thought of his father was a welcome reminder of how brutal the nobility could be, regardless of how fine their quarters. Luc, scanning the hall for some sign of Gavin, still did not see the man. 'Twas no coincidence that his sire avoided him thus far, Luc knew well enough.

Gavin would see his own desire fulfilled first. The nobility, after all, cared for themselves alone. Luc's lips thinned.

If naught else, 'twas clear that if this Princess Brianna desired attention, she had gained her full measure on this day. Not only was the hall packed to capacity, but all were garbed in their richest finery. Damask gleamed on all sides, the lustre of silk shot through more than one garment, feath-

ers bobbed and jewels flashed. Though Luc's simple clothing was his best, it paled in comparison.

But he did not care.

He *would* not care.

Luc spotted the familiar crest of Montvieux and guessed
that his brother would know Gavin's whereabouts. As he
strode across the hall, Luc noted that Burke had changed
little over the years since last their paths had crossed.
Broader of shoulder than he had been all those years past,
with a few threads of silver at his temple, Burke had, if
anything, grown yet more handsome.

Which was reassuring. This troublesome princess would
not be able to resist Burke, Luc decided. She would take one
look at the three of them and melt with desire for the noble,
chivalrous, prosperous Burke. Then, Luc would settle the
issue of Llanvelyn with Gavin and head home in short order.

To ensure the sheaves were stacked properly. Luc pushed
that prospect of delight from his mind, and looked hopefully
for his father's shadow behind the favored son. He was only
to be disappointed.

But Burke smiled and closed the distance between them,
lithe grace in his every step. "Greetings, Luc, 'tis long since
we have met."

"Indeed." Luc shook the proffered hand. His brother's
grip was sure, and he felt again that old admiration that
Burke had steered his course well through waters Luc had
chosen not to navigate. "How fares your dame, Margaux?"

"Well enough. And Llanvelyn?"

Luc nodded. "The season was a good one. Have you seen
Gavin?"

"Not yet this day." Burke turned his gaze, assessing as he
glanced over Luc's garb. "I could lend you a tabard, if you
desire."

Luc shook his head stubbornly. His linen shirt was clean,

his green wool tabard and darker green hose were unadorned, but suited his life well. His leather boots were
rougher than Burke's, which doubtless had been fashioned
in some Italian city, but were functional.

Even without spurs.

"There is no need," Luc declined firmly, refusing to give
any credence to a whisper in the back of his mind. "I am
what I am. The woman might as well see as much."

Burke smiled wryly. "And may the best man win her
hand?"

"And may *you* win her hand," Luc corrected, seeing no
risk in letting his true feelings show. "And quickly, if you
please. Llanvelyn awaits my return."

Burke frowned. "I understood there was a steward there."

"Pyrs died two years past." Luc's words were curt, the
only sign of how deeply the old man's passing had affected
him.

Burke watched him for a long moment, but Luc frowned
and looked again for his father.

"And you have no regrets in the choice you once made,"
Burke finally commented, his idle tone not disguising his
interest.

"I?" Luc shook his head and his words were emphatic.
"Nary a one."

A gleam of appreciation lit Burke's eye. "Who would
have imagined such a simple life would suit you?"

"It suited my mother and her family well enough."

"Hmmm. So, here you stand, garbed like a farmer amidst
wealth and privilege, untroubled by the disparity." There
was a note of mild wonder in Burke's tone. "You are a
nobler man than I, Luc Fitzgavin."

Luc smiled. "I doubt that."

Burke's gaze was steady as he smiled slightly himself.

"The most astonishing thing is that you begrudge me naught."

Luc shrugged easily, never having seen any reason to be jealous of his brother's many accomplishments. "We are different men, Burke, born of different women, raised in different ways. 'Tis only good sense that our lives should differ as well."

"Once they did not," Burke noted softly. Luc stiffened at the reminder and looked away, but Burke would not leave it be. "You could have won all I call my own by now, or perhaps more, if you had not given up your blade." A lump rose in Luc's throat but he kept his expression grim. "Luc, you have to know that your talent was rare," Burke added.

"Perhaps." Luc cleared his throat. "But 'twas not a life that suited me as well as it evidently does you."

"Is that the truth?" Burke glanced away, dissatisfaction in the line of his lips. 'Twas not an expression Luc had seen upon Burke's visage before, but a fanfare of trumpets sounded before he could ask after it.

The assembly turned as one to face the dais. Tullymullagh's elderly steward appeared at Luc's elbow, tsking under his breath. "Quickly, quickly! Over here, both of you. Now, where is the third? There must be a third!"

The steward clucked his tongue, anxiously eyeing the assembly. The crowd fell back behind the two brothers, just as that sought-after third man joined the pair, his russet hair gleaming.

Rowan. Luc flicked a curious glance to his youngest brother, as tall and handsome as ever. Luc was surprised to see that Rowan's usual cavalier smile was lacking.

'Twas clear that Rowan was here against his own desire, as well. Luc's lips thinned at the reminder, and he folded his arms across his chest at the inconvenience wreaked upon them all.

"There!" the steward crowed. "Now, come along, come along, we must not keep Princess Brianna waiting on this day of days."

She could not wait, but they had been compelled to travel long and far to serve her will. The spoiled princess of Tullymullagh had indeed made all dance to her willful tune.

Luc imagined a sullen and demanding woman, pointing petulantly to all she desired and winning it each time. She was likely ancient and unable to make a fitting match in any way other than this frivolous game. Or pretty but with the wits of a stone, insistent that all made her the center of attention.

The center of attention she would evidently be on this day, at least. Luc folded his arms across his chest and impatiently waited out the moments until he could consult with his sire.

The minstrels plucked a tune and every head lifted in anticipation. A bevy of maidens burst into the hall, spilling flowers to the left and the right, their hair bedecked with ribbons. New garments for this very day, Luc concluded, disgusted with the cavalier waste of hard coin.

"The lady Brianna," bellowed the steward, "Princess of Tullymullagh!"

With that, the most beautiful woman Luc had ever seen stepped through the portal into the hall. The princess smiled shyly as she descended the stairs from the solar. She stepped on to the dais with the grace of a swan, and Luc's protesting thoughts screamed to a halt.

Luc stared, for he could have done naught else.

Brianna was the perfect, tiny fairy queen of Pyrs' bedtime tales. Luc had never imagined that such beauty could exist outside of fanciful stories and was clutched with a desire so primal that it curled his toes.

Indeed, the admiration flooding through Luc put his response to Tullymullagh to shame.

Luc's heart began to pound as he sought some flaw or hint that he had named her wrong. But nay. The lady Brianna's face grew only more fair as he looked longer upon it. Her hands were as delicate as butterflies, her skin as creamy as new milk. Her smile was heart-wrenchingly innocent, her cheeks flushed slightly with attention of all fixed upon her. Her green surcoat was laced tightly at the sides and revealed her slender curves.

Luc could imagine her curled up to sleep in a flower bud all too readily.

She was not at all the woman he had anticipated.

Luc swallowed and reminded himself that *this* was the selfish woman who would make them all do her bidding. No doubt her temperament was an unattractive one and her heart as dark as her face was fair. She would be selfish and indulged, slow of intellect. This was not a woman given to conversation or likely even one who would permit her loveliness to be marred by the rigors of childbirth.

Even knowing that, Luc could not cease his staring.

"She is a beauty," he whispered in wonder, without even meaning to do so.

"I suppose." Burke shrugged with an indifference that Luc found hard to match. "But beauty is as beauty does."

Aye, 'twas much Luc's own conclusion and reassuring to have Burke give the thought voice. He glanced at his brother. "But you will still wed her when she chooses you?"

Burke flicked a telling look Luc's way. "You presume much, Luc."

"Do not be so modest, Burke." Rowan's murmured comment barely carried to their ears. "If she has not the wits to make a sensible choice, no doubt there are those who will make the decision for her."

Rowan looked at Luc and that familiar roguish twinkle

glinted in his dark eyes. "She will choose neither a farmer nor a bastard rogue, of that you may be certain," the man continued. "Nay, Burke, 'twill be you burdened with the duty of deflowering this beauty."

The very thought made Luc's heart clench in a most unexpected manner. What was wrong with him? Women never had such an effect upon him. Had he caught some ague upon the ship?

That would be another inconvenience to lay at this lady's feet. Luc's lips thinned grimly, and he looked back to the perfection of the princess. To his own surprise, annoyance toward his brother Burke stirred to life within him for the very first time in all his days.

'Twould be Burke who would meet this beauty at the altar; Burke who would bed her; Burke who would look upon her lovely face for the rest of her days. It did not seem right that Burke did not appreciate her allure.

As Luc would have done.

That thought brought Luc up short. How could such senselessness invade his thoughts? He folded his arms across his chest and glared at the lovely noblewoman, deeming her responsible for addling his wits.

Brianna looked over to the brothers with open curiosity. She would not even glance at him, Luc well knew. Aye, she would weigh her choices by their outward appearance, caring naught for the inner man. 'Twould be Burke's evident wealth and success that would draw her eye, Luc knew it.

What he did not know was why that troubled him so.

The lady looked at Rowan and smiled with a politeness that wrenched Luc's heart. She looked at Burke and he was certain her gaze brightened with the surety of the choice she must make.

Then she glanced at Luc. A jolt ripped through him as

their eyes met. Her full lips parted ever so slightly and Luc had the distinct sense that they were the only two in the hall.

And Brianna smiled, the gesture curving her lips as slowly as dawn slips over the horizon. Luc could not bring himself to look away.

'Twas suddenly cursedly warm.

Luc knew well enough that he was not a handsome man, though neither was he that hard upon the eyes. He was tall enough and his shoulders were broad enough, though his features lacked the chiseled perfection of Burke's profile.

Indeed, Luc was possessed of a grand nose.

And a shock of white, white hair above his right brow. Pyrs had called it a mark of uncommon fortune; Gavin dismissed it as a curse. Otherwise Luc was dark of hair and blue of eye and not particularly distinctive to his own thinking. 'Twas clearly the oddities of his appearance that held the woman's gaze.

Perhaps he should have accepted Burke's offer of finer garb.

"Ladies and lords, damsels and knights," Brianna began, her voice pitched lower than Luc had expected. 'Twas quite a pleasant voice, actually, and hinted at a cleverness unexpected.

The assembly applauded politely, but Luc could not move. Indeed, it seemed Brianna addressed him directly, though Luc could not imagine why.

'Twas Burke she would choose, after all. And he would be glad to see the matter resolved.

"I bid you welcome to the keep of Tullymullagh," Brianna said with a minute nod at Luc. "And I hope the hospitality of the hall has not failed you." She held his gaze for a long moment, as though inquiring after his own treatment and Luc found himself nodding ever so slightly.

Her smile broadened as though she were pleased and Luc's heart skipped in a most unexpected way.

Aye, a chill from the ship. It could be no more than that.

"On this day, many have gathered in the hopes of witnessing a wedding, but I fear I must disappoint you all." Brianna smiled into Luc's eyes, a vision of feminine softness, as though inviting him alone to indulge her.

And he was sorely tempted to grant this princess whatever she desired. Luc scowled at his own gullibility. An agitated murmur rippled through the crowd and he belatedly understood the princess' words.

"You were bidden to choose a spouse from my sons!" Gavin declared, stepping into view for the first time. The steward frowned, but Gavin shoved his way to Brianna's side.

Luc was not surprised to see that his father's rough manner had changed little. He took a half step forward, but the lady gave Gavin a quelling look.

"Which does not ensure the wedding be performed on this day," she declared with resolve. She tossed back her veil, the move revealing the end of a blond braid, then fixed the trio of brothers with a bright glance.

And she looked again to Luc. His mouth went dry to be so singled out. "I will take no man to wed who has not proven himself to me," Brianna declared. "As I know naught of the three of you beyond your pedigree—" her expression and quick glance to Gavin made her opinion of that clear "—I can only grant a fitting test of your suitability as spouse."

The murmur became a growl as the assembly exchanged comments on this unforeseen development. They had come for a wedding and were to be cheated of it.

But Luc found himself surprisingly intrigued. Perhaps he had been too quick to condemn the lady's intellect.

And that alone was most interesting.

Brianna raised her voice with determination over the rumbling, clearly not one to be cowed by dissent around her. "I challenge you each to go forth into the world and bring me a gift that will persuade me of the honor of your intent."

A *gift?* Luc's dawning estimation of the lady dropped like a rock falling from a cliff. Trust a spoiled woman to base her choice on the richness of gifts!

"A gift?" Gavin roared. "You cannot do this thing! You cannot change the arrangement!"

This time, Brianna's glance was positively scathing. "I will *not* wed a stranger, especially one with no regard for me." She pivoted to glare at the brothers anew, her words spoken with crisp authority. "I bid you bring me a gift that will make me laugh. He who makes me laugh loudest and longest, I shall willingly take as my husband."

The crowd gasped as one, then broke out in excited chatter as the princess swept regally from the hall.

A gift to make her *laugh?*

Luc blinked in astonishment and his opinion of Brianna changed course yet again. 'Twas unexpected indeed.

Brianna was not the foolish woman Luc had expected, even if she was careless about interfering in the lives of others. Indeed, her request showed not only wit but a rare determination to affect her own fate. Few women would have been so bold as to make such a demand.

The last of Brianna's maidens disappeared up the stairs just as Gavin came to life. "You cannot do this thing!" he raged.

A silver-haired man shook his head and stepped regally into Gavin's path. " 'Tis already done," he said simply.

"I am the new Lord of Tullymullagh!" Gavin bellowed, launching into a characteristic tantrum. Rowan rolled his eyes. Gavin's manner was in marked contrast to the composed and gracious man who opposed him. "I am in charge of this keep! And I demand that your daughter return to the hall. I command her to make her choice this very day from my three sons!''

The older man shook his head with quiet resolve. Indeed, a faint shadow of a smile lurked upon his lips. ''My daughter will do no such thing.''

This then was the king Gavin had ousted.

''I shall compel her to do my will!'' Gavin pushed past the former lord of the keep. The old king fell back against the wall, clearly surprised by Gavin's forceful move, though his eyes blazed with anger. The steward swore and dove to steady his master, even while Gavin darted up the stairs.

Steward and former king glared disapproval as Gavin muttered unpleasantries. The last of the maidens looked back, squeaked and lunged skyward. She disappeared through the portal.

And the door closed behind her with a resounding slam.

Gavin fell upon the wrought iron handle just as there was a click of a bolt sliding home. The old king unsuccessfully tried to hide his smile, though the steward did not even try. Rowan chuckled outright.

Luc could not help but be amused himself by the lady's foresight. 'Twas not often that anyone bested his sire. Indeed, 'twas not often that anyone even tried, for Gavin's lust for vengeance over the smallest slight was renowned.

'Twas clear the lady Brianna did not guess the manner of foe she engaged. An unexpected protectiveness surged within Luc, but he shoved it aside, knowing such sentiment had no place here.

He was, after all, a knight no longer. Damsels in distress had best look elsewhere for their champions.

And, no doubt, this lovely lady's champions were legion.

All the same, 'twas clear that though she might be willful, this noblewoman had much experience in seeing her own wishes rule the day. Luc glanced over the hall, intrigued at how many were caught in the snare of her desires.

But he would not join their numbers.

Indeed, her challenge had ensured that Luc be gone from Llanvelyn even longer than expected. Should Burke linger over this task, Luc might not be able to return home before the spring. The very sowing could be interrupted. Not one harvest but two could be jeopardized!

Curse the woman for her demand!

Gavin shook the handle of the door. "I demand admission to these chambers! I insist that the lady Brianna choose her spouse immediately!"

Gavin pounded on the heavy oak door to no avail as the whispers rose to a crescendo in the hall. Finally, Luc's father turned to confront the sea of upturned faces, his face turned ruddy with embarrassment.

"She has locked the door," he confessed unnecessarily.

"Aye," the former king agreed without surprise. "And she will not descend before your agreement."

A chuckle rippled through the assembly and Luc noted how many eyes shone with interest. Truly, they had witnessed more than expected on this day. Gavin stalked back down the stairs like an unhappy toddler and glared at the former king.

He looked over the assembly and his lips thinned before he confronted the old king anew. "I will wait her out! She cannot stay up there forever!" He pounded his fist into his other hand. "I will not permit this disrespect!"

"She can remain there for quite a while," her father said mildly. "Brianna oft lays in provisions before staging such a feat."

Gavin's face turned yet more red. "This insolence is intolerable! Her deeds are a direct violation of King Henry's will!"

His eyes narrowed dangerously and he took a step closer to the old king, his voice low with threat. "Perhaps hearing that her sire was in the dungeons would prompt the lady to change her mind."

The old king inhaled sharply, but he had no chance to speak.

Burke cleared his throat and all looked at him as one. "The king did grant her the right to choose," he commented smoothly.

Gavin glared at his prized son. For his part, Luc was amazed that Burke should encourage the lady's whim.

Brianna had found an unlikely ally, indeed.

But Burke glanced mildly over the assembly. "And I remind you all that King Henry, after all, did not specify that Brianna make her choice on this very day."

Luc blinked. Could it be that Burke truly did not want to wed this beautiful woman?

Gavin's lip curled. "Do you then accept the whim of a mere woman as your command?"

Burke shrugged. "I see little harm in the lady's test of character. Indeed, whoever wins her hand might well gain her heart as well."

The old king beamed at this chivalrous sentiment. Luc watched his father noting this glance and saw that man's mind change in a heartbeat.

"If Burke declares the challenge a just one, then the lady's challenge will stand," Gavin declared.

"To the quest!" the old king called with decided vigor.

"How good to know that you still can do no wrong," Rowan murmured with no small measure of irony. Burke ignored the comment. It had always been thus between these two, but Luc bore Burke no ill will.

Indeed, he would not have wanted the burden of fulfilling

Gavin's lofty ambitions, a burden that Burke carried so effortlessly.

Hundreds of fists punched the air in that moment, the gathered souls stomped their feet and applauded their approval.

"To the quest for a bride!" they roared, no doubt delighted at the tale they would have to recount to others. Several minstrels already huddled together, one plucking a tentative tune on his lute.

"To the bride quest!"

The hall erupted into cheers, the assembly forming an avenue of their own accord for the brothers to depart. They began to chant, their eyes bright upon the brothers as they clapped together.

"The bride quest! The bride quest!"

Gavin fixed his sons with a stern eye. "Away with you, then!" he cried with a wave of his hand. "Search far and wide for a trinket to make the lady laugh!"

The chanting grew yet louder and Burke bowed low to both Brianna's father and his own. Luc followed suit, though he noted Burke's easy grace with unfamiliar envy. Luc even began to consider what might tempt the lady to laugh before he caught himself.

Marriage was not on his agenda, after all, no matter how clever or lovely the lady Brianna might be.

Aye, the sooner Burke returned with his prize, the better to Luc's mind. He forced himself to think of crops and harvests and matters of good sense—as dull as they were in comparison to a certain blade-bright princess—as the threesome strode through the cheering throng and out into the courtyard.

And there, the sadly neglected orchard of Tullymullagh caught the late afternoon sunlight.

Luc paused to look. There was no shortage of weeds tangled about the fruit trees' trunks, their branches were in dire need of pruning. The drainage was good here, he noted quickly, the slope angled very well to the south.

The trees, though, had been abandoned. 'Twas a tragic waste.

Perhaps one like Pyrs had passed away and none had replaced him. A sadness claimed Luc's heart that such a legacy should go unappreciated.

And he broke ranks with his brothers without another thought. He had to go and look at the trees, see how badly they had been neglected, see if there was anything he might do.

"Luc! The stables are this way!" Burke called, evidently thinking him disoriented.

"My labor lies this way," he declared without slowing his pace.

Rowan frowned. "You will find naught to make a woman laugh there."

"You find something to make her laugh," Luc retorted, his gaze lifting to the trees once more. Aye, someone had once toiled to see each spaced well from the other.

"You cannot decline to participate!" Burke called.

Luc glanced back with a smile, liking the idea as soon as he heard it.

He simply would not go on Brianna's quest.

No more than that. He did not want a bride, after all, and an indulged princess certainly would not have any use for him. And if Luc remained here, in his sire's presence, he might sooner obtain the seal of Llanvelyn.

'Twas perfect.

"I have just done precisely that," he retorted.

Burke's astonishment was clear. "But—"

"But naught! I know my place and it is not with a princess by my side." Luc's tone was resolute as he waved his brothers off. "Go! Go in haste and bring her gifts. Win her hand before the snow flies, for I have much work to do at Llanvelyn."

Rowan laughed, though there was no malice in his merriment. "Ah, Luc, what has happened to the man who once you were?" When Luc ignored the comment, Rowan shrugged and turned to the stables, leaving Burke staring after their eldest brother.

Luc forgot them both as the bark of the first tree came under his hand. He was yet the man he always had been, though Luc did not care whether any understood that. Luc noted the scars of insects, the bushiness of growth in dire need of pruning. He frowned and immediately made plans for the tree's recovery.

This, Luc resolved with a nod at the forgotten tree, this he would do for the memory of Pyrs.

• • •

FENELLA BOUNCED INTO Brianna's chambers, her eyes sparkling. No doubt she had been by the hearth in the kitchens again. Brianna considered how difficult the young maid would find her inevitable transition to lady of her family manor, for she would be unwelcome in her own kitchens then.

Or, at least, the gossip would cease when she arrived. 'Twould nigh kill Fenella, Brianna was certain.

The hour was late, the light fading so from the room that Brianna had just laid her detested embroidery aside. The hoofbeats of the horses had faded away hours past, leaving the princess wondering how long 'twould be before one of the brothers returned.

This day had been reassuring, both in the fact that she had won her way, after all, and that none of her maids had been able to induce her to laugh, despite their best efforts to the contrary.

Brianna might win this battle yet. Indeed, she could do no less. Already her sire showed more vigor than he had since the loss of Tullymullagh. Throughout the day, Brianna's restless imagination had conjured fanciful dreams of her father restored to the throne.

And how he would smile as the last stone was finally set into Tullymullagh's walls.

"You will never guess what has happened," Fenella enthused. She rocked slightly on the stool opposite, her toes tapping restlessly as though the news would burst from her of its own accord. The other handmaidens looked up from their work with curiosity.

"Then you must tell me." Brianna smiled, tucking her needle into the embroidery.

"Oh my lady, you will never believe it!" Fenella clasped her hands together and leaned toward her mistress, her eyes round. "One of them did not go."

The women gasped at this, but Brianna frowned. "You mean one of the brothers? He did not go on the quest?"

"Aye, the one on the end in less fine clothes. You must recall him, though he was the least remarkable of them all."

Brianna might have argued that point, though her handmaidens quickly concurred. She recalled the man in simple garb all too well, for his gaze had been steady with disapproval when he met her own. Her own response to that level blue stare had been startling, for he was the least handsome of the three, with a great nose and a perfectly white forelock stark against his dark hair.

Yet there was something compelling about him, perhaps born of his disapproval. Uther had confided that he was, in fact, the eldest one whom Gavin had not wanted to invite.

Perhaps Brianna was but curious as to what this Luc had done to earn his sire's dismissiveness.

Never mind that this son had looked at her as though he

could not wait to be free of her presence. That had been a first for Brianna and a feeling that she could not forget.

Perhaps Brianna only had a natural urge to see this Luc's obviously low opinion of her corrected. But even speaking directly to him and turning her charm upon him had earned her naught, 'twas troublingly clear.

'Twas no less troubling that Brianna could conjure his visage perfectly in her mind's eye.

No less his scowl. Indeed, Brianna had already wondered what such a humorless man might fetch to make her laugh. And now, she was to be denied that answer.

That must be why Fenella's news was so annoying!

"But he *has* to go," Brianna insisted. "That is the wager, after all. It is a *quest*. They all must go, at my bidding, like one of the old tales."

But Fenella shook her head and leaned even closer. Her voice dropped to a scandalized whisper and the maids gathered closer. "I hear that he bade his brothers win you quickly that he might return home to his fields."

"Nay!" One of the maids laughed in disbelief.

"How could he not want to wed our lady?"

The maids erupted into giggles but Brianna straightened with a nearly audible snap.

'Twas a critical part of Brianna's plan that all three brothers abandon Tullymullagh. They must go on the quest in order to *fail* at the quest! That alone must be why she felt so irritated.

The man muddled her plan.

Who did he think he was?

"In fact," Fenella continued with a delighted giggle, "he has taken to Tullymullagh's own orchards. Cook said that the ostler said that he said he would make his time count for something of *merit* in this place."

"He would rather labor in the orchards than compete for a princess' hand?" The handmaidens tittered like little birds at this news.

This she had to see! Brianna pushed to her feet and strode to the window as her maids chattered behind her.

There, within the circle of the orchard's trees, in the fading light of the dusk, she could just discern the silhouette of a man.

And Brianna knew with absolute certainty who it was. Her heart skipped a beat.

'Twas true.

"But Lady Brianna is a renowned beauty! Men have come to compete for her hand for years!"

"Indeed, I heard tell of some offering to pay hard coin to join the ranks of Gavin's sons!"

"Imagine!"

"What is amiss with the man?"

There appeared to be naught amiss in the world of Gavin's son. From here, it looked as though he was trimming the trees and working diligently at the task as though he had not a care in the world.

And so intent was this man upon his labor that he apparently did not even note that the light was fading. The very sight of his concentration did naught to assuage Brianna's pride.

Outrage rose within her. Why, she had set the rules of the game, she had laid out a quest, she had a plan to regain both her independence and her father's holding—this man had no right refusing to even participate!

If he did not even deign to go, then Brianna could not refuse to laugh at his gift—which meant she could not refuse *him*.

And that simply could not be permitted to happen.

Fortunately, Brianna had no compunction about setting Luc Fitzgavin straight.

She sailed out of her chambers, her handmaids gossiping excitedly in her wake, and stalked toward a man in dire need of revelation.

Chapter Two

*L*UC WAS NOT PARTICULARLY SURPRISED TO SEE BRIanna striding through the courtyard toward him, her kirtle flying out behind her.

What did surprise him was that it had taken her so long to come. In his experience, indulged women were quick to note deficiencies in their attendance. Brianna tugged off her veil and cast it impatiently at the ground with a marked disregard for convention. The orchard was clearly her destination and her mood was evidently less than prime.

What doubly surprised Luc was the wave of anticipation that rolled through him. Indeed, Brianna was even more alluring in her anger than she had been in the hall and Luc's blood quickened that he was the target of her anger.

As she drew nearer, Luc saw that Brianna's eyes flashed, a flushed spot burned in each cheek. She gathered up her skirts and strode into the orchard with purpose, indifferent to the survival of her fine shoes. Burrs and dried weeds snatched at her gown but she strode on, eyes flashing emerald fire, oblivious to every obstacle.

She was magnificent. Luc found himself turning to confront her and bracing for a battle of words, without ever having had any intention of doing so.

"You!" Brianna jabbed one finger through the air. "You cannot stay here. You simply cannot!"

Luc folded his arms across his chest and surveyed the approaching princess with feigned indifference. "I just have." He shrugged, purely to infuriate her.

It worked.

"Oh! You are *insolent!* I am the princess of Tullymullagh and I will not permit you to remain." Brianna snagged her kirtle on the branch of a tree and gave the garment a frustrated tug. A slight tearing sound resulted. If Luc had expected her to moan over the damage, he would have called her response wrong.

The princess glared at Luc, cursed, and clutched even more of her voluminous skirts before continuing toward him. She came to a breathless halt before him, tipped up her chin, and looked him in the eye.

And she had a dangerous allure with such proximity. The ripe curve of Brianna's breasts was within a handspan of Luc's chest, the fan of her breath brushed his skin. A waft of a feminine scent—Luc fancied 'twas attar of roses—set a heat unfurling in his belly.

Ye gods, had he ever met a more beguiling woman?

"I shall *force* you to follow my quest!" she declared vehemently, her eyes flashing.

Luc let himself smile. Brianna was a good bit tinier than he and 'twas amusing to consider how she might single-handedly compel him to depart.

"Indeed?" he could not help but ask.

His smile clearly did naught to improve her mood. "Indeed!" Brianna retorted. "Why, I shall call the gatekeeper this very moment and have him escort you to the road."

Luc arched a brow and glanced toward the gates. "The gates have been closed since sunset."

Brianna spun to look, her golden hair whirling around her

shoulders, the wavy tresses evidently having worked free of her braid. Luc was certain he had never seen hair of such an incredible color. It made him want to touch it, but he had no more than lifted his hand before she spun back to face him.

Her lips had thinned that he spoke the truth, but she squared her shoulders regally and looked him dead in the eye.

Indeed, the lady did not surrender the field readily. Luc could not help but admire her persistence.

"You may pass through the broken wall, as the invaders did," she charged.

"Ah, but 'twould not be seemly," Luc returned solemnly.

"Seemly?" the lady echoed in an indignant hiss. "What is not *seemly* is your lingering here when I have granted a quest."

"Yet here I will remain." Luc turned and deliberately nicked a spur from the closest bough with his blade, knowing that his indifference would trouble her greatly.

'Twas impossible to resist.

"There is no place for you to sleep," she claimed, with a toss of her wondrous hair. "I am quite certain that all pallets are claimed this night."

"I will sleep in the stables. 'Tis no trouble at all." Luc granted the lady his most winning smile.

Her nostrils flared. "I shall forbid it!"

"But the arrangement is made." Luc leaned casually against the tree, intrigued by her determination to be rid of him. "Indeed, your ostler is most kind."

Brianna stamped her foot. "You cannot do this! You *must* leave on my quest." She fixed Luc with a bright eye and her voice lowered. " 'Tis how it works in every bard's tale— how can you be so cursedly stubborn?"

Before Luc could ask her the same question, the lady took a deep breath and glared at him anew. "Have you forgotten that you were summoned, after all, to compete for my hand?"

"That may be so," Luc acknowledged easily. "But I *came* for an entirely different reason."

The lady blinked and was momentarily at a loss. "You did?"

"Aye. I came to discuss another matter with my father."

The lady appeared uncertain how to proceed in the face of this information. She looked at Luc, at her hands, at the ground. From what he had already witnessed, Luc suspected 'twould not take her long to chart a new course. He watched and waited, expectant.

He was not to be disappointed.

"You mean that you do not want to win Tullymullagh?" Brianna asked in evident amazement, the very idea clearly unthinkable to her. "Or my hand in marriage?"

Luc shook his head decisively. "Nay."

She caught her breath at his blunt denial and her eyes widened in astonishment. Luc could see now that Brianna's eyes were a thousand shades of green, their depths lit with remarkable golden flecks. They tipped upward at the outer corners, like those of a cat or an Eastern seductress, her lashes were of deepest gold and thick beyond all.

Luc saw in their depths a glimmer of intelligence and his resistance to the lady's allure slipped dangerously. His heartbeat began to echo in his ears and Luc was very aware that he stood in a twilit orchard with the most beautiful woman he had ever seen.

Brianna licked the ruddy fullness of her lips, frowned, then scanned the decrepit orchard in disbelief. When she spoke, her low tone was incredulous. "You truly prefer the company of ancient fruit trees to the pursuit of a quest that might make you a powerful lord?"

"Oh, without a doubt." Luc watched the lady consider

his assertion, clearly never having heard the like, and enjoyed that he was challenging her belief that all would dance to her will.

He realized he liked surprising her. Luc had the distinct sense that Brianna was seldom surprised.

Much less denied.

Her ruby lips parted and Luc wondered, at a most inopportune time, what 'twould be like to kiss this determined Irish princess. Her lips would be softer than soft, he guessed, and his hands would fit right around her waist. She would kiss sweetly in her innocence, though Luc guessed that experience would make her passion burn with a bright flame.

He felt a sudden, quite unreasonable, desire to be the one responsible for that awakening. Indeed, Brianna stood so close to him in this very moment that Luc had but to bend his head to brush his lips across hers. 'Twould be so easy.

The thought was more than tempting.

But that would be wrong! He had no interest in marriage and noblewomen like Brianna could not afford to dally. Nay, 'twould be her chastity that won her a fine match, no more and no less.

All the same, he could not shake his desire for her kiss.

Clearly Luc was even less well suited to the life of a knight than he had previously believed.

Brianna, oblivious to his inner turmoil, wrinkled her nose in a most enchanting way. "But, *why*?" she asked in genuine confusion. "All men desire to be lords or barons or kings or otherwise greater than they were born. Surely you desire more than you have to your own hand?"

Luc arched a brow at her assumptions. "Which would be what?"

"Well, some holding smaller than Tullymullagh." Her conviction and her words faltered. "I would assume. I mean, your clothing is like that of a farmer. . . ." A soft flush suffused the lady's cheeks and her gaze dropped away from Luc's in her embarrassment.

Her blush deepened when he said naught. "Unless, of course, I misconstrue the import of your simple garb."

When she flushed with such maidenly sweetness, 'twas difficult to recall that she was the one who had summoned the brothers here on a mere caprice. Indeed, she looked so innocent and vulnerable that Luc had a errant urge to protect her from harm.

As might better befit the chivalrous knight Luc had long ago decided he would no longer be.

Luc took a deep breath. He would not protect this princess or pursue her quest, but still, he could not be churlish with her for thinking her home fine.

"You guess aright. I administer a Welsh barony in lieu of my sire," Luc acknowledged quietly. " 'Tis a modest manor, but suits my needs well enough."

Brianna slanted a bright glance through her lashes, her cheeks bright pink. "I would apologize if I gave offense. I meant no insult."

Luc shrugged, unable to keep himself from smiling in reassurance. The lady smiled ever so gently back at him and his heart began to pound once more. "Most nobles think naught of what makes their board groan with abundance." Luc tried to sound unconcerned by her broadening smile. "But 'tis the farmers and laborers, after all, who break their very backs that they might pay the lord's tax."

Those words dismissed her smile before 'twas full.

"Oh!" Brianna drew herself up proudly, the fire back in her gaze. She shook a finger beneath Luc's nose. "My sire does not overtax his villeins!"

"Nay?" Luc rolled his eyes at her naive trust, then nodded toward the stone keep looming behind them. "And what built Tullymullagh? Such a keep is of great cost to construct, and coin comes from but one source on a holding.'' He propped his hands upon his hips and stared down at the defiant princess. ''Unless your sire wished thrice upon a clover leaf and had the fairies conjure Tullymullagh in the night?''

Her eyes flashed emerald lightning; when she spoke, her voice was low. ''My sire crusaded to the Holy Land,'' she declared, fairly biting out the words. '' 'Twas upon his return that he began to build Tullymullagh's keep, the labor funded by what he had earned there.''

There was misplaced righteousness! Luc knew well enough how crusaders ''won'' their spoils!

''Earned?'' he echoed skeptically. ''There is naught *earned* by crusaders to the East.''

The lady's eyes narrowed. ''What do you mean?''

''That riches brought from Outremer are oft stolen from infidels and heathens, naught more noble than that.''

Brianna gasped. ''My sire is a knight of honor and repute! How dare you slight his intent, when you know naught of him or of crusade?''

''Naught?'' Luc barely bit back an explanation of his own past before 'twas uttered. He glared at Brianna, as annoyed with himself for responding to her as with her ability to conjure old memories.

Crusade had naught to do with his life any longer. Luc gritted his teeth and turned back to the tree, removing a spur with more force than was necessary.

''Then you do know something of crusade,'' Brianna observed.

Luc flicked a quelling glance her way. ''Naught worth discussing.''

The lady was not quelled, but then he had hardly expected as much.

"You are a knight," she charged softly.

Luc pivoted to face her and folded his arms across his chest in turn. He met the lady's gaze steadily and determinedly changed the course of their conversation. "It seems to me that matters are most simple. You expect me to depart on your quest. I do not intend to do so. The hour is late, my lady, and I would suggest that you retire, despite your evident urge to be rid of me."

To Luc's surprise, his last words were greeted by a flash of fear in the lady's remarkable eyes. Clearly she wanted him gone—why was she afraid that he understood the truth?

Luc had a sudden sense that something was in the wind.

He took a step closer and the lady, remarkably, backed away, her retreat fueling his suspicions. "Why are you so anxious to see me gone?" he asked. Brianna fairly danced backward, but Luc was in hot pursuit.

"I am not!" she protested, her guilt more than clear.

"What difference does it make whether I linger in the orchard or not, my lady?" Luc asked smoothly. "Have you some scheme concocted?"

Brianna blanched tellingly. What was she planning? "Nay! Not I!" she lied hurriedly. In her haste to escape his questions, the lady stepped on her skirts and stumbled.

Luc lunged forward and caught at her elbow. Brianna gasped as he scooped her off her feet in the nick of time. She clutched his shoulders for a tantalizing moment before she was safely upright again.

Luc could feel her heart hammering against his chest with a fear disproportionate with the potential of falling. Her small hands landed on his shoulders, her toes stood on his sturdy boots, her elbows rested in Luc's grip. Luc looked into the lady's luminous eyes, totally unprepared for the jolt of desire that rolled through him.

She was so tiny, so exquisitely feminine.

And she was so very clever. Luc had never been able to resist a puzzle, and Brianna of Tullymullagh was proving to be more of one than he had expected.

He wanted very much to know what plan was hatching in her mind. "I must go," she insisted and tried to step away.

Luc adjusted his grip ever so slightly, summoning a smile to reassure her. He had no intention of hurting her, but neither would he release her when he was so close to an answer.

"Tell me first what you are scheming," he suggested.

Her eyes widened. "Naught!" Brianna declared breathlessly.

Luc arched a brow. "That seems unlikely. Why else would you fear my remaining here?"

"I simply want you to go on my quest." Her words tripped over each other in their haste to be heard.

Luc was not persuaded. "Why?"

Brianna swallowed, she looked away, then she looked up at Luc. "I like you best," she said, then her cheeks flamed.

'Twas so obviously a lie—both from her manner and the simple truth of Burke's greater desirability—that Luc laughed aloud.

"Indeed?" he said finally. "I believe, my lady, that you are merely trying to make me do your will."

Brianna's flush deepened. "Nay, not I." She opened her eyes wide and stared up at Luc, as though willing him to believe her. " 'Tis true." She patted his shoulder. "Truly."

Luc did not believe Brianna for a heartbeat, but that did not stop a wicked idea from dancing into his mind.

He arched a brow, enjoying the prospect of surprising this woman yet again. "Aye? Then, if you favor me so very much, why not grant me a token of your esteem?"

Brianna blinked. "My sleeve?" she asked hopefully, as though she knew 'twould not suffice.

Luc shook his head firmly. "Your kiss."

Brianna's mouth opened in a perfect circle of surprise. She paled, then another flush stained her cheeks. She dropped her gaze with maidenly modesty but not before Luc saw the sparkle of curiosity in her eyes.

That alone shattered his resistance.

Luc inclined his head and brushed his lips once across hers, not wanting to frighten her. Even that minute taste of Brianna's lips proved to be sweeter than honey and left him hungry for more. Indeed, Luc wanted naught else but to gather Brianna closer and kiss her so deeply that she could think of naught else.

He paused, though, and waited for her consent.

Her gaze flicked to meet his once more, that sparkle dancing in the emerald depths. "One kiss," she whispered breathlessly.

Luc did not grant the lady a chance to change her mind.

This, he resolved, would be a kiss worth remembering.

Luc lifted Brianna against his chest, his fingers spreading across the back of her tiny waist. To his delight, his hands did fit perfectly around her slender waist. He slanted his mouth across hers, claiming her lips with tender possessiveness. Brianna tasted of wine and honey, she smelled of roses, she felt more soft than anything Luc had ever felt before.

'Twas but a moment before she tentatively kissed him back.

Luc needed no further encouragement. He deepened his kiss, caressing her lips with his tongue until she opened her mouth to him.

When he took advantage of her move, Brianna gasped, then sighed. Luc swallowed both sounds, his heart thundering when her tiny fingertips landed against his jaw. Her touch was as light as a feather, the press of her curves against him a temptation that was nigh impossible to put aside.

But her kiss revealed her innocence and 'twas not Luc's place to take more than his due.

Even if he savored what she granted to him.

Finally, Luc set Brianna on her feet and reluctantly lifted his lips from hers. The lady appeared delightfully flustered, yet she would not meet Luc's gaze.

Remarkably, she seemed to have naught to say for herself. Her breathing was hastened, those fingertips had fallen to Luc's shoulder. He captured her hand securely within his own.

Brianna's flesh was so creamy, her hand so fragile within the roughened breadth of Luc's own palm. That protectiveness returned with a vengeance at the sight of her uncertainty, yet Luc could not resist his urge to plant a single chaste kiss in her palm.

Even her palm was breathtakingly soft.

Brianna caught her breath at his gesture, her other hand rose to her lips. Luc looked into Brianna's eyes as he folded her fingers over his salute and pressed his lips to her knuckles. She stared at him, clearly well aware that she trod new ground and entirely uncertain how to proceed.

Luc grinned slowly, liking very much that he had surprised her.

Again.

This could well prove habit-forming.

"Off to your chambers, my lady," he murmured. " 'Tis late to be wandering about in the orchard with fallen knights, after all." Brianna glanced up as though surprised by his words and Luc winked, unable to resist teasing her. "Even the one who is your *favorite*."

Brianna turned absolutely crimson. She inhaled sharply and snatched back her hand, spinning away to flee across the orchard. She did not glance back until she had reached the safety of the orchard's perimeter.

Then she shook a finger at him. "I shall not forget this, Luc Fitzgavin!" she huffed. "You have gone too far in this."

"On the contrary, my lady," Luc grinned. "I only did your bidding. Is that not what you prefer?"

"Oh! Oh, you are insolent beyond all!" Brianna clearly struggled to find a better argument and failed. She opened her mouth and shut it again, glared at Luc, then pivoted and stalked across the bailey. The princess snatched up her veil en route and continued to the doorway to the hall without stopping.

No doubt she thought Luc would miss her single backward glance.

He saluted her with a single wave when she did look back and was nigh certain he could hear her snort of disapproval. "I shall learn your secret, my lady," he called softly after her. "Make no mistake about that."

Though he knew his words must have carried across the silent bailey, Luc was not surprised that Brianna did not answer him.

A tuneless whistle on his lips, he turned toward the stables, acknowledging that Tullymullagh was proving much more interesting than he had expected.

Not to mention a certain princess. 'Twas Brianna's cleverness alone that snared Luc, no more than that. And the puzzle of whatever scheme she had concocted, of course.

Though, oddly enough, 'twas the taste of her kiss that kept him awake long into the night.

• • •

THE AUDACITY OF the man!

Brianna stormed through the hall, not caring who she troubled in her passage. How dare he insist upon a kiss? A nagging voice in her mind insisted that 'twas her own fault, but Brianna ignored it.

What else could she have done but insist he was her favorite? The man was too perceptive by half! Who else would have discerned that she wanted merely to have him gone and cared little for the quest?

And now, he was determined to remain at Tullymullagh and ferret out whatever plan Brianna had.

She could just spit.

Brianna climbed the stairs to the solar, seething all the while. Surely, Luc could not unravel her plan further? 'Twas bad enough he refused to leave, 'twas quite disconcerting how he delighted in denying her, but surely, he would never figure out her true plan?

Unfortunately for her peace of mind, Brianna was not nearly as certain of that as she might have liked to have been.

Her fingertips rose to her burning lips as she reached the second floor and in the shadows there, Brianna confronted another unwelcome truth.

She might not truly have been lying when she called Luc her favorite of Gavin's sons. He was by far the most interesting of the three, for he alone defied expectation.

'Twas just a first impression, no more than that, and Brianna knew well enough that such impressions could be deceiving. After all, even the mercenary Gavin thought his eldest son unworthy of note.

All the same, Brianna could not help but wonder why Luc was no longer a knight.

No less what he would do on the morrow.

• • •

CONNOR OF TULLYMULLAGH stood at the solar window and watched the waxing half moon rise over what he had wrought. The pale moonlight fell over the bailey below, the curtain wall, the village beyond, the spire of the parish church, and rows of fields lying fallow for the winter.

Connor's roving gaze came back to the curtain wall over and again. Not one, not two, but three places there were where the wall was yet incomplete. Three breaches—beside the gate—to hold against attack, three weaknesses in Tullymullagh's defense.

Three reasons why the keep had fallen into alien hands.

Too late, Connor cursed his own foolish trust. He had thought himself secure in his pledge of fealty to the high king, thought Tullymullagh too minor an estate to attract an avaricious eye, thought Ireland a kingdom of peace.

And he had been wrong.

In the wake of that error, Connor could not help but wonder whether his secret had been breached. He had been so very careful for so very many years, but had he merely fooled himself? Had it been his secret that brought Gavin and England's king to his gates? Connor fought the urge to turn, fought against even looking, let alone checking that all was secure.

A man like Gavin Fitzgerald could not possibly know.

Connor took a shaky breath, frowned, and studied the holding spread before him. The keep that he had spent two decades building, the keep that housed his memories and treasures, would soon be occupied by the spawn of Gavin Fitzgerald.

And there was naught he could do about it. 'Twas a bitter root to swallow. Connor had long planned of Brianna continuing here. He had planned upon Ruarke de Rossiers taking Brianna's hand and the pair of them bringing son after son to light.

Connor scanned the long empty road for some sign of his champion knight, but found only stillness. He gripped the sill, feeling suddenly old and ineffective. Aye, Connor had had plans aplenty and now had naught to show for it.

He ran his hands across the smooth stone that formed the lip of the window, letting his mind flood with memories of better times instead. Connor felt the heat of a foreign sun upon the back of his neck, tasted the tang of alien spice within his belly, watched a king's ransom in gems catch the light as they filtered through much younger versions of his hands.

And Connor heard a much-loved voice instruct him upon the differences in pearls, as those same gems—those marvels who snared the very moonlight in their sheen—rolled across his tongue.

Salt from the Red Sea, the precious rarity of sweet from Oman.

Connor stared at the vacant line of the road and wondered whether he could yet taste the difference. This window looked at the distant sea, and beyond, to Outremer, and Connor scanned the horizon in recollection.

He remembered all too well the first stone keep he had seen. By the time he had travelled all the way to Outremer, Connor had seen castles more wondrous than ever he could have imagined. The castles had seized hold of his imagination and, by his return, Connor had been determined to build his own fortress of stone.

As he had. Still he marvelled at the cleverness of the garderobes hidden in the corner of each floor and the wooden ramps outside that guided the refuse to the river swirling around the north side. Basins there were, carved into the very walls, and designed to snare rainwater for the occupants' use.

The hall itself was high and massive, lofty enough for any king and large enough for any gathering Tullymullagh might host. The floor in the hall was fitted stone, a massive fire-place was nestled into the north wall, its mate into the south.

A stair rose on the wall farthest from the dais, climbing to the second floor with a heavy door at its summit. This tier, with its heavy wooden floor, was divided into three, one of which was occupied by Brianna, the others used for maids and retainers.

The stairs rose again to Connor's own solar, a lavish chamber that filled the third floor and overflowed with memories for him. Each plank had been laid with care, each stone placed with perfect craftsmanship. The windows here, as elsewhere, were small openings fitted with wooden shutters. By and large, they faced east and south, to diminish the bite of the winter winds.

A tiny staircase wound against one wall of the solar, leading to Connor's own private chapel at the peak of the tower. The bishop himself had blessed the cross that rose from the roof.

Below Connor's window was spread the bailey itself, a large courtyard filled with activity each day. The well was here, the armory, the smithy. He could see the portcullis of the gates to this sanctuary.

Connor's gaze fell on the cursed curtain wall and he knew now that he should have built it first, not last. Though indeed 'twould have been inconvenient for moving the great quantities of stone.

But experience taught the lesson too late.

Behind Connor, to the east of this high tower, lay the garden his beloved Eva had treasured. 'Twas a sign of the differences between them—that he had to look to the mysteries beyond the horizon while she was content within the circle of her garden walls.

'Twas a tribute of a kind that he let the garden tumble into disrepair after Eva's passing. In truth, Connor had not been able to bear the possibility that the garden Eva so loved continued to flourish after she was gone.

Perhaps 'twas good he could not look upon its tangled waste from here. Perhaps its neglect—and the reason for it—was not a fitting image for a man to carry to his dreams.

Connor frowned. Beyond the gates, a ribbon of road wound through the tightly clustered homes of Tullymullagh's village, the smoke of peat fires meandering skyward on this chill night. The cross on the roof of the parish church was etched in silhouette against the darkness of the sky, the outlines of distant hills could be seen in the moonlight.

If he squinted, Connor imagined he could see the glint of the sea. It had been so long since he had ventured away from Tullymullagh. Now, he remained by a mercenary's whim. He might well be forced to leave.

Connor did not know where he would go.

He looked down at his hands, the moonlight making them appear more frail than he knew them to be. He was no longer young; he was no longer idealistic, for time had taught him otherwise.

Aye, he was tired and aged indeed.

There were but two things Connor had left to do in this life. He would see Brianna safely wed to a man of honor, and he would see the legacy he had saved for her safe within her own grip. His eye strayed of its own accord to the stairway rising to the chapel and he turned back to the window with an effort.

A hue and cry burst on the stairs, tearing Connor away from the jeweled treasury of his memories. He spun in dismay, just in time to find the rough Gavin Fitzgerald bursting into his chambers. Connor's steward, Uther, raced behind him, his expression echoing the horror Connor was feeling.

"My lord! I do apologize!" Uther declared, nearly breathless from a quick climb. "He *insisted* upon coming to

the solar and there was little I could do to stop him!'' The
steward's expression was scathing, but the mercenary
clearly cared naught for such disapproval.

"Ha!" Gavin declared with satisfaction. "That fool child
of yours left the door unlatched. Now I shall claim what
should be mine!"

And Connor's heart clenched in fear.

Did Gavin know his secret?

Gavin's very presence in Connor's chamber was offensive, every rough line of his being in marked contrast to the
grace of the solar's decor.

Never mind its precious secret.

Connor's heart hammered with the fear of discovery.
"Nay!" he argued with rare vehemence. "This solar is
mine, at least until one of your sons wins Brianna's hand."

Gavin swaggered into the room and waved dismissively to
Connor. "Nay, old man, I have been patient enough. King
Henry divested you of Tullymullagh and granted its posses-
sion to me."

Connor could hardly argue with that, though he dearly
desired to do so.

Gavin poked himself in the chest proudly. " 'Tis *my* keep
now, it has been my keep for a month and 'tis time there
were changes made within its walls. I shall savor each one
of Tullymullagh's pleasures, as its rightful lord." He openly
ogled the fine chamber. "Including this one."

All the same, Connor was not at all prepared to vacate his
abode for this savage excuse for a man. And certainly not
immediately. 'Twas imperative that Connor see his last two
objectives realized.

He folded his arms across his chest and rose to his full
proud height. "I shall not move from this chamber. 'Tis to
Brianna and her spouse I will yield and none other."

Gavin sneered. "You have little choice, old man." He

hauled his blade from its scabbard with unexpected speed, then smiled as he touched the tip to Connor's throat.

Uther gasped. Connor held his ground, letting his contempt for Gavin filter into his gaze.

"Unless you would care to settle the matter with steel upon steel?" Gavin taunted.

Connor stood in regal silence and seethed. His keep might have been granted to Gavin, but 'twas clear enough the man was devoid of chivalrous intent, or indeed any grace.

Yet 'twas also clear that he was younger and more fierce than Connor could hope to be. 'Twas not a swordfight Connor could win, as much as he hated having the truth made so bluntly clear.

But, despite the odds arrayed against him, Connor would only abandon his chambers on his own terms.

Indeed, he could risk no less.

" 'Tis indeed a bold knight who confronts an unarmed man with Toledo steel," he commented and valiantly tried to summon the quelling glance for which he was reputed.

Gavin inhaled sharply but before he could rant, Connor pushed the blade aside with one determined fingertip. He was not at all certain Gavin would permit the move, but breathed a silent sigh of relief the other man did.

His cold eye must not be without effect, even in these days.

Encouraged, Connor cleared his throat and spoke sternly, as though he addressed a wayward child. "You cannot expect me to abandon the chambers of a lifetime at your whim. Had you informed me sooner of your wishes, I would have removed my belongings earlier this day."

To Connor's delight, Gavin did not seem to know what to say.

"As 'tis, the hour is too late to stir the help." Connor inclined his head slightly. "First thing on the morrow, I shall prepare the chamber for you—'' he gritted his teeth to utter the next words ''—as befits Tullymullagh's new lord.''

As Connor had anticipated, those last words stole the last of the wind from Gavin's sails. The man looked around the chamber greedily, then narrowed his eyes as he looked at Connor again.

''I shall hold you to an accounting of the solar's contents,'' he growled. ''By noon on the morrow.''

Connor's lips twisted wryly. ''I would have expected no less.''

''And your daughter, she must become a suitable lady of the estate for my son.'' Gavin continued. ''Burke shall have no impulsive creature by his side, but a woman who can be relied upon to see his home in order.''

Connor bridled at the insinuation that his daughter was less than perfect, but Uther stepped forward. ''We have already begun such tutelage,'' he lied and Gavin grunted his approval.

''Good. Then, we all understand each other.'' Gavin's eyes narrowed as he looked back to Connor. ''I shall have your hide if that bed is moved, or that chest, or that inlay trunk or—''

''I shall take only those belongings most personal,'' Connor interrupted crisply. Uther looked positively lethal over the vulgarity of this transaction, but Connor gestured for the loyal steward to say naught.

Indeed, Connor would ensure the one token of value was gone so completely as to not even be missed.

''There will be no trick?'' Gavin demanded with a suspicion that made Connor fear anew that his thoughts had been discerned. ''You will not lock me in the hall below once more if I leave?''

Connor's lips thinned and he spoke with great precision. ''I give you my word of honor.''

Gavin snorted. "Words!" he sneered. He jabbed his sword through the air at the older man. "I shall take my rest on the floor directly below, that you or your wayward daughter cannot deceive me again. This chamber shall be mine by noon on the morrow, Connor *once* of Tullymullagh, make no mistake."

He leaned closer, brandishing the sword. "And do not push the limits of what you deem *personal* effects."

Connor held the man's gaze stubbornly as Gavin shoved his blade back into his scabbard. Gavin turned and stalked to the doorway, pushing aside the scandalized steward.

"Make no mistake yourself, Gavin Fitzgerald," Connor uttered with quiet resolve. Gavin paused on the threshold to look back. "I shall always be *of* Tullymullagh. 'Tis in my blood, as 'tis not in your own."

The two men's gazes held for a long charged moment. Perhaps something of Connor's old indomitability shone in his eyes, for Gavin evidently thought better of arguing the point.

Then mercifully, the man swore and was gone.

"Barbarian," Uther muttered under his breath.

"Beyond doubt," Connor agreed. The exchange had left him newly decisive, and the path before him lay clear. "Summon Brianna. I will not have her slumbering in any ways near that man. She has defied him—as have I—and I imagine this Gavin is not one to forget a slight."

'Twas as good an excuse as any to see his daughter close at hand, though Connor did not truly believe that even Gavin would sully a prize destined for one of his sons.

Uther, though, inhaled sharply at the very prospect, then bowed low and clicked his heels. "Aye, my lord. I shall ensure that the lady Brianna arrives with all haste."

But Connor was already thinking ahead. He must find some way to work his prize into Brianna's possession, and thence to safety, without his daughter ever guessing the value of what she held.

Sadly for his ends, the princess of Tullymullagh shared her mother's keen intelligence. Connor frowned and tapped his toe as he thought.

Brianna also shared Eva's love of a romantic tale. At that recollection, the old king permitted himself an indulgent smile.

Forgive me, my Eva, but the ends do justify the means.

Chapter Three

T WAS LATE WHEN LUC STILL LAY AWAKE, TRYING TO both cast the woman from his mind and find comfort in the hay. On either side of the stall he had chosen, warhorses and palfreys stamped in their stalls and nosed in their feed bins. Otherwise the stable was shadowed and silent.

A whisper sliced through the quiet like a knife through fresh cheese. Truly there was naught more effective than a hushed voice just beyond earshot to make any man stop and listen.

Which Luc did.

"What has taken you so long?" the voice demanded, frustration evident even in the low tone. "I have been waiting and waiting, with no word at all."

"The land is besieged," retorted a second even lower voice, tinged with impatience.

Two men 'twas, of that Luc was certain. He could not guess their identities when their voices were so low. And in this keep, there was no shortage of options, for a good hundred people—few women among them—made their homes here.

But why meet in the stables in the midst of the night? There could be no good reason for such secrecy. Did this have something to do with Brianna's scheming? Luc strained his ears to catch their words.

"One cannot simply come and go in these times. Surely you have the wit to realize it. Now tell me, what news?"

"The keep is lost to a Welsh mercenary, seeking both territory and the favor of the English king," retorted the first.

The second swore eloquently.

"He has already pledged fealty to that king."

The second muttered another curse. "Who is it who holds Tullymullagh, then? Who is this mercenary?"

"Gavin Fitzgerald, though he only holds the seal in trust."

There was an incredulous pause. "What is this?"

"The mercenary is wed, so the king decreed Brianna should wed Gavin's son. He has three sons and the princess sent those sons on a quest to compete for her hand."

Now the second man's low chuckle throbbed through the stable. "Trust Brianna to unwittingly play to my hand."

"What of your news?" Now the first voice was impatient. "What have you learned?"

"Ah, only that all we heard rumored is true."

The first man exclaimed in delight. *"All* true?"

"Aye, the Rose of Tullymullagh is more a prize than anticipated, though I did not plan for this intrusion. It complicates matters considerably."

"One son remains."

"Nay!"

Luc's ears pricked at this mention of himself.

"Aye, the princess tried to dissuade him of his course, but to no avail."

The second man swore again. "That is less than good news. The Rose of Tullymullagh *must* be mine!"

Silence echoed once more through the stables and Luc did

not dare even breathe for fear of discovery. Who were these men—and what dark intent did they have for Brianna?

"Perhaps matters yet can be turned to our advantage," mused the second man.

"We have need of a plan," declared the first.

Luc dared to ease closer to the stable door and inadvertently rustled the straw. The stallion in the next stall tossed his head and snorted at the disturbance. He snapped the reins with vigor and Luc froze.

"What is amiss?" demanded the first man anxiously.

"That fool stallion Raphael," the second said dismissively. "Never have I laid eyes on so witless a steed. No doubt, the ostler will come along to see what ails him. 'Twould be better if we talked elsewhere."

There was a stealthy tread of footsteps and Luc leapt for the stall opening. He peeked around the edge just in time to see the last of a man's boot disappear around the far corner. He could not even discern its color in the wan light.

Then, both whispers and footfalls faded to naught.

The inconveniently sensitive stallion snorted and stamped impatiently as Luc tossed himself back into the straw. Indifferent to Raphael, Luc folded his hands behind his head and stared into the shadows of the rafters.

'Twas clear the men spoke of Brianna and 'twas equally clear that she would be a markedly fine prize of a bride for any ambitious man. There was naught precise to be gleaned from the words he had heard, though Luc had an undeniable sense of foreboding.

Why else meet in the stables when all were abed?

And whisper.

Luc could not stop a protective urge from rising to the fore. 'Twas his cursed training at root, and Luc wished heartily that his finely honed instincts would let him be.

• • •

"GAVIN MEANS TO sleep *here*?" Brianna stood before her sire, incredulous, as a trio of her maids busily set her belongings to rights in the solar. Uther grimly supervised the move.

The difference in Brianna's sire was remarkable—but a month past he had been bent beneath the weight of his loss and old beyond his years. But now he stood tall and straight, regal as he had been before Gavin came. On this night, a gleam of resolve shone in his grey eyes the like of which Brianna had never seen. Her sire fairly bristled with determination.

She had had but a moment to marvel at this before he confessed his intent to vacate his own chambers for none other than the mercenary himself.

And that news had stolen Brianna's very breath away. It had nearly driven all thought of Luc Fitzgavin from her mind.

But not quite.

"Aye." Her father bit out the word. "On the morrow, the solar will be made ready for Tullymullagh's new lord."

What madness was this? "Father, we cannot permit it! The solar is *your* chamber, and it is fully my intention to ensure—"

"Brianna!" Connor's voice cracked like a whip. Everyone in the room straightened to look, for 'twas rare for the old king to chastise his child. Brianna could not look away from her father's blazing glare.

She understood all too clearly that she had said too much.

Brianna felt her cheeks heat with self-awareness but stood proudly and tried to pretend that she was finishing her sentence as she had intended to begin it. "To ensure that the transition, when it comes, is an orderly one. Indeed, it is hardly reasonable to expect my maids and Uther to toil at this hour to see my belongings moved here."

The fire abated in her father's eyes and Brianna knew she had read him aright. He cleared his throat now and assumed a more benign expression.

"In truth, 'tis not Gavin responsible for this change," he conceded with an apologetic smile to the busy foursome. All of them responded to his charm, any displeasure fairly melting from their faces.

"'Tis only I who would ensure that my daughter sleeps securely this night." Her father met her gaze once more and Brianna knew his next words would be significant. "Gavin declared he would sleep on the floor below," he added softly.

"He did not!" Fenella exclaimed, freezing in the act of plumping a fine feather pillow.

"He did that," Uther confirmed grimly. "He was sorely vexed that our lady saw him locked out of the tower—" Fenella giggled at the recollection, but the steward did not smile "—and he is determined that 'twill not happen again."

Brianna digested this morsel of news and concluded that her sire was being overprotective as was his wont.

Uther's tone turned petulant when Fenella did not resume her labor. "How many times must I tell you to turn down our lady's linens? She must be sorely tired after this day."

"Aye, Uther." Fenella flushed and hastened to the older man's bidding.

"Immediately, Uther." The other two maids fussed with the linens in question.

"And how many of you does it take for such a simple task?" the steward demanded testily. "You and you, fetch the lady's embroidery and her garb for the morrow." He snapped his fingers impatiently.

"Aye, Uther." The pair scurried away.

"And where is the lady's bath?" Uther continued, evidently put in poor temper by these quick arrangements. "Has everyone in this abode forgotten how to manage the simplest matters? Must I oversee every little concern?" He inhaled sharply once more, his bright gaze sweeping the chamber in disdain.

"I shall check upon the bath," Fenella offered with a low curtsey that clearly won her naught in the steward's estimation.

His lips thinned. "And become lost in the kitchens when the first gossip reaches your ears, no doubt." Fenella blushed as she hurried from the room, but Uther was quick on her wake.

He pivoted on the threshold and bowed low to Connor. "I do beg your pardon, my lord. The keep is in an inexcusable uproar, but I shall endeavor to set matters to rights in short order."

"Of course, Uther."

"And on the morrow, I shall begin to teach the princess all she needs to know."

"Impeccable, Uther. As always."

The steward bustled off and Brianna had no doubt that he would lay siege to someone's misconceptions. She turned back to find her father's gaze bright upon her.

But they were alone. This was her chance to not only confess her plan but to win her father's counsel in privacy.

"Do not give me that look," Connor chided softly. "Gavin would have you learn the duties of a lady of the keep and 'tis not such a poorly timed thought. Uther will see that you know all you need to know."

"Father, I care little of that." Brianna closed the space between them with a quick step and seized her father's hands. "We need not let Gavin gain the solar," she said urgently. "You see, I have a plan to ensure that I need not choose *any* of his sons. And as Henry declared, Gavin cannot wed me himself for he already has a wife. So, once the sons have failed, then all we have to do to ensure that you regain suzerainty of Tullymullagh is to persuade Gavin to abandon—"

"Brianna!" Connor's tone was chiding and he gave her fingers a firm squeeze. "Understand that Gavin will not abandon Tullymullagh, for any price. 'Tis his prize and one he labored to win."

Brianna cared little for any sacrifice Gavin might willingly have made. To her it seemed her sire was bearing the full price of this change.

And unnecessarily so.

"But Father, Tullymullagh is *yours!* You have labored to build it from the ground and 'tis unfair that you should lose Tullymullagh on the eve of its completion."

Brianna got no further before her father silenced her with a single fingertip touched to her lips. She looked into his eyes and her heart wrenched at the profound sadness she found there.

"Fair has naught to do with the way of the world, child," he said sternly. Brianna tried to protest, despite the weight of his finger, but Connor pushed more firmly against her lips. "Brianna, you must face the truth. I will never be King or even Lord of Tullymullagh again."

"But—"

"But *naught*!" Her father's eyes flashed once more. "One does not win the war by fighting a single battle again and again and again."

Brianna stepped back, confused by this claim. "I do not understand."

"Tullymullagh is lost to me, but not to you," her sire

asserted. "Know this, child, you will be Lady of Tullymullagh, if 'tis the last deed I see done in this world."

Brianna frowned. "But I do not intend to wed any of Gavin's sons and Henry will not make me lady without a lord."

Connor smiled slowly, his eyes sparkling silver. "Do you imagine, child, that I have not considered that issue?"

As Brianna stared at her father's expression, she knew beyond doubt that she was not the only one with a plan.

Though she was sorely confused by his claim. "But, Father, how could you have found my one true love without my even knowing of it?"

Her father's eyes narrowed. "I beg your pardon?"

"My one true love." Repeating the words evidently did naught to enlighten her sire. Brianna smiled. "I will only wed my one true love, Father. If there is to be a Lord of Tullymullagh who claims me as his bride, that can only be my one true love."

Connor seemed slightly dumbfounded by this confession.

Undeterred, Brianna squeezed her sire's hand. "Father, surely you know that your own tale, the power of the love that you and Mother shared, could only inspire me to desire the same manner of match?"

Connor released Brianna's hands and strode across the room, rubbing his temple. He pivoted to face her where the shadows cast by the oil lanterns obscured his expression.

When he spoke, his words were strained. "Have you, perchance, *found* this one true love of yours?"

Brianna was surprised to find herself assaulted by the memory of a very steady, very blue gaze. 'Twas a gaze that lurked between an impressive nose and a startlingly white tuft of hair, a gaze that sparkled when a certain man teased her unexpectedly.

Nonsense! 'Twas no more than her vigorous curiosity at work.

"Of course not!" she declared with unnecessary vehemence. "But I am certain that I shall know him the very moment my eyes land upon him."

Connor's words carried an affectionate smile. "Will you now, child? And how will you know?"

Brianna shrugged. "Why, the way that you and Mother knew. Because your hearts were as one." She took a step closer to her father. "Tell me exactly how it was that you knew the truth."

Connor cleared his throat. "I did not guess the truth when first we met. Indeed, I was long away from your dame before I knew that she had captured my heart," he confessed quietly. "And I feared then that I had guessed the truth too late to ever win her hand."

"In Outremer," Brianna breathed, loving every nuance of this tale.

"Abandoned for dead in Outremer," her father corrected sternly.

"But you came home to Mother. 'Tis so romantic!"

"Aye," Connor admitted. His eyes glittered even in the shadows. "But never was there a certainty in my heart that the lady felt the same regard for me. 'Twas no more than a hope, a distant hope, until I returned and saw the welcome in her eyes."

Brianna smiled. "But she *did* love you. And she was feeling precisely thus about you. How can you imagine that I would not want the same love in marriage for myself?"

Connor stepped closer, his gaze fixed on Brianna. "Child, understand that what we felt then was but a faint shadow of what ultimately grew between us. You may well have already met this one true love you seek."

"How would I know?"

"Think, child. Think of a man who stands by you with honor, a man who prompts your smile, a man you would be proud to call sire of your sons. A man who will take his place beside you in this solar and command Tullymullagh as his own."

Brianna could not quite stifle a feeling that her sire had very definite ideas who that man might be.

She might have thought further upon the matter if she had been able to evict those blue eyes from her memory. But Brianna knew that Gavin's uncooperative son was not for her.

Luc Fitzgavin had as much as told her that he had come to precisely the same conclusion.

'Twas odd how Brianna did not find his words encouraging.

Her sire laid a hand upon her shoulder, his voice sounding low in her ear. "Make no mistake, Brianna, there is much yet at stake. Use the wits granted to you and consider our situation. Already our forces have lost to Gavin's own, and many valiant knights have paid the price. Beware that any further protest against this invader may bring his retribution upon us."

This was precisely Brianna's concern, but her sire granted her no opportunity to speak. "Understand, Brianna, that Gavin Fitzgerald is not the manner of man who ever forgets a slight granted against him."

A chill hand closed around Brianna's heart as she realized that she had already proven most defiant of the mercenary's will. But she was only defending what rightfully belonged to her father!

Outrage rolled through Brianna once more, but her father granted her no time to indulge it. "On the morrow, Gavin lays claim to this chamber," he continued intently. "But

there is one thing I would see safe from his hand and I have
need of your aid.''

Brianna's eyes widened. ''What is it? What can I do?''

A footstep sounded on the stair and Connor started. ''We
must not be overheard!'' he whispered. His fingers tightened
on Brianna's shoulder as Uther's complaints carried to their
ears.

''By the saints above, one would think you never had
brought a bath to the solar! Have you so soon forgotten the
Lady Eva herself taking her leisure in these chambers?''
The wooden tub was rolled into the solar by the cook's
largest helper who smiled apologetically at Connor and Brianna.

Uther was dissatisfied, though, and fussed over the place-
ment of the tub. He continued to fret, even when three men
carried steaming buckets of water into the chamber.

''Nay, nay, nay, move it over *there*. There will be a draft
from that window. Now, you and you—fetch those two braziers from the floor below and we will have need of more
wood from hall. The princess must not catch a chill!'' Uther
clapped his hands and servants scattered.

Connor winked so quickly at Brianna that she nearly
missed the gesture, let alone prepared herself to follow his
lead in whatever he might say.

''What is this, child?'' Connor declared suddenly when
Uther might have spoken. His tone was shocked. ''You
missed the Mass this day?''

Brianna had not, but she hung her head all the same.
'Twas clear this was some plan of her sire's to win them
their privacy once more. ''I am sorry, Father,'' she murmured, as she thought she should.

''An apology to me is naught before God!'' Connor retorted. He squared his shoulders and spun to face Uther, the
very image of moral indignation. ''Uther! Please send my

goodwill to Father Padraig. Ask whether he would be so good as to come and sing the Mass for Brianna and myself. In the private chapel.''

Brianna understood immediately. They would have a few moments in the chapel alone for her father to finish telling her what he wanted secured from Gavin.

Uther bowed. ''Of course, my lord. I believe he was just in the hall below. I shall have the lady's bath prepared by the time you have made your prayers.''

''Excellent, Uther. As usual, you have matters well in hand.'' Connor turned a stern eye upon his daughter. ''Child, you must learn that there is no excuse for failing to give thanks on each and every day you draw breath.''

''I am sorry, Father.'' Brianna bowed her head as though ashamed of her behavior. Her father led her toward the tiny stair on the far side of the solar, then paused as though in sudden recollection.

His gaze, though, was markedly steady. ''And bring your cloak, child,'' he murmured with feigned casualness, his words loud enough for Uther's ears. ''The chapel is cold these nights.''

Brianna quickly did as she was bidden, curious beyond all as to what she was going to learn. Connor picked up a small oil lantern and followed immediately behind his daughter. As they climbed the stairs, the maids spilled back into the solar with all the belongings they had been sent to fetch.

''Make haste!'' Connor murmured urgently.

Brianna did as she was bidden. ''But why summon Father Padraig?'' she whispered.

''We may have need of a witness to declare we took naught from the chapel,'' Connor responded quietly.

And Brianna realized that her father's secret was hidden there.

• • •

FATHER AND DAUGHTER reached the floor of the chapel above and Connor genuflected before he lifted his lantern high. The light flickered off the simple contents of the chamber and, as always, Brianna was awed by its beauty.

A simple altar carved of wood spanned the middle of the room, a silver chalice and plate reposing in its center. A square linen cloth adorned the altar, IHS worked in gold thread on the corner hanging to the front. A thick rug was cast across the wooden floor that the family's knees might be protected. 'Twas a small chapel, by any calculation, the roof was so steeply pitched that only the very center was usable.

But behind the altar on the east side rose a massive crucifix that had fascinated Brianna since her childhood. Wrought of wood, the juncture of the arms was marked with a great quartz half-sphere polished to a gleam. No matter where the light was in the chapel, that stone seemed to shine with an inner light.

'Twas said that a fragment of the True Cross was trapped within the stone, though Brianna had never had the opportunity to see it closely for herself.

Her father quickly lit the two plump beeswax candles on the altar and the wicks sputtered fitfully before they caught the flame. The tiny room suddenly danced with warm candlelight, the gold of the crucifix gleaming mysteriously. The quartz glowed, as always it did.

In the blink of an eye, Connor had set aside his lantern and reached for that very stone. Brianna watched as he ran his hands over it. Her father moved so quickly that Brianna could not have said precisely where he touched the great jewel.

She did, however, see it open like the lid of a box and hear the faint creak of a hinge. Brianna gasped, her father fired a quelling look across the chapel, and footsteps sounded below in that very moment. Connor reached inside what looked to be a tiny chamber hidden behind the stone, removed something roughly square, then closed the compartment again.

Then the priest's blessing echoed from the solar below. Brianna heard the servants' murmured greetings to the man of the cloth passing through their ranks. She smelled the tang of the incense in the censer Father Padraig always carried and heard his footfall on the ladder.

Her sire fairly flew across the chapel. He pushed Brianna to her knees before the altar and pulled her cloak closed.

And just as the priest's shaved pate glowed in the shadows of the stairs, Connor shoved whatever he had retrieved into Brianna's hands. 'Twas a flat cold box and she immediately pulled it beneath her cloak. Her fingers told her 'twas metal and unadorned, about the size of her hand laid flat and as thick as both hands together.

"Letters penned to me by your dame when we were betrothed," Connor whispered. "We must hide them anew."

Brianna clutched the precious relic of her mother and hid it deep within the folds of her cloak. "But where?" she murmured, barely daring to give voice to the words as the priest drew near.

"In Eva's crypt," her father declared without hesitation. "You know the place. Your dame will see that they are held secure, for she intended them to be yours."

Brianna's fingers curled around the cold metal hidden within the heavy wool folds of her cloak. "I shall read them!" she breathed, unprepared for her father's fierce glare.

"Nay! They must be hidden, *immediately,* and none must see you at the deed." Connor's hand closed tightly over

Brianna's own when she wondered at his urgency. "Swear to me that 'twill be precisely thus," he whispered urgently.

Brianna had only a moment to make her pledge, even though she did not fully understand her father's reasoning. The tension eased from his features and they both inclined their heads to pray.

"Good evening," the priest declared from the stairs behind.

Connor raised his voice then and turned slightly. "Good evening, Father Padraig. I would thank you for coming to us this night."

The priest smiled as he stepped across the room. He was a man of middle years, so slender as to be nearly gaunt. The hair left from temple to temple below the tonsure that marked his profession was iron gray and bristly. His expression, though, was always contemplative and Brianna found his presence remarkably peaceful.

Indeed, Father Padraig was a walking testament of the tranquility that could be found in contemplation.

" 'Tis my vocation, Connor," he said mildly now and swung his brass censer to perfume the air of the chapel. "When the flock needs tending, 'tis my pledge and my task to be there."

Brianna's sire inclined his head slightly. "And how fortunate we are to have you in Tullymullagh. I have bidden Brianna pray these past few moments and reflect upon the import of taking daily Mass."

The priest's smile widened slightly as he came forward. Reaching into the vial of holy water hanging from his belt, he anointed his finger, then traced a damp cross upon Brianna's brow. "You have naught to fear. She is a fine child, Connor, and her heart is pure." He arched a brow and smiled. "And I recall the Lady Brianna's presence at the Mass this morn, even if she does not."

The priest made his mark upon Connor, his smile turning thoughtful. " 'Tis the mark of the mortal father to occasionally err in punishing too severely." Father Padraig turned to genuflect before the altar. He gave the censer one last swing before setting it beside the altar and folding his hands together. "Let us pray to the Father who never errs."

And Connor bowed his head without a glance to his daughter. Brianna clutched the token of her dame, closed her eyes, and prayed fervently that one day, she would have the opportunity to open the box and unfurl these precious pages.

One day, she would run her fingers across her dame's own confession of love and hear the echo of that woman's voice in her ears once more. One day, she would read her mother's own telling of how a woman might know that a man had captured her heart.

'Twas a gift beyond anything Brianna had ever dreamed. As Father Padraig began to sing the Mass, Brianna vowed that no man would ever steal this token away from her.

Her father might be overly cautious, but Brianna would do as she had pledged. Indeed, she could not risk losing this valuable gift.

Chapter Four

LUC WAS AWAKENED BY THE ECHO OF RAPHAEL stamping his feet. The beast snorted with displeasure and snapped his reins temperamentally. The cold grey of a winter's dawn had crept into the stables and Luc felt the chill of it in his bones.

He sat up, shoved a hand through his hair, and wondered what had troubled the stallion at such an early hour. 'Twould be too soon for the fires to be lit in the hall, he wagered.

A woman's voice rose shrilly in that moment. "Whatever do you *mean,* there are no stalls available? Why, Tullymullagh has always boasted an ample stable and I see no reason why *you* should deign to turn us away at this early hour."

Luc stood up with interest and brushed the straw from his chausses. He straightened his chemise, tugged on both boots and tabard, tucked his knife in his belt, then peered over the stalls.

At the far end of the stable, near the portal, a woman tapped her toe with unconcealed impatience. She might have seen few more than twenty summers, but her lips were drawn so taut as to be unattractive. Her eyes were small and mean, her gaze darted over the stable with displeasure. Her garb had once been rich, but now was stained; the hem of her kirtle was crusted in mud.

But 'twas her manner that more accurately revealed her noble birthright. She railed at the ostler who looked extremely unhappy with his circumstance.

A solidly built giant of a man who was a good ten years Luc's senior, Denis the ostler was clearly a simple man. His pate was as bald as an egg and Luc had already noted that his single brow, which ran from temple to temple, worked vigorously when he was concerned.

Denis' great gift was his ability with horses. In but a day, Luc had noted that Tullymullagh's ostler had been born to his labor. Denis murmured in the ears of the horses and they adored him, each and every one, following his bidding when they would permit no other near them.

But Denis' skill with people was markedly less. In this moment, he stood sleepily, his linen sleeves shoved past his elbow, his boots already mired, his brow wrinkling busily as the lady heaped demands upon him.

Luc could only sympathize with his plight. There could be naught worse than denying a shrewish noblewoman what she expected as her due, especially so early in the morn.

"Truly!" the lady exclaimed. "How can you expect me to believe that there is not a single empty stall at Tullymullagh? Tell the truth instead! Tell me that this new overlord refuses to receive his closest neighbors." She jabbed a finger at the ostler's chest, her voice rising another increment. "Is that not the way of it?"

Raphael snorted and shuddered as though he could not bear the high pitch of her voice.

Denis, meanwhile, bowed low. "Nay, nay, 'tis not that at all, Lady Ismay." He cleared his throat slowly, as though he needed time to seek an explanation. His words fell heavily. "I am fully certain that Gavin Fitzgerald would be delighted to host you, but he has many guests already."

"Is that so? I cannot imagine that any of them come from

as fine a lineage as we.'' The lady tossed her veil and Luc glanced dubiously over her steeds.

If she truly had coin to her name, she did not spare it on either garb, attendants, or steeds. The mare lurking behind the lady was decidedly grizzled.

Denis straightened and wrung his hands when he saw how little effect his argument was making upon the noblewoman. ''Some of King Henry's party have remained and the new lord's men, as well.''

Lady Ismay snorted disdain. ''Say naught to me of that English king! His minions are welcomed while loyal neighbors like ourselves are not? What manner of barbarian is this man?''

The amiable ostler fairly squirmed, his hands working together as he fought to appease the lady. '' 'Tis the hour, Lady Ismay. Much of the keep remains asleep, including Gavin Fitzgerald himself—''

''*Disturb* him immediately!'' The lady's anger rang through the stables. She pointed demandingly to the keep and drew herself taller, the gesture doing little good for her profile. ''Hasten your sorry hide to him this very moment and *demand* that we be properly received!''

Denis looked sorely dismayed by the prospect and Luc could not blame him. Gavin was not a man who took well to interruption, particularly early in the morn, and no doubt Denis had already tasted the bite of Tullymullagh's new lord. On the other hand, this Lady Ismay would stop at naught to see her own way fulfilled.

Had it not been for the ostler's predicament, Luc would have been content to let this noblewoman stew in her own dissatisfaction.

But Denis was a kindly man undeserving of such nonsense.

Luc cleared his throat and stepped out of the stall. ''Good

morning to you," he said and the arguing pair turned as one to confront him. Relief washed over Denis' visage while the lady merely looked more grim.

"Ostlers from every side and nary a hand to take a steed," she snapped. "All of Christendom has gone straight to hell in this year." Denis looked shocked, but Luc waved off any protest he might have made.

"How many steeds have you?" Luc asked mildly.

"Three," the lady supplied, her tone waspish. Even the black mare whose reins Lady Ismay held tightly appeared embarrassed to be seen with her mistress. The silver-snouted beast stepped back, standing as far away as she could, the reins stretched taut. She had never been a fine beast, Luc could see now, for she was comparatively short and stocky.

Not a noblewoman's steed, by any means. Clearly Tullymullagh had neighbors with lofty aspirations. Luc imagined this woman was one who came regularly to fill her belly at another, more ample, board. There were nobles he had known who never troubled themselves to remain at home, simply savored the hospitality of others all the year long.

The possibility said little good of her character.

"Dermot!" the lady bellowed suddenly, the single word loud enough to deafen a man. Luc winced and heard Raphael shake his harness in vexation.

A man dressed with slightly more care than the lady appeared in the portal of the stable. He was fair of hair and fair of skin. Even his eyes were unnaturally pale, the very shade of rainwater. He seemed a man of ice and water, so fair was he. His gaze flicked to the woman and Luc caught the barest glimpse of raw animosity in his eyes.

Then the expression was gone and the man summoned a limp smile. "I am here, Ismay," he said softly, his voice as insubstantial as his coloring. "At your very side, as always."

"Hm!" Ismay sniffed disapprovingly. "You certainly were not very *close* by my side. I could not even see you, Dermot! Where had you gotten yourself? And what took you so very long to come from gate to stable?"

"I thought I caught sight of an old friend, my love, but I erred. 'Twas no more than that." Dermot's voice was low and quiet, not unlike a whisper. Though Luc could not have said whether 'twas one of the voices he had heard the night before, the mention of encountering a friend made Luc prick up his ears.

That and the malicious glance Dermot had briefly cast toward Ismay. Luc wondered exactly who that man's friend might have been.

"A likely story. A *friend*." Ismay rolled her eyes. "More like, you lost your way! In all truth, Dermot, you would lose your very head were it not firmly attached. Where have you *been?* And what on earth have you been *doing*?"

Dermot smiled with the quiet grace of a Madonna. "In truth, it matters little, my love, for we are together again. Have you already seen to the stabling of the horses?"

" 'Twas an adroit change of subject, but the lady did notice that her attention had been firmly redirected. Indeed, she smiled at her mate or lover, whichever Dermot happened to be.

Then she pivoted and glared at the ostler anew. "I should have done so if there was any excuse for *efficiency* in this place! What do you mean to do about this appalling situation?"

"There is a stall here," Luc interjected and saw gratitude light Denis' eyes.

"I knew 'twas a malicious lie that there was no space!" Lady Ismay declared angrily.

" 'Tis the stall I slept in," Luc countered evenly, "and one that was well occupied until but a moment past."

The lady grimaced. "You mean to stable my mare in a stall where the help have slumbered?" She shuddered, then scowled at Denis. " 'Twill have to be mucked out thoroughly, you understand, for one never knows what manner of vermin live in these people's garments."

Neither Luc nor Denis observed the state of the newly arrived couple's garments. Indeed, the pair looked as though they had slumbered in the fields.

Denis drew himself up proudly. "I am well aware of how a steed should be treated, Lady Ismay." He reached out for the mare's reins and the lady slapped them into his palm.

The black mare, though, sidled tentatively closer to Denis. That man smiled, then conjured an apple from his chausses for the wary steed. The beast abandoned her mistress' side without another thought, nuzzling Denis and partaking noisily of his offering. Luc watched the ostler smile as he stroked the horse's nose and did not miss Denis' fleeting frown when he checked the mare's bit.

The beast had been reined in hard, Luc would wager.

"Well! See that it does not get *fat*." Lady Ismay's lips drew tightly together and she glared now at Luc. "And what do you mean to do with the other two?"

"I am certain that in the course of the morning's comings and goings, more stalls will become available," Luc responded. "Why not simply leave your steeds in the ostler's good care while you break your own fast?"

Before the woman could protest, Luc stepped forward and laid claim to the reins Dermot held. Their hands touched in the transaction, the arrival's skin colder than cold.

Luc barely suppressed an instinctive shiver.

Lady Ismay sniffed. "At least there is *someone* with a measure of consideration for his betters in this place."

They had another black mare with a star on her brow, though she had a slight sway to her back. A small dappled grey palfrey obviously carried the pair's possessions. Even as meagre as they appeared to be, the beast was so gaunt as to hardly be up to the task.

Luc felt his lips thin at such cruelty and he immediately relieved the palfrey of its burden. The creature shuddered when the weight was lifted from its back, and Luc was not surprised that neither Ismay nor her companion seemed to notice.

Denis noticed and his brow began to lower in a most unfriendly manner. "Edward! Cedric! Andrew! Get yourselves from bed!" he bellowed. "There are steeds to be tended with all haste." He touched the horses with gentle hands.

Denis turned his back upon the arrivals, clearly reassured to be on familiar ground. In no time at all, he would be alone with the steeds and, Luc knew, all the happier for it. Luc handed off the second mare's reins to the tow-headed and sleepy-eyed squire that came running a moment later.

The ostler's eyes shone with gratitude when he glanced at Luc once more. "I do thank you for your aid in this matter, sir."

" 'Twas naught, Denis." Confident that all had been set to rights, Luc made to step away.

But the lady Ismay froze in the act of rummaging through her belongings. *"Sir?"* she echoed incredulously, her sharp gaze flicking between Luc and the ostler. Her lip curled with disdain. "You call *him* sir?"

Denis grinned, no doubt delighted to know something she did not. "Aye, Lady Ismay. This is Luc *Fitzgavin,* after all." He placed an emphasis on Luc's surname, drawing even Lady Ismay's attention to the moniker that revealed his parentage.

Son of Gavin.

Lady Ismay paled and Luc knew that she had no doubt precisely which Gavin was his sire. A bright glint of consideration flashed in Dermot's eye before 'twas concealed.

Before Lady Ismay could recover herself and make some pathetic apology, followed no doubt by a plea for an audience with his father, Luc waved to the ostler and strode toward the orchards.

He took a deep breath of the morning air. Crisp and clean as only it could be in the autumn. Luc's thoughts and his footsteps turned to the orchard as he scanned the sky. The morning sunlight was thin, he noted with pleasure, but there was no chance of rain.

The exchange with this noblewoman made him doubly glad he had left that life behind. Aye, 'twas no life for a sensible man. Luc ducked beneath the canopy of the apple trees, a merry whistle was on his lips.

Gavin would doubtless slumber late, particularly if he had indulged himself the night before. In the meantime, Luc would do Pyrs' memory proud with the labor he did in this orchard. He wondered what Lady Ismay would have thought if he had declared a Welsh steward to have been more of a father to him than his own blood sire.

Luc could readily guess. The very thought made him smile.

But Luc's whistle stilled when he realized that he could not have so readily guessed what Princess Brianna would make of such news.

Aye, she was one difficult to predict.

An *interesting* woman, there was no doubt of that.

Despite himself, Luc's eye roved the high walls of the keep. What scheme did Brianna concoct? And did it have anything to do with the whispers he had overheard?

• • •

'TWAS NOT UNTIL the next morning that Brianna realized one very critical fact. Fenella and the maids were busily moving Brianna's effects back from the solar and her father's belongings to the adjoining chamber. Gavin was pacing irritably and generally underfoot, but not interested in taking the advice of either Uther or Connor to wait in the hall.

'Twas when Brianna arrived back in her usual chamber that she saw the truth. She stared across the bailey to her dame's stone sarcophagus resting on the very perimeter of the garden.

It lay directly alongside the orchard. 'Twould be impossible to secure the letters safely within her mother's tomb, as her sire had bidden her, without Luc seeing her.

The simplist solution, of course, would be to ask Luc to leave her be beside her mother's grave. Brianna chewed her lip in thought, knowing that had no hope of working. Not only did the man seem determined to defy her on principle alone, her request would no doubt feed his suspicions that something was afoot.

Luc would watch her, Brianna guessed, and that would not do.

Unless, of course, he had abandoned the orchard to seek out his sire. Or perhaps he still slumbered! Newly optimistic, Brianna peered through the shutters, oblivious of the chill of the wind through her chemise.

Even as the morning mist rose from the river beyond, Brianna could discern the silhouette of Luc Fitzgavin striding from the stables with purpose.

She leaned back against the wall and frowned. Curse the man! 'Twas as though he awakened early to vex her!

Again.

Brianna peered through the shutters to covertly watch Luc wander amidst the trees. She could not help but wonder about his past. Why would a knight cast aside all he had earned? A knight lived a life of privilege, of danger and splendor; by contrast, a farmer's existence was deadly dull. Brianna could not imagine exchanging her life for that of the alewife, for example.

Unless she had an extremely good reason. That made her frown in thought. What had compelled Luc to make his choice?

Brianna was surprised by how very much she wanted to know.

She told herself that she was curious, no more than that. Her interest had naught to do with the way this man looked at her, truly *looked* at her, instead of merely ogling the fairness of her features. He listened to her, he even argued with her, despite his obvious disapproval of all she was.

And, well, she would not consider his kiss. Just the recollection made her feel warm and tingly.

Nay, she was merely intrigued by a puzzle.

Yet Luc had been very reticent in providing details. He seemed to enjoy pestering her—what if she pestered him? Brianna could ask about Luc's past! She guessed that he would not welcome her inquiries.

Could she drive him away from Tullymullagh with mere questions?

'Twas worth a try. Once Luc departed from the orchard, Brianna could hide her mother's legacy. Then, she could turn her attention upon finding a way to convince Gavin to renounce his claim.

That would be the true challenge, she well knew.

Her course decided, Brianna spurned the embroidered gown that Fenella offered and dug in her trunk for a tunic that fell to her knees and a pair of heavy chausses.

Fenella's face fell. "But, my lady, you have not worn such

garb in all my days with you! 'Tis unfitting for an eligible woman of your rank!''

"But, Fenella, if I wear a fine gown to labor in the orchard, you shall spend all your time restoring it to rights.'' Brianna hauled on the woollen chausses with purpose and flashed a reassuring smile to her maid. The maid had only just finished clucking over the damage to her kirtle from the night before.

But Fenella gaped. "You mean to *labor* in the orchard?''

"Not truly labor.'' Brianna tossed her maid an easy smile. "I would merely talk with this Luc while *he* labors.''

Fenella's eyes widened at the prospect of a tale to share in the kitchens. "The one who would not go?'' She slipped closer to the window and peered down at Luc, widening the gap between the shutters with her fingertips.

She glanced back to her mistress coyly. "Is he most charming?''

Brianna grimaced. "Hardly that.''

"But you spoke with him long last evening.'' Fenella giggled. "Do you *fancy* him, my lady?''

"Nay!'' Brianna laced her chausses decisively even as her cheeks heated. "I but tried to persuade him that 'tis in his best interest that he be gone from Tullymullagh.''

"In the moonlight.''

Brianna glared at her maid. "'Twas of no import. In point of fact, we argued. He is a most vexing man.''

Fenella could not completely hide her smile. "Of course, my lady. 'Tis oft the way of things when a man and a woman first acknowledge each other.''

"We do not *acknowledge* each other!'' Brianna pushed to her feet, more than ready to end this discussion. "Might you trouble yourself to find my old boots?'' she asked deliberately. Fenella hastened to dig in a trunk on the far side of the chamber.

"Have you not cleared your belongings away yet?"
Gavin's impatient roar echoed in the hall and Brianna realized she could not leave her dame's treasure in these chambers. Her sire had made her promise to keep the box safe,
after all. The tunic Brianna wore was full and she reasoned
that with a sash about her waist, she could secure the precious box against her belly.

At least until she found her chance.

"Here they are, my lady, but such boots are hardly fitting
for you these days." Fenella's lips drew in a disapproving
line. "Look at the wear upon them! All will think your sire
lost his entire fortune."

"I care little what the others may think," Brianna said
calmly and took the boots. Fenella looked so disappointed in
her mistress' choice, that Brianna's defiance melted slightly.
"Perhaps you could do me a favor this day, Fenella."

"Aye, my lady."

"I should like to wear my finest garb to the board tonight.
The blue kirtle edged with gold. Could you perhaps see that
all is made ready?"

"Oh!" Fenella clasped her hands in delight. "And the kid
slippers I so admire?"

"Of course."

The maid smiled at the very prospect. "Oh, my lady, you
will look most lovely. Here, I will braid your hair, for if you
mean to be in the orchard all the day, you cannot have it
loose. But on this night, I will use those blue ribbons that
suitor from Dublin left for you. . . ."

Brianna fought to stand still as Fenella's fingers slid deftly
into her hair. The maid's tales of who said what the night
before slid over her mistress unheard. Brianna was too busy
trying to think of a way to retrieve the box from its hiding
place without Fenella seeing her.

Salvation came from the most unlikely of places.

A horse snorted in the bailey and the maid flew to the window, casting open the shutters, her task forgotten in her thirst for news. Brianna caught the end of her braid and knotted a lace about it as she gauged the distance to her dame's box.

"Oh, my lady! Is that Lady Ismay?" Fenella hung out the window unashamedly.

Brianna grimaced. Lady Ismay was the last person she wished to see this morn.

Or on any other morn, for that matter.

All the same, Brianna took the opportunity of Fenella's distraction to delve the box from her linens and secrete it beneath her tunic. She tucked it into the top of her chausses and scanned the chamber for a suitable sash, barely aware of her maid's chatter.

"And Lord Dermot fast by her side, as always," Fenella mused. "Truly, he is a most devoted spouse. 'Tis a marvel to me that any man could adore such a woman with such ardor. And the way she talks to him!" The maid rolled her eyes. "'Tis clear she fancies herself more eligible than ever she was. Lord Dermot must be a veritable saint. Look! Ismay is hailing your master Luc."

Those words distracted Brianna from her task.

"He is not *my* master Luc," she retorted, but could not keep herself from edging toward the window in turn. Brianna did not even trouble to note Lady Ismay, her gaze flying of its own accord to the orchard.

Where Luc Fitzgavin looked directly and steadily toward her.

Brianna's heart took an unruly skip. She drew back into the shadows, her finger clutching a fistful of cloth where her dame's box was hidden.

Though she could not precisely see from this distance, Brianna knew how Luc's blue gaze had not wavered from her own. 'Twas as though he knew about both the box and her intention, the very steadiness of his glance most unnerving.

Her lips tingled in recollection of Luc's kiss at that very inopportune moment. Brianna felt her cheeks flush scarlet and deliberately turned her back on the window.

"Not your master Luc indeed," Fenella muttered, a knowing glint in her eye. "Do you imagine that I have not noticed your preoccupation this morn?"

Brianna could not stop her flush from deepening. To divert her maid's attention, she waved to the window once more. "Is it only my eye or is Lady Ismay garbed rather more poorly than usual?"

Fenella leaned out the window anew, greedily seeking details. "Aye, you speak aright! Has she no shame? Why, her gown is *filthy*!"

Brianna did not care what Lady Ismay wore or did not wear, much less how she conducted herself. She was merely glad that Fenella was sufficiently interested to remain at the window.

The maid wrinkled her nose in disapproval. " 'Twould be an improvement to grant her the one you damaged last evening, unless I miss my guess. And not a single servant in their wake." Fenella clicked her tongue like an elderly matron. "What has possessed the woman? Has she no pride? She comports herself like one born common and without grace."

Brianna hastily tied a sash about her waist, knotting it so that the box was secure, then passing it twice more around herself so that the bulk of the fabric hid the box's shape.

Fenella looked suddenly as though she might turn back to her duties. As she fumbled with the knot, Brianna blurted out the first words that came to her lips. "Do you think Dermot looks well?"

"Not so very good, though he is always very pale," Fenella acknowledged, leaning back out the window again. " 'Tis his coloring, I think. So delicate in a man." She sighed and her tone turned wistful. "Do you think he is happy with the match he has made?"

Brianna shrugged without interest. The box was securely hidden, she was certain of it. "I would not dare to guess."

"Zounds!" Gavin's bellow sounded just a few feet away. Both women jumped. "How long can it take a man to move a few trinkets? I would have occupancy of the solar *now*!"

Brianna suddenly had a much better idea of how she could disconcert Luc Fitzgavin than with a few questions. After all, Luc confessed he had come to Tullymullagh only to speak with his sire.

That could definitely be arranged.

• • •

"LUC FITZGAVIN! What is this you do?"

Luc's head snapped up at his sire's shout. He grimaced at the sight of an enraged Gavin striding lop-sidedly across the bailey. Behind that man danced the princess Brianna in markedly sensible garb, clearly anxious to see the result of what she had wrought.

For Luc had no doubt that 'twas her hand behind his father's visit. 'Twas clear she had informed Gavin that Luc yet remained at Tullymullagh. Luc's lips tightened to a grim line.

Aye, he should have expected her to make trouble wherever she could. She was bound to see him gone, after all.

Although this was not the circumstance under which he had hoped to discuss Llanvelyn with his sire, it seemed Luc would have little choice. All the same, he had no intent of providing a certain princess with the result she desired.

He was not leaving Tullymullagh without Llanvelyn's seal.

Luc braced his feet against the ground and awaited his father. Gavin was in fine form, his heavy features dark with rage, his fury making him fairly spit when he spoke.

Fortunately, Luc had borne the brunt of his sire's ire before and lived to tell the tale. Brianna, Luc noted, hesitated on the periphery of the orchard. Evidently she was intent upon hearing every word but, belatedly, was seized with some discretion.

Well, she would witness no display of temper from Luc. He would not provide whatever entertainment she sought. Luc was bound and determined to not play to the lady's rules.

'Twas a matter of principle.

"Luc! You faithless cur!" Gavin bellowed. He let loose a string of profanity, then poked his finger angrily through the air toward his errant son. "From the very day you drew breath, you have been a curse upon me! Why do you remain at Tullymullagh? Did you understand naught of what was transacted yester morn?"

"I understood that you intended Burke to win Tullymullagh," Luc retorted calmly.

Gavin paused momentarily at the truth of that, then scowled and continued onward. "Get yourself gone from this place and seek a gift for the princess! Take a steed, any steed, take mine own, but get on your way. A prize beyond all else hangs in the balance, you witless fool!"

" 'Tis a prize I do not wish to win," Luc countered.

His sire's eyes narrowed at this claim. "What manner of fool declaration is that?" he roared after a moment's pause, then flung his hands skyward. "Your dame's intellect is showing in that claim! You wear the mark of her unworthy kind upon your very brow, as ever you did!"

That accusation prompted Luc to respond heatedly. "My

dame's character—much less the coloring of my hair—has naught to do with this."

Gavin snorted and propped his hands on his hips. "Blame *me* for your circumstance, will you? 'Tis always thus with you—never can you see the opportunities hung right before your very eyes."

"I see the opportunity well enough," Luc retorted. "But all the same, this is not one I desire."

Gavin fired a baleful glance at his eldest son. "Naught has changed in all these years," he charged in a low voice. "To Llanvelyn alone do you cling, *afraid* to reach for more."

Luc bristled at the accusation, though he fought to hide his rising anger. He was very aware of a certain golden-haired presence. "I have *never* been afraid of reaching for what I truly desire. That 'tis not the warring legacy you would have me pursue says more of your character than of mine."

Gavin snorted, though his eyes flashed dangerously. " 'Tis the taint of your dame's blood." He spat on the ground between them. "You hold yourself above the necessary brutalities of life."

"There is naught 'necessary' in the brutality of your life," Luc retorted angrily. "And certainly naught necessary in slaughter that serves no more than your own greed." Gavin inhaled sharply, but Luc took the remaining step between them and stared into his father's hardened gaze. "How many must die before you deem your coffers full enough?"

Gavin's eyes flashed and he responded, as he oft did, with his fist. Luc heard Brianna gasp as his father's blow landed against his jaw.

Ye gods, but the man had not weakened with age! Luc refused to give either his father or Brianna the benefit of seeing how much the blow hurt. He took but one step back, straightened, and looked his sire steadily in the eye.

" 'Tis not half what it used to be," he lied. "Are you eating well enough these days?"

Rage lit Gavin's eyes. "Yet you do not strike back," he declared with scorn. "No better than a woman are you."

"Unlike you, I see no good in violence."

"Coward!"

"I chose my path," Luc said quietly. "And still I cleave to it."

Gavin snorted. "And still you have not the sense to be afraid of me. Truly *naught* has changed."

Luc rolled his eyes as though the idea were ludicrous. "There is naught to fear from the likes of you." He nodded deliberately toward the wide-eyed Brianna, who looked suitably startled at what she had set in motion. Luc turned back to his sire and managed a cool smile despite the ache in his jaw. "Unless you have become so foolish as to leave witnesses of your deeds."

Gavin spun, eyed the princess, swore, then pivoted back to face his son. "One day," he growled with a shake of his heavy finger, "one day I shall shake your cursed composure. You have always been too clever for your own good."

Luc's lips thinned. "A clever man has no need to win his way with his fists."

Gavin looked as though he were sorely tempted to strike his eldest again. He shook his head, though, and stalked a few paces away. When he turned to survey Luc anew, suspicion was bright in his eye. "Why did you come if you did not mean to compete for a bride? Why respond to my summons at all?"

Luc arched a brow and could not keep a thread of humor from his tone. "I but desired to speak with you, Father."

For, as remarkable as that fact was, 'twas true.

Gavin's brow furrowed. "With *me?* What idiocy is this?" He jabbed an indignant finger through the air. "My missive made the situation most clear!"

"As it made equally clear your intent to break an old pledge." Luc met his father's gaze squarely. "I came only to remind you of a promise you made to me."

Although Gavin did not look away, a tinge of red claimed his neck. "I cannot recall every word tossed aside to appease a child," he snapped.

" 'Twas no appeasement and you know it well," Luc retorted in a dangerously low tone. "You promised me Llanvelyn in a decade's time. Eleven years have passed since that pledge was made, and I have yet to hold Llanvelyn's seal in my own hand."

Luc extended his hand, palm flat.

Gavin's lips tightened as he stared at Luc's outstretched hand, then he shook his head. "Llanvelyn! What do you care for a petty Welsh barony?" He gestured to Tullymullagh's high keep. "*This* is a prize for a man who walks proudly! This is the prize you should pursue!"

"This is a prize you may keep for Burke," Luc retorted firmly. "I have no desire for it."

'Twas most odd but those words had a ring of untruth when they fell from Luc's lips, but he stubbornly held his ground.

"Llanvelyn is humble."

" 'Twas *pledged* to me." Luc folded his arms across his chest. "What is your pledge worth these days, Gavin Fitzgerald?" Luc arched a brow. "Surely not even less than I recall?"

Gavin glared at his son in outrage, his fists clenching and unclenching. The moment stretched long between the pair and Luc was well aware of Brianna's assessing gaze.

"I owe you *naught*," Gavin snarled.

"I but offer to relieve you of a burden, Father, a manor that must remind you of simpler times." Luc lifted that brow again. "And more common roots than you might prefer to profess in these days."

Gavin fired a sly glance his son's way. "Pursue the quest and, win or lose, I shall grant Llanvelyn to you in exchange."

Luc snorted. "Another promise that you might break? Nay, your obligation is already long past due. Grant me the seal now."

Gavin's lips drew to a disapproving line. "How should I even know that you are a fit lord of Llanvelyn?"

Luc refrained from commenting on his father's belated interest in the state of his first holding. "You could see the estate yourself. It prospers these days."

Gavin grimaced. "I would not burden myself with the sight of the pitiful place again."

"Your sire thought it a fitting prize for a man of ambition," Luc felt compelled to observe.

Gavin rolled his eyes. "My sire was a man who understood naught of the world. A man of meagre ambition." His gaze turned assessing. "Perhaps 'tis *his* taint that courses through your veins."

Luc had a rather good idea where any taint in his veins might have originated, but he bit back his words. In truth, he had already provoked his father enough.

Gavin waved dismissively. "But you speak aright, in this at least. 'Twas by the king's decree alone that you and Rowan were even included in this folly." Gavin took a deep breath and eyed the stone keep with pride. "Aye, Burke alone will make a fitting master of Tullymullagh."

The assertion was curiously irritating. Luc certainly had the training and the wits to administer an estate like Tullymullagh.

Although he had never been irked by his sire's low assessment of his talents before. He glanced to the wide-eyed princess, her lips parted, and readily recalled their brief kiss.

A kiss that Burke would likely savor over and over again. Luc's annoyance rose markedly at that thought, yet he forced himself to think of the issue at hand.

He was *not* interested in a spoiled princess.

Burke was welcome to Brianna.

"And Llanvelyn's seal?" he prompted sharply.

Gavin frowned and sighed. "When Tullymullagh is settled upon Burke," he conceded with obvious reluctance. "The seal of Llanvelyn shall be yours. And not one moment before."

Luc was surprised that the concession did not please him more than it did. That must be because the value of his father's pledge had yet to be proven. Obviously, holding the seal in his own hand would be the only proof of Luc's success.

He bowed slightly to his father. "I thank you for your generosity."

But Gavin's lip curled with scorn. "Do not thank me, Luc. And do not blame me in your dotage when you regret all you have cast aside." He fixed his son with a stern glance before turning away and snorted once. "Llanvelyn will no doubt prove to be a poor prize."

And Gavin limped out of the orchard, not even acknowledging Brianna before continuing across the bailey to the hall.

But Gavin's departure brought Brianna to life. She ran across the orchard toward Luc, her eyes wide with alarm. Despite his annoyance with her attempt to force him to her bidding, Luc's errant heart took a skip as she drew near.

"Did he hurt you?" she demanded breathlessly, hovering a few feet before Luc as though she wanted to come to his side but dared not do so. She truly looked as though she were concerned for his welfare, though Luc could not believe 'twas so.

All the same, his heart began to pound.

Luc grimaced, ran his tongue over his teeth and assured himself that they were all yet in place. He spat in the grass and was relieved to see no blood in his spittle. "Nay. Indeed, 'tis time enough he grew feeble."

Brianna heaved a sigh that might have been born of relief. "I cannot believe that he struck you!" she exclaimed.

Luc granted her a wry glance. "When you merely wanted him to have me cast bodily through the gates."

Brianna flushed scarlet and looked guiltily at her toes. 'Twas all the confirmation of her plan Luc needed.

All the same, he was no closer to knowing why she wanted him gone so badly. Brianna licked those lips, then unexpectedly impaled Luc with a glance. " 'Tis appalling he should treat you thus! Are you not his eldest son?"

Luc shrugged. "And neither favorite nor the spawn of a heated infatuation. Indeed, there is none he would rather strike." The princess' eyes were still filled with concern and disbelief. Luc smiled wryly. "I remind him of beginnings he would prefer to forget."

"Oh!" She blinked. "Are you bastard born?"

Instead of answering, Luc folded his arms across his chest and considered the woman before him. "You are full of questions this morn, my lady. Is this some further part of your plan to see me fleeing from Tullymullagh?"

A flush stained her cheeks as it had the night before, but this time she held Luc's gaze with resolve. "I would simply know more of you," she declared with bravado.

Luc could not help the slow grin curving his lips. He took a long step to close the distance between them and savored the alarm that flashed through her eyes.

Brianna held her ground, though, seemingly determined to hide her response.

Undeterred, Luc treated her to his most engaging smile. "But, then, I should have expected no less," he said silkily. "Seeing as I am, after all, your *favorite*."

Luc leaned down to kiss the tip of Brianna's perfect nose, then pulled an increment away to look deeply into her eyes. She caught her breath in a most satisfactory way. "Is that not so, my lady?"

Chapter Five

BRIANNA STARED INTO THE INDIGO GLEAM OF LUC'S eyes and swallowed. She had absolutely no choice but to lie.

Again.

Matters were definitely not proceeding according to her plan. Luc had not been sent away from Tullymullagh by Gavin, indeed, he had apparently not even been troubled by the man striking him.

Brianna felt a grudging admiration for the way Luc stood up to his sire's bullying. But admiration was the last thing she wanted to feel for this man!

Not only did Luc show an annoying ability to read her very thoughts, but he had had the audacity to kiss her nose! 'Twas difficult indeed to think anything of merit at all with her heart skipping as it did now.

Brianna was very aware of those perceptive blue eyes so dangerously close to her own. She took a deep breath and prayed she would not be struck senseless by repeating her lie.

Father Padraig was full of such dire warnings.

"Aye, you are," Brianna managed to utter despite the lump in her throat. She hoped Luc interpreted her flush as one borne of maidenly modesty. " 'Tis only natural to be curious, I would think.'' Brianna summoned her brightest smile and desperately tried to disguise how much Luc's featherlight kiss had troubled her.

When his smile broadened, she was quite certain she had failed. 'Twas uncharted territory Brianna had entered—there was little doubt of that. And there was less doubt that she would continue onward nonetheless.

Brianna would not reflect upon the import of that.

"And equally natural for a man to be reticent about his past,'' Luc countered smoothly. He stepped an increment closer and Brianna could not help herself from stepping hastily back.

Then she cursed her weakness when Luc smiled and closed the distance between them once more. Brianna slid back one step, then another, yet one of Luc's long steps was all it took to put them toe to toe once more. She retreated, Luc lazily laid chase, until Brianna felt the trunk of a tree collide with her back.

Fool! Brianna closed her eyes in defeat, fully expecting to open them to find Luc close.

But he lingered a few feet away, his warm gaze yet upon her. There was something of his smile that reminded Brianna of a hungry wolf on the hunt.

But she was supposed to be making *him* flee! Frustration rose within Brianna as she became newly aware of the box pressed against her belly. She needed Luc out of the orchard, out of the bailey, and out of Tullymullagh! How could she turn this tide?

But Luc *had* conceded disinterest in talking of his past. Perhaps Brianna's plan to plague Luc with questions until he willingly departed Tullymullagh had promise, after all!

'Twould have to do. Indeed, the warm scent of Luc's skin was so merrily addling Brianna's wits that she could not possibly have conjured an alternative.

She was thinking instead of a certain bone-melting kiss granted beneath the stars.

Brianna pushed such recollections from her thoughts. She tipped up her chin with defiance as though she had planned all along to back into this tree. "So," she inquired brightly, "are you indeed a bastard?"

To her disappointment, Luc appeared supremely untroubled by her question. "So many questions," he mused, "and those of a man disinclined to answer." Luc met Brianna's gaze with startling suddenness. "What shall we do?"

Pinned by that steady regard, Brianna had a hard time taking a breath. "You *must* answer me," she declared in a rush. "I am the princess of Tullymullagh, after all."

And Luc, to Brianna's surprise, laughed aloud.

'Twas a rich and merry sound, all the more so because 'twas unexpected. His eyes twinkled in a most intriguing way, the crinkle of laugh lines revealed that he was not oft so sober as he had been thus far. Luc looked markedly younger, and when his warm regard collided with Brianna's own, her heart skipped a beat.

"And I, like all others here, must dance to your bidding?" he inquired mildly, then arched an ebony brow.

Brianna cleared her throat, quite certain the prospect had never sounded so whimsical before. " 'Twould only be fitting," she said stiffly, "as an acknowledgement of my station."

"Ah!" Luc scanned the orchard for a moment, then flicked a bright glance at Brianna. "Perhaps 'twould be *more* fitting if we made a wager."

There was something in Luc's teasing tone that warned Brianna she would not be enamored of whatever wager he had in mind. Aye, a decidedly mischievous gleam had taken up residence in those blue eyes and Brianna had the sense she faced an unpredictable man.

All the same, she was very curious.

"What manner of wager?" she asked not troubling to hide her suspicion.

His smile was fleeting, and Brianna knew he had not missed the import of her tone. " 'Twould be a simple enough wager," he confided easily. "For each question you would have answered, I would take a toll of one kiss."

"Oh!" Brianna straightened, hating how his very words sent the heat of anticipation surging through her. Curse her lips for choosing to burn in recollection now! "That would hardly be appropriate!"

Luc shrugged. "Ah, well, 'twas but a thought." He pulled out his knife and turned his attention upon the tree bough beside him, frowning as he nicked away a tiny spur.

"But what is this you do?" Brianna demanded, not in the least bit pleased by how readily Luc appeared to forget her.

He glanced up in apparent surprise. "I must await Burke and might as well do something of merit in my days here." And Luc turned back to the tree.

Brianna nibbled her lip. This was not right at all. Luc was supposed to go on her quest, Gavin was supposed to force Luc to depart, Luc was supposed to flee from her prying questions.

But none of that had happened. She surveyed the apparently engrossed man through her lashes and considered her predicament. 'Twas clear enough that Luc Fitzgavin would challenge Brianna's every expectation.

Could she surprise him instead? 'Twas evident that he did not expect her to accept his wager. Surely she could bear a few kisses—her heart raced at the prospect—to see her ends achieved?

Surely she could devise questions that would make a reticent man writhe?

There were precious few options left to Brianna. She had

to see this man gone, one way or the other. She took a deep breath and straightened. Luc flicked a very blue glance her way and she wondered whether he was truly as indifferent to her as he would like her to believe.

The very prospect cheered Brianna immensely.

"I accept," she said with a toss of her hair and was gratified to glimpse surprise lighting Luc's eyes. 'Twas gone as quickly as it appeared, but Brianna had the distinct sense that she made progress on her course.

She would see her way yet!

Brianna stepped forward and shook her finger before Luc. "But I have a condition of my own for this wager."

"Aye?"

"Aye. You must answer what I ask of you, fully and honestly, regardless of this reticence you claim."

Luc folded his arms across his chest and his glance was chilling. "You doubt my intent is noble?" he asked coldly.

Brianna echoed his pose and lifted her chin. "*You* are the one who calls yourself a fallen knight!"

Luc stared at her for a long moment, then muttered something beneath his breath and shook his head. He then inclined his head, but not quickly enough that Brianna did not note the brightness of his gaze. "Fair enough," he conceded in a low voice that made Brianna shiver in anticipation.

Had she made a fool's wager? Surprisingly enough, Brianna did not care.

Then Luc's sapphire gaze bored into her own and Brianna was aware of naught but the way his words echoed with conviction. "You have my oath, my lady, that I shall answer each of your questions as fully as I am able."

Brianna could not help but believe Luc. There was a grim line to his lips, a certainty in his words, that made her trust in his pledge. 'Twas a fiercely determined knight who faced her in this moment, despite his garb, and Brianna recognized

Luc's rare resolve. He must once have been a formidable knight.

'Twas no petty reason that had made Luc set aside his spurs, Brianna guessed.

The thought made her eyes widen in excitement. *There* was a tale Luc would not be ready to relinquish! Brianna parted her lips to ask her question, but Luc stepped closer and silenced her with a single finger laid across her lips.

His flesh was warm, his skin roughened. Brianna could feel the strength of Luc's hands even in that gentle touch and thought suddenly of the possessive way he had gripped her waist the night before. Brianna stared into blue, blue eyes and could think of being nowhere else in Christendom.

Then, that twinkle made a reappearance and Brianna knew well enough to brace herself for this unpredictable man's next words. Luc lifted his finger from her lips with deliberate slowness and Brianna wondered whether he truly could read her thoughts.

Or discern the tingle his touch awakened within her.

"I do believe, my lady," Luc murmured amiably, "that the tally stands in my favor."

Brianna gasped in astonishment. "But we have just made the wager!"

"And we have only just met." Luc shrugged. "Surely 'tis only fair to make an accounting?"

"You! You have an audacity beyond all!"

Luc grinned. "And you do not?"

Brianna flushed and sputtered as she sought an argument. Truly this man conceded naught to her. " 'Tis *different*!" she finally declared.

"Ah! Because you are a princess and I am no prince? Or because you are a woman and I am a man?" Luc watched her avidly and Brianna knew she needed absolutely no reminder of the difference in their genders.

Indeed, she had never felt so utterly feminine as she did in this man's presence. 'Twas clear he had awakened some part of her that had long been slumbering. Brianna stubbornly resolved to grant him no inkling of that.

If she could. Aye, perhaps she had merely come of an age when she was susceptible to the allure of men.

It could have naught to do with *this* man. He was most irksome!

Brianna lifted her chin and counted out kisses on her fingers for the man before her. "You kissed me last eve," she recounted, "and again this morn."

"I?" Luc feigned innocence. " 'Twas you who agreed to that kiss last eve."

Brianna's lips thinned. "At your behest!"

Luc shook his head. "And an onerous burden 'twas for you to bear." Brianna might have heatedly agreed, but Luc arched a brow and she knew he had not been fooled.

"It counts," she insisted instead.

"But not the one this day," he argued. " 'Twas no more than a peck."

"A *kiss* 'twas," Brianna maintained stonily. "And I demand it be counted as such."

"Fine," Luc agreed with an alacrity that immediately fed Brianna's suspicions. He lifted his own fingers. "And now, we count your questions. Last eve alone . . . " he rolled his eyes. "Oh, my lady, in truth, I cannot recall them all, they were so numerous." His gaze slid to meet her own. "Shall we call it a dozen, for the sake of simplicity?"

Brianna felt her cheeks heat. Aye, she had asked him so many questions the night before. "Nay! 'Twould not be fair to count them all!" She jabbed her finger toward him grimly. "We begin from the kiss itself."

Luc frowned. "Oh, I am not certain that is truly fair, my lady, after all—"

"After all, you have won your way in more than your share already this day," Brianna interrupted tersely. She granted Luc her most steely glare. "Truly you are the most irritating man I have ever had the misfortune to meet."

Luc merely grinned, unrepentant. "If I did not have impeccable manners, I might well return that compliment, my lady," he teased.

"I am not irritating!"

"Not to those who immediately do your bidding, no doubt." Luc grinned and folded his arms across his chest, clearly not counting himself among their number.

Brianna did not care for the way that confident smile loosed an army of butterflies in her belly. What a perfectly vexing man!

She took a deep breath and glared at Luc. "We begin the tally from last eve's kiss," she stated.

"Your questions from this morn, then?"

"Aye." Brianna folded her arms across her chest, quite certain this accounting would come in her favor.

"Let us see, then," Luc mused, then tapped his left index finger with the right. "You asked if I was injured," he recalled, fixing her with that disconcertingly blue gaze.

'Twas true enough. Brianna wrinkled her nose. She had forgotten that, but even conceding this question would leave the count in her favor. She nodded mutely.

Luc tapped his second finger and Brianna found herself noting the lean strength of his fingers once again. He had a considerable tan, though as soon as she noted that, she tore her gaze away from his fingers. "And you asked if I was Gavin's eldest son."

"That does not count! I *knew* that already!"

"Then why did you ask?" Luc asked mildly. That twinkle revealed that he knew well enough that he was right and Brianna hated that she had been so foolish.

No longer. She would beat this infuriating man at his own game.

Or die trying.

Brianna gritted her teeth. "Aye, I did ask that."

Luc grinned then, tapping his third finger in a very disconcerting way. "And do not forget, my lady, you asked if I was bastard born."

God's wounds, but she had! Did the man remember everything?

Perhaps she *had* made a fool's wager.

Nay! She would see this through.

Luc's voice dropped low enough to melt Brianna's very bones. "Do you truly want an answer to your question, my lady fair?" he asked silkily.

And his gaze dropped pointedly to her lips.

'Twas more than clear the price that answer would bear.

Brianna opened her mouth to protest but nary a sound came out. She felt her color rise, she stared into Luc's eyes, and she silently acknowledged that she wanted Luc's kiss more than his answer.

But that was nonsense!

All the same, Brianna found herself nodding before she could even question the wisdom of her impulse. Luc's eyes flashed like sapphires, then he closed the distance between them in a heartbeat. He bent and, once again, gently captured Brianna's lips beneath his own.

Luc tasted as seductively masculine as he had the night before. As before, he kissed Brianna gently, his tongue running across her lips as though he would cajole her into participating. Luc's fingertips touched Brianna's chin, then slid along her jaw, leaving a breathtaking tingle in their wake.

His gentle tenderness was irresistible. When Brianna opened her mouth to his embrace, Luc's strong hand cupped the back of her head with a possessiveness that made her heart pound like thunder. He slanted his mouth over hers and kissed her with a thoroughness that stole her very breath away.

And Brianna did not care.

Her hands found their way to his broad shoulders, she stretched to her toes. There was something in Luc's caress, perhaps 'twas the way he lingered for her approval before continuing, perhaps 'twas the tenderness with which he held her, which made Brianna certain that she could but step back if she chose.

The very possibility made Brianna want the very opposite. Shivers ran over her flesh, an alien heat unfurled in her belly. She felt her nipples grow taut as Luc's tongue rolled warmly between her teeth. 'Twas all new sensations and even more wondrous than what Luc's earlier kiss had roused within her.

When Luc eventually lifted his head and stepped away, Brianna was honest enough to admit that she was disappointed. She made good note of how sharply Luc inhaled, as well as the vivid blue of his gaze, and her heart pounded anew. Indeed, it seemed that he gritted his teeth.

Was it possible that Luc had not been unaffected by their embrace?

Not that Brianna cared, of course. She pushed the very possibility away. She wanted naught but to see this man gone; she wanted naught but to spurn his gift; she wanted naught but to see her father restored to suzerainty once more.

She wanted to *trouble* him.

Sorely.

Although holding that steady gaze clearly had a tendency to make Brianna forget those objectives.

Or at least, grant them less weight. What whimsy seized her wits when Luc kissed her? Was this the fate of all women—to be affected by the merest touch of a man once the prospect of marriage loomed in their future?

"And your answer." Luc gazed down at Brianna, a half-smile curving his lips. "I am no bastard, my lady, but the product of a dutiful coupling."

Brianna frowned but Luc slid his thumb across her bottom lip. He watched its course as though he could not look away, then visibly swallowed.

The thumb paused at the corner of Brianna's mouth, then retraced its course. Brianna could not bring herself to move or look away.

And Luc's nostrils flared ever so slightly. She could discern the brilliant blue of his eyes through his lashes and instinctively knew that 'twas not her heart alone that raced.

"Fear not, my lady," Luc said softly, "you shall have your full answer. My pledge is not worth so little as that."

He smiled for her alone and Brianna's heart galloped.

"My grandfather, Gavin's sire, realized that his only son had ambitions far beyond the family saddlery," Luc confessed. "When Gavin first rode to war—taking the side of Matilda as did so many in Wales—my grandfather worked busily to cultivate an arrangement that would suit my sire's worldly aims."

Luc shook his head, his voice no more than a confidential murmur. That thumb moved back and forth across her lip with leisurely deliberation and Brianna stifled the urge to shiver. She found herself watching Luc's firm lips as he spoke, greedily noting every little change in his expression.

'Twas only that she might be as perceptive as he, of course.

"He was proud when a local minor baron, that of Llanvelyn, agreed to let his sole daughter wed Gavin. The baron was aged. Wales was restless in those days and many of the nobility had not returned from war. No doubt the baron appreciated the prospect of not only seeing his daughter's future secured, but that an heir with a talent for war would be present to protect his holding.''

Luc's ebony brows drew together briefly. "Gavin, as you might expect, found the holding of Llanvelyn too paltry for his attentions. The marriage contract was signed, however father and son argued bitterly. 'Tis a testament to my sire's character that he only agreed when the old baron suddenly expired.''

"And he would step into that man's place," Brianna concluded.

Luc looked to her and nodded. There was a warmth lingering in his eyes, as though he approved of her quick understanding, and Brianna felt her cheeks heat slightly.

"Gavin was the Baron of Llanvelyn as soon as the marital vows were exchanged. Still he had no interest in the holding, though, and hastened back to war and prospect of greater spoils.'' Luc's smile turned rueful. "I was the result of that wedding night." His lips twisted. "As was my mother's death in the labor of me. Gavin did not deign to remain or return.''

Brianna's eyes widened at this admission, but Luc's thumb fell away. He stepped back, the matter clearly closed to his thinking, and Brianna immediately shivered in the absence of his warmth. Luc ran a hand over the bark of the tree once more, as though preoccupied with his chosen task.

But his grim expression revealed to Brianna that the recollection had troubled Luc more than he might prefer her to believe.

Indeed, Brianna had the urge to console him. How dreadful to know that you were undesired, to never have known the woman who granted you breath, to be spurned by your own sire. Luc must have been abandoned to the care of servants.

'Twas entirely different from Brianna's upbringing as a cherished child.

Though she missed Eva sorely in the years since that woman's death, at least Brianna had known her mother. At least Brianna had been raised in the circle of her mother's love. She flicked a glance to Eva's sarcophagus and suddenly was recalled to her real objectives.

Luc was a thorn in the side of her plans, after all. Brianna's lips tightened. She was to drive him away, not feel compassion for him! Indeed, 'twas his presence that kept her from fulfilling her vow to her father to secrete Eva's letters.

Viewed in that context, his dismay was the most promising sight Brianna had seen this day.

Luc flicked a sudden glance her way. His confident manner had already been restored, Brianna noted with disgust, wishing heartily that she might trouble the man as thoroughly as he did her.

Indeed, his very glance made her cursed lips tingle anew.

"That is your answer, my lady." Luc's gaze dropping pointedly to her lips as though he could discern their burning. "Unless you have another?"

"Nay!" Brianna danced away, her thoughts whirling. Although she knew the question she must ask him, Brianna had to bolster her resolve before another of this man's kisses.

But she would be back.

She halted a few feet away from Luc, her pride demanding that she make a suitable departure. The man must not believe she was fleeing him! "Do you intend to go to the kitchens and break your fast?" she asked.

Luc shook his head. "Nay. There is much labor to be done here and I had best begin."

Brianna frowned. "Surely you do not intend to remain here all the day?"

Luc glanced to her and back to the tree. "That I do. There is precious little daylight in this season and one must make use of it all."

Nay, this was not right at all!

"But you must eat!" Brianna charged.

Luc shrugged. "No doubt Denis will be able to send a lad to fetch some morsel or another."

Brianna stamped her foot. "Nay! You *cannot* do this! You must go into the hall."

Luc looked up, assessment bright in his eyes. Brianna cursed herself for such vehemence, even as she fought to find a plausible excuse for her protest.

" 'Tis unseemly," Brianna declared. "You are, after all, a guest of Tullymullagh." She smiled as graciously as she could manage, desperately hoping that for once Luc would believe her lie. "I could not hear of it."

To Brianna's dismay, Luc stepped closer to her and Brianna had the distinct sense that he had not been fooled. "Indeed?" His lips quirked slightly. "Your concern is misplaced, my lady, for I am well accustomed to such labor."

His steady gaze made Brianna want to squirm or retreat, but she somehow managed to hold her ground. "There is no need," she managed to say. "Please, come and enjoy a meal in the hall."

That dark brow rose. "My lady, if I did not know that you wanted me merely outside of Tullymullagh's gates, I might conclude that you wanted me out of the orchard, as well."

Brianna caught her breath and she knew her eyes widened slightly. She could not summon a timely protest to her lips.

"Indeed, the only question would be *why*?" Luc scanned the orchard as though he might spy the very reason for her argument. A lump rose in Brianna's throat when Luc's glance lingered on Eva's sarcophagus.

The glance he flicked her way was cat-bright. "And who is laid to rest in the garden?"

"My mother." Brianna's words were more breathless than she might have liked. She forced a smile. "She was fond of spending time here."

Luc's glance slid to meet Brianna's and she had the distinct sense she could hide naught from him. "And you?"

"I know naught of gardening."

"I could teach you, if you had the will."

Brianna's heart leapt. 'Twas only because this would be a perfect opportunity to needle Luc further. First though, Brianna had to retreat and compose herself.

The man had her all a-tangle this morn. " 'Tis most kind of you." Brianna struggled to find a plausible excuse for leaving him to his labor and uttered the first thing that came to mind. "But I have duties in the kitchens this morn."

Luc smothered a grin and frowned with mock surprise. "Indeed? A *princess* has labor in the kitchens? Truly I thought Tullymullagh better staffed than that."

Brianna loathed how quickly she flushed, no less how he let her escape with naught.

Though in a way, 'twas refreshing not to have the upper hand surrendered so readily. Brianna refused to reflect upon that.

"Decisions need to be made," she said breezily, "about the meal for this day."

"And I thought I could smell the meat roasting already," Luc mused. "How odd."

Brianna gritted her teeth and stifled the urge to cast something at him. "For the *morrow,* then."

Luc flashed a heart-wrenching smile Brianna's way. "Of course," he conceded, his tone revealing that he was far from fooled.

Brianna propped her hands on her hips and glared at him. "I *do* have duties here."

"Embroidery?" Luc asked mildly, no censure in his tone.

Brianna opened her mouth to declare that she loathed embroidery, then closed it again.

'Twas true enough, as much as she hated to admit it, that she did precious little. A telltale flush rose over her cheeks under Luc's steady perusal.

"Lady Brianna!" someone cried and Brianna jumped. She turned back to find one of the scullery lads running from the portal to the kitchens.

"Lady Brianna, if you please, there is a great ruckus in the hall!" he confessed in a rush. "Cook asked that I seek you out, for Uther is sorely beset in settling our new guests."

Oh, Ismay.

Brianna groaned inwardly at the reminder of that woman's presence and felt an immediate wave of sympathy for Uther. She could well understand how the meticulous steward would feel overwrought by the recent events. Uther took great pride in both elegant manners and a fastidiously run household.

It seemed he would see neither again any time soon.

"We have great need of your aid!" the boy pleaded.

Brianna cast an arch glance back at Luc, and he inclined his head. "Do not let me keep you when you are in such demand, my lady," he murmured, then his lips quirked. "Duty does call."

Their gazes locked and all seemed to halt for Brianna. She watched the way that hint of a smile toyed with Luc's firm lips and understood that Luc knew 'twas fortune alone that had saved her in this.

Brianna felt her own lips curve in response, but determinedly dismissed her amusement. She knew suddenly that she would accept Luc's offer. She would learn more of this man, even if the price was another heady kiss or two.

Indeed, Brianna looked forward to the challenge. But, in this moment, she could not abandon poor Uther to Ismay.

Brianna turned and smiled for the boy. "Of course. Cook is right. Betwixt the two of us, Uther and I shall find a solution, perhaps even one that Lady Ismay finds fitting."

The boy's relief was visible and immediate. "I thank you, Lady Brianna!" He bowed deeply. "They are in the hall, and we should hasten."

As she crossed the bailey, Brianna felt a steady gaze follow her progress. 'Twas true enough that she did virtually naught at Tullymullagh. Clearly, the time had come to make a change. Brianna was a child no longer, after all, and she was able enough to contribute more than embroidery to the keep.

Aye, one day she would no doubt have to manage a household herself. Even Tullymullagh would not always have Uther's efficiency at its bidding. 'Twas resolved. Brianna would set Ismay to rest, then ask Uther to teach her all he knew.

She could not help but wonder what Luc Fitzgavin would make of that.

• • •

LUC COVERTLY WATCHED the lady Brianna retreat to the kitchens. He had no doubt that she welcomed the opportunity to leave him be, just as he had no doubt she wanted him gone.

He wished he knew why.

Further, Luc knew without doubt that this was the most intriguing woman he had ever met. Her sweet kiss was intoxicating, her determination a delight. As much as Luc enjoyed surprising her, the lady was not without a surprise or two of her own.

Luc had never expected her to accept his impulsive and bold wager. But now that Brianna had, Luc had marked difficulty concentrating on pruning the tree at hand.

He was thinking of honey sweet lips and keeping one eye on the portal to the kitchens. If naught else, waiting for Burke would be more interesting than any had expected.

That thought soured Luc's temper and he set to pruning with a vengeance. Marriage was for fools, and Brianna was a bride for a knight ready to take an estate like Tullymullagh to hand.

Yet for the first time in eleven years, Luc's reasons for putting aside his spurs seemed less than compelling. Indeed, he almost questioned his very resolve.

'Twas a woman addling his wits, no more and no less.

And Luc had *pledged* to have no part of that life again. A man who could not keep his word was worth little in this world—and Luc Fitzgavin took great pride in keeping his word. He had that lesson from his sire, as well as a lesson upon the foolhardiness of marriage.

Why, after all, would Luc have need of a bride?

Especially a troublesome one like Brianna of Tullymullagh? Nay, she was not the kind of woman for him. He but enjoyed teasing her.

And kissing her. That realization did markedly little to improve Luc's mood, no less the growing feeling that the orchard, in the absence of a certain princess, was rather dull.

But Luc would not leave. After all, 'twas what the lady wanted. And the longer he denied her will, the greater the chance Brianna would return to set Luc straight.

'Twas that prospect alone that finally coaxed a tuneless whistle to his lips. Luc would keep his eyes and ears open, and merely wait for Brianna's inevitable return.

'Twas but the anticipation of matching wits with the lady

again, Luc told himself, but in his heart, he called the assertion a lie. Aye, the lady Brianna had a way of capturing a
man's attention.

Luc could only hope she never guessed the truth.

Chapter Six

UTHER WAS NOT A HAPPY MAN.

His lord Connor had been ousted from the solar—where that man rightfully belonged, to Uther's mind—in favor of the barbarian Gavin. 'Twas an insult not readily endured.

This might have been onerous enough, if Gavin had not insisted upon prowling constantly while the men labored to complete the move quickly enough for his taste, interfering in every possible way with the process.

'Twas a far cry from the level of organization Uther preferred.

Gavin insisted he wanted to ensure he was not cheated, but the steward was not convinced. Uther guessed that Tullymullagh's new lord wanted to make it so difficult to move anything from the solar that Connor simply abandoned all he held dear in that room.

Uther was not prepared to let that occur. Connor had treated him well for nigh on twenty years and his sire for thirty before that. The sweet concern of Lady Eva yet burned bright in Uther's mind, as well. If need be, he would single-handedly ensure that Connor paid no greater price than absolutely necessary to this conquering barbarian.

'Twas the least Uther owed this family.

The arrival of Lady Ismay was a chore that Uther could have done without. And as for her spouse, Dermot was a man who had always made Uther's flesh creep. He was too pale for a mortal man, and indeed, he had a way of disappearing like a wraith.

As he had already done.

"How dare you not offer suitable accommodations for Dermot and myself?" Lady Ismay demanded shrilly. "In all honesty, Tullymullagh long had a reputation for being an abode of fine manners and decent service." The lady's lip curled in scorn while Uther fought back an impolite response. "What has befallen you, Uther? You *used* to have exquisite taste in such matters."

Uther tried not to glare at this most unwelcome guest. This day had already frayed his patience severely and Ismay pressed him further. He barely restrained himself from observing that the accommodations he had already offered her were far superior to whatever she knew at her home estate.

Tullymullagh, after all, was a wondrous keep. Not long ago, it had been constructed of timber and boasted but a single hall, with the lord's solar to one side. Though Tullymullagh had the privacy of a wall separating solar and hall even before Connor's grand vision, Uther well knew that Lady Ismay's keep, Claremont, sported only a curtain betwixt the two.

For this woman to demand a chamber of her own on the second floor, particularly when all were making do with less rather than more, was beyond audacious. Uther would not compel Connor to share quarters with any other, and he had already conceded that the princess must share her chamber with the noblewomen in residence. There was little choice but to let the noblemen occupy the third and last second-floor room, while all others slept in the hall.

Uther did not appreciate such a quick repetition of

Gavin's insistence that all be ousted for his convenience. Gavin could not be denied.

The lady Ismay was another matter entirely.

Uther dug in his heels.

"Might I remind you, Lady Ismay," he said coldly, "that Tullymullagh has been conquered. There is much beyond the realm of my influence in these days."

Lady Ismay sniffed. "Then, what miserable excuse for a hovel do you mean to offer us?"

Uther looked the lady dead in the eye. "You will have to make do in the hall."

"What?" Lady Ismay sputtered. Uther indulged himself in the guilty pleasure of enjoying her fury before he chided himself at the impropriety. "What travesty is this? How dare you expect *me* to sleep in the hall, like a common serving wench?"

"Is your solar at Claremont not part of the hall?" Uther asked coolly. "Or has there been great construction since last I was there?"

Ismay glared at Uther and inhaled so quickly that her nostrils pinched shut.

Before she could summon a cutting response, the lady Brianna appeared by Uther's elbow. He barely concealed his sigh of relief. Aye, Brianna was yet young, Uther thought with pride, but already her dame's natural grace in awkward social moments shone within her.

She would make a fine lady of this keep.

And she would know how to soothe this woman.

"Why, good morning to you, Lady Ismay," Brianna declared smoothly, her words like balm on an angry wound. "What a delight to find you travelled to Tullymullagh, and this when winter is in the air. How are matters at Claremont?"

Lady Ismay straightened primly. "Not well," she snapped.

Brianna's eyes showed her concern. "But what is amiss?"

Lady Ismay swallowed. " 'Tis lost," she murmured, her voice low with bitterness. "We have *lost* Claremont and all within its walls."

"All?" Uther was astonished into speaking when he had no place doing so.

"To whom?" Brianna asked, her quick question hiding Uther's slip.

Lady Ismay, to her credit, held her chin high. "An English baron, allied with that cursed Strongbow. His forces overran our own and he claimed the holding two months past."

"But we heard naught of this," Brianna declared.

Lady Ismay slanted a glance in her direction. "I preferred to have none know my shame and hoped aid would come, especially when the barbarian rode out with most of his troops a month past. But he rode only to Cashel, where he evidently pledged the lands—" her voice trembled with anger *"—my* ancestral estate—to the hand of Henry II."

Lady Ismay shuddered from head to toe and even Uther felt the tiniest twinge of sympathy for her plight. 'Twas true the woman did not show the grace one normally expected from the nobility, but she was high born, after all.

The lady Brianna laid a hand upon the older woman's arm. "Did you fight his return?"

"We were sorely outnumbered and Dermot, Dermot is not a strategist, 'tis most clear." Lady Ismay's lips twisted, her anger making her look yet older than her years. "Once that invader won the keep anew, he cast Dermot and myself into the night with what was upon our backs alone."

Lady Ismay swallowed proudly and her tone turned tart. "I believe he meant for us to die in the wind."

"Surely your villeins took you in?"

Lady Ismay glanced up at Brianna's anxious question. "The miller alone had the boldness to defy his new lord, but we could not endanger even him overlong. He found us some sorry excuse for steeds and we slowly made our way here upon the wretched beasts."

Lady Ismay choked back a sob and Uther wished he were anywhere else in Christendom. Saints above, but he could not bear to see a woman weep!

"We have lost *everything*!" Lady Ismay wailed and her tears began to fall.

Brianna patted the noblewoman's arm and Uther was doubly glad she had been in attendance for this confession. "Surely you have relations to aid you," she suggested quietly.

Lady Ismay fired her a glance filled with loathing. "Nay! Everything is gone! My home, my heritage, every coin within the treasury is stolen from beneath me. I have only what I could secure hastily within my skirts. Every steed, every knight, every heart has been pledged to that usurper, while I—the true blood of Claremont—have been cast out like *chattel*!"

Ismay shook her fist at a somewhat startled Brianna. "I will not be treated like chattel!"

Then her face crumpled as defiance gave way to despair. "I am *not* chattel," she whimpered and began to cry in earnest.

Brianna stroked Ismay's dark hair. "I have slept in a miller's abode!" Ismay blubbered. "I have slept in a field, I have ridden a mare bred to haul ale to market. Never have I been forced to endure such indignity in all of my days!"

"I am sorry, Ismay," Brianna said softly.

Suddenly, Lady Ismay took a deep, uneven breath, straightened, and fixed Brianna with a glance. "I beg of you, as one noblewoman to another, do not prolong my humiliation. Do not compel me to sleep in the hall amidst laborers and mercenaries, as your steward would insist."

Brianna met Uther's horrified gaze with sympathy shining in her own. The sight melted some of the frost around the steward's old heart.

Aye, she was Lady Eva's daughter, that much was clear.

"Perhaps we could arrange for the lady Ismay to sleep in my chambers, as well," she suggested quietly. "Lord Dermot can join the other noblemen or settle his pallet in the hall, as he chooses."

"I suggested this alternative earlier," Uther said stiffly, "but it did not meet with the lady's satisfaction."

"I must sleep with Dermot!" Lady Ismay cried. She clutched Brianna's chemise. "I must bed with Dermot. We must have our privacy." She turned upon Uther. "Can you not see a chamber cleared for us, with all haste?"

Uther had had enough. "As we discussed, if you must slumber together, then you will both have to sleep in the hall," he retorted crisply. " 'Twould be entirely inappropriate for any man—be he your spouse or not—to enter my lady Brianna's chambers at night. And I refuse to be responsible for your own fortune should you choose to slumber in the noblemen's chamber. Together in the hall or separately in the noble's quarters. 'Tis your choice."

Lady Ismay eyed him with dislike in her small eyes, then her tears welled anew. She turned back to Brianna and sniffled most pathetically. "How low we have fallen in so little time," she moaned.

"Perhaps we should see Ismay settled upstairs quickly, Uther," Brianna suggested, a silent plea in her eyes. "It seems she might appreciate a few moments to herself. Perhaps a hot bath might be welcome after Ismay's journey?''

''I have not had a bath in weeks!'' Ismay wailed and began once again to sob with vigor.

Aye, Uther would have guessed as much. ''Indeed.'' He nodded crisply to the lady Brianna and began to organize a plan within his mind even as he turned away.

'Twas then that he spied the errant Dermot.

The dispossessed lord was seated at a bench among the serving men of Tullymullagh, putting away ale at a ferocious rate. Despite his wife's concern, Dermot seemed markedly untroubled by the prospect of being separated from her.

Uther frowned as he recalled all too well the tales that had circulated when Lady Ismay, then recently orphaned, insisted to her guardian that she must accept the suit of the mysterious and newly arrived Dermot.

Aye, there had been a rumor that Dermot was not nobly born at all, that he was no more than a man of common but foreign origins, bent on winning himself a fortune. The guardian had not been inclined to entertain the heiress' whim. There had been whispers that Ismay forced his hand by sacrificing her chastity to Dermot.

'Twas one way for a woman to see her will done. Uther could not help but wonder whether the ploy had been devised by Ismay or by Dermot. 'Twas true enough that in those days, Claremont had been an estate of rare wealth and a prize to be coveted. Uther supposed 'twas still a prize, despite years of poor administration, for some Englishman had seen fit to besiege it.

'Twas curious how a body forgot such matters over the years, like those tales of Dermot, then they were recalled with startling clarity at the oddest moments.

A scullery lad appeared at Uther's elbow with a question

and practicalities claimed the steward's attention, leaving him no more time to wonder the relations of neighbors.

• • •

DESPITE BRIANNA'S DETERMINATION, 'twas the following morning before she could return to the garden again. Uther had taken to her request with a vengeance and Brianna had spent the day fast on his heels, desperately hoping she would recall half of what the steward explained to her.

'Twas interesting, though, that much she had to admit. Even if she did keep peeking to see whether Luc remained at work.

He was there every time Brianna looked.

'Twas a blessing that Ismay snored so loudly, for Brianna awakened when the chamber was yet dark. She dressed in haste, hoping she might actually secure her mother's letters before Luc appeared.

Brianna raced down the stairs and burst from the hall into the bailey. Her heart leapt to find a familiar figure already in the orchard, even though the dawn light was just tinging the sky.

Curse the man! Luc had *still* beat her to the orchard.

Brianna did not like the way her heart began to pound with anticipation. She was prepared, she told herself firmly. She knew the question she must ask, she was ready to tolerate the kiss Luc would demand in return.

'Twould be better to see the matter resolved.

Brianna's lips thinned and she strode across the cobbled bailey. She had the distinct sense that the passing of each day diminished her sire's chance to regain Tullymullagh yet further. Gavin might hire more forces or more of his men might arrive. Time was of the essence!

But 'twas of kisses Brianna was thinking, not time, when Luc glanced up. He smiled slightly, as though he had been expecting her, and Brianna felt the oddest flutter within her belly at his acknowledgement. Luc immediately sheathed his blade to watch her approach.

Had she not known better, Brianna might have thought Luc had missed her.

"Duties done?" he asked mildly, then his eyes twinkled. "Or did it take this long to see matters arranged to the lady Ismay's satisfaction?"

Brianna almost smiled in return. "You have met her, then?"

Luc rolled his eyes. "Her arrival would have been difficult to slumber through. She seems to be one much indulged."

"Like me?" Brianna could not help but tease him in turn as she trudged through the undergrowth of the orchard.

The flash of Luc's eyes was quick and he hesitated for a moment before he spoke. "Nay," he admitted softly, his gaze assessing. "Nay, not at all like you."

The concession sounded like a compliment. And one that Luc was surprised to find himself making.

Brianna was prepared to ask for details, when Tullymullagh's portcullis creaked. She glanced back to the gates at the gatekeeper's unexpectedly merry shout of welcome. Who had arrived so early in the day?

A tall knight dismounted in the bailey with a flourish, his white stallion stamping proudly. The beast, caparisoned with brilliant red that matched the hue of the knight's tabard perfectly, stepped tall and his nostrils flared.

The knight's mail gleamed. His squire was quick by his side to take the helmet he removed. A shout rang across the bailey and Denis the ostler scurried out to look, his expression changing from confusion to astonishment.

"Ruarke!" Brianna cried.

The knight grinned cockily, his sandy hair tousled by the wind. "Brianna! Wench of my heart!" he roared, then laughed with his characteristic merry rumble.

"You are back!"

" 'Tis true enough," the knight retorted cheerfully. Denis welcomed Lightning with a murmur and the warhorse deigned to have its ears scratched. Squire and ostler led the stallion and pair of palfreys toward the stable.

Ruarke fixed Brianna with a bright glance. "Now, come, and let me have a look at you!"

But Brianna halted on the perimeter of the orchard. She propped her hands upon her hips and glared cheekily at the new arrival. "Where have you been?" she demanded with a sternness that was not completely feigned. She was very aware of Luc attending this conversation. "What manner of champion knight are you to abandon your lord's keep in its most dire hour?"

Ruarke sobered and folded his arms across his chest. He looked most stern and forbidding when he assumed this pose. "And what, child, do you imagine I have been doing?"

Child. 'Twas how Ruarke treated her, that much was for certain. Irritation slid through Brianna even as Ruarke strode closer and she felt her color rise in indignation.

Luc did not think she was a child. Brianna could not halt the comparison that came immediately to mind.

'Twas odd, but even though Luc had awakened these new urges within Brianna, she felt no similar tingle of anticipation when Ruarke strode toward her.

"I saw you speak with Father two months past," she charged quietly and a flame lit in the knight's eyes.

"Then you know I did not abandon my liege lord," Ruarke retorted in an undertone.

"He sent you for aid," Brianna guessed.

Ruarke shook his head and frowned in clear disappointment. "And there was none to be had. All of Ireland has been beset."

Brianna frowned. It seemed to her that it should not have taken Ruarke so long to work his way back to Tullymullagh. Indeed, if he had arrived sooner, Tullymullagh might not have fallen into Gavin's hands.

Brianna tilted her chin. "And you returned via . . . France?" she challenged.

Ruarke smiled sadly and his voice dropped yet further. "Brianna," he chided gently, as though he explained a matter of great complexity to a dimwitted child. "I had to ask at every keep. I had to knock at every door in my quest to bring aid to your sire."

His eyes turned sad and he glanced behind himself. "To return alone was a defeat I never hoped to face. Know this, never would I willingly fail in any quest your sire did grant me."

Brianna immediately felt guilty for judging him so harshly. How like Ruarke to exhaust every possibility before he conceded defeat! He had tried, even if his prolonged absence had not aided Tullymullagh in the least.

Ruarke could not have known precisely what transpired here.

"Now, come here and let me see you," he suggested.

Brianna drew herself up proudly and eyed the knight with mock hauteur. "I come to you? 'Tis *you* who should bend your knee to me!"

Ruarke chuckled, cast aside his gauntlets, took the two steps left between them, and dropped to one knee. "Your wish, my princess, is my very command."

Brianna caught her breath, certain she would feel something when Ruarke captured her hand within his.

But she felt naught. 'Twas true his hand was warm and just as rough as Luc's, not to mention as tanned. His fingers were strong, and her hand looked small within his.

But Ruarke might as well have been her father for all the

tingles he set in motion. He even brushed his lips across her knuckles and Brianna felt naught at all.

She did not want to think about the import of that and hauled her hand out of the knight's grip. "Fool," she charged, achingly aware that Luc was witnessing this.

Luc, who awakened tingles aplenty, seemingly without even making an effort to do so.

"Fool? Not I!" Ruarke lunged to his feet, caught Brianna around the waist and spun her in the air. "What is this? Why are you not garbed in one of your fine kirtles?" He frowned and fumbled, as though he would drop her to the ground. "And God's blood, child, what have you been eating? You have gotten *fat* in my absence!"

The twinkle in the knight's eye belied his words and Brianna gave him a hearty swat on the shoulder. "More likely 'tis *you* who have been losing your strength, playing chess instead of swinging your sword!"

At the charge, Ruarke sobered anew, his glance flicking to the alien standard that fluttered from the roof of the gatehouse. "Come," he murmured. "I have need of a cup of ale and whatever you can tell me of matters here."

Brianna glanced back over her shoulder before she could stop herself. Her own heart took an unruly skip when she found Luc staring directly at her, his arms folded across his chest and his expression grim.

Indeed, she could fairly see the blazing sapphire of his eyes, even at such a distance.

She hesitated at the sight of his annoyance. 'Twas unlike him to be visibly irked, Brianna knew it well, and the fact that his look was directed at her suggested she might be responsible.

If she left in this moment, she might well be missing another opportunity to drive Luc away. Luc would compose himself in her absence and Brianna would have to lay siege to his defenses anew.

On the other hand, Ruarke might be persuaded to aid her in this and he could be a formidable ally.

Brianna chewed her lip, torn between her choices.

"What is this?" Ruarke demanded. "Do you pursue a dalliance with some garden laborer?" Though his tone was yet teasing, there was a dark thread running beneath his words that startled Brianna. She looked at Ruarke to find his expression anything but jovial.

Indeed, he looked most displeased. His lips had drawn taut and his eyes were narrowed. Brianna blinked, for she had always seen Ruarke smiling and amiable.

"Does your sire know of this?" he demanded, his manner bristling with disapproval.

And Brianna was immediately reassured. How like Ruarke to think of honor and her father's pride, to fear for her reputation! Brianna smiled and tucked her hand into his elbow.

"There is naught for him to know about. We have but talked of the trees," she said, feeling the tension ease out of the knight's arm. "He is going to teach me to restore the gardens as they were when Mother tended them."

She might have introduced the pair, but Ruarke fired a hostile glance over his shoulder to the eerily still Luc. " 'Tis inappropriate labor for you," he said curtly. "Leave the man to his task. We shall see you garbed properly and set before the fire with your embroidery before midday." He tapped her on the nose. "You should have naught to trouble yourself save which color of silk to ply next."

And that apparently was that, at least to Ruarke's mind. Brianna gaped at him, astonished that he could expect her to waste time with her embroidery when the future of Tullymullagh was at stake.

Then Ruarke winked at her playfully, his earlier manner restored. "Shall we steal a loaf of fresh bread from the kitchens?"

"Cook will have words for you," Brianna warned, as always she did. "You know he likes to guard every single loaf until midday."

"Ah! It shall be just as old times." Ruarke grinned mischievously. He waggled a finger at Brianna. "Indeed, I *dare* you to steal a second at the same time."

'Twas their old game all over again. Aye, Cook would bellow, Ruarke would charm and they would be chased from the kitchen by Cook wielding a wooden spoon dripping with gravy. On the threshold of the hall, Cook would abandon the chase, though not without dire warnings regarding their next visit to the kitchens.

Then, they two would collapse onto benches in the hall and devour their prize. 'Twas familiar enough and had proven a source of amusement time and again.

But why did an oft-played game suddenly seem childish beyond all?

'Twas just her concern for her sire coloring Brianna's mood, she knew it well. She forced a smile for Ruarke and nodded assent. They turned their footsteps toward the kitchen, but, as they reached the portal, Brianna could not help looking back to the orchard one last time.

With determination, Luc was pulling weeds from around the roots of the trees quickly and efficiently, apparently oblivious to her departure. Brianna nibbled her bottom lip and wondered what he truly was thinking.

There was no doubt that the man would not tell her, even if she asked. Brianna turned back to Ruarke, certain he had not noticed her backward glance.

But Brianna was wrong.

• • •

LUC PULLED UNDERGROWTH with a savagery he had not known he possessed. He told himself that he was but unnerved by the interview with his sire yester morn, but recognized the lie. His jaw still ached slightly in recollection, particularly when he gritted his teeth with vigor.

As he did in this moment.

Luc certainly had not missed the lady Brianna's annoying presence all the day before. He had not looked for her, he had not listened for her voice, he had not replayed the intoxicating sweetness of her kiss countless times.

Not Luc. He was a man with labor to be done. And he certainly had not missed the board yesterday because he wished to avoid the lady—or her obliviousness to him. Nay, he had merely forgotten the midday meal.

The great hall of a keep like Tullymullagh was not Luc's place, after all.

At least not anymore.

Luc was certainly not thinking about his spurs and sword safely tucked away at Llanvelyn. He refused to recall his own splendid caparisoned warhorse or the weight of a blade within his grip or to consider himself arriving much as this Ruarke had.

Nay. Luc had made a pledge and he would keep it.

Indeed, the touching reunion he had just witnessed told Luc all that he needed to know. 'Twas hardly news that he had been merely a diversion for the princess Brianna.

No doubt this knight had already sampled the princess' kisses most thoroughly.

The very idea was infuriating.

Luc ignored the tiny voice reminding him of the innocence he had sensed in the lady's response.

Perhaps she only toyed with him, Luc insisted to himself. Noblewomen were known to do as much for their own enter-

tainment. And how much, truly, did he know of the work-
ings of a woman's mind?

Precious little.

Which had suited Luc well enough every day of his life
and would suit him well enough now. Yet even that resolution did naught to alleviate Luc's uncommonly foul mood.

He simply could not shake the memory of the knight
Ruarke falling to one knee before a blushing Brianna.

'Twas like a cursed bard's tale and Luc already knew the
lady's fondness for such whimsy. What he could not fathom
was why it troubled him so. Whether she cared for Ruarke
or romance had naught to do with him. Indeed, if Brianna
were busy with Tullymullagh's champion, she would cease
to pester Luc.

The prospect of that was markedly flat.

And so 'twas that Luc was thoroughly relieved by the
interruption when the ostler Denis came bustling across the
orchard, his features lined with concern.

• • •

BRIANNA HAD BARELY crossed the threshold to the kitchens
and taken a deep breath of the warm scent of yeast when she
realized the room was unnaturally quiet. Cook fired a glance
of trepidation toward the new arrivals and 'twas not an expression that suited his amiable features well.

It had naught to do with the prospect of their thieving
bread.

"What . . . ?" was all Ruarke managed to say before
Brianna realized the reason for the strained atmosphere.

Gavin was standing over Uther, what looked to be a sheet
of parchment clutched in his fist. The mercenary's face was
ruddy with indignation, a blue vein throbbed in his temple
as he shook the list. "You all mean to cheat me!" he roared.
"The ledgers are rife with errors!"

Uther cleared his throat. "Sir,"—'twas clear he believed

he used the term loosely—"I can only, once more, give you my assurances that the inventory was fastidiously executed—"

" 'Twill be you who is fastidiously executed," Gavin retorted. Uther paled but held his ground as Gavin shook the list beneath the man's nose. "This keep is of such a size that there cannot be such a shortage of sugar and spice. 'Tis inconceivable that the salt alone could have sunk to such minuscule levels."

He leaned closer to the older man but Uther did not back away. Gavin's voice dropped to a hiss. "I would suggest it would be best for your health to find the errant inventory."

How dare he threaten Uther! Brianna made to step forward and protest this treatment of her father's loyal servant, but the scrape of steel on steel interrupted her.

Ruarke stepped past her, swung his blade high and pointed it at Tullymullagh's new lord. "And I would suggest it prudent to your own survival to treat this household with respect."

The room fell as still as a tomb.

Gavin pivoted leisurely and his eyes narrowed as he assessed the new arrivals. He did not draw his own blade, his gaze almost insulting as it raked over Ruarke. He seemed to gauge the knight's ability with his eyes alone.

Then Gavin arched a brow and his voice dropped dangerously low. "Who is this man so bold that he enters my own keep carrying a blade unpledged to my hand?"

Ruarke straightened proudly. "I am Ruarke de Rossiers, the—"

"The so-called champion of Tullymullagh," Gavin completed with a smirk. "Your arrival is somewhat less than timely."

From her vantage point, Brianna could see the flush of red

that suffused the back of Ruarke's neck, though his manner
did not change. "I had errands abroad."

"Aye, I know well enough of your *errands*," Gavin
sneered. He smiled in a most unfriendly manner. "As well
as how thoroughly they failed. Make no mistake, Ruarke de
Rossiers, your ride to the high king to plead his aid for
Tullymullagh has been duly noted."

Brianna inhaled sharply, but Ruarke did not seem to so
much as breathe. Gavin sauntered across the kitchen toward
them, the stiffness of his lamed leg seeming worse than
Brianna had noted before. He paused just beyond Ruarke's
reach with the blade and cast a scornful glance at the sword.

"An heirloom blade?" he asked conversationally.

Brianna felt rather than saw Ruarke ease slightly. "My
sire's own and his before him," he declared with evident
pride. "It has been in our family these nine generations."

With lightning speed, Gavin drew his blade and slashed at
Ruarke's own. The two swords clanged together with terrific
force. 'Twas clear Gavin's blow was ferociously strong.

And Ruarke was evidently caught by surprise, both by the
blow and its savagery. He cried out as the hilt was fairly torn
from his hand and Brianna caught her breath when Ruarke's
sword clattered to the ground.

Gavin spat upon it, then sheathed his own blade.

The kitchen help had collectively taken a step back. Belatedly, Brianna saw that Ruarke's sword had been slightly
bent.

"And not fine Toledo steel for all its age," Gavin said
coldly. "A man is only as good as his weaponry, chevalier,
and sentiment has never served a warrior well." He snapped
his fingers and his cowed squire scurried to fetch Ruarke's
fallen blade.

Ruarke stood so straight that Brianna knew he must be
mortified.

Gavin threw the parchment in Uther's direction, then fixed
the Cook with an equally quelling eye. "You might find it
prudent to lend your assistance in the steward's recalcula-
tion of the inventory."

"Aye, my lord!" Cook bowed low, all his scullery boys
and maids bowing and scraping in turn.

A fleeting smile graced Gavin's features, then he turned
back to Ruarke and sobered. "On your knees, chevalier.
Your excuse for a blade will be pledged to my hand before
you stand upon your feet in this keep again."

Every eye widened in the place. Brianna's hands went
cold. Her father's champion could not be pledged to Gavin!

"Ruarke, do not do it!" she whispered.

Gavin lifted his gaze to hers and smirked. "No knight
survives within this keep without cleaving to me and me
alone. And I will not suffer a potential enemy to leave alive.
Make your choice, Ruarke de Rossiers."

Brianna's heart sank with the certainty that Gavin meant
his words.

Ruarke took a deep breath, then glanced back to Brianna.
"Forgive me," he said quietly.

Brianna was shocked as Ruarke turned his back upon her
and reluctantly dropped to his knees. Though she knew the
knight had little choice, still she felt betrayed by his seemingly quick agreement.

Then she felt guilty for daring to judge him. Ruarke's life
hung in the balance, after all! What else could he have
done?

With a lump in her throat, Brianna watched as Ruarke
bowed his head and lifted his hands, palms pressed together,
to the new lord of Tullymullagh, prepared to make his oath.

But Gavin did not step forward.

"Nay." Gavin eyed the expectant knight, clearly enjoying
his submission, then shook his head. " 'Twill not be that

simple for you, chevalier. I would know for certain the depths of your commitment—and would have all within Tullymullagh witness your change of allegiance." He snapped his fingers again. "Follow me. Upon your knees, *sir*."

Gavin left no time for argument, pivoting upon his heel and limping from the kitchens with surprising speed.

And Ruarke, a bold, successful, powerful knight, followed the man destined to be his new liege lord, crawling on his knees.

• • •

'TWAS A FAR cry from the homecoming Ruarke had envisioned for himself. He was humiliated beyond all else, shuffling through the deadened herbs cast across the floor of the great hall.

'Twas no circumstance for a knight and Ruarke quietly seethed with the indignity of it all. How *dare* this man, this creature who was no more than an exalted mercenary, set out to embarrass the likes of Ruarke! How dare this excuse for a lord insult his betters!

Yet there was no question of leaving Tullymullagh. And remaining, alive, at least, meant submitting to Gavin Fitzgerald.

No matter how lethal the blow to Ruarke's pride.

Everyone within the keep had come to watch his humbling, it seemed to Ruarke, and he hated Gavin Fitzgerald with a newfound and considerably more personal passion. Ruarke slanted a baleful glance to his tormentor and caught the smile playing upon Gavin's lips.

Aye, the new lord of Tullymullagh knew well enough what he did. Ruarke gritted his teeth. He would not consider the ruin of his chausses, the scratches to the fine leather of his new boots.

Fact was, he had sorely underestimated this new foe.

And Ruarke had some recalculating to do. He could only hope that he lived long enough to have that chance.

Gavin turned his steps toward the dais. The burly Welsh ruffian propped himself up in the high chair of Tullymullagh and Ruarke shuffled to a halt before that man's feet.

The bile rose in Ruarke's throat at the travesty of what he was compelled to do. There was no other man in all of Christendom to whom Ruarke would like less as a liege lord.

But he had seen the gleam in Gavin's eye when he made his threat. This was a man who had killed oft before and thought naught of repeating the deed.

And Ruarke de Rossiers had no intention of dying when he had so much for which to live. No mere pledge was going to stand in the way of all he had envisioned.

'Twas only words, yet those words would let him live.

One day, vengeance would be his own.

Ruarke bowed his head, before Gavin could see the rebellion in his eyes. He lifted his hands once more, praying the appalling deed would at least be completed quickly. Gavin's calloused palms closed immediately around Ruarke's own, as though he too were anxious for this pledge to be made.

Ruarke pledged himself to Gavin by the age old formula. He closed his eyes as Gavin kissed first one of his cheeks, then the other, bracing himself against the man's powerful odor. Ruarke bit down on his certainty that he had sworn his blade to a man no better than a barbarian.

"Kiss my boot."

Ruarke blinked, certain he could not have heard aright. He glanced up and Gavin smiled a cold smile down from his perch. "I bade you kiss my boot, oh noble knight. I would see that your heart follows your words."

The hall fell into astonished silence. Ruarke eyed the boot in question and fought against his urge to flee this charade.

But 'twould serve him naught to irk Tullymullagh's new lord. And he had already granted his word before dozens of witnesses. Likely this last humiliation would satisfy Gavin.

Ruarke gritted his teeth, leaned forward, and brushed his lips just barely across the toe of one heavy black leather boot.

And was stunned when Gavin kicked him right in the jaw.

Pain exploded in Ruarke's face, the assembly gasped in unison, and the knight fell backward into the rushes, dazed.

"Nay!" Brianna cried from a distance. "Do not hurt him!"

"I shall do what I will with any enemy within my walls," Gavin retorted as Ruarke caught his breath.

Before he could collect himself, two men seized his arms and Gavin came to stand over him. Ruarke struggled for freedom, but to no avail.

Gavin leaned close to Ruarke. "I did not care for your reluctance in this, chevalier," he purred. "And it seems to me that your heart is not at one with your words at all." Gavin glanced at the men holding Ruarke's arms. "Strip him of his weaponry and cast him in the dungeons. His own company should convince him of the bounty of my hand."

Anger flashed within Ruarke. Never had he been treated so disgustingly in all of his life! 'Twas unjust! 'Twas wrong! He would not go willingly into the dungeons, like some common criminal!

"You cannot do this!" Ruarke bellowed before he could stop himself. "I am the champion of Tullymullagh! I am a knight and not to be shamed in this way!"

Gavin's lips twisted in a sneer as he leaned close to Ruarke's face. "Precisely," he whispered. "And that is why I will break you before I let you stride freely through this keep."

Ruarke spat in the barbarian's eye.

Gavin did not miss a beat before backhanding the knight so hard that Ruarke's breath was stolen away. The knight sagged in his captor's arms as another kick landed in his gut and his face was pummelled.

But Ruarke was far from defeated. The anger he already carried in his heart now burned the ferocity of a white-hot flame. Ruarke knew he would have his due—and if Gavin Fitzgerald should step into his way, so much the better.

Then Ruarke knew naught at all.

Chapter Seven

"CEASE!" LUC CRIED AS SOON AS HE SAW WHAT WAS happening in the great hall.

And to his astonishment, Gavin did precisely that. The man paused, fist raised, and looked from the powerless and battered knight on the floor before him to his son.

"You!" Then his lips twisted mockingly. "Who are *you* to challenge my authority?"

"I merely challenge your wits," Luc retorted, well aware of the gasp that echoed in the hall. His father's eyes flashed, but Luc strode closer. He had never been afraid of Gavin before and he would not begin now.

And he would not permit Gavin to ruthlessly beat a defenseless man. 'Twas unconscionable, 'twas *wrong,* and just the sight infuriated Luc beyond all.

"To what purpose do you even strike another blow?" he demanded angrily. "The man cannot defend himself and already he is beaten to a stupor."

"He needs to learn a lesson," Gavin snarled. "He needs to know who is the new lord of Tullymullagh."

Luc inclined his head to indicate the unconscious knight and could not keep the sarcasm from his tone. "Aye, he looks to be attending your lesson well."

Gavin's lips thinned and he took a menacing step closer to Luc. "I should see you whipped in his stead."

"To what purpose?" Luc not only refused to retreat, but he folded his arms across his chest. "I already know that you prefer to speak with your fists—there is no lesson to be learned there."

Gavin inhaled sharply. "Insolence!" he roared. Anger flared in the older man's eyes and it seemed the entire assembly held their breath when he raised a fist toward Luc.

But Luc did not so much as breathe, his gaze unswerving from his father's own. Gavin swore and his hand fell to his side before he completed the blow.

"You always were *unnatural*," he growled, then glared at the fallen Ruarke with dissatisfaction. Gavin waved at his men impatiently. "Take him away! Grant him the hospitality of the deepest and darkest dungeon within this keep that he might think upon his loyalty."

The knight was dragged from the hall by a trio of men. His crime was no more than being allied with the loser rather than the victor, but the price he was to pay disgusted Luc. His father had learned naught of honor in their years apart.

Luc caught a glimpse of the greyed visage of Connor of Tullymullagh and knew he had felt every blow upon his knight as though it struck his own hide. He felt a wave of sympathy that Brianna's father must endure the loss of all he had wrought, especially in his sunset years.

The old king paused and met Luc's gaze for a long moment, leaving Luc with the distinct sense that he was being assessed. Then, Connor turned for the stairs, his shoulders more bowed than they had yet been.

A flicker of movement revealed Brianna as she tried to follow her sire. "Father? Are you well?" Her voice was strained and Luc knew he had not been the only one to note the burden Connor bore.

Connor summoned a weak smile for his daughter. "I but need a rest, child. Perhaps you might visit me later." He beckoned to his steward. "Uther, if you will." The pair shuffled their way up the stairs, looking markedly elderly, and Luc's lips thinned that his own sire should be behind this disservice.

He knew well enough that 'twas greed alone that made Gavin set his sights upon Tullymullagh. None had slighted him here, the keep had no strategic import, 'twas far from Gavin's other holdings. Gavin had merely decided 'twas fine enough for his Burke and cared naught for how many were killed or maimed in the acquisition.

Perhaps that was why Burke appeared to have mixed feelings about wedding Brianna. He had, after all, witnessed the assault. Luc's gaze fell on the princess in question and everything within him quickened at the sight of her dismay.

And Luc suddenly wished that he could make all come right for this fetching woman. She was so vivacious, as bright as a harbor beacon, that it seemed unfair she should have to face such a challenge.

Brianna watched her sire ascend, clearly not in the least convinced that he had need of so little, but aware that she had been dismissed. 'Twas evident that she felt needed by both sire and champion. Indecision warred on her lovely features, until she made a motion to continue behind the party heading to the dungeon.

Gavin apparently noted her move, for he swivelled to jab a finger through the air after his men. "And see that he has no visitors for two days and nights!" he bellowed.

Brianna blanched and her indignation was clear when she turned upon Gavin. "But he is wounded! He needs tending!" Luc had to admire that even after what she had wit-

nessed, she was not afraid to speak her mind to his abusive
sire.

Yet that very audacity made him fear for Brianna's safety.
Luc took a step forward that Gavin not court any ideas about
treating Tullymullagh's princess as he had treated its champion.

To Luc's relief, Gavin satisfied himself with a glare in
Brianna's direction. "He needs naught that solitude and dis-
comfort cannot provide."

Brianna looked after the knight worriedly. Luc feared suddenly that she would not heed his father's demand any more
than she heeded that of any other. His innards writhed at the
prospect of what Gavin might do to her in retaliation for
such defiance.

Indeed, she asked for little but the opportunity to show
consideration for a man's injuries.

Luc cleared his throat. "Surely 'twould hurt naught to
ensure that his injuries will readily heal." Gavin glared at
him and Luc knew he would have to put matters in his
father's own terms. " 'Twould serve none if an able knight
expired when he need not do so."

Consideration dawned in Gavin's expression and he slid a
calculating glance around the hall. Luc guessed his sire
could well use an experienced blade in his ranks.

And no doubt even Gavin realized the popularity of the
knight he had struck. Should Ruarke die, many here would
turn completely against their new lord.

If they had not already done so. The assembly drew back
against the walls, almost as though they collectively flinched
before Gavin's very regard.

"Perhaps," Luc further suggested. " 'Twould hurt little to
let the princess herself see to the knight's injuries. 'Tis the
place of the lady of the keep, after all."

Gavin pursed his lips and Brianna seemed to hold her

breath. The older man looked to the princess and Luc knew Gavin was weighing that woman's acceptability as Burke's bride.

"Not until the morrow," Gavin decided abruptly. "One night he shall have alone and untended to consider his path."

"But—" Brianna began to protest.

"Nay!" Luc declared. His mouth went dry that Brianna would so recklessly endanger her own hide.

She looked fleetingly at him, a confused frown upon her brow at his single word. Despite his certainty that she would not heed him, Luc sought to compel her to silence with a single curt shake of his head.

And to his immense relief, Brianna bit her lip and said no more.

Gavin looked scornfully to Luc, his quick glance revealing that he had not missed the exchange. A nasty gleam in his eyes made Luc doubly fear for Brianna's welfare.

He would have to ensure that she steered a wide path of Gavin, at least until her nuptials were performed. Gavin might restrain himself from doing injury to a prize destined for Burke, but Luc resolved in that moment to be doubly certain his princess was safe.

"Have you come only to urge *compassion*?" Gavin snarled.

"Nay." Luc straightened. "The ostler would have your permission to build a temporary addition to the stables. It seems the ranks of horses at Tullymullagh far exceed the capabilities of the existing stables." He arched a brow. "And those beneath your hand seem anxious to have your explicit approval before they act."

Gavin waved off the question. "He may do whatsoever he will. No doubt *you* can grant him better advice than I on such paltry domestic matters." His lip curled. " 'Tis the mark of a man to concentrate upon warfare alone."

Luc deliberately did not take his father's bait.

Gavin rolled his eyes, then frowned at the high table, his interest turning to more mundane concerns. "Is there naught to eat within this hall?" he roared and all jumped in unison. "Faith, a man could starve in this place!" He snapped his fingers at the plump cook. "Stir yourself, Cook, or I shall be compelled to find trusty help to replace you."

"Aye, my lord. At once, my lord!" Cook, Luc noted, ran for the kitchens with an agility that belied his weight. Gavin stormed toward the high table, berating all that crossed his path, and Luc heaved a sigh of relief that the storm was passed.

Then, he saw the lady Brianna bearing down on him, her eyes shining, and was not nearly so certain of that. She might have conceded agreement for the moment, but Luc suspected the battle was far from won.

Indeed, he found himself looking forward to whatever she might say.

Or do.

"Luc!" Brianna breathed. "That was wondrous, indeed!"

" 'Twas naught," Luc insisted gruffly, not the least bit certain why her praise made him feel self-conscious. He nodded, thinking the matter closed, and made a trio of steps toward the portal before Brianna darted to his side.

"Do not go! I would thank you properly for aiding Ruarke."

Luc glanced over the hall, now erupting into characteristic chaos, and had the sudden urge to be alone with the lady. It had naught to do with her use of the word "properly" he was certain.

"Not here," he counselled, and to his astonishment, Brianna nodded ready agreement.

She chattered amiably as they matched steps and headed into the bailey. Luc marvelled that she had so readily agreed to his recommended course.

What was awry? 'Twas most unlike the lady, Luc well knew.

"I cannot even think of how much longer Gavin would have struck Ruarke," she confided. " 'Twas horrible to watch, and all the more so because there was naught I could do. Do you think he is sorely injured?"

Her concern for Tullymullagh's champion knight grated on Luc. Such a man was hardly deserving of such loyalty. What had he done to deserve it? Abandoned Tullymullagh in its hour of need? Luc stalked toward the orchard, his mood growing more foul with every word the princess uttered about marvelous Ruarke.

Until a sudden thought brought Luc up short. He halted in the midst of the bailey, deeply afraid that he knew precisely why the princess was so concerned about this knight. Luc pivoted to face a wide-eyed Brianna, equally certain of why she wanted him gone from Tullymullagh.

It all fit together beautifully and he knew well enough that this woman had her wits about her.

"Is this then what you are planning?" Luc demanded tersely. "Do you want me gone so that your champion can challenge Gavin's claim, so that there are none whom Gavin might summon to aid him?"

Brianna gasped, the way her hand rose to her lips and her face paled telling Luc all he needed to know. "I do not understand what you mean," she whispered, but Luc knew the words were a lie.

She knew *precisely* what he meant! And Luc had guessed

aright! Anger rose hot within him that she would be so cavalier with her own welfare.

But then, men like Gavin Fitzgerald were beyond this lady's experience.

Ruarke, though, should have known better. Another black mark was struck beside that knight's name in Luc's mind.

Luc stepped closer to Brianna, his words low and hot. "What manner of fool is this man to let you take such a risk?" he demanded. Brianna's eyes widened. "Can he not see that you could well be injured? And what of the pledge he just granted my sire?" Luc flung out his hands. "Does his oath mean so little as that? How can he believe that Gavin will *forget* such a pledge?"

Brianna shook her head. "But Ruarke knows naught of this," she began, then bit her lip as she realized her concession. Her guilty gaze rose to Luc's as though she hoped he had not caught her slip.

But he had.

And Luc knew full well that he had rightly discerned the turn of this woman's thoughts. He muttered an expletive beneath his breath, scowled at the proximity of the keep, then laid claim to Brianna's elbow and marched her toward the orchard.

"What is this you do?" she demanded, even as she fought to free herself from Luc's grip. "You cannot simply drag me about the bailey or expect me to follow your whim!"

Luc fired a dark glance her way. "This is for naught but your own good, my lady, and you *will* attend what I have to say."

Brianna blinked, then ceased to struggle. She fairly ran beside Luc, taking two steps to each angry one of his, evidently thinking better of arguing the point.

Luc halted in the midst of the orchard where none might overhear and captured the lady's shoulders within his hands.

She was so tiny, so fragile, it sickened Luc to imagine what his father might do to her for even *thinking* of treachery.

How that man would savor the marring of such a perfect fairy queen.

"My lady," Luc said with a grim glance into her eyes. "Tell me that you have not been planning to challenge Gavin's claim to Tullymullagh."

Brianna opened her mouth, then closed it again. She frowned, she looked away, then she peeked through her lashes at Luc.

"Do not even imagine you can lie to me," he growled.

She flushed and lifted her chin, that spark of defiance bright in her eye. "And what if I did?"

Luc wanted suddenly to shake Brianna until her teeth rattled. This was serious beyond all! "My lady! Use the wits God granted you. My sire *never* forgets a slight—nor does he let one go unrewarded. He will ensure that you rue any such course, for *none* defy him with success."

Brianna's lips set stubbornly and Luc knew this battle would not be readily won. Indeed, she folded her arms across her chest, then glared up at him. "That is not true! *You* defied him just moments past!"

"I have naught to lose."

The lady tipped her chin. "What of Llanvelyn?"

Luc shook his head, forced to make the concession. " 'Tis true, he could deny me the seal, as he has done all these years. He could turn all of my labor to make the estate prosperous to naught, readily enough." Luc let his gaze bore into the lady's emerald one. "But, even then, 'tis a comparatively small claim Gavin has upon me."

Brianna shrugged. "He has *no* claim upon me."

"Nay!" Her very insouciance was infuriating and Luc gripped her shoulders more tightly. "My lady, you must understand that my father is not a man of compassion! You have just seen the kind of success your champion can expect to meet when facing him.''

Brianna rolled her eyes. ''I told you Ruarke knows naught of this.''

Luc stared at her, aghast as he realized the import of what she said. ''You would defy my sire *alone*?'' He could not keep the edge of incredulity from his tone. ''What manner of idiocy is that? I thought you a woman of sense!''

She drew herself up proudly. '' 'Tis not idiocy to fight for one's home! *You* fight for Llanvelyn.''

''Yet if it were denied to me, I would not be scarred for all my days,'' Luc retorted. Brianna's eyes widened and he nodded grimly. ''Aye, Gavin would see your beauty marred for his own twisted vengeance alone.''

Brianna fought to hide how his words startled her and failed. Her words fell in haste. ''My looks are of little import.''

'Twas clear the lady would not be readily swayed. Luc forced himself to voice his worst fears. ''And what of your maidenhead? What of your innocence, if he grants you to his men for a night?'' Luc glared down at her, willing her to understand the magnitude of what Gavin might do. ''My lady, what of your very *life*?''

Brianna paled and sagged slightly beneath his hands. ''He would not,'' she whispered, though Luc saw new uncertainty in the depths of her eyes.

Luc nodded sadly, infinitely relieved that Brianna finally recognized her peril. ''That and more, if the whim took him,'' he admitted, then gave her shoulders a squeeze. ''You *must* abandon this course.''

Brianna, though, bit her lip and looked across the river, apparently indecisive.

Luc gritted his teeth, knowing he had never met another so cursedly stubborn. ''My lady, consider who would aid you if your plan went awry.'' She flicked a very green glance Luc's way. "Your champion could do naught to aid you, especially while imprisoned. Your sire is aged, as is his steward, all knights are pledged to Gavin's hand."

Luc lowered his voice and leaned closer. "No one dared step forward to aid Ruarke. You must consider who would or could aid *you*."

The lady turned an appealing glance upon him. "Would *you* not do so?" she asked softly. Her hand lifted to his shoulder and Luc was seized by an urge to pledge himself to her from this day forward. "You aided Ruarke."

Luc swallowed the lump in his throat with difficulty. Brianna would be Burke's bride—'twas not his place to pledge himself to her protection.

And he had left the life of a knight behind.

Yet even knowing that, Luc could not bring himself to deny her. "I will not always be here," he reminded her gently instead.

Tears welled in the princess' emerald gaze. Her hand rose to grip Luc's fingers, as though she would draw upon his strength. "But Luc, it wounds my father so to witness this change." Her voice was soft, her heartbreak evident in every word. "Did you not see his face when Ruarke fell?"

Luc's heart tightened. He was awed that this woman saw no further than her father's dismay, that she would put even herself in jeopardy in an attempt to ensure her father's happiness.

'Twas an impulse so noble and selfless, so uncommon, that Luc could only gaze at her in admiration. She stared up at him, her tears accenting the myriad shades of green in her wondrous eyes.

"Aye, Brianna, I did," Luc managed to agree. He gave Brianna a minute shake, still feeling the need to persuade her of the danger before her. "But you must consider—

would it be easier for Connor to see you bear the brunt of Gavin's temper?''

"Nay!" Brianna's tears spilled suddenly, cascading over her cheeks like sparkling jewels. "I do not know what to do," she whispered unevenly and bowed her head.

Luc could not resist her. Indeed, to see her defeated manner tore his heart in two. Luc bent over Brianna as though he would shelter her from an ill wind, slipped an arm over her shoulder, and wiped her tears away with a gentle thumb. Brianna leaned her brow upon his shoulder and Luc felt her tears wet his tunic as she silently wept.

He felt humbled that she leaned upon him, even as much as this, for he had the sense that this woman seldom relied upon others for strength. Indeed, she had a wealth of it to call her own.

"Wed Burke. 'Twould be the best course for you," he counselled quietly, ignoring the scream of protest that erupted within him.

Brianna made no acknowledgement of his words and Luc sought some way to reassure her. Had she not protested wedding a stranger? And what could she know of Burke, after all.

"He is a good man, a knight noble and true," he murmured. "He will see you safe."

But to Luc's surprise, the lady responded most violently to his low words. He caught but a glimpse of the angry flash of her eyes before she shook off his grip and stepped back. "I will *not* wed Burke!" she snapped, her eyes flashing as she propped her hands upon her hips.

Luc blinked at this abrupt change of manner. The marks of Brianna's tears still shone on her cheeks but her determination was back with a vengeance. What had he said to so rile her? "But whyever not?"

"Because I do not love him!" Brianna impatiently wiped

aside the vestiges of her tears. "Indeed, I barely *know* him!"

Ah, 'twas the issue of wedding a stranger. "He is a good man—"

"I do not care!" Brianna glared at Luc stubbornly.

Luc folded his arms across his chest and regarded her. "You do not care whether he is a good man?"

"I care only that I do not love him!" Luc's lack of understanding must have shown, for Brianna shook her head and heaved a sigh. "Luc, I pledged long ago to wed only my own true love. I shall do that, regardless of what you, or my father, or your father or even the King of England himself have to say about the matter!"

Luc stared at Brianna, doubting what he had heard, then shoved a hand impatiently through his hair. "What whimsy is this? Truly, you do listen overmuch to the bard's tales."

"I do not!"

Luc spread out his hands. "Then where, my lady, did you seize upon such whimsy as this?"

" 'Tis not *whimsy*!" Brianna poked her finger in Luc's chest. He stood still, marvelling at her spirit as he watched her. "My parents had a rare love, one that they recognized *before* they wed."

Luc could not help his skepticism. "Indeed?"

"Indeed!" Brianna pursed her lips and looked away, then shook her head before meeting Luc's gaze once more. Her voice, when she spoke was surprisingly soft, her tone cajoling. "I know it must be hard for you to believe as much, for your childhood cannot have been easy," she said urgently. "But mine was *different*."

She hesitated, as though uncertain whether she should confide more. Her gaze was luminous, her expression expectant.

Luc knew she waited for reassurance from him.

"You cannot know what the future holds," he said quietly. "You might well come to love Burke."

"And I might *not*!" Brianna retorted. "I must *know* before any nuptials! Can you not see the good sense of that?"

" 'Tis not the way of things and you know it well. Marriages are made for alliance, not for love." Luc shook his head, but Brianna caught at his sleeve.

Her cheeks pinkened slightly as she held Luc's regard and he felt his heart begin to pound anew. "Could I share with you a tale, that you might understand? Please?"

And truly, when this lady regarded him so hopefully, Luc knew he could deny her naught. To listen to a mere tale was precious little indeed.

And what else had he to do this day? Naught of more import than ensuring Brianna abandoned her quest to oust Gavin—naught more critical than ensuring this charming beauty was safe.

Until Burke's return.

The conclusion was souring. Luc forced a smile for Brianna, knowing there was no reason for him to be so irked at the very prospect of his brother's return. "Of course."

Yet when the lady smiled up at Luc, a smile destined for him alone, any thought of Burke completely fled his mind.

And that suited Luc perfectly. When Luc offered his hand and the lady shyly put her fingers into his grip, Burke de Montvieux was as far from his elder brother's thoughts as ever he could be.

• • •

THEY SAT TOGETHER on the low wall that marked the river side of the orchard and Brianna swung her feet as she sought the words to begin. In truth, she had been noting the lean strength of Luc's legs, his boots firmly planted on the ground.

Aye, she liked that he was concerned for her and had the

distinct sense that while Luc was at Tullymullagh, naught ill could happen to her.

That must be why his reminder that he must leave had been so disappointing.

"You must have cared deeply for your dame," Luc commented idly when the silence had stretched long.

"Aye." Brianna glanced up, Luc's gaze colliding with hers in the wake of his words, and she noted the brightness of the blue. She would wager her answer interested him more than he might care to admit. Aye, it might well be that the shade of his eyes grew more vivid when his passion was aroused.

Did his eyes not glow as blue as a summer sky when he kissed her?

Brianna's lips tingled in recollection of those kisses, but she forced herself to answer his question. "Aye, I did." Brianna frowned. "It has been quiet here since she passed, though she was the most tranquil soul that ever I have known. As I told you, 'tis her sarcophagus there."

Luc's glance followed her pointed finger and he nodded. "Because she loved the garden."

"Aye. That she did." Brianna blinked back an unexpected tear. Luc, to her relief, seemed to sense her dismay and feigned interest in the distant hills. Brianna appreciated having the moment to collect herself and marvelled again that Luc was content to let her take her own time.

"And you say that your sire and she shared a rare passion."

"Aye." Brianna smiled at the recollection of the tale she had oft been told. "They met afore my sire took the cross." She slanted a glance to her companion, suddenly shy. " 'Tis a tale I love for 'tis romantic beyond all, but I fear you may find it tedious."

That errant twinkle danced briefly in Luc's eye and he

arched a brow mischievously. "For I am clearly a man with no regard for romance?" he teased and Brianna cursed how quickly she flushed.

"I know little of what you hold in regard," she argued, well aware of Luc's sparkling regard, even though she stared at her toes.

'Twas not exactly true, she realized suddenly, for she knew already that Luc held a pledge in high esteem. And he had disliked seeing Ruarke attacked when the knight could not defend himself. Luc showed concern for her own welfare, with a determination that warmed Brianna's heart.

Indeed, Brianna could not help but think of a knight's pledge to uphold his sworn vow and to ensure the protection of those unable to see to their own welfare.

Why *had* Luc ceased to be a knight? It seemed the labor was perfectly suited to the turn of his mind. Brianna knew well enough the strength of Luc's grip and guessed he was a formidable opponent.

She could ask him, but that would be a question. Her flush deepened with the certainty that Luc would demand his toll.

They had made an agreement, after all. 'Twas not, Brianna admitted to herself, so onerous an arrangement.

Brianna slanted a glance Luc's way to find his gaze bright upon her and once again, had the odd sense that he read her very thoughts. The hint of a smile curved those firm lips, as though he did not find her conclusions troubling in the least.

"Tell me your tale," he urged.

Brianna deliberately cleared her throat. "Well, when Edessa was lost and the call came from Rome to regain that city, 'twas nigh upon the eve of my sire's knighting. He insists now that he took the cross for 'tis the bane of youths and fools to believe they can set the world to rights single-handedly."

Luc snorted softly at that, though Brianna could not imagine why. She paused, but he said naught, so she continued.

"At any rate, he was knighted by the high king himself and 'twas there my dame first caught sight of him. There were a full dozen men to be knighted that Easter Day, each from prominent families, and, as you can imagine, virtually everyone upon the isle had come to the high court to celebrate."

Brianna smiled in recollection of all the times she had begged her mother to share this beloved tale. She folded up her legs and wrapped her arms around them, setting her chin upon her knees. "My dame said she knew Connor of Tullymullagh was the man for her the very moment her gaze landed upon him, for there was a twinkle in his eye that she found most fetching."

"No more than that?" Luc asked with soft skepticism.

Brianna clicked her tongue with disapproval and granted him an arch glance. "You were to listen alone!"

Luc grinned and inclined his head slightly. "My mistake, my lady," he said with mock formality. "Please, do continue."

"They were *destined* to love," Brianna informed her companion haughtily. When Luc said naught to that, she tossed her hair and continued. "After they had danced several times, my mother's suspicions were confirmed, but my sire confessed that he had already pledged to take the cross. My dame, though disappointed, held her tongue for she had no right asking anything of him while he undertook a quest of such import.

"And so, my sire went upon his way, travelling south to follow the Holy Roman Emperor and the Frankish king to the Holy Land." Brianna frowned. "But the war went awry. King and emperor fled the field at Damascus when 'twas clear the battle would be soundly lost. My sire was among those knights abandoned by their leaders and left to fend for themselves.

"He awakened to find himself stripped to the flesh and among the dead left to rot beneath the sun. My sire wandered as well as he could, hoping in some way he might yet find some sanctuary."

Brianna glanced up to find Luc staring at his boots, his expression grim. Had she inadvertently reminded him of something?

Or someone?

Brianna could not tell and so she continued on. "My sire had the rare good fortune to be found by a merchant who cared naught for war. He took my sire to his home and had his wife tend my sire's wounds.

"And as my sire healed, he thought oft of a fair maiden he had met dancing at the high king's court. He recalled how she laughed and how her eyes shone when he teased her and he wondered how he could not have seen the truth.

"But my sire resolved that he could not return to Tullymullagh with naught to his name, for 'twould shame his family overmuch. He persuaded the merchant to let him labor in his employ, that he might earn enough to at least replace his steed and blade.

"The merchant was readily convinced, for he had no son of his own and his business was a thriving one. And my sire, once he regained his health, was young and strong. In those days, my sire's hair was dark and he sat in the sun that his skin might darken and attract less notice. The merchant kept him from view as much as possible, their home being on the perimeter of the town and one already known for many comings and goings of foreign traders.

" 'Twas gemstones this man bought and sold, rubies and emeralds from the east, amber from the north, amethysts from Europe and pearls from the sea. My father oft told me tales of the wonders of this man's treasury, for they would spend evenings marvelling at the beauty of these treasures God had wrought. He always speaks of those two with great fondness in his words.

"When my sire's wages were due, he took his payment in gems. For two years he labored and the merchant was well pleased, but then the man suddenly fell ill. My sire was as troubled as the merchant's wife, for over the years, they had grown very close.

"In the darkest hour of his illness, the merchant seized my sire's hand and bade him go home, bade him return to his homeland and find a merry wife—he bade him bring children to light. 'Twas the merchant's single regret that he and his wife had never conceived a child. The merchant told my sire that he thought of him as a son and that he wanted to be remembered by him as he was alive, not dead. So, he granted my sire a legacy of gemstones and sent him from his door, even as he lay dying.

"My sire, with the merchant's wife's aid, stitched the stones into his humble clothes. She packed him food and kissed his cheeks and sobbed when he left their door for all time. And my sire wept as he walked home in that simple garb, to all appearances a pilgrim returning from Jerusalem."

Brianna felt her voice fade. "He oft said the voyage was a long and lonely one, for he knew his old friend had passed away behind him and the man's widow was left alone."

Brianna took a deep breath and flicked a glance to Luc. He was watching her avidly, his features tense with his attentiveness. "Once home, my sire sold the gems, precisely as the merchant had bid him do, a few at a time, first in London, then at the Champagne Fair, then in Paris. Never too many at once, never too conspicuously, never two remarkable stones together. And as the gems were sold, Tullymullagh's stone walls began to rise from the soil.''

Luc cleared his throat and Brianna paused in her tale to meet his steady gaze. ''I owe you an apology,'' he said softly. ''Your sire did not build this keep upon the sacrifices of others. I am sorry that I accused him of such misdeeds without asking after the truth.''

Brianna smiled, liking well that Luc had the fortitude to admit when he was wrong. ''No doubt you have known many others guilty of those crimes.''

Luc looked away and frowned, deliberately changing the course of the conversation. ''And what then of your dame?''

Brianna's smile broadened, her enthusiasm restored. ''Ah, that is the *best* part of the tale! You see, she had heard no good from the East and she feared greatly for my sire's survival. She prayed for him, but evidently to no avail, for the years passed and he did not return. Her own sire eventually insisted that she must wed, for she grew no younger, but her heart weighed heavy at the prospect. She dallied over her choices, wanting none other than the man she knew she could not have.

''And then, on the day her sire insisted she must choose, Eva came down to the hall, still undecided, only to find a pilgrim awaiting her there. A pilgrim, with a merry twinkle in the shadows of his eyes.'' Brianna sighed with delight. ''A pilgrim who dropped to one knee and asked for the honor of her hand in marriage.''

''Ah, romance,'' Luc murmured, but the gleam in his own eye revealed that he did not mock her.

Brianna poked his shoulder playfully. '' 'Tis a marvelous tale! It had been five years since they had danced at the high king's court and my dame could not believe Connor stood before her once again. Her sire, of course, was only too glad to accept the suit of the sole heir to Tullymullagh.''

Luc's lips twisted into a smile. " 'Tis no wonder you put such credence in bard's tales," he commented. "You seem to have been spawned of one."

Brianna kicked her feet. "I think 'tis wondrous!"

Luc nodded and scanned the orchard. "Aye, 'tis. Would that every child had such a tale to call their own, hmm?"

Brianna caught the sadness in Luc's tone and felt a sudden sympathy for his own upbringing. 'Twas true enough that he had no such happy tale of his parents' union and she realized as she eyed Luc's profile how very much her parents' love had shaped her own life.

She wanted suddenly to know more of what had shaped Luc's life. Brianna laid a hand on his arm, following impulse before she could consider the wisdom of it. "Why did you cease to be a knight?" she asked breathlessly.

Luc impaled her with a very blue glance, then leisurely lifted one brow. "Is that a *question,* my lady?" he asked, his voice thrumming low.

Brianna's gaze fell to his lips, her heart hammered in anticipation, and it seemed she could not draw a full breath. She was warm from head to toe, she tingled in anticipation of the shivers she knew Luc would awaken, she yearned for the sense of security she felt within the circle of his arms.

But Brianna could not summon a word. She nodded, transfixed as Luc leaned toward her, his eyes blazing like sapphires. She closed her eyes as his lips closed demandingly over her own.

Her fingers landed on Luc's chest and Brianna sighed with satisfaction as she felt the hurried pace of his own heart. 'Twas encouraging to know that she was not alone in being affected by these kisses.

Then Brianna thought of naught but Luc and his embrace. 'Twas thrice her name was called before Brianna even heard the summons. Luc lifted his head and frowned at the portal to the hall, then drew away from her. "You are sought," he said softly, his brilliant gaze dropping to Brianna's lips.

"I would have my answer," she insisted and Luc smiled.

He leaned forward and tapped the tip of her nose. "On the morrow, my lady. The tale is not short, but you shall have it all." His gaze bored into hers as though he would will her to believe him. "I promise it to you."

Brianna flushed and smiled, knowing that Luc would keep his word. "I know," she whispered and their gazes clung for a breathless moment.

"Lady Brianna!" Brianna jumped guiltily at Uther's impatient call. "The lord Connor asks for you!"

"Go," Luc urged.

Brianna bounced to her feet and ran across the orchard. She looked back from the portal of the hall, her heart skipping a beat when she found Luc watching her departure.

"On the morrow," she whispered to herself, then fled to her sire's side. On the morrow, she would know considerably more about Luc Fitzgavin, Brianna was certain.

And that prospect put a decided dance in her step.

Chapter Eight

"**F**ATHER?"

Connor started at the sound of his daughter's voice and propped himself up in his bed. He scanned the room and his tension eased when he saw Brianna's familiar silhouette in the portal. Aye, he had been slumbering and this in the midst of the day.

Truly, he had become an old man.

Brianna stepped out of the shadows of the portal, her features etched with concern. She was so vibrant that Connor's heart contracted with pride. Her golden hair snared the light from the brazier Uther had lit, her cheeks glowed with youth and vitality. And in the tilt of her chin was something of a young woman who had once granted him a kiss farewell.

As was there in the radiant sparkle of her eyes. Was this due to Ruarke's return? Did he dare to hope his plan might come to fruition?

"Are you well, Father?"

"Tired, child. I am but tired." Connor forced a smile and patted the edge of the bed. "Come and chat with me for a moment. What news of Ruarke?"

"Gavin would have him left to rot, but Luc stood for my request to tend his wounds." There was a thread of pride in his daughter's voice that caught Connor's attention. That 'twas not in reference to Ruarke was doubly interesting. "I may visit him in the morn."

Connor glanced beyond her to the door to assure himself that no one was there, then dropped his voice all the same. "And our task?"

"Oh!" Brianna gasped and flushed. " 'Tis not done yet, Father. I am sorry." Her hand rose to the wide belt twined around her waist and Connor knew the box he had granted her was yet safely in her possession. "I have not yet had an opportunity, for Luc is oft in the orchard." Her blush deepened in a most intriguing way.

Connor sat up a little straighter, but tried to keep his tone idle. "This Luc is the son who did not go on your quest?"

"Aye." Brianna swallowed visibly and seemed fascinated with her hands.

Perhaps his daughter had seen a similar glimpse of that man's character. 'Twas appealing how this Luc had confronted Gavin, at Ruarke's behest.

Perhaps one of Gavin's sons at least had been spared that man's cruel character. 'Twas a matter to watch closely. For as much as Connor believed his daughter's conviction to wed for love whimsical, he still would prefer to see her happy in the end.

'Twas his great weakness.

And Ruarke, 'twas true, had proven somewhat disappointing thus far. Why *had* he taken so long to return?

Faced with his daughter's uncharacteristic silence, Connor seized the chance to deliberately steer their conversation in a direction he wished to pursue. First, he cleared his throat. "It seems to me that this Luc is as unlike his sire as any man could be."

Brianna glanced up quickly, too quickly for her to be disinterested in the subject. "What do you mean?"

"It takes no small courage to defy a man like Gavin Fitz-

gerald, yet this Luc does so, and on the side of honor.''
Connor watched his daughter carefully. '' 'Tis rare indeed to
meet a man of such lofty principle. Did I not understand that
he tends a small Welsh barony?''

''Oh, but Father, Luc was a knight!'' Brianna's eyes
shone.

Connor arched his brow. ''But now he tends the fields?''

''Something happened, I know not what, but he—'' she
blushed once more ''—he has promised to tell me of it on
the morrow.''

Connor interpreted the blush as a sign that his daughter
had bent her considerable will upon uncovering this man's
secrets.

He found that most intriguing.

Brianna looked to him then, sympathy shining in her eyes.
''It must have been a blow of rare power, for he is not a man
to lightly cast aside anything of merit.''

Nay, Connor would have guessed as much. There was a
strength about Luc Fitzgavin that he found appealing—and
Connor understood well enough that the life of a knight
could provide many an incentive to seek a more peaceful
life. 'Twas a burden upon the spirit to always be at war, to
always be a witness to death. Connor could not blame a man
of honor for taking a more peaceful course.

And from events of this day, Connor had the distinct sense
that Luc was just such a man of honor. He thought of
Ruarke and long-laid plans as he watched his daughter, still
reluctant to cast aside a cherished scheme.

But Brianna's eyes had never shone like this when she
spoke of Ruarke. Would Connor's course ensure his daughter's happiness? Surely, Ruarke had just been unavoidably
delayed? The man's loyalty was beyond question, as was his
affection for Brianna.

Connor would have to reflect upon the matter and keep his

eyes open for this Luc. He forced a smile and flicked an affectionate finger across Brianna's nose.

"Ah, you must be feeling better!" She kissed him on the cheek and smiled with a sunniness that warmed Connor's old heart. Brianna looked so much like her mother when she smiled so merrily. "I suppose then there can be no harm in confessing that Cook has candied some elecampane, just for you."

"You all indulge me overmuch," Connor said gruffly, knowing that 'twas evident he was pleased. A boy from the kitchens tapped on the door, his nervousness evident in how carefully he balanced the dish he bore. The considerable bulk of Cook hovered behind.

"You must be surprised," Brianna whispered, then turned with a welcoming smile. "Enter!"

Aye, she was a rare one, Connor thought with a surge of pride. Brianna would cheat none of even the most simple pleasure. 'Twas as Father Padraig said—she had a heart that was pure.

And a compassion that knew no rival.

Connor coughed and donned a puzzled expression when the pair drew near. "Uther brought me soup earlier," he began, then feigned astonishment at the confection proudly presented to him. "Cook! You outdo yourself in these times! Elecampane! 'Tis my favorite and you know it well."

Cook beamed. "I hope 'twill lift your spirits, my lord."

"Aye." Connor accepted a pink sweet and rolled it around in his mouth. "I feel better already! Ah, Cook, your talents increase every day. Come, child, move these cushions that I might sit up."

Cook snapped his fingers and the boy quickly ducked to aid Brianna. When Connor thanked the pair, they bowed low. Cook was positively radiant as he lumbered back out the door.

"Well done!" Brianna declared, claimed a sweet herself, then eased farther on to the massive bed. "Come, Father, tell me again of your travels in the East. Tell me about returning to Mother."

"You have heard it oft enough," he grumbled, as always he did.

Brianna smiled. "And I would hear it again."

Connor returned his daughter's smile, then settled back to recount the tale he knew—and loved—as well as his own name.

• • •

LUC WAS IN a conundrum. He spent the day working diligently in the orchard, his thoughts churning as he sought some escape.

But there was none. Not only had Luc pledged to answer any question Brianna might ask, but he had given her his word *again* that he would confide this particular tale on the morrow.

And Luc Fitzgavin was a man who kept his word.

Even if the story of why he had abandoned his spurs was one he had never before shared. Nay, Luc had never even considered sharing it! The very prospect left Luc feeling as though he rode to battle with no ranks behind.

But he had granted his word.

Luc created arguments aplenty, but there was not a one that could counter that responsibility. He cursed his own weakness in the waning light of the afternoon, a weakness that had seen him grant such a pledge in exchange for a woman's kiss.

For Brianna's kiss.

Truth was, Luc was coming to desire the lovely princess. And 'twas not just because of her sweet kisses or the nectar of her lips.

Luc liked how Brianna's eyes flashed, her cleverness, her

determination. There was something exhilarating about matching wits with her, for Luc could never be certain of reigning victorious.

'Twas more than intriguing. And Luc liked very much that her resolve was bent on ensuring the happiness of those she loved, even with a disregard for her own welfare.

He had seen enough of selfishness in his days.

Aye, Brianna was a woman unlike any Luc had met before. And her kisses were not to be spurned either.

Luc cast a glance to the keep where he knew she was, then frowned and turned back to his labor. Denis and the boys were busily gathering stones for the addition to the stables and the bailey was filled with activity.

But Luc missed a certain golden-haired woman. He told himself that he was just concerned for Brianna's welfare and took reassurance in Gavin's periodic appearances in the bailey. Hopefully, Brianna merely remained with her sire. 'Twould be like her, Luc concluded, to cheer that man in this trying time.

He hoped with sudden fervor that Burke was as protective of his princess as Luc knew he would have been in his brother's stead. He recalled Burke's indifference to the lady's charms and was far from reassured.

Indeed, the request from Denis for advice distracted Luc from his thoughts at a most welcome time.

• • •

BY THE TIME the evening meal was called, Luc could not resist the lure of the hall any longer. He was certain 'twas only because he had need of a warm meal in his belly, but found himself anxiously seeking Brianna.

He wanted to be assured of her welfare, no more than that.

But Luc's first glimpse of the lady made his heart thunder with more than relief. Brianna was already at the high table, resplendent in sapphire embroidered with gold. Though her garb was rich, 'twas naught compared to her vivid beauty and Luc stood silently for a moment to watch her.

She was a veritable fairy queen.

Brianna's grace was no less than Luc had first perceived and 'twas clear from her manner that she was in fine health as she had been earlier that day. Luc forced the tension to ease from his shoulders.

He watched as Brianna initiated conversation all along the dais, a perfect hostess, even in the face of trial. Her sire sat by her side, a small smile toying with his lips, his color markedly better than it had been earlier. Connor was once again the wise, if deposed, king. Luc was quick to lay the credit for the improvement in the elderly man's manner at Brianna's feet.

Dermot sat to Brianna's left, Ismay upon his left, and even that man seemed to be contributing to the conversation. Ismay, Luc noted, seemed overly interested in the contents of her chalice.

But, like a moth to the flame, Luc's gaze was drawn back to Brianna. The lady nigh sparkled—indeed, the mood in the hall was markedly lighter than when Luc had last crossed its threshold.

Gavin had absented himself, but Luc guessed a good measure of the change was due to Brianna's efforts. To be sure, none had forgotten Gavin's cruelty or the knight imprisoned far below, but some festivity at the board could lighten a man's heart.

Brianna glanced at Luc and smiled, her entire face brightening when she spied him. Luc stared back at her, snared by her regard, his heart thumping painfully.

And he thought unexpectedly of Pyrs. The memory of their last venture into Llanvelyn's gardens together pushed its way into Luc's mind uninvited. There had been no swaying the older man from the walk, no matter how painfully he coughed that day.

They had gone because 'twas of such import to the man who had asked so little of Luc, even while he gave so much.

Pyrs had made his way painstakingly to a gnarled ruin of a tree and commanded that Luc look upon it. Luc had, seeing in its blackened heart the tale of the disease that had struck it dead. He had turned to Pyrs, uncomprehending their pilgrimage to this place.

Luc could still recall the resolve burning in Pyrs' tired gaze. "I had not the wit to see what ailed it," the older man had confessed. "By the time I cut out the illness that milked its will to survive, 'twas too late."

Pyrs had fixed Luc with a demanding glance, one that insisted Luc see the import of his words. "You must have the courage, Luc, the courage to cut deeply when a wound embitters the heart. You must remove all of the poison that taints the future. And you must do so afore 'tis too late."

At the time, Luc had assumed Pyrs was confessing guilt for letting any plant falter beneath his fastidious care, but in this moment he wondered. Had Pyrs been granting Luc more personal advice?

Had his loss, the same loss that made him abandon his spurs, embittered Luc's heart? He did not know, but he was suddenly afraid it might be so. Luc stared into a lady's eyes, distance obscuring their marvelous color, and wondered.

Perhaps Pyrs had seen aright.

Before Brianna could invite him to the high table, if indeed she intended to, Luc sat down hastily at the closest table. He needed a moment's solitude to reason this matter through.

Luc glanced to the dais and acknowledged the rare compassion that Brianna carried. He had seen ample evidence of it in the sympathy she extended to Ismay, indeed, in the understanding she showed of her own father's history in Outremer.

He instinctively knew that Brianna would not judge him or his decision harshly. And that was the only certainty Luc needed to make his choice.

After all, one could not be too careful with one's own heart.

• • •

THE WINE WAS GOOD, the meal better, the companionship fine, and Luc savored them all in the wake of his decision. He felt more at ease than he had in years and more alive. More than once, Luc caught himself glancing to the high table.

The candles were burning low when an overwhelming fog of musk and ambergris surrounded him. Luc coughed, certain there had been no harlots at Tullymullagh, then met the unsteady gaze of the Lady Ismay.

"Aye, here you are!" The kohl with which Ismay had outlined her eyes had run slightly in the heat of the hall, half the carmine from her lips graced the cuff of her chemise. Her cheeks were flushed, her veil askew, and she was far from a fetching sight.

She wavered slightly on her feet, the ruby contents of her chalice slopped over one side, then she winked at Luc. "I have been seeking you, Luc Fitzgavin," she confided unevenly.

Luc could not imagine why. "Indeed?"

Ismay leaned toward him and lowered her voice, a drunken and aged would-be seductress. Her kirtle gaped open to grant Luc a view he would rather have been spared. Luc knew 'twas deliberate that both chemise and kirtle were unfastened, just as he knew that the tired breasts revealed would not have incited lust in any healthy male.

'Twas an awkward moment.

"Oh, aye." she purred. " 'Tis clear enough that you are a man who sees a task completed." She hiccuped. "A man who does not back down before a challenge. An *effective* man." Ismay slanted a killing glance toward the high table, before smiling once more at Luc. Luc had but a moment to consider how he might best escape her amorous intent before the lady stepped closer.

Inadvertently, Ismay trod on the dirtied ends of her trailing sleeve. She lurched suddenly forward. Her eyes widened as her wine took to the air, she wailed, and she toppled.

Luc could do naught but catch her before she hit the stone floor.

Ismay swooned in his arms and one breast burst free of her chemise. Her besotted smile turned to a parody of coyness and Luc fairly dumped her on to the bench beside his place. He hauled her kirtle hastily over her nakedness and heartily wished he were anywhere else in Christendom.

Luc looked around for relief, but Dermot had disappeared. Uther was carrying a candle toward the stairs, while Connor and Brianna embraced, clearly before the old king retired.

And no one took any note of Luc's plight at all.

He fell upon Ismay's now-empty chalice like a drowning man seizing upon a straw. "I shall fetch you some more wine, Lady Ismay."

But the lady propped her elbow on the table, thunked her chin into her hand and eyed him dreamily. "I have no more need of wine, master Luc. What I need is a man's love."

'Twas truly an inopportune moment for Dermot to be absent.

"Come." Ismay patted the bench beside herself. "Come and talk with me, Luc, for I am in dire need of companionship."

Luc could not be rude. He could not walk away, yet he

could not take the seat beside her. Mercifully, the bench on the opposite side of the table had become vacant, so Luc sat there.

He turned the chalice restlessly in his hands and silently begged Dermot to make all haste.

Wherever that man was.

Ismay leaned across the table, her eyes gleaming, and her breast fell out of her kirtle again at the move. "What ails you, Luc? Have you no desire for me?"

Luc cleared his throat and strove to look anywhere other than at the pallid breast lying upon the board. "Surely Dermot claims that honor?"

Ismay grimaced. "No more often than he feels is necessary to ensure his place."

If Luc had thought matters were awkward before, he now understood his own folly. Truly, the last thing he wanted to know was the state of intimacy betwixt Ismay and Dermot!

But when he might have excused himself, Ismay snatched at his hand, claiming it with surprising strength. Luc looked reluctantly to her eyes and found an unexpected anger burning there.

"Do not imagine that my husband has any tender feelings for me. There was a time when I was so foolish as to believe that Dermot was all he seemed, but those days are long gone."

Her lips twisted ruefully and she seemed suddenly somewhat less inebriated. "As, indeed, is the only reason he saw fit to wed me. Aye, 'tis only now that I clearly discern the sorry excuse for a man who has lain beside me all these many nights." Her lips twisted. "And lain elsewhere on so many others."

Luc could not keep himself from looking to the high table in search of that man. He saw that Brianna had risen from the board and the flutter of maids about her indicated that she too intended to retire.

Yet Dermot had not yet returned.

But Luc could not sit and hold Ismay's hand all the night long. Truly this conversation grew awkward, and he was tired. "I am sorry, Lady Ismay . . ." Luc began, intending to excuse himself.

Ismay snorted laughter. "As am I, you may be certain."

Luc did not know what to say to that.

But Ismay squeezed his hand. "Why should I be the only one to hold my marital vows in esteem?" She walked her fingers up Luc's arm and struggled to look beguiling.

Luc was put in mind of an old whore who had followed an invading army of knights from the many years past when he had been young and impressionable. Yet even then, he had felt naught but sympathy for the sorely used creature.

As he did now.

"Lady Ismay!" The priest of Tullymullagh clucked his tongue gently as he passed their table. He was of the lanky and quiet class of priests, and Luc did not imagine the man had ever truly smiled.

He arched a brow as he paused alongside, his gaze never falling to the wedge of flesh Ismay exposed though Luc knew the priest was well aware of it. "Do you not imagine that you are somewhat casually attired for the hall?" His disapproval was more than clear.

Ismay had the grace to flush and clutched at her chemise with a mumbled word or two. As she fumbled with the tie of her chemise, Luc extricated his hand from hers.

The priest looked pointedly from Ismay to Luc. "I expect I shall see you both at Mass on the morrow?"

Luc contented himself with a nod, but Ismay held the priest's gaze defiantly. "Aye, Father Padraig. If all goes well, I shall have a confession to make."

The priest straightened, clearly appalled by the noble-woman's words. He might have made a quelling comment, but Ismay snatched up her chalice and bellowed for wine. In that moment, Luc saw that Father Padraig realized Ismay's drunken state.

"If not more than one," the priest murmured with a frown. He nodded to Luc and moved to the next table.

"Come, master Luc, let me show you the merit of the woman that I am," Ismay cooed. 'Twas clear the priest's manner had not altered Ismay's intentions, but Luc straightened with purpose.

"I am sorry, Ismay, but 'tis not my way to dally with wedded women."

Ismay eyed him for a long moment, then sat back, her lips tight once more. Then she glanced to the high table and Luc fought his urge to follow suit.

When Ismay looked back to him, a knowing glint lit her eyes. "The Rose of Tullymullagh," she said mockingly and Luc hated that his interest was so transparent. "Every man loses his heart with but a single glimpse."

Before Luc could argue the state of his heart, Ismay leaned forward and shook a finger beneath his nose. "But know this, son of Gavin, I remember much of the Rose of Tullymullagh that others have forgotten." Her eyes narrowed. "There is a tale here that has not been told for a long time, a tale that will change your thinking about much of what you see."

But Luc was not inclined to sit with a drunken noble-woman this night. Ismay was drunk, Luc was bone-tired from helping Denis, and Brianna was being safely ushered to her chamber by her maids.

All would be well this night.

"Perhaps another time, you might share the tale with me," he said politely, then bowed. "I wish you a good evening, Lady Ismay.'' And as Ismay's brow furrowed, Luc made for the portal.

Little did he guess he would have no chance to hear Ismay's tale, on the morrow or any other day.

• • •

BRIANNA AWAKENED WITH a sense that something was amiss.

The steady drum of rain fell against the shutters. The keep was cold, 'twas yet dark, the deep breathing of the other women carried to her ears.

Aye, November had come with a vengeance. 'Twas when Brianna snuggled deeper into her bedlinens that she realized what was wrong.

Ismay snored like a bull.

But no one snored this morn.

Brianna sat up and scanned the slumbering women, disregarding the chill upon her skin. She frowned and looked again with growing concern, but there was no avoiding the truth.

Ismay was not there.

Had she perhaps found some private place to mate with Dermot?

Nay, Dermot had not remained long at the board, though Ismay had lingered, imbibing heavily of the wine. Brianna's heart clenched as she recalled the last glimpse she had had of Ismay.

She had been holding fast to Luc's hand and staring into his eyes.

In Dermot's absence.

Brianna gasped in horror. She was out of bed in a flash and hauling on her chausses and boots and tunic, suddenly very certain where Ismay had spent the night. And with whom.

Luc Fitzgavin was no man of honor, after all!

A cold lump rose in Brianna's throat, though she knew 'twas only because she had been deceived.

She did not care for Luc.

She *could* not care for him.

Nay, 'twas the knowledge of adultery at Tullymullagh that troubled Brianna. Aye! Her father had always insisted that all beneath his roof adhere to a high moral code. That was what upset Brianna. It made perfect sense, though the explanation did little to account for the sick feeling in her belly.

Fortunately, Brianna had no compunction about making the error of their ways clear to both Luc and Ismay.

Regardless of what state they might be in at this early hour.

• • •

LUC FOLDED HIS arms behind his head and listened to the rhythm of the rain upon the stable roof. The thatched roof was so close above his head that he could have stretched out his fingertips and fairly felt the impact of the drops. Instead, he breathed deeply of the mingled scents of the wet straw overhead and of the many steeds housed below.

And he uncharacteristically lingered abed. 'Twas warm here in the loft and Luc was loath to rise. 'Twas early yet at any rate, for even Denis' footsteps did not carry from below. The horses snorted quietly, the dogs whimpered in their sleep, the squires around him stirred as they dreamed.

They all had taken to the loft the night before, tethering steeds throughout the length of the stables' corridors until the new structure could be completed, pushing aside the straw that squire and soldier alike might nest like mice. 'Twas only in the middle of the loft, where the ladder rose from the stable, that a man could stand straight.

Luc eyed the many sleeping here and wondered where Dermot had taken himself the night before. He was notably absent. More importantly, where had he disappeared earlier?

Had Dermot been one of those who schemed within these very stables but two nights past? Luc heartily wished he could know for certain—no less that he knew the truth of those conspirators' intent for Brianna.

He had a feeling 'twas naught good.

It seemed there was no end of perils confronting his princess.

Of course, Brianna had no need for Luc's errant chivalrous impulses. Indeed, once she wed Burke, she would have chivalry aplenty within her very bed.

The thought annoyed Luc more than it should. He cast back his linens, suddenly impatient to rise. He had just hauled his chemise over his head when the door to the stables abruptly creaked open. A wedge of faint light shone through the loosely placed floor of the loft and illuminated the top of the ladder.

And a voice rose in an imperious whisper from below. "Luc Fitzgavin, show yourself!"

Luc's heart skipped at the familiarity of those enraged tones before he grinned. 'Twas as though he had summoned her with his very thoughts!

He was only relieved because he wanted the telling of this tale behind him. Luc was certain of it and quickly hauled on his chausses.

The lady, though, was not patient.

"Luc!" she called again.

"Be silent!" Luc hissed through his teeth. "You will wake every soul within this place."

Mercifully Brianna did as she was bidden, though Luc could well imagine that would not last. He sought his boots in the shadows, trying to dress with haste.

Before he had even completed his task, Brianna had climbed the ladder to the loft. She stood directly before him, her eyes flashed in fury, hot color burned in her cheeks, and her full lips were taut with disapproval. Raindrops, snared in the loose cloud of her hair, shimmered like jewels, but there was no mistaking the lady's mood.

The only question was what could have angered her so.

Luc had no chance to ask.

"You!" Brianna charged with low heat, her voice rising slightly in her anger. "I believed you to be different from the others! I believed you were truly a man of honor and repute!"

Luc blinked—one boot on, one boot off—and struggled to think of what he had done to challenge that conclusion. "And now?" he dared to ask.

"Where is she?" Brianna hissed.

Luc frowned, yet kept his voice low. "Who?"

"Ismay!" Brianna fairly seethed. "Do not toy with me, sir. I know well enough that she is here!"

Luc was not nearly so certain of that. Why would Ismay be *here?* "I do not know what you mean," he began, but was to have no opportunity to finish.

Brianna advanced upon him, shaking a finger the entire way. "I do not know what you have done with Ismay this morn, but I know well enough what you did last evening and I will have you know that no man—no man!—shall be allowed to behave thus within this keep!"

Luc donned his other boot, glanced at the still slumbering boys, then strode toward the infuriated lady with purpose. 'Twas clear there were matters muddled, for he knew he had done naught wrong.

"We shall talk elsewhere," he informed Brianna, his voice quiet but firm. Luc captured her elbow within his grip, meaning only to guide her in the darkness.

But Brianna snatched her elbow away. Luc marvelled that she could be so troubled by what he had done, especially when he could not imagine what it had been.

"You will *not* take me away from here!" she charged. "You will not distract me while Ismay sneaks from your pallet!"

Luc eyed the princess incredulously, then glanced pointedly back to his decidedly empty bed. "From *my* pallet?"

"I saw you with her last eve and she did not come to chambers at all," Brianna retorted, her chin held defiantly high. " 'Tis clear enough she found another pallet to share and by the looks of your discussion last eve, 'twas with *you* she found companionship."

Brianna pointedly refused to meet Luc's gaze. "I thought you were a man of honor," she said with low heat. "I thought you were a man who would not seduce a woman already wed, let alone while her spouse lingers nearby."

Brianna took a ragged breath that tore at Luc's heart before he could defend himself, her vehemence was undiminished. "Ismay is vulnerable, she has lost much of late. I *never* would have believed that you would take advantage of her or any other woman in such distress." She clenched her fists and glared at Luc. "Such behavior is lower than low, you, you *adulterer*!"

Ismay? She thought he had bedded *Ismay?* Luc could not completely quell his smile. How could Brianna even imagine that he could be tempted by the likes of Ismay? The very idea made Luc unwillingly chuckle.

"Oh!" Brianna's eyes flashed and she made to swat his shoulder. "Do not mock me!"

Luc snatched her hand out of the air and folded it within his own. She fought his gentle grip and fairly spit sparks at him. "Brianna!" Luc spoke with low urgency and bit out his declaration. "I did not bed Ismay."

"So you say!"

"Where is she, then?" Luc challenged.

Brianna scanned the loft and Luc knew she saw only men

and boys. She flicked a glance to Luc, as though she wanted to believe him but did not dare. "But I saw her with you last eve. You held her hand!"

"She held mine," Luc corrected. "Ismay was lonely last eve and Dermot not to be found. I spoke with her, 'tis true, but I assure you, my lady, I left Ismay in the hall when I retired."

The princess studied Luc with more than her usual intensity, as though she would discern his every secret in his eyes. Luc did not dare break her gaze, for he wanted beyond all else for this woman to know he was honorable.

Though he did not dare to consider why 'twas of such import to him.

"You did not bed her?" she asked hopefully.

"Nay!" Luc shook his head with resolve. "I did not. How can you imagine I would even be tempted?" He grimaced comically and was relieved when Brianna's tension visibly eased.

"You are uncharitable to say as much," she charged, though 'twas clear she thought the opposite. A decidedly mischievous gleam lit her eyes. "I shall have to tell Father Padraig."

Luc grinned down at her. "Now there is a threat to curdle a man's blood. Your priest is dour, indeed. Does he *ever* smile?"

Brianna shook her head, then her brow puckered with concern. "But what of Ismay? She did not come to our chamber to sleep, Luc." She squeezed his fingers with concern. "Do you think something is amiss?"

Luc's heart swelled that Brianna not only believed him, but trusted him to resolve her concern.

"Perhaps she found Dermot," he suggested with a shrug. "And they found a corner together. Last evening, she seemed in need of . . . *reassurance*."

Brianna's lips quirked at Luc's discreet choice of word. "Yet you gave her none." There was no question in her tone, no doubt of his intent, and Luc found himself relieved.

'Twas just because he took pride in his credibility, no doubt. "None," he agreed, just to ensure matters were clear.

And the lady smiled.

The change in her regard warmed Luc like the sun appearing after a hard rain. He could not look away from the shine in her eyes. Brianna's hands fell upon Luc's chest, the steady pounding of the rain hammered overhead. He could smell the sleepy musk rising from her skin mingled with the rose scent she favored and he guessed that she had leapt from bed to make her accusation.

Before he could reflect further upon the warm intimacy of that, a squire rolled over and snorted loudly in his sleep. The lady started and looked for the source of the interruption.

'Twas only a moment that she broke his gaze, but 'twas long for Luc to realize the lady's folly.

"My lady, you should not be seen here," he counselled quietly. "It could be misconstrued. I would not have your reputation sullied within your own home."

Brianna sighed and wrinkled her nose. "But I do not want to go back to my chambers. And no one is up as yet."

"Then, come," Luc invited, gallantly offering Brianna his elbow. "I have the perfect solution."

"And what might that be?"

"Let us walk in the rain while I grant you the tale you are owed this day." Luc summoned a smile for Brianna, knowing this telling would not fall easily from his lips.

But he had promised it to her, and he would keep that pledge.

Chapter Nine

T HE RAIN FELL AROUND THEM, A MIST HAD CLAIMED the distant peaks and vales, and all within view was etched in myriad shades of grey. The orchard was silent but for the muted patter of raindrops on deadened leaves and the echo of their footsteps.

Brianna was fiercely glad to be sharing this moment with this man. She wanted very much to hear his tale. Luc guided her gently by the elbow until they halted beside the stone wall, then the heat of his hand fell away.

The River Darrow chortled far below, a chill whisper of winter in the rushing water. The lands of Tullymullagh swept into the distance, veiled by the rain, but Brianna looked at her companion. She shivered, folded her arms beneath her cloak and waited.

When Luc flicked a vibrant blue glance her way, she knew he was to begin. Anticipation rolled through her, for Brianna guessed that this was no trivial tale. She was honored that Luc had chosen to confide it in her.

Luc's words came in a low murmur. " 'Tis true enough that once I was a knight," he acknowledged, propping his hands upon his hips and surveying the distant hills with unseeing eyes. "And I suppose, in some way, I must yet be. 'Tis meant to be a pledge a man makes for his entire life and, though I have left that life far behind me, the words I once vowed yet color all I do.''

Luc paused for a long moment, as though he sought where to begin. ''You must understand that Llanvelyn was all that I knew of life, for through my childhood I never left its lands. My sire was a man of distant repute and when he rode into Llanvelyn's bailey in my eighth summer, I was dazzled by his person. He was more richly garbed than any man ever I had seen, his steed was larger and prouder than any of my limited experience.''

Luc grimaced. ''Perhaps 'tis a reflection upon the simplicity of my life thus far that I was so readily impressed. Perhaps I did not want to believe that the whispered tales of cruelty could be true of my own blood sire. At any rate, when he declared he had arranged for me to train for knighthood at an estate adjacent to Montvieux, there was naught that could have kept me from going.''

He flicked a glance to Brianna, his lips twisting wryly. '' 'Twas beyond belief, that this man would sweep up his forgotten child and set that boy upon a path to win his spurs.''

''Like the tale of a troubador,'' Brianna commented, and Luc's answering smile warmed her heart.

''Indeed.''

''But where *is* Montvieux?'' Brianna asked, uncertain of the connection to Luc and Gavin. ''Why squire you there?''

''My sire's second and current wife is Margaux of Montvieux,'' Luc explained. He leaned his hips against the wall, the move setting his gaze on a level with her own. ''When my dame passed away, Gavin won Margaux's hand and they brought Burke to light.''

''And Rowan.''

''Nay.'' Luc shook his head firmly. ''Rowan is the result of one of Gavin's dalliances.'' He met Brianna's gaze somberly. "With a woman in a travelling troupe of entertainers."

"Oh."

"Oh, indeed." Luc grinned. "Though Margaux had considerably more to say of the matter. She is a woman of strong opinions and Rowan's delivery to Montvieux at four years of age, when his dame died, was the reason Margaux finally cast Gavin out of her bed. 'Twas a vicious battle, from all accounts."

Brianna frowned in recollection. "But when King Henry was here, Gavin said that Rowan was with Margaux."

"Aye, she took a fancy to him, and to her credit never blamed the child with the circumstance of his conception. She raised Rowan as her own and they are yet close. 'Twas Margaux who saw Rowan named for her hereditary estate, much against Gavin's wishes. He is not heir, for that is Burke's honor, but carries the appellation 'de Montvieux' all the same."

While Brianna puzzled over this, Luc shook his head. "But, Rowan must have been yet a babe, if indeed he had been conceived, when Gavin came to Llanvelyn. Both Burke and Margaux were unknown to me in those days. I knew only Pyrs, the steward of Llanvelyn, who treated me as a son though he himself had never wed."

Luc pursed his lips. "Pyrs was not pleased by my father's sudden arrival, no less by my departure. I was so delighted, though, and he held his tongue." Luc shrugged. "I was but a boy and did not realize the reason for his reservations."

"He knew the manner of the man Gavin was," Brianna guessed.

Luc nodded, then continued. "Gavin and I rode to Cardiff, then sailed to Normandy. We were met by a grand party of knights and squires who escorted us to the luxurious keep perched on a cliff high above. Gavin left me there, to that lord's care, and I trained more determinedly than any of the dozen boys consigned to squire within those walls.''

"You wanted to please your sire," Brianna suggested softly.

Luc's intent glance told her that she had found the truth. "I wanted to be worthy of his continued attention," he admitted quietly, then frowned anew. "Though he never returned. In two years, though, I earned the right to serve as the lowest of the lord's own squires.''

Luc paused for a heartbeat.

'' 'Twas then that I met Tyrell. He was another of the lord's squires, a year older than I but markedly less driven. To be sure, Tyrell had a grand legacy awaiting him as the eldest son of a mighty lord. But he was a merry lad, always interested in a jest or a prank. He even could coax the stern marshal to chuckle. He seemed to take naught seriously beyond his own amusement and I had never met the like of him.

"It seemed we were as dissimilar as chalk and cheese, yet Tyrell took me beneath his tutelage in the lord's service. He aided me when I knew not what to do, he took pains to show me court manners of which I knew naught. 'Twas evident to all that I did not share their privileged background, but Tyrell cared naught for my rural past. It became clear that we actually held many convictions in common.''

A half-smile of recollection tweaked Luc's lips. "We were inseparable, Tyrell and I, and we pledged—one night when some scheme of Tyrell's had landed us in disfavor together—that we would serve together for all time once we earned our spurs.''

Brianna grinned and leaned against the wall beside Luc. She was very aware of the strength of his leg so close to her own, no less the heat emanating from his flesh. '' 'Tis difficult to imagine you possessed of such whimsy,'' she teased and Luc's grin broadened.

"I was young,'' he declared and winked. "Tyrell, like you, had a great fondness for bard's tales and chansons. Over the years, we spun grand tales of the damsels we would rescue, the fortunes we would win, the castles we would besiege. Six years we trained together, six years we drank of the conviction that the world of men is a good and just place.''

Luc looked at his boots and his voice dropped low. "But that was a childish conviction, destined to be lost.''

And he halted his tale for a long moment. Brianna did not dare interject her opinion of that. He was serious, too serious for her taste, his thoughts clearly on some painful memory.

Brianna feared that she had asked too much.

She thought Luc had forgotten her presence, he stood still for so long, but he abruptly threw back his head to stare into the distance again.

There was a suspicious shimmer in his eyes.

Words fell quickly from Luc's tongue now, his tone flat as he recounted the tale. "We were granted our spurs on the same St. John's Day, in the midst of a grand fête whence six of our companion squires were also granted their spurs. The lord knighted us with his own blade, Tyrell's sire had swords forged for each of us, our patron granted us each a fine steed.''

Luc's voice softened slightly. "Mine was a dapple, name of Grisart.'' He swallowed visibly and continued. "I had never known such generosity and, on that day, I truly believed that I had joined the ranks of a fine and exalted elite.''

"And your sire's gift?''

Luc snorted. "He was not there and he sent naught.''

Brianna was outraged that Gavin would have missed such

an event in his son's life. "How could he not attend? 'Twas a day of great import to you and one he had set in motion!"

Luc glanced at her and away. "He cared naught for *my* training. 'Twas all for his own ends. He had some grand scheme to win alliance with this lord by entrusting me, his eldest son, to the care of that man's household. Evidently the plan had failed, for the lord yet loathed my sire. 'Tis a testament to that man's fine character that he expended the coin to train me, all the same."

Brianna could well imagine that this lord had immediately discerned the difference betwixt Luc and Gavin. "He must have seen promise in you," she suggested.

"Or determination." Luc's gaze burned into her own. "I wanted those spurs, my lady, I *wanted* them with all my heart and soul. I believed that their absence alone was what kept me from this gifted circle of the nobility, from the respect of a family such as that Tyrell knew. Indeed, I could not have been more wrong, but I was young and had much to learn."

"What happened?"

"Tyrell pledged immediately to his sire's hand and I, of course, followed suit. We were to be together, as you recall, and I had no demands upon me."

Brianna smiled slightly. "Aye, you two had damsels to save and keeps to storm in the name of righteousness."

Luc nodded but did not smile. "Tyrell's sire dispatched us to support a distant cousin in Norman Sicily. 'Twas the best of possibilities, to our thinking, for our destination was distant and exotic; our responsibility solemn in representing Tyrell's own sire. It seemed our glorious fates were to begin more quickly than could have been hoped."

Luc kicked at the dirt and his tone turned grim. " 'Twas not exotic. 'Twas hot beyond all else and filthy, and we both were briefly ill. We marched south from this cousin's holding and thence across the sea to Ifriqiya where the battle raged.

"The true horror began when we rode first into battle, for the slaughter was no game. Men with whom we had ridden died, and they did not die nobly. 'Twas all over a patch of land unfit for any purpose but prized for its location. The Moors desired to connect their far-flung kingdom, the Normans wanted it to control trade in the Mediterranean Sea.

"The battle for it was brutal.

"And yet more brutal was the price paid by those unfortunate souls living upon that land. Golden and brown of hue, they were unlike any folk I had seen before, yet they tilled and toiled much as those I knew well at Llanvelyn."

Luc swallowed awkwardly. "I could not look upon them without thinking of Pyrs."

Brianna did not fill the silence that stretched between them. She watched Luc closely, knowing she could barely imagine such an alien world. She knew little of battle, naught of what men faced on the field itself.

"Yet they were as chattel or dogs to the nobility sweeping through their lands." Luc's voice echoed with low outrage. "Those knights took anything they desired for their own with no care for what damage they left in their wake. *Any-thing.*"

Brianna did not know what to say. She could barely imagine the horror of what Luc had witnessed, yet she saw in his eyes that he recalled every detail. She realized suddenly how very sheltered her life had been, at least until two months past.

Luc shoved a hand through his hair. "In the eternity of those two years, I cannot list the crimes I witnessed. I cannot imagine how many bastards were left in the wake of those two armies."

Brianna gasped. "Nay!"

"Aye. Homes were pillaged and churches defiled, goods stolen from people unfortunate enough to profess a different faith. Our troops left devastation in their wake."

The bile rose in Brianna's throat at the very thought. Indeed, when the minstrels sang of battle, 'twas a noble undertaking, but Luc's recounting made the savagery most clear. His words conjured such a vivid image that Brianna knew he shared the truth.

Luc, after all, would not lie to her.

Luc's lips tightened and his voice dropped low. "Yet, oddly enough, all the knights had taken the very same pledge of honor." He flicked a glance to Brianna and she could only watch him.

"You may believe that we made our disagreement clear, though such argument was not welcome among our companions. After one particularly vicious brawl over the matter, Tyrell and I conceded that we could not change the ways of these marauding knights. We could but hie to our own moral code. Indeed, we were convinced that these Norman men, so long in Sicily that they no longer spoke or even looked as us, had lost the true way of knighthood."

The conclusion made good sense to Brianna.

"I dare say we were relieved when the holdings in Ifriqiya were finally and irrevocably lost. There were rumblings of war upon our return to Sicily, for the Pope had implied the Holy Roman Empire was but a papal fief and Frederick Barbarossa was prepared to make his argument with bloodshed. But Tyrell's sire had sent a missive, summoning him home."

"And you went with Tyrell."

"Aye." Luc nodded. "We were both convinced that our dreams would be confirmed upon more familiar soil. We believed Tyrell's sire to be a man of honor and repute, and that beneath his hand, our vows would see their full glory."

There was an undercurrent to Luc's words that caught Brianna's attention. "Do not tell me that you were wrong."

Luc slanted a glance her way that spoke volumes and indeed, its steadiness chilled her heart.

But he did not immediately answer her question. "Imagine, if you will, our return to Tyrell's home estate after nigh upon three years abroad. The entire keep turned out in festivity for the eldest son and heir. To them, Tyrell had gathered glory in his service, though I saw the shadow our experiences had cast into his eyes.

"His sire, though, saw naught of that. That great man raised a chalice in the hall that eve and drank the health of his returned son. He declared that Tyrell would lead his assault upon an acquisitive neighbor in dire need of a lesson."

There was a tightness in Luc's voice that made cold fingers clench around Brianna's heart. His gaze was determinedly locked upon the orchard, but she glimpsed the brilliant sapphire hue of his eyes.

Luc cleared his throat deliberately, but did not look at her. His voice thrummed low, his words fell in haste. " 'Twas uncommon cold that April, and the march to the keep took nigh on a week, all of it through chill rain. Naught could have dampened our spirits, though. When the fortress rose above us, silent and dark, Tyrell suspected 'twas virtually undefended."

"He did not send spies?"

Luc's gaze was deadly blue. "He believed his sire had ensured this would be an easy victory, a homecoming *gift* for his heir."

Brianna raised a hand to her lips, suddenly fearing the

outcome of this tale. She held Luc's gaze for a moment, then he continued, again in that low monotone.

"On the eve of our assault, the rain turned cold and driving. 'Twas slick on the roadway, the horses lost their footing, the men were coated with ice. The wet soaked through the leather of our gloves and nigh froze our fingers, the very wind had a bite. By the time we stormed the gates, our troops were sorely weakened by the cold.

"But we took the gates and it seemed then that Tyrell would be victorious. We surged triumphantly into the bailey, knowing the keep was virtually our own, and stepped into a baited trap."

Brianna gasped, but Luc continued grimly. "There were hundreds of men waiting in the shadows, many times our small force, many battles more seasoned. My steed was hacked from beneath me before I saw the fullness of our peril. I was on my feet alone and facing attack from all sides.

"In a heartbeat, the bailey was ankle-deep in blood and rain, the surviving horses had bolted and fled in terror. I spotted Tyrell just as a wicked swipe of a mercenary's blade slashed his belly open. I ran to defend him, but 'twas too late."

Luc closed his eyes and paled slightly at the memory. " 'Twas too late. His own innards spilled from between his own fingers as Tyrell caught at the wound. He was yet aware of all around him, he knew what he held, that was the true horror of it all."

A lump rose in Brianna's throat, Luc's words stealing her very breath away. She could not imagine how she might have faced such a challenge.

Luc swallowed heavily and clearly fought to keep his voice dispassionate. "I held him while he died, I tried to grant him some dignity amidst such chaos. Suddenly he cried out, I thought in pain, but too late I realized it had been a warning. The hilt of a sword was cracked over my head, I saw my own blood flow, and then naught.''

Luc sighed and his eyes narrowed. ''I awakened outside the walls, amidst the carcasses of all those who had ridden with us.'' He took a steadying breath, his gaze clouded with memories. '' 'Twas cursed cold. Beside me lay Tyrell, who never would jest again.''

Brianna bit her lip, knowing that this man would take the loss of such a friend even harder than most.

''I could not leave him there,'' Luc confessed with a shake of his head. ''I could not do him such disservice. He was my friend, my partner, my companion. So, beneath the eagle eye of the keep's sentry, I lifted Tyrell onto my shoulders and began the long walk to his sire's gates. They let me go, I know not why.''

He fell silent and Brianna ached for what Luc had endured.

A moment later, she dared to touch his sleeve. ''They must have wanted your lord to know what had transpired,'' she suggested softly.

Luc's expression turned yet more grim. ''That man never doubted the outcome.''

Brianna frowned. ''But why? I do not understand. Surely he must have been devastated by the loss of his heir?''

Luc's lips twisted and his words were cold. ''On the contrary, he informed me that he had yet two more blooded sons to call his own.''

Brianna was horrified. ''He could not have known the battle would be lost!''

''Aye, his manner made me believe as much. Indeed, he was quite delighted that the loss of Tyrell had won him the seal of a prosperous monastery.''

''I do not understand.''

Luc pursed his lips. "Tyrell's sire was a strategist beyond all. I am convinced that he knew all along that his forces would lose this fight. But he had a hankering for a prosperous monastery endowed by that other lord, one that nearly bordered upon his own holdings. And he guessed that if his eldest son—his heir, no less—marched to attack the other lord's keep, 'twould provide a fitting distraction for his real intent. He dispatched six mercenaries to claim the monastery while the lord defended his keep. 'Twas an easy victory and Tyrell's sire won precisely what he desired."

Brianna gasped. "He deliberately sacrificed his *son* to win property?"

Luc merely held her gaze, challenging Brianna to believe that such cruelty was possible.

"But that is barbaric!"

"He told me that 'twas good I had returned Tyrell because he could now fittingly bury his son at this monastery," Luc confided with disapproval. "He openly gloated how Tyrell's popularity would no doubt increase the offerings made in the chapel there."

Brianna gasped. "How appalling!"

Luc frowned and his words rang with mingled anger and disappointment. " 'Twas then I understood that Tyrell and I had been mistaken. There was naught corrupted in the nobility of the south that has not similarly gone awry in the north. Nobility like our fathers took whatsoever they desired and cared naught for what it might cost another."

Luc continued in an angry monotone. "That a man could cast aside his son for such a minute gain showed me that this was a world of which I wanted absolutely no part. 'Twas then I knew that the most honorable person I had ever known was the one who had raised me." He flicked a telling glance at Brianna. "And Pyrs was common-born."

"Was?"

"He died two years past." The tightening of Luc's lips revealed how strongly the man's passing had affected him.

Brianna laid a hand on Luc's arm. "I am sorry. He must have been a wondrous man."

Luc smiled sadly and closed his fingers over Brianna's own. "He was."

She took a step closer, unable to resist the urge to console this strong man who asked so little of those around him. "And Tyrell, as well."

Luc almost smiled as he met her gaze. "Aye."

Brianna toyed with his fingers. "And you gave up your spurs?"

"I put them aside, as I put aside all the trappings of knighthood. My steed was gone, the rest was quickly consigned to a trunk in Llanvelyn's storeroom." Luc frowned. "But 'twas the *sword* I pledged never to hold within my hand again. 'Twas the blade of a knight, after all, that was responsible for all the wickedness I had witnessed."

Luc's gaze bored into Brianna's, the hue of his eyes an unearthly blue. "A knightly blade grants a man the opportunity to take more than his due, to slaughter any who defy him, to wreak carnage in his wake. A sword is a weapon I will *never* wield again. I left that life, I abandoned my blade, and I will not return to it."

Brianna suddenly recalled another detail. "And your blade was a gift from Tyrell's sire."

Luc nodded once. "A taint 'twill never shake. I will never do him the honor of holding it within my grip again."

"But," Brianna frowned. "Surely you do not need to cast all aside?"

"Do you suggest that I break my pledge?" Luc's tone was frosty.

Brianna flushed for she knew well enough that that was

out of the question. Indeed, Luc's determination to keep his word was one trait she admired about him.

"Nay, of course not. I know you would not do as much." His manner eased slightly, even as Brianna fought to find some way to explain herself. "But surely you could find some compromise!"

Luc stared at her for a moment, then abruptly shook his head.

When he finally met her gaze, she was relieved to see a glimmer of humor lurking there. "You seem most concerned about my prospects, my lady," he mused and she had the distinct sense that Luc was deliberately changing the subject.

She had no chance to wonder at that, though, for Luc took a smooth step closer and Brianna knew better than to trust the mischievous twinkle in his eye. "Do you show such interest in all who come Tullymullagh's way?"

Brianna flushed scarlet. She took a hasty step backward.

"And it seems to me that you have asked a number of questions this morn," Luc continued, a wicked glint in his eye. "Shall we tally them?"

"Nay!" Brianna danced away. She was certain she should protest, even if the prospect of Luc collecting his due made her catch her breath. "They did not count!"

Luc frowned with mock severity. "They *all* count, my lady," he insisted. " 'Twas our wager, after all." He paused and folded his arms across his chest. "Unless *you* plan to break your pledge?"

Brianna barely bit back a chuckle. Truly the man let her escape with naught.

And she liked that very much.

"One kiss," she suggested.

Luc's dark brows shot skyward. "At least four," he retorted, then counted on his fingers again. "You asked after

Ismay in the stables, the location of Montvieux, the reason I was squired there, why Rowan travelled with Margaux—"

"That was no question!" Brianna darted toward Luc, shaking an indignant finger. "I took care to make that a comment alone!"

Luc grinned. "Oh, I am not at all certain it sounded as such, my lady." He shook his head solemnly. "Nay, not at all." He winked quickly then began to count again. "Let me see. You also asked of Gavin's gift for my knighting, what happened to Tyrell . . ." Luc glanced up at her with twinkling eyes. "I should think that four kisses would be a bargain you would leap to accept."

"You!" Brianna sputtered momentarily. "You are audacious beyond all!"

"And you called me your favorite," Luc clicked his tongue, then his smile broadened. "Four, or shall we continue to count?"

"Oh!" Brianna paced a few feet beyond Luc, wondering how she would survive four of his kisses in short order, then pivoted to face him anew. She lifted her chin as though undaunted by the prospect and braced herself for a sensory assault.

In truth, her heart was already hammering wildly; she was not precisely certain she was losing this negotiation.

"Four, then," she declared. "I accept your terms."

But Luc's gaze had drifted past Brianna's shoulder and his gaze sharpened. He frowned at the river coursing below, as though uncertain of what he saw there.

Brianna turned to look, but Luc immediately stepped closer and gripped her shoulders. "Do not look, my lady!"

But Luc did not move quickly enough to prevent Brianna from seeing the body broken on the rocks below.

Nor from recognizing it.

"Ismay!" Brianna gasped. "She fell! Luc, we must aid

her! Who knows how long she has lain there? She must be injured—''

''My lady!'' Luc interrupted Brianna tersely. She met his steady gaze and saw a hint of the truth there, though it made her blood run cold.

''Would you fetch the priest?'' he asked with quiet certainty. '' 'Tis all Lady Ismay needs now.''

Brianna felt the color drain from her face. She blinked back tears of shock, looked to the left and the right, as she struggled with her realization.

Ismay was dead.

''Father Padraig,'' she confirmed in a voice too small to be her own.

''Aye,'' Luc agreed. He gave Brianna's shoulders a minute shake, his voice dropping lower. ''And, my lady, do not look back when you go.''

Brianna nodded, appreciative that Luc tried to protect her from another glimpse of Ismay's broken body. Indeed, she wished belatedly that she had heeded Luc's advice to not look at all.

For 'twas an image that could not be dismissed. 'Twas not the way she wanted to remember Ismay, not at all.

Brianna nodded again, feeling her tears rise, then slipped from beneath the warmth of Luc's grip to do his bidding. She knew she did not imagine the weight of his gaze upon her as she made her way across the bailey, but she did not look back. And she did not stop until she found Father Padraig already awake in the hall.

• • •

As Brianna walked, then ran, across the bailey, Luc could not tear his gaze away from her departing figure. Even when she disappeared, the lady remained at the fore of his thoughts. He wanted more than the lady's kisses, that much was certain.

Aye, Luc wanted more even than *four* kisses.

He realized that he had never confided in another soul these past eleven years as much as he had confessed to Brianna in a few days. 'Twas the way she listened, the way her eyes sparkled, the way she made each word seem of import.

'Twas the way she *cared*.

Luc turned back to watch the river churn around Ismay and let unexpected relief roll through him. 'Twas a relief born not only of knowing the telling of what had happened to Tyrell was over, he realized, but that 'twas shared. He had given voice to all his frustration and hurt, and the task had been easier than anticipated.

Indeed, Luc felt markedly lighter as a result. The world seemed full of possibilities he had barely glimpsed before.

For bringing the tale to light had made it seem less dire. Luc stood and questioned whether he had given his experience more than its due. 'Twas true enough that he had made a decision while he was riled and stubbornly clung to that choice even after the pain of his loss had faded.

Luc's lips quirked despite himself. 'Twas a move not uncharacteristic of another determined soul he knew.

In that moment, the priest erupted from the keep, Brianna in his wake, Connor and Gavin, Uther, Cook, and the entire household trailing sleepily behind. The arrivals streamed across the bailey and lined the wall, each peering to the body fallen in the river below.

Father Padraig vaulted the wall with unexpected agility and scrambled down the muddy river bank. Luc was quick on his heels once he noted that Brianna hung back from the wall. It pleased him disproportionately that she heeded his advice on such a small matter.

The angular priest bent over Ismay just as Luc reached the bank, then closed his eyes in acknowledgement of her state.

The rain had wreaked havoc with what remained of Ismay's kohl and the dark line had spread down her cheek. There was a hint of carmine lingering upon her bottom lip, though her face was pale beyond all.

What had possessed her to leave the hall the night before and wander through the shadowed garden? She must have been pickled indeed to have climbed the wall without realizing the peril of what she did.

And she had more than paid the price for her recklessness.

As Father Padraig began to intone last rites, Luc could not tear his gaze away from Ismay's impassive features. Would Tyrell have expected Luc to spurn all in the wake of his death?

Luc knew his friend would not.

'Twas time he made a change.

The priest's "amen" hung in the air as boys bearing a litter drew closer, then the priest closed Ismay's widened eyes. Luc watched him mark a cross on the fallen lady's pale brow. The track left a dry line for the barest moment before the raindrops washed the symbol away.

" 'Tis a sign," Father Padraig muttered, his glance rising ominously to those peering over the wall. His voice grew louder. " 'Tis a sign that the hand of God takes retribution for the wages of sin."

The priest looked both grim and smugly satisfied when he turned his regard upon Luc. "I was not the only one who noted her wayward manner in the hall last eve, 'tis clear, for the eye of the Lord is ever vigilant."

Luc could not bring himself to speak poorly of the unhappy woman who now lay dead at their feet. "Ismay may have overindulged in the wine," he conceded when 'twas clear the priest expected his agreement.

"May have? She did—and I can only guess where such weakness of the flesh did lead in the end!" Father Padraig spun and flung his hands into the air for the benefit of his audience. "Gluttony! Pride! *Fornication*!" Father Padraig hissed the last word, his eyes blazed, then he looked coldly back to Ismay. "You see the Lord's judgement before you."

The boys came to an uncertain halt beside Luc, the priest glancing to each of them in turn. "I shall expect you immediately at the Mass. We shall have need of every voice to intercede in prayer for Lady Ismay's immortal soul."

"Aye, Father." The boys nodded agreement, clearly uncomfortable in the priest's forbidding presence.

Luc stepped forward and directed them with the litter. He lifted Ismay's broken body from the cold riverbed, considered the chattering souls lining the wall above, then cast his own cloak across Ismay as a shroud. There was little to be done for Ismay, but he suspected she would have been appalled to be viewed in such a state.

The cold rain soaked his tunic in a heartbeat, but Luc savored the chill tingle against his flesh. He was *alive*.

And time 'twas he did something about the matter.

"Someone must ride to Endlist," Father Padraig asserted as they all began to climb up the bank. He punctuated his words with a solemn glance to Luc. "The monks at that priory have always dressed Tullymullagh's dead."

"Where is it?"

Father Padraig lifted a lean hand and pointed back to the north. "The road winds past that hill, and there a trail breaks to the right. Two miles down the track is the priory that Connor's father endowed."

Luc impulsively decided that he would perform this errand. The opportunity to indulge his newfound vitality was irresistible. "I will go."

Father Padraig nodded once, then gestured regally to the litter as he reached the wall. His voice rose as he addressed the assembly. "This sheep stumbled from the path of righteousness last eve and paid a toll for her wandering ways."

The household fidgeted like errant children caught at some prank.

" 'Tis a *sign* that the eye of the Lord is upon us. 'Tis a *sign* that sin will not be left unaddressed." The priest cast a quelling glance over the dampened assembly. "Come to the Mass. We shall raise our voices together in prayer for Lady Ismay's immortal soul."

The priest swept across the bailey, the village church his obvious destination. The boys carrying Ismay's litter trudged behind, every inhabitant of Tullymullagh fell into step after the sad party.

The rising sun made an orange streak through the dreary grey clouds, the silhouettes of the party etched dark against the heavy sky. Connor offered Brianna his elbow and the pair took their place at the front of the group.

Luc watched the lady and savored the quickening within him at the sight of her. He felt as though he had slumbered since Tyrell's death, or at least, buried himself in obscurity, but now Brianna had awakened him with a vengeance.

Dermot pushed past Luc, his features as expressionless as a mask. Ismay's own accusations against her spouse echoed in Luc's ears once more.

What had Ismay recalled about the Rose of Tullymullagh that all others forgot?

Would Luc ever know?

Chapter Ten

*L*UC CAUGHT UP TO THE OSTLER JUST OUTSIDE THE stable doors. "Have you a swift steed I might ride this day, Denis? Father Padraig requests I ride to Endlist Priory and I would make haste."

Denis' brow worked for a moment as he thought the matter through. " 'Tis not far, but to make it there and back with speed and Brother Thomas in tow, you will need a strong mount, indeed."

"Brother Thomas?"

"Aye, 'tis always he who stitches the shroud." Denis' glance was telling. "He is a most *ample* man."

"Ah." Luc nodded understanding. "Will I need two horses?"

Denis shook his head. "Brother Thomas insists upon riding pillion." The men ducked beneath the dripping portal of the stables and were welcomed by a skittish snort.

Luc glanced up to find the great dapple grey destrier housed in a stall halfway to the back eyeing them warily.

The ostler evidently noted the direction of his glance. "Raphael would be a good choice, if indeed he would bear you."

Raphael flared his nostrils as though expressing his opinion of that. Luc's mouth went dry. He had not ridden a destrier since the day that Tyrell died.

Indeed, he had refused to do so.

But now the prospect was tempting.

"Would his knight not be troubled by the intrusion?" No knight whom Luc had ever known had suffered another man to ride his warhorse. 'Twas imperative that there be a great bond betwixt the two, for they oft had only each other to rely upon to survive.

Denis shook his head and his brow gathered darkly. " 'Tis the trouble. Chevalier Gaultier is dead this last month and none has been able to ride Raphael in his stead."

"Gaultier was killed in the assault of Tullymullagh?" Luc guessed and Denis nodded sadly.

"Aye, and a tragic waste 'twas. Never have I known a knight of such gentle strength. Gaultier had ridden years past with my lord Connor in Outremer and had come here in search of peace."

"They must have been of similar age, then."

"Aye, Gaultier told me once he had seen fifty summers, though he was hale enough still." Denis' expression turned grim. "And he was a man who could be relied upon, unlike some others hereabouts. When Tullymullagh was besieged, he rode out in our last defense."

" 'Tis a daunting task for a man in his winter years."

Denis' disapproval was clear. "He was not a man to shirk a duty, however grim it might have been."

"Yet Tullymullagh's champion was not to be found on that ill-fated day," Luc said quietly, guessing the reason for the ostler's displeasure.

Denis snorted. "Not he!"

Luc felt a surge of irritation that this Ruarke had abandoned his rightful duty, not only leaving an older man to do his labor, but returning jubilantly when all was over and done.

Denis took a deep breath. " 'Twas a wicked day, I tell you. Gaultier was struck down early, but Raphael stood over him, defending his master from further harm. They had ridden long together, those two, and the steed did his utmost. Sadly 'twas too late for Gaultier by the time Raphael had his relief."

Denis leaned against the stall and considered the stallion, who watched them both with open distrust. "And now I have a fine dapple grey stallion, bred of champions and worth a king's ransom, who will not permit another to draw near him, save myself. And even I, he will only tolerate to bridle him and lead him to run in the bailey."

Denis swallowed and shook his head. "I fear he misses Gaultier overmuch."

The destrier blew out his lips as though he would agree with this sentiment. His gaze landed anew upon Luc and there was a light in his eye that put Luc in mind of a steed he had once known better than himself.

"I once rode a dapple grey stallion," Luc admitted.

"Aye? What happened to him, sir?"

Luc frowned and fought the constriction in his throat. "He died too soon, Denis."

And Luc had never taken another steed because there could be no other who could compete with the affection he had had for Grisart. There was no denying the crystal clarity of the truth. Indeed, Luc had not wanted to care for another creature the way he had cared for that steed.

But he had resolved this day to lay the past to rest.

Before the ostler could ask another question, Luc lifted a brush from the shelf and stepped into the destrier's stall with purpose. Raphael looked over his shoulder, his gaze assessing, but Luc murmured soothingly to him and lifted the brush to his haunches.

"Do not fear, Raphael, I have done this afore," he declared softly. The brush fitted Luc's hand with a familiarity almost forgotten, and as soon as Luc touched its bristles to the stallion's flank, he was deluged in memories.

The smooth gloss of a healthy horse's hide, the smell of hay cast beneath one's feet, of leather, of dung. These had all been part of Luc's life, once, as had the tightening of a steed's muscles in gallop, the bite of the wind, the echo of hoof on road.

No less the weight of steel in a man's hand, upon his back, at his heels.

Luc made long, easy strokes with the brush, as always he had when Grisart was unsettled. After but half a dozen strokes, a shudder ran over Raphael's flesh. Luc felt some angst ease from the beast as he made another leisurely stroke and another.

And he began to murmur to the beast, as once he had murmured to another. "Aye, you are a fine creature, indeed, Raphael."

The horse shifted his weight from foot to foot, as though he acknowledged the words.

"But you must be in dire need of a run after two months in only stall and bailey. Do you not miss the road unfurling beneath your feet, Raphael? Do you not miss the rush of the wind?"

The stallion snorted less vigorously than before. He leaned into the stroke of the brush, though he tried to hide his interest by nosing in his feed bin.

Luc was not fooled. He had seen these ploys before.

"I would ride you to Endlist Priory," he murmured. "I would ride you, Raphael, if you would bear me there."

The destrier turned to watch Luc steadily, as though he considered the question.

"Aye," Luc continued, brushing as he spoke. "I expect you know the way better than I and, in such foul weather, I would have a surefooted steed beneath me. A swift and fine beast, like yourself."

Luc stepped farther into the stall and Raphael did not impede Luc's progress. Nor did he flatten Luc against the wall of the stall. The stallion but waited and watched, tentative in the trust he had shown thus far.

"Has Denis cleared your hooves?" Luc asked softly. "Or would you even permit him?" As he began to brush Raphael's charcoal-hued mane, the steed could not disguise his delight.

He tossed his head proudly and Luc thought suddenly of silver bells on a fine harness. They were long lost, as was the beast who had jingled them with such pride.

His eyes welled with unexpected tears.

"Aye, Raphael, I once rode a fine dapple grey," he admitted huskily. "As finely wrought as you and every measure as loyal."

Luc shook his head and felt his lips curve in a bittersweet smile. "I remember how high he stepped when he fancied himself well groomed and finely caparisoned." Luc swallowed and his voice dropped. "And I remember how he would never permit any other but me to clear his hooves."

In that moment, beside that grey steed, the years blurred. The stable could have been a hundred others, the stallion could only have been one. Without thinking of what he did, Luc leaned against Raphael and reached up to scratch the stallion's ears.

As he had done to Grisart so many times before.

The muscled heat of the stallion's flesh was against Luc's chest, the scent of steed and stable rich in his nostrils, the familiar brush clutched in one hand and the yet more familiar grey fur beneath the fingers of the other.

Luc tasted the salt of a tear he had not known he had shed.

"Aye, Raphael," he whispered unevenly. "I *remember.*"

Luc stood there for a moment that stretched long, permitting himself to indulge in those memories he had long denied. 'Twas as though he opened a forgotten trunk and removed each treasure stored within it, holding each to the light and marvelling at them in succession.

He not only remembered but Luc acknowledged the gaping hole his choice had made in his life. If he had not pursued his knighthood, he would have seen naught of the world, he would never have known Tyrell, he would never have ridden Grisart.

And Luc realized that he sorely missed the gifts knighthood had brought his way. Like most matters, his experience had been a mix of good and bad.

For so long, Luc had chosen only to see the darkness, but now he would look into the sun. Raphael bent to nuzzle his neck, as though he had heard and approved of that sentiment.

Luc froze, the stallion persisted in nosing his chemise. Luc glanced up and saw in Denis' wondering expression that this was the first the destrier had touched another of his own volition.

It seemed they both had stepped beyond an obstacle on this day. Slowly, the knight who had set aside his spurs so long ago turned and reached to scratch those silken ears anew.

"We ride then, Raphael," Luc said quietly. "We ride to Endlist in the rain, you and I, and return with an ample friar name of Thomas." He smiled crookedly up at the stallion. "That will teach you to take pity upon a knight who cast aside his spurs."

Raphael snorted unrepentantly and stamped his hooves with new impatience. Luc heard Denis dance away, that man's voice unsteady as he bellowed for a squire.

"Edward! Raphael has need of his saddle. Hasten yourself, boy!"

• • •

BRIANNA DARTED DOWN the stairs, her sire's old cloak clutched to her chest. She had found the news of Luc's departure profoundly disappointing, though that made little enough sense.

Was Luc's departure from Tullymullagh not the one objective she had sought?

Even so, in that moment, Brianna knew that she did not want Luc to go. If naught else, she intended to see Luc once more before he rode through Tullymullagh's gates.

She stepped through the portal to the courtyard, breathless from her run, and pulled up her own hood against the onslaught of the rain. Brianna halted in astonishment at the sight that greeted her eyes.

Gaultier's destrier Raphael had finally permitted someone to ride him.

And that someone was Luc.

The stallion trotted around the bailey, his neck arched, his nostrils flared, his hooves lifting high with each step. He toyed with the bit as though unfamiliar with its obstruction, though Brianna knew he had always made such a display. There was an exhilaration in his every step, as though he was overjoyed to be ridden once more.

Brianna looked at Luc and her breath caught in her throat. His attention was fixed upon the steed and Brianna heard the low thrum of his voice, though she could not discern his words. He gripped the reins with one hand, the other stroking Raphael's neck. Luc's chemise was soaked and clung to his muscled torso like a second skin, his ebony hair hung wet against his brow.

He was a vision of mingled strength and gentleness that Brianna found extraordinarily compelling. She had never seen a man ride with such assurance—let alone one fixed so attentively on his mount.

"Rides as one born to the saddle, does he not?" Denis the ostler demanded with a pride more fitting of a man for his own son.

Brianna smiled. "Aye. I thought Raphael would bear none."

"He would not, before this day." Denis nodded to the pair as they made another round of the bailey. "There is a bond between those two, mark my words, Lady Brianna. They both of them know what 'tis to shoulder a loss."

Mine was a dapple, name of Grisart.

Brianna's eyes widened as Luc's low words echoed in her mind once more. She marvelled that a man who had seen such cruelty could not only keep from going mad, but retain such essential kindness. She could see that gentleness in Luc's hand upon the stallion's neck.

Indeed, she had sampled that tenderness herself in his kisses.

Luc turned Raphael and headed suddenly toward them, the stallion tossing his head proudly. When Luc's gaze collided with hers, Brianna had the guilty sense that he had heard her very thoughts.

She flushed as Luc suddenly brought Raphael to a halt beside them. The horse snorted at the interruption, stamped his feet, but waited with a docility he had not shown these two months.

Denis beamed.

"He seems anxious for a run, Denis," Luc commented.

He flicked an approving glance to Brianna, a half-smile curving his lips.

"Aye, 'tis more than time," the ostler agreed with obvious approval. "Take him to Endlist Priory, sir, take him with my blessings. Show him what 'tis to feel the road beneath his feet and we will not be able to keep him in the stall."

"You will have need of a cloak," Brianna interjected. "My sire does not use this cloak any longer, but 'tis warm. I thought it might serve you well."

Brianna's color rose yet higher as Luc's smile broadened and she shoved the garment toward him. Curse the man, he seemed amused by her discomfiture! Their fingers brushed in the transaction and at the heat of Luc's touch, Brianna's mind flooded with inopportune memories of his kiss.

And her own desire for more.

"You have my thanks, my lady."

Even his low voice was enough to awaken that tingle of desire within Brianna. How she hated that he would be gone, even for a brief time!

Luc tugged Raphael's reins. "Good day, my lady," he said with a bow of his dark head. "Denis." Luc turned Raphael adroitly and tossed the cloak over his shoulders in a wide dark arc. He clicked his tongue, gave the steed his heels and they galloped for the gate.

"Born to the saddle," Denis pronounced with satisfaction.

Aye, 'twas true enough, Brianna had to admit. In fact, she could not tear her gaze away from Luc's retreating figure. It seemed that he loved to ride, that he was one with the beast beneath him, that he cared about naught else in all of Christendom.

In marked comparison, when Ruarke rode, he was always looking to see who had noted his finery or his skill. But Luc apparently cared naught for how he looked, who was watching, or what he wore.

'Twas odd, for though they were both knights, Luc was as little like Ruarke as ever a man could be—

Ruarke!

Brianna's mouth dropped open in shock. She had pledged to see to Ruarke's injuries this very morn! She made her apologies to Denis, then fled into the keep, the women chattering in her wake.

How could she have forgotten?

• • •

RUARKE DID NOT smile this day.

Brianna had a moment to observe her father's champion knight while Gavin's man-at-arms sought the key to the knight's prison. She peered through the tiny grate in the armored door and felt a wave of pity.

Ruarke was slumped in one corner of the shadowed cell, his gaze fixed on the fickle flame of a small oil lamp burning in the center of the floor. His expression was sour, his eye swollen to purple splendor, his mail gone, and his chemise stained. He moved with a stiffness that revealed Gavin's savagery.

Brianna suspected the light made the knight look markedly worse than he truly was. All the same, 'twas clear Ruarke's mood was less than prime.

"Here 'tis," the man-at-arms growled suddenly beside Brianna's elbow, the jingle he gave the keys making Ruarke's head snap up. Brianna summoned her best smile and stepped into the cell with a confidence she was far from feeling.

She was not reassured when Gavin's man locked the door securely behind her. Ruarke glowered at her, his swollen eye looking red and mean in the midst of the bruising.

"I had thought you might come sooner," he growled.

Guilt surged through Brianna that she had kept him waiting for the only event of his day. "And why are you still garbed in less than your finest kirtle? You do your sire disservice—do you not understand your place in this keep, Brianna?"

Brianna lifted her chin proudly, disliking his tone. All the same, she could scarcely blame Ruarke for being dissatisfied. Although Tullymullagh's dungeon was dry and relatively devoid of vermin, 'twas still dark and chill.

And 'twas still a prison. It must chafe sorely upon a man like Ruarke to be so confined, he who was so used to being free in the wind and sunshine.

So, Brianna deliberately did not take offense at his poor temper. "There was much awry this morn," she said smoothly as she stepped into the cell. "Lady Ismay fell from the orchard wall last eve and was found dead in the Darrow."

Ruarke's brows rose in surprise and his expression brightened with curiosity. "Truly? What was she doing upon the orchard wall?"

Brianna shrugged and dropped her voice, resolving to leave Luc's suspicions out of this discussion. "She was besotted last eve."

Ruarke shook his head. "And missed her step, like as not. I tell you, Ismay has never been a woman with her wits about her. Was Dermot not close at hand to keep her from such foolery?"

"Ruarke! You must not speak so ill of the dead!"

The knight grinned roguishly. "I am but bored to tears, my lady, and hungered beyond all."

Brianna could not help but smile in return. " 'Tis fortunate indeed that I considered that possibility this morn." She crouched beside the knight and pulled back the linen to reveal the contents of her basket.

The aroma rose from the fresh bread secreted there and

Ruarke's smile flashed wider even as his belly growled. "You are an angel of mercy, my lady," he declared, then reached for the bread like a starving man.

Brianna was startled by his enthusiasm. "Have they given you *anything* to eat?"

"Naught." Ruarke made short work of the bread as Brianna wished she had thought to ask Cook what food had been brought to the dungeon. She had assumed Gavin would not deny the knight the simple grace of a meal.

It seemed Brianna had much to learn of men and their ways.

Luc's tale wound into her ears once more, and Brianna knew she had never believed such cruelty possible before this day. But there was no doubt that Luc told her the truth, for the telling had been painful for him.

Could she have continued, with the bitter burden of such experience upon her heart? Brianna did not know. The uncertainty made her admiration for Luc grow an increment more.

She noted Ruarke's glance expectant upon her and forced herself to think of something to say. "Then, you must not eat too quickly," she counselled. "Look, there is a rind of cheese below and a few apples from the garden."

"Is there wine?" Ruarke demanded, peering into the basket with obvious anticipation.

"Nay." The knight's face fell and guilt suffused Brianna anew. "I did not imagine that you had naught to eat at all," she explained hastily. "I thought only to bring you better fare, some of Cook's fine bread instead of the rough biscuits and cheese."

Ruarke's lips twisted. " 'Tis a prison I inhabit, my lady, not a tavern."

Brianna flushed at his gentle chastisement. "I did not understand," she said quickly, then forced a smile. "On the morrow, I will bring you more."

Ruarke snorted and glanced around the cell. "If the cur keeps his word, then on the morrow I shall be free," he muttered darkly, then glanced at Brianna and smiled apologetically.

"Then, of course, you would not have to sully your shoes by coming to this place," Ruarke amended and reached to cover Brianna's hand with the warmth of his own. "It ill suits you to be here, though indeed, I appreciate your presence."

Brianna stared at Ruarke's hand and marvelled that she felt naught. His flesh was no less warm than Luc's, his tone no less confidential.

But it still left Brianna completely untroubled. Perhaps she was not merely awakened to the touch of men in general, but to one man specifically. Brianna bit her lip, for there was a matter deserving of reflection.

She looked up to find Ruarke's regard bright upon her and smiled more genuinely. 'Twas reassuring, at the least, to see Ruarke returning to his usual charming manner.

"What other news do you bring from the hall?" he asked with characteristic cheer. "Share with me all of the gossip, even that which you fear is wildly untrue."

"Let me look at your eye first," Brianna suggested with a smile. "Is it painful?"

The knight shrugged. " 'Tis my pride that is most sorely wounded," he admitted, then grinned crookedly. "Have you a salve for that, my lady fair?"

• • •

THE GUEST CHAMBER at the priory was simply furnished, the bed hard, the linens stiff. It had been farther than Luc anticipated to Endlist Priory, one look at Brother Thomas convincing Luc that Raphael needed a rest before repeating the journey.

All the same, he was restless at the delay. Luc lay in the darkness, listening to the rain, studying the ceiling.

And thinking of a certain beguiling woman.

'Twas true the lady Brianna had a rare effect upon Luc. They were not dissimilar, they two, both resolved to keep their promises, to care for those they loved, to uphold honor and justice. Even Brianna's thoughts seemed to follow a similar course to Luc's own. He had been startled when Brianna asked him of compromise, for Luc's own thinking had veered in the very same direction.

Aye, 'twas more than desire for Brianna at work in this, though Luc's desire was greater than any he had known. Kisses were one matter, but 'twas unthinkable that he dishonor the lady with any greater sign of his admiration.

Which made Luc consider an old conviction. He frowned and folded his arms behind his head, unable to clear his mind of Brianna's tale of her parents. They had been happy in their marriage.

With only the example of Gavin before him, Luc had never considered the possibility that marriage might be a happy state. 'Twas clear the match from which he had sprung had not been a merry one and even his fleeting experience of Margaux had convinced Luc that he could never have borne the bickering of that match.

But Brianna did not bicker. And Brianna knew what wrought a happy match. Luc had never followed his father's example in any facet of his life—why should he assume that he must do so in marriage?

Pyrs had never seen value in marriage, or indeed in women. Tyrell had faced an arranged match without complaint, Gavin had made a muddle of two marriages. But Luc had a choice.

He had a chance for something much better.

'Twas not only a time to heal, to put the ghosts of the past behind him, and to start anew. 'Twas time to take a chance.

'Twas time, Luc resolved, to make a certain defiant princess, one with fire in her eyes and honey in her kisses, laugh aloud.

And preferably *before* the infinitely eligible Burke returned. He rolled to his feet and paced the narrow room, anxious to be on the road to Tullymullagh as soon as humanly possible.

• • •

THE SUN WAS sinking low when Brianna climbed the stairs from the dungeon, its light a dull glow behind the low clouds. She hesitated in the corridor betwixt dungeon and hall, struck by the silence in the bailey beyond. Brianna crept stealthily to the portal and stared out into the bailey, Ruarke forgotten in a heartbeat.

There was not a single soul within eyesight.

And a metal box still pressed against Brianna's belly. She yet carried her cloak.

'Twas as though the moment had been made to serve her end. Aye, this might well be Brianna's first and possibly her only opportunity to see her sire's mission accomplished.

Luc was gone, much of the household were involved in arranging for Ismay's funeral, the stableboys were evidently off at some task for the ostler. The partially completed addition to the stable stood silent in the rain, temporarily abandoned.

Not wanting to waste time, Brianna cast her cloak over her shoulders, hauled up the hood, and dashed out into the drizzling rain, her fingers working busily at the knot of her sash.

Brianna knew the perfect place to secrete her mother's letters so that no one would ever be able to steal them away from her. Connor would be relieved to know all was secured. Brianna would be quick about the task.

And if anyone saw her in the bailey, she would declare that Ismay's death had put her in mind of her mother's passing and that she had felt the need to offer a prayer by her grave.

'Twas perfect.

• • •

BROTHER THOMAS TOOK to the respite from his vow of silence like a fish to water. Indeed, the monk barely paused to draw a breath as he recounted anecdotes all the way to Tullymullagh.

Denis had made no jest, for Brother Thomas was of considerable size. It had taken no small effort to get him perched on the pillion behind Luc's saddle.

Raphael had been decidedly unimpressed with the result.

Mercifully, Brother Thomas had not seemed to note the steed's haughty manner. The monk chattered like a veritable magpie as the road unwound before them, each curve bringing yet another tale or memory to his lips.

When Tullymullagh's keep rose from the horizon, Brother Thomas dropped his recounting of distant gossip. "Ah, Connor has done himself proud with this structure, that much is certain. And look how the high wall is progressing! Indeed, there was no more than the keep itself when last I came this way eight years past. Is that a cross on the top of the tower?"

"Aye. I believe there is a private chapel there."

"Magnificent!" Brother Thomas tapped a finger on Luc's shoulder. " 'Tis the example of faith set by Connor and his sire before him that ensures the prosperity of their holdings."

Luc cleared his throat carefully. "You do realize that Tullymullagh was captured?"

"Pshaw!" Luc caught a glimpse of Brother Thomas' plump fingers waving dismissively. "Invaders come and invaders go. 'Tis the burden of Ireland to be plundered time and again by foreigners consumed by greed. 'Tis only a matter of time before this Gavin Fitzgerald makes his way back to Wales."

"And what of his sons?" Luc could not help but ask.

"Ah! We shall aid the lady Brianna in making a true man of whichever one she chooses, despite his sorry lineage."

Luc deliberately bit his tongue at that, though he could not completely suppress his smile. They crested a rise, the village spread virtually before their feet painted in the silvery hues of the incessant rain.

Brother Thomas let out a little cry of delight.

"They have extended the mill! 'Tis a great sign of prosperity. And look! There is a new gatehouse rising high over Tullymullagh's own gates." The monk clicked his tongue with approval. " 'Tis a fine estate that Connor has built upon his sire's lands. Indeed, the old man would be proud beyond all."

"You seem well acquainted with Tullymullagh," Luc commented. "Are there often dead to be dressed?"

Brother Thomas chortled. "Nay, not so many as that." The warmth of his bulk leaned closer. "But I was raised in Tullymullagh. Indeed, my sire was once the miller, God rest his soul, and despaired of me." The monk laughed aloud. "Ah, I was a challenge to him, that much is certain."

"What do you mean?"

"I had no aptitude for his trade. My sire, he could fix any device with only a glance upon it. He could not understand how I, his own son, could not fathom the most simple mechanism."

The monk's tone turned thoughtful. " 'Twas to his tremendous relief that my younger brother shared his aptitude.

Indeed, when last I was here, Matthew was running the mill himself with great success."

"Your sire has passed away?"

"Aye, both my parents. Taken in the winter of a decade past, 'twas hard upon the elderly and the weak." Brother Thomas cleared his throat. "But Matthew always did our sire proud."

"You must visit him while you are here."

Brother Thomas' tone brightened. "Aye, aye, that I must! His wife, fine woman, makes the most splendid dumplings that ever have crossed my palate. And she has a nose for a tale, that much is certain. Oft is the time that my old recollections of who is related to whom and what tale was whispered years past shed light upon current circumstance. What goes around does eventually come around, you may be certain of that."

Before Luc could agree with that, the monk tapped him on the shoulder once again. "There is no question that I must spend at least one night at Matthew's board. The winter nights are long at the priory and 'tis imperative we have tales to share amongst ourselves."

A mischievousness in Brother Thomas' words snared Luc's attention. He glanced back to find a merry twinkle in the monk's eye. "I take it as my most solemn duty to my brethren to gather all the gossip I can hold," the man confided, then patted his considerable girth. "And you may be certain, I can hold a great, great deal," he said with a wink.

Luc found himself not only grinning but liking his companion. "And how did a miller's son become a monk?"

"Ah, now there is a tale!" Brother Thomas gestured to the high keep as they rode beneath its shadow. "Connor's father was a man who heeded well what happened in his holding, you may be certain of that. He had founded the priory with a generous endowment and 'twas the talk of the village in those days. Such generosity in the name of the Lord!

"One day not long afterward, he sent word to my sire and asked if I might aid in the castle. Now, Tullymullagh's keep was not nearly so fine in those days, being as it was a wattle and daub construct. Connor has made marked improvements in what he holds to his name. But all the same, 'twas intimidating indeed for a young boy to be summoned to the lord's own hall."

That finger tapped again. "You may be certain that I was more quiet than most children, for this figure of mine has been much the same since I first drew breath. As a boy, I was markedly shy and kept to myself. My sire, I suspect, thought I had found some trouble and was to be called to task by the lord himself.

"To my eyes, even in those days, the hall was a vision of wealth and splendor. The very sight was dazzling, no less the richness of the lord's own garb. But that man called me to his side, he even deigned to put a hand on my shoulder, and I saw a kindness in his eyes that eased my every fear."

"What did he want from you?"

Brother Thomas chortled. "He had a son, one Connor of Tullymullagh, his heir and my contemporary. And the lad was not driven to learn his letters, as needs demanded he do in order to run this great keep. Aye, Connor was more concerned with learning to manage his sword. His sire decided Connor should have some competition beneath the scribe's tutelage."

"And he chose you."

"Aye. The old lord read me aright, for I took to my letters like naught else in my short life. Here was my place! Here was the labor that made my heart sing! I gave the young heir a fair contest, of that you may be certain."

Brother Thomas chuckled at the recollection. "Ah, my

dame was fiercely proud that her eldest son lived at the keep itself. And when Connor took his spurs as a properly educated young man, the old lord offered me my heart's desire in gratitude.''

''What did you ask him to grant you?''

''I asked him to let me be with the books.'' Brother Thomas' voice dropped low. ''I had hoped he would but let me work as his own scribe, but his gratitude extended far beyond that. He petitioned the priory and sent me with a generous endowment, one that came from his own purse, and one that overwhelmed any protest against my humble origins.''

The monk's voice broke. '' 'Twas more, far more, than I could have dreamed he might have done.''

He caught his breath and sniffled slightly behind Luc. '' 'Tis a fine strain of blood that courses through the veins of Tullymullagh's kings, make no mistake. I have no doubt 'twill overwhelm whatever deficiencies this son of Gavin's brings to the hall.''

Indeed, Luc already knew what marvels a child of Tullymullagh's lineage could make possible. He smiled secretly to himself and touched his heels to Raphael to urge him on.

Short moments later, Luc dismounted before the chapel where the chanting of prayers echoed and looked expectantly to Brother Thomas. He remained seated, clearly not yet done with his tale.

''And ever since that day, I come to Tullymullagh to dress their dead,'' Brother Thomas confided solemnly. '' 'Tis but a small gesture of gratitude for all the old lord granted to me.''

There were tears in the monk's eyes and Luc realized suddenly the youthfulness of his appearance in comparison with Connor. ''You and Connor are contemporaries?'' he asked, before he could halt the words.

Brother Thomas smiled, then frowned as he assessed the distance to the ground. "Aye, though those years in Outremer were hard upon Connor. They forged his spirit, though, and he was tested in ways that I can barely imagine. And indeed, that journey made his treasury what 'tis today."

Luc was momentarily startled that the monk made such easy reference to the tale Brianna had shared. Did everyone in these parts know the source of Connor's wealth?

"Why do we halt here?" the monk demanded with an abruptness that stole away Luc's musings.

"Lady Ismay was brought here."

"Ah!" The monk stretched out his hand. "Aid me, sir, if you will. 'Tis markably far to the ground and I fear for these fragile old bones of mine."

Luc could not help but think of his own bones as he reached a hand to the considerably-sized monk. He thought of the struggle to see Brother Thomas in the saddle and feared the worst.

But evidently, descending from the saddle was not an issue. Brother Thomas swung his leg with surprising grace, gripped the saddle, and grunted as he dropped the very tips of his sandalled toes to the ground.

Raphael stepped to one side and snorted relief. The monk patted the stallion's rump, then smiled at Luc. " 'Tis a fine steed you ride for your station. Do you not aid the ostler?"

"Aye," Luc conceded, unable to resist the opportunity to grant the monk an unexpected morsel of news. "But 'tis by my choice, not by rank." The monk frowned, not understanding, and Luc continued with a smile. "My name is Luc Fitzgavin."

Brother Thomas' eyes widened in mingled surprise and delight. "You are the one who did not go!" he crowed. "Ah, everyone will be astonished that you were within our very midst at the priory and they did not guess the truth!'' He grinned and slapped Luc on the back. ''Ah! I shall have tales to tell after this journey, you may be certain of it!''

Voices rose from within the chapel once more, a familiar benediction carrying clearly to Luc's ears. The Mass was nearly over, and Luc had a very good idea where a certain princess would be at this moment on a Sunday morn.

''The 'Ave,' '' Brother Thomas exclaimed. ''How I do love the 'Ave Maria.' ''

''As do I,'' Luc said firmly and knotted Raphael's reins to a fencepost. He could not resist the opportunity to see his princess as soon as possible. ''Shall we?''

Chapter Eleven

WHEN BROTHER THOMAS SLIPPED INTO THE CHAPEL and smiled at the entire assembly, Brianna's heart began to hammer. For if the monk was here from Endlist Priory, then the man sent to retrieve him must also be returned.

She peeked to the back of the chapel, her heart leaping when she found not only Luc standing there, but his blue, blue gaze fixed upon her. Brianna felt herself flush, noted her father's glance to her and thence to the back of the chapel.

"Hmmm," Connor murmured, and Brianna did not miss his sharp look her way. She held up her chin, but could not stop anticipation from flooding through her.

Luc had returned!

Finally. Brianna had spent all of the previous evening hoping for his reappearance in the hall.

At least, she had done so when she had not been run ragged with making arrangements for Ismay's funeral. Much to Brianna's surprise, Dermot had no more than a perfunctory interest in such matters and it had been left to her to decide.

Since Ismay's holding was lost and the new lord there as yet unknown, Brianna and Uther concluded that Ismay should be buried in the cemetery of the Tullymullagh parish church. If she could be moved later to join the remainder of her family, 'twould be done then.

Truly, the management of a keep was a task like no other. Until these past few days, Brianna had had no idea how hard Uther labored. 'Twas interesting to plan menus and assess inventory, far more fascinating than merely plying a needle at embroidery.

Brianna felt that she was truly contributing to the household and possessed new satisfaction in her role. She owed a debt to Luc for his prompting her to do more.

Aye, Brianna's anxiety to see him could only be because she wished to tell him as much. She tapped her toe impatiently as Father Padraig lingered over the Mass and fairly fled when he breathed the last "amen."

Her father took due note of her hasty departure, she knew.

But Brianna found 'twas no easy task to make her way to the back of the chapel when all else proceeded the same way. Brianna exchanged more than one glance of exasperation with the man she would meet, her heart pounding when he resolutely waited for her.

No sooner had Brianna come within a few steps of Luc, than Uther waylaid her. She heaved a sigh of frustration and felt herself flush when Luc's smile broadened in understanding.

Silently, Brianna urged Uther to hasten himself.

"My lady, I had considered that due to lack of suitable space within the keep, Ismay might lay in the parish church itself until the funeral on Tuesday," Uther declared. "If you are amenable." He guided Brianna firmly through the chapel doors and toward the castle gates, while she cast an appealing glance back to Luc.

Luc shook his head, strolling behind Brianna's group with casual ease. It could be no accident he lingered so close.

Could Luc be as interested in speaking with Brianna as she was in speaking with him?

The very prospect made Brianna lose the thread of whatever Uther told her.

"My lady!" Cook called from the other side of the assembly. "When you have a moment, I should like to review the menu for the week."

"And perhaps check the tallies for the week?" interjected Uther. "There is still the issue of Gavin's concern with the spice inventory."

"My lady, what garb shall we make ready for the funeral?" Fenella chimed in.

Brianna had thought no further than how quickly she might be finished with her growing list of responsibilities when Gavin cried out.

"Burke!" he roared. " 'Tis *Burke*!"

All spun to watch the mercenary dart as well as he was able to the gate of the churchyard. Gavin's heavy features were transformed with glee when he turned back to the assembly and pointed triumphantly to Tullymullagh's gate.

"Burke is returned!"

Brianna immediately spotted a knight astride the midnight stallion, waiting just outside Tullymullagh's gates.

Brianna felt her lips part in dismay and her blood run chill. Burke could not be back so soon! She glanced to Luc, only to find his expression grimly fixed on the gates.

What was she to do? Luc had told her to accept Burke's suit, indeed he had insisted 'twas the choice to make. Brianna knew Luc's counsel was good, yet still she hesitated to do his bidding.

For if Luc's kisses had awakened her to the touch of men, why did Ruarke's touch leave her cold?

Aye, what if Brianna did not feel the same fire from Burke's touch as she felt from Luc's?

What if Brianna could *not* come to love Burke, despite Luc's endorsement of his brother?

The very prospect was terrifying. 'Twas everything Brianna had sworn not to endure! Her own defiance warred with her trust of Luc's judgement.

Was she merely avoiding what was best for her, simply for the sake of calling her own tune? If she declined Burke, would she regret her choice? Had Luc not already known better than she?

Brianna wished fervently that she could talk to Luc but once more. Just for a moment. He would aid her to make a sensible choice, Brianna knew it well.

Aye, it might well be that the response to men he had awakened now slumbered once more and her flesh would not tingle beneath Luc's touch either.

Oh! How Brianna wished she knew more of such matters! And 'twas too late to consult with Luc.

The assembly surged forward and began to chatter merrily, carrying Brianna in their enthusiastic tide. Denis ran to take the steed's reins, Burke dismounted, and Gavin clapped his returning son upon the back. Connor smiled with anticipation as he offered Brianna his elbow and hastened her onward.

The moment of decision was upon her.

And Brianna did not know what she should do. In the absence of her own decisiveness, she took a deep breath and resolved to put her faith in Luc's assessment.

She would laugh at whatever Burke brought.

• • •

BY THE TIME she was seated in the hall, Brianna's heart was racing. She sat between her sire and Gavin on the dais, her hands clenched together in her lap. Her fingers were cold, her palms were damp, but she held her chin high.

A hard lump took residence in Brianna's throat, she ached

with awareness of Luc standing at the back of the hall. But one glimpse had been enough of his grim countenance. His arms were folded across his chest, his gaze bored into Brianna as though he would will her to heed his counsel.

Aye, she was so agitated, she knew any laughter that broke from her lips would sound fey. Surely, none would be fooled?

One part of her hoped that Burke had truly brought something amusing.

Another part only wanted the moment behind her, the issue resolved.

But Luc was relying upon her to use the wits God had granted her. And Brianna did not want to disappoint him.

Uther cleared his throat and the chattering in the hall ceased expectantly. Every face turned toward the dais, every visage was bright with curiosity. Brianna gripped her own fingers tightly.

"Lords and ladies, people of Tullymullagh." The steward spoke in his most authoritative tone and the last of the murmuring fell silent. "Not even a week has passed since we assembled within this very hall to hear the challenge of the princess Brianna for Gavin Fitzgerald's three sons. As well you may recall, the lady requested each son to bring her a gift, a gift intended to make her laugh, and pledged she would wed the man who made her laugh loudest and longest."

The crowd nodded approvingly and nudged each other as they looked at Burke. He stood patiently to one side, a massive saddlebag at his feet. Brianna thought it moved of its own accord, but when she looked again, 'twas still.

She swallowed and gripped her fingers more tightly. Luc's determination seemed to bear down upon Brianna but her heart pounded with trepidation.

What if she could not love Burke? What if she never felt

more for him than she did at this moment? He was a complete stranger to her, despite Luc's endorsement.

"And now," Uther continued, "the first of those sons is returned. Chevalier Burke de Montvieux comes with a gift for our princess fair. Let us see how well he succeeds at coaxing the lady's laughter."

Burke bowed slightly at this introduction, acknowledging the applause that swept through the hall. "I thank you for such a welcome," he said smoothly, though his deep tones prompted no response from Brianna.

She bit her lip, knowing full well that if it had been Luc before her, but one glance from him would have sent a quiver dancing through her.

Brianna glanced to that man, still at the back of the hall, and felt that very quiver.

Meanwhile, Gavin's favored son crossed the room with easy grace, his saddlebag perched on his hip. The troubadours poked their noses out of the assembly and avidly whispered details to each other. Brianna forced herself to look at the man before her instead of watching Luc.

This Burke was a handsome man, she supposed. His nose was too small to have much character, to her mind. And the silver hair threaded through the ebony at his temples was rather too predictable for her taste.

She found it hard to believe that he truly could surprise her.

As Luc did.

Would Burke challenge her, question her, compel her to use her wits? Would Burke agree to all Brianna asked, or would he insist she have good reason for asking it of him? Would his kisses make her tingle, his touch make her shiver?

Brianna could hardly believe as much.

She wondered anew what Luc would have brought her, if indeed he had deigned to depart on her quest. There, she was certain, would have been something of considerable interest.

"I am certain Burke has found the perfect gift," Gavin growled on Brianna's one side.

Brianna was not nearly so convinced.

Burke's saddlebag wriggled quite definitely as he set it upon the floor with care. Fenella, near beside him, peeked under the flap and giggled.

Brianna bit her lip and tried to convince herself to do as Luc had bidden her. The assembly leaned closer in anticipation.

"My lady Brianna," Burke said solemnly and bowed impeccably low. "This gift is for you and I hope that it will bring delight."

Brianna could not help but notice that Burke looked as though he hoped precisely the opposite. His very manner was indifferent beyond all and she sat back with a slight frown.

'Twas one thing to wed a stranger upon the advice of one she trusted. 'Twas quite another to wed a stranger *indifferent* to the prospect of those nuptials. Aye, if Burke wanted to win her hand, he ought to show some enthusiasm!

If the man was not enamored of the thought of wedding Brianna, she could not imagine she would win his attention in the wake of the deed.

'Twas clear enough that Luc did not know his brother's heart.

But, mercifully, Brianna had discerned the truth in time. In the blink of an eye, she resolved *not* to laugh.

Regardless of what this man had brought to her. Brianna took a deep breath, entangled her fingers, and sat ramrod straight.

Burke bent and, with nary a glance Brianna's way, opened the flap with a flourish.

For a moment naught happened.

Then, the overly large noses of three young wolfhound puppies appeared in unison, the dogs blinking at the sudden light. The women in the assembly cooed, the men snorted, and Brianna sat back with a barely restrained sigh of relief.

Dogs might be amusing, but they were not that funny. This she could manage.

As though it had heard her thoughts, one dog erupted from the bag and attacked Fenella's hem. The maid squealed and danced back, the pup stumbled over its own ungainly paws. The second pup leapt after the first and tackled it. They rolled into a tangle of soft fur, wet noses, and massive feet, coming to an abrupt halt against Dermot's foot.

That man smiled coolly, then obviously aware of the crowd's eyes upon him, bent and tentatively scratched one puppy's ear. Brianna could tell that 'twas not a comfortable gesture for him and wondered whether Dermot disliked small creatures.

The dog, however, was oblivious to any reservation on Dermot's part. It leaned back and promptly lost its balance, rolling bonelessly to its back. The assembly chuckled. The second pup climbed shamelessly over the first to be scratched in turn.

Dermot's touch behind this puppy's ear sent the small creature into throes of pleasure. Its back leg working vigorously, its large paw thumping its fallen brethren in the nose. The first dog yelped, then clambered to its feet, and gave that offending foot a vigorous chomp.

Chuckles echoed around the hall. The second pup yowled, the two began a merry chase. They dodged knees and tables, ducked beneath skirts, scattered the rushes, and generally set everything to chaos. Brianna sat stone-faced while the assembly laughed lightly at the puppy's antics.

Brianna was not even tempted to smile.

The third pup, no longer the center of attention, pushed a cautious nose out of the saddlebag. It had evidently been watching from within the security of the bag, for when it trotted out, it headed straight for Dermot.

But it wanted Dermot's leg, not his finger.

And 'twas a male.

Dermot inhaled sharply when the pup latched onto his shin with vigor and began to hump. The assembly howled while Dermot tried to shake the amorous pup loose without success.

Fenella fought against her own laughter even as she bent to aid the beleaguered Dermot, but to no avail. Denis laughed so hard that he had to wipe away tears from his eyes. Burke strode across the floor and lent his assistance, but the pup was naught if not determined.

'Twas Dermot's horrified expression that was nearly Brianna's undoing. She bit her lip painfully against her own laughter and clutched her fingers more tightly together.

She would not laugh.

Connor finally let out a hoot of laughter when the pup finished his deed. For when Burke scooped up the dog, the pup's souvenir upon Dermot's chausses was clear to view. Dermot's eyes looked as though they would drop from his head, he was so appalled.

The assembly nigh rolled upon the floor. Ruarke slapped his thigh, Gavin chortled, even Father Padraig made some sound that might have passed for laughter. Brianna bit her lip to keep back her own.

But she managed the deed.

Within moments, the din had settled, the pups were back in the saddlebag and Burke was bowing low. He did not look the least bit disappointed by his failure and Brianna knew she was not the only one to note that fact.

She had made the right choice.

Burke had barely straightened before Gavin erupted from his seat, his pointed finger shaking with fury as he shouted at his favored son. "*You!* I would talk with you! *Now*!"

Burke's eyes flashed, then he inclined his head to his sire, the very image of elegance and deference. Any hint of his anger was gone as the knight pivoted smoothly to follow his sire's bidding.

Gavin's departure was in marked contrast to his son's grace, both from his distinctive hobble and his obviously poor temper. The hall fell into awkward silence as they left, then conversation and speculation swelled to a roar.

Brianna smiled with satisfaction. She sought Luc's gaze once more, only to find that he had slipped from the hall.

Aye, he could not have discerned Burke's indifference from the back of the hall. And he might well be displeased by her decision to ignore his advice. Brianna had to talk to Luc, she had to explain her choice.

Brianna was certain Luc would understand once she voiced her doubts.

He was a man of good sense, after all.

"Well done!" Ruarke declared as he came to lean against the dais. He winked as he grinned up at her and Brianna wondered why her sire's champion would be so concerned for her nuptials.

Then her sire's words stole away her thoughts. "You were not amused by the pups?" Connor laid his bent hand over Brianna's own and gave her fingers a squeeze. "This Burke *is* Gavin's heir, child."

Brianna patted her sire's arm with confidence. "He seemed little enough interested in me, Father. Indeed, I know naught of the manner of man Burke is, much less whether he is my own true love."

Connor sobered and his voice dropped low. "Child, you must not put too much stock in such whimsy. A man and a woman can find love between them, even if their match is arranged."

"Perhaps they do, Father," Brianna conceded with a smile. "But I will not take that risk."

Connor's glance was compelling. "Have you found this one true love whom you seek so diligently? Is there a man who stands beside you with honor, ready to defend what you hold dear? A man you trust beyond all others and upon whose word you can rely?"

Brianna stared into her father's concerned eyes and her mouth went dry. There *was* such a man, a man whose company she sought, a man whose word of honor she could trust, a man who treated her with respect.

A man whose kisses enflamed her.

"Have you, Brianna?" Ruarke demanded silkily when she said naught.

Brianna blinked, certain only that she had to talk to Luc. Immediately.

"I—I do not know," she managed to say, hoping her tone was light. Brianna smiled pertly, squeezed her sire's fingers, then slipped from her chair, and quickly crossed the hall.

Luc would be in the orchard, she guessed, and turned her steps in that direction. Aye, Luc would be irked with her, there was little doubt of that, but Brianna knew she could make him understand.

And she owed him no less than four kisses, after all.

Her heart skipped a beat, her feet flew in anticipation. So occupied was she with her thoughts that Brianna did not see Ruarke scowl far behind her.

Nor did she see her sire frown, then gather his robes to lend chase.

• • •

THE WAVE OF relief that swept over Luc when Brianna did not laugh had been dizzying. Indeed, he had left the hall for a breath of fresh air in an attempt to clear his head.

The lady had spurned Burke, and now Luc had need of a plan.

He headed for the orchard, struggling to think of some way to make Brianna laugh. The pups had been amusing, he knew, though 'twas Dermot's predicament that tempted Luc's own chuckle.

Brianna had sat impassive, though, throughout. It seemed the lady clung to her conviction to wed only for love.

And Luc knew well enough how stubborn she could be. He frowned at the apple trees, uncertain how he might circumvent that obstacle. Aye, he could well imagine that Brianna would ensure she did not laugh at any jest he made.

If Brianna guessed Luc's intent—and the lady was not weak of intellect—she might even avoid him.

And that would serve naught.

But *how* to make Brianna laugh? Luc paced and puzzled. Unlike Rowan, he did not have a store of humorous tales, nor an arsenal of amusing tricks he could perform. He had been spared his brother's upbringing among troubadours and entertainers and only now felt the lack.

Luc froze as he realized his own folly.

For if Brianna desired a man to keep her amused, then Burke was not the brother whose gift she awaited. 'Twas *Rowan* who could coax a smile from a stone; 'twas Rowan who could keep Brianna laughing for the rest of her days. And the very nature of Brianna's quest hinted at the import of merriment in her life.

Rowan might return at any moment.

Luc's heart clenched at the possibility, even as he spun to eye the vacant gates. Nay! He had to win Brianna! He had to surprise her, conjure her laugh, then make her his bride, even if he knew not how to begin.

Then, once all was resolved, Luc could set to the task of winning Brianna's heart.

"Luc!"

He spun to find the lady in question running across the bailey to him. Her eyes sparkled, she had gathered her fine skirts in fistfuls, her legs flashed beneath the hems. Her veil had slipped askew, her smile made Luc's heart begin to pound.

It had been but a day, and he had missed her sorely.

"I did not laugh!" she confessed with breathless delight when she came to a halt before him.

Nay she had not. In the wake of his relief, Luc decided 'twas as good a time as any to discover what the lady found amusing.

"And why did you not?"

Brianna laid a small hand upon his arm and leaned closer, a waft of her beguiling perfume making Luc's toes curl within his boots. Ye gods, had he ever desired a woman more?

"Luc, you must not be angered with me," she said hastily and Luc could not imagine why he might even consider the possibility. "I know you advised me to accept Burke and I tried to follow your counsel, I truly did, but you must believe that 'tis not because I distrust you that I did not laugh."

Luc blinked as he tried to make sense of this unexpected revelation. What counsel?

Brianna heaved a sigh, her fingers kneading the cloth of Luc's chemise. She flicked an appealing glance his way. "But I could not do it! Burke was so *indifferent*." She took a hasty breath. "I know you could not discern as much from the back of the hall."

Ah! Luc had advised her to wed Burke.

He had forgotten.

And Brianna had nearly done it, on his counsel alone.

Brianna rolled her eyes. "Luc, 'tis one matter that Burke is a stranger, though 'tis one mitigated by your reference to his character, but if he is disinterested in the match—" she leaned closer, her fingers tightening on his arm, her eyes wide with concern "—then how might love bloom between us after the nuptials?"

Ye gods, but Luc had nearly brought disaster upon his own intentions, without ever meaning to do so!

But all the same, there was something encouraging in the very fact that Brianna had heeded him. Luc had to hear that fact fall again from her lips.

He captured her hand beneath his own and stilled its agitated movement. "You truly thought to accept Burke, merely upon my advice?"

"Aye." Brianna smiled with a shyness that wrenched Luc's heart. "You were most certain that he is a man of honor and the one I should choose. Indeed, Luc, Burke is no stranger to *you*."

To think that Luc had nearly lost Brianna because of his own misguided advice! One day, if all came aright, Luc knew he would find the matter amusing.

In this moment, though, he was seized with an urgency to take advantage of his chance.

But how to make the lady laugh?

"You must not be insulted," Brianna urged, obviously misinterpreting Luc's silence. " 'Tis not because I do not trust you."

Luc captured both of her hands within his own and leaned toward her with intent. "My lady," he murmured, his voice thrumming low with affection. "Make no mistake, I am most delighted that you did not laugh."

Brianna blinked in evident confusion. Then she frowned. "But, you counselled me—"

"I did."

"But . . ."

Luc could not resist the ripe curve of Brianna's lips any longer. He laid one finger across their fullness to silence her protest, his loins tightening at the soft touch of them beneath his finger. "Aye, but I erred," he admitted. "I am most relieved you did not take my advice."

"You erred!" Brianna's eyes flashed dangerously as she shoved Luc's fingertip away. "You *erred* and you did not see fit to tell me?" She jabbed an angry finger in the direction of the hall, then railed at Luc. "I might have laughed apurpose! I would have been compelled to wed that man as a result! And you tell me merely that you erred?"

"I am sorry," Luc began in all sincerity, but got no further.

"Sorry? *Sorry*?" Brianna turned that finger upon him and beat a staccato in the midst of Luc's chest. "And what is that worth if I were to wed the wrong man? You should have come to me immediately and set this matter to rights!"

"My lady, I tried to speak with you this morn but you were busy—"

"Too busy to be concerned about the remainder of my life?" Brianna snorted with indignation. "I should think not!" She folded her arms across her chest and regarded Luc haughtily. "You, sir, owe me an apology."

Luc shoved a hand through his hair, then nodded. " 'Tis true enough," he conceded. "And I am sorry. 'Twas my intent to speak with you upon my arrival, but events conspired against me. I am also glad that you are a woman of such good sense."

Brianna sniffed as though she fought to remain cool. But

the quick glance she fired at Luc revealed that she was touched by his apology.

And the fact that she did not leave him be was most encouraging.

Perhaps he might make the most of this. There was more than one way to cajole a smile from a lady. "Though 'tis true that you yet owe me four kisses, my lady," he reminded her with a smile. "Shall we settle all our obligations this very morn?"

"Oh!" Twin spots of color burned in Brianna's cheeks.

Luc grinned. She was not immune to him, by any means, nor to even the prospect of his kisses.

That could only be a good sign.

Brianna retreated half a dozen steps and glared at Luc, her veil slipping farther askew. "You are incorrigible!" she charged heatedly. "And demanding. And disrespectful. And, and . . ."

Luc folded his arms across his chest to regard her with good humor. "And dare I hope, interesting?" He arched a brow as Brianna sputtered. "Intriguing? Challenging?" Luc paused for a heartbeat and deliberately met the lady's gaze.

"Or perhaps *amusing*?"

Brianna gasped, then caught the tail of her fury once more. "How could you possibly be amusing? You have no interest in making me laugh, you refused to depart on my quest, you refused to bring me a gift, you refuse to do *anything* that I ask of you!" She flung out her hands. "You are the single most infuriating and confounding man that I ever have met!"

"Because I do not *rush* to do your bidding?" Luc let his skepticism filter into his expression. "You cannot convince me, my lady fair, that you would harbor any respect for such a sorry excuse of a man." He shook a finger at her in turn.

"Indeed, you would not even deign to speak with me if I were as biddable as a trained pup."

Brianna blinked. Her cheeks pinkened as she held Luc's gaze, and then, ever so slowly, a smile spread across her lips.

"Nay," she confessed softly. "Nay, you speak aright. I would not come to talk with you, then."

Luc was satisfied to see his point made, but Brianna tilted her head to regard him. "I wish you *had* gone on my quest," she admitted softly.

'Twas a promising and unexpected admission.

And an opportunity not to be lost.

Luc held the lady's gaze, determined to get to the root of this. "Why?" he asked smoothly.

Brianna seemed to guess his interest in her response, for her flush deepened. She stepped backward, her gaze flicking away from Luc's. " 'Tis a test of character," she said lightly. "I would but know what you might bring."

"Nay." Luc shook his head and her alarmed gaze danced back to meet his own. "Your quest was no test of character and you know it well."

"But 'twas!" Brianna caught her breath when Luc stepped closer.

But she did not step away.

"My lady! Do you imagine that I have forgotten your plan to see your father rule Tullymullagh again?"

Brianna blanched. "I . . . I . . ."

"You had a scheme," Luc supplied firmly, "a foolish one that could have seen you sorely injured." He arched a brow. "Your quest was no more than a ploy to see all three brothers departed from Tullymullagh while you followed that scheme."

Brianna bit her lip, clearly caught.

Luc had no desire to torment her, so he took the last step

between them and captured her chin in his hand. "Fortunately, all ended well," he concluded.

"Because of you," Brianna acknowledged quietly, her cheeks flaming.

"My lady, I am glad I did not go upon your quest," Luc said, wanting her to hear his resolve. "For that alone granted me the chance to persuade you of your folly in defying Gavin."

The lady swallowed. "No one has ever refused to do my will," she confessed quietly, then lifted her gaze to meet Luc's. "No one but you."

She looked so vulnerable, so astonished that this could be, and so shaken by the fact that it was true, that Luc wanted only to reassure her. He wanted to make her smile again.

"Ah!" Luc arched a brow and winked playfully. "That, then, must be why you *missed* me so!"

Brianna choked, his comment clearly an unexpected one.

She chortled, her eyes danced. She lifted a hand to her lips, but to no avail.

For then, the lady laughed.

• • •

'TWAS TRUE ENOUGH, that Luc never did her bidding.

And equally true that Brianna would have thought less of his character if he had.

But the realization that she had indeed missed him sorely—and that because he defied her every expectation—was what brought the laughter to her lips.

And once Brianna loosed her laughter, it seemed she could not stop it.

Until Luc grinned, grasped her shoulders within the heat of his hands, and tipped back his head to bellow. "The lady Brianna laughs for me!"

Brianna sobered with a snap.

What was this?

Her laughter halted, she stared at Luc, only now realizing the import of what she had done. Brianna glanced back to the rustle of the assembly bursting from the hall, calls echoing over the walls as each passed the news to the other.

The entire household came running to witness the truth. Brianna turned back to Luc with horror.

"You tricked me!" she charged.

That man grinned cockily and Brianna saw his delight with what he had wrought. "You laughed," he reminded her firmly.

How dare he try to fool her? "It did not count!"

"It certainly did," Luc confirmed, his eyes dark with intent. "You laughed at the jest of one of Gavin's sons, and now, my lady, we shall be wed."

Wed?

To Luc?

"But this does not follow my plan!" Brianna protested, certain that events had never run so surely from her grip before. "You did not depart on the quest!"

Luc flicked a bright blue glance her way. " 'Tis clear I did not need to do so."

"But . . . but . . ." Brianna wildly sought some grounds of protest. This man could not best her at her own game! Why, the entire point of the quest was to ensure that she was not compelled to wed any particular man! "Aha!" she crowed with delight. "You did not grant me a gift!"

Luc hesitated for a moment and Brianna knew she had bested him.

"No gift was granted, so the laughter does not count!" she repeated, liking well that Luc seemed flummoxed by this.

Ha! She would have the last word!

But someone cleared his throat pointedly. Brianna pivoted to find her sire advancing into the orchard. He shook his head sagely. " 'Tis not so, child. Luc has granted you a rare gift indeed.''

Brianna was indignant that her father would take Luc's side. "What gift?"

Connor smiled. "The wisdom that no one should dictate to one's spouse, for the strength of a marriage is in partnership and understanding."

While Brianna fought to find an argument to that, Connor granted a nod to Luc. "I confess that I have listened to your discussion," he admitted without embarrassment.

Luc inclined his head, clearly untroubled by this. " 'Tis not beyond reasonable to attend to your daughter's future happiness."

Connor beamed at that sentiment, then turned his bright gaze on Brianna once more. " 'Tis clear enough to me, child, that this man, this man who challenges your will and cares for your safety, is a man you may be proud to take to your side."

Brianna gasped, not in the least bit pleased to find her heart making a similar case. She pivoted to face Luc. "How can you insist upon this course?" she demanded heatedly. "You know full well how I feel about the necessity of love in a marriage."

No sooner had she uttered the words, than Luc's grip on her fingers tightened. "My lady," he murmured, his voice pitched low. "I understand that this matter is of import to you, and thence, 'tis to me."

Brianna swallowed and stared into the vivid sapphire of Luc's gaze, the intensity of the color telling her that he meant whatever he would say.

"I would see you happy, I would see you satisfied with your match. My lady, you may be assured that I *shall* persuade you to love me."

Brianna's heart began to race. She stared at Luc, her heart

hammering at his unexpected words. Luc lifted her hand, his gaze unswerving, brushed his lips across her knuckles.

Brianna was certain the entire household saw her shiver.

"Indeed, Brianna," he murmured, his tone pitched for her ears alone, "I pledge it to you."

Luc had never uttered her name before. The very sound was so intimate, it conjured recollections of kisses and the heated promise of mysteries yet to be learned. Brianna caught her breath and looked away.

She knew well enough that Luc kept his word with a vengeance.

Could he make her love him? The very possibility was both tantalizing and terrifying. Brianna already admired Luc, she already trusted him, she already knew she could rely upon him.

She already was haunted by his smile.

But more importantly, would Luc come to love her? His words made it sound as though he had no intention of doing so.

And that was troubling indeed.

• • •

LUC WAS NOT encouraged by the lady's uncertainty, not in the least. Was there something here of which he knew naught? He had anticipated Brianna's concern with regards to love and tried his utmost to persuade her that he took the issue most seriously.

But Luc did not trust her uncharacteristic silence, nor the way she looked into the distance and frowned.

What was Brianna thinking?

"Let me pass!" Ruarke pushed his way through the ranks of those watching. He glowered at Luc, no less at the man's claim upon Brianna's hand, then stormed closer. Luc straightened, preparing for a verbal assault. Indeed, each time he saw this man Luc liked him less.

"What is this?" Ruarke demanded. "I heard some nonsense that Brianna laughed."

" 'Tis not nonsense," Luc retorted, not caring for the man's manner. "She did and we shall be wed."

"What?" Ruarke's eye flashed angrily. "This cannot be! Why, this lady cannot wed the likes of you! You are not even a knight!"

"On the contrary," Luc declared coldly. Well aware of the way the lady watched the exchange, Luc did not so much as flinch before Ruarke's noisy display. "I have been a knight for nigh on fifteen years."

He refrained from commenting upon Ruarke's loose interpretation of those knightly duties. To Luc's mind, the man had no place abandoning Tullymullagh in its hour of need, be he champion or merely a knight of the household.

And he did not like how quickly Ruarke had pledged his hand to Gavin. A man like Connor deserved greater loyalty from those beneath his hand.

Ruarke could have chosen to leave Tullymullagh, if only to make a point about the change of its lordship. There was no doubt that an able knight could find employ elsewhere and simultaneously keep his honor intact.

Ruarke blinked. "You do not dress as a knight."

"Garb does not make the man." Luc could not halt his cool and pointed assessment of Ruarke's fine garb. Indeed, Luc was not surprised that this champion had absented himself while the keep was under assault.

Battle might have mired Ruarke's fine tabard, after all.

The two men's gazes held in silent challenge and Luc guessed suddenly that this knight had aspirations of claiming Brianna as his own bride.

He could not help but wonder what the lady thought of that.

Ruarke straightened angrily, apparently reading Luc's

glance aright. "What of the other brother?" he demanded of Connor. "Was the wager not that the lady should wed whosoever made her laugh loudest?"

"Aye, 'twas!" Brianna insisted immediately. "Bless you, Ruarke, for recalling that detail!"

What madness was this?

Surely Brianna could not have affection for this man of so little merit? She was possessed of markedly good sense—why would it abandon her in this matter?

Luc looked to the lady in shock.

Indeed, he had his answer, and 'twas not the one he had expected. Luc's pledge to win her heart meant naught, for the lady was already in love.

The very thought launched an ill tide in Luc's belly. He abruptly released Brianna's hand and stepped away, not wanting to interfere in this plan. Brianna looked to him with alarm, but Luc could not imagine what else she expected of him. He had made her laugh, he had declared his honorable intent, yet she had insisted upon spurning his suit.

A man of honor pressed no further.

Ruarke pounced upon Brianna's hand when she hesitated and swept it possessively into the crook of his elbow. He fired a lethal glance at Luc, then summoned a charming smile for her alone.

"Come, my lady, come break your fast with me."

"But . . ."

Luc was not surprised that Brianna did not appreciate having Ruarke make her decision for her. The lady was naught if not determined to see the course of her own mind.

Whatever foolish path it chose to tread. He still could not conceive of why she would have interest in Ruarke.

"But *naught*," Ruarke declared, as though he scolded an errant child. " 'Tis time you lingered with finer company than this. And what of your embroidery?'' Ruarke fairly dragged Brianna from the orchard.

Brianna cast an appealing glance over her shoulder from the periphery of the orchard, but Luc deliberately turned away. He would *not* rush to her aid in this. Brianna had chosen her knight and could no doubt see matters her way in the end.

Luc folded his arms across his chest and scowled at the River Darrow. Aye, he had been seven kinds of fool, indeed.

Chapter Twelve

HE KITCHEN PORTAL SLAMMED WITH VIGOR BUT A heartbeat after Brianna and Ruarke disappeared into the hall. Burke strode across the bailey, oblivious to anyone or anything in his path. Luc glanced up and acknowledged that he had never seen his brother so angered.

Then Gavin erupted in his favored son's wake, his fist shaking in the air as he hobbled out into the bailey. "Go then! Go! You are no son of mine, Burke de Montvieux!"

"Fine!" Burke bellowed with a defiance Luc had never before witnessed in him. Luc's eyes widened and he, along with most of the household, straightened to watch the exchange. " 'Tis a shame I cannot purge the taint of your blood from my very veins!"

Gavin looked fit to explode and his face reddened dangerously. He pointed his finger after Burke. "I shall reclaim all of your holdings! I shall see that you do not inherit Montvieux! I shall lay claim to every coin that ever you have won if you do not return this very moment—on your knees, chevalier—and apologize."

Burke pivoted and propped his hands on his hips as he glared back at his sire. "Take it and welcome!" he roared. "The price of your favor is too high!"

Luc blinked in astonishment. He had never seen his brother angry; he certainly had never suspected Burke would defy their father. But Burke swivelled and stalked to the stables with nary a backward glance. Gavin seemed sufficiently stunned that he fell silent, even while the assembly burst into excited chatter.

A jingle of trap announced Burke's return but a few moments later. He rode his black destrier out of the stables, heading directly for the gates with nary a glance to either side. Luc noted his brother had loaded no saddlebags and left with only his garb, his blade, and his steed.

He looked again. 'Twas unthinkable that Burke spurned Gavin's approval.

But that was precisely what Burke did.

Gavin hastened forward and raised his voice to a bellow. "If you leave this place without seeking a fit gift for the princess, I shall never speak with you again!"

Burke spat on the stones of the bailey. "There is a loss in my life!" he retorted.

While Gavin sputtered, Burke touched his spurs to his steed and rode through the gates, apparently oblivious to the storm behind him. Luc marvelled that patient, dutiful Burke had finally been pushed too far.

"I shall see you destroyed!" Gavin raged too late to be heard by his departing son. "I shall see you penniless!" He jumped up and down in his impotence. "I shall see you unwelcome in any keep in Christendom!"

But Burke was gone.

'Twas but a moment later that Gavin realized the truth. He wandered to the gate like a man in a daze and stared down the unfurling road.

Hoofbeats faded from earshot, yet Gavin still stood, staring through the gaping gate. He was clearly stunned by this development. Finally, he slumped to sit on the outside of the gatehouse.

The gossip in the bailey erupted with a vengeance. If his father intended to await Burke's return, Luc had a feeling Gavin would be waiting a very long time.

• • •

CONNOR OF TULLYMULLAGH had not only witnessed the fleeting wonder on his daughter's visage when her laughter faded, but he guessed the import of that look. Aye, Brianna resembled her dame strongly in that moment, and Connor recalled well enough what Eva had had in mind when she turned that soft-eyed glance upon him.

It had always been followed by a confession of the most sentimental kind.

And Brianna had turned that glance upon Gavin's eldest son.

Connor watched Luc assessingly, the pair's heated exchange echoing in his ears. The younger man was sorely wounded by Brianna's denial of his pledge, though he fought to hide the truth.

Aye, there was passion aplenty between those two, that much could not be denied. Their very confrontation made Connor feel young again, sending a recollection of the early misunderstandings he and Eva had shared.

Aye, in those days, he had been a man of war, unable to tell a fine lady exactly what troubled his heart. In time, Eva had taught him much—and she had learned to read what Connor dared not put into words.

But on the way, there had been battles aplenty. As painful as they were, the reconciliations—Connor's smile broadened—the reconciliations were nearly worth the price.

Connor knew Brianna had found her one true love, even if she was not prepared to admit the truth as yet. He liked well that the man in question was one of rare honor. He had noted Luc's intercession for Ruarke, noted his resolve in both denying to follow Brianna's will and in defying his own sire.

No wonder Brianna had not laughed at Burke's pups. Stubborn child. His lips curved with affection, Connor took a step farther into the orchard, lending chase to the man who would govern Tullymullagh in his stead. Connor realized as he walked that this Luc had labored to save these forgotten trees and his heart swelled a thousand-fold.

Eva's dream was being restored. Tullymullagh would prosper beneath Luc's hand, Brianna would bear sons to make the hall ring with laughter.

Connor's smile broadened. "You will be good tonic for her," he charged softly when he reached the younger man.

Luc merely shrugged and frowned. "With all due respect, that seems unlikely, sir."

But his gaze trailed tellingly to the portal.

"Aye? How so?"

Luc nodded toward the keep. "Her heart, it seems, is securely held by your former champion." His lips thinned. " 'Tis not my place to steal what he has fairly won."

"Nay," Connor said with resolve. "Brianna does not love Ruarke." He enjoyed Luc's surprise.

"But she must. She chose to leave with him."

Connor shook his head. "I know Brianna enough to know she was but startled." He leaned against a tree and ran his hand over its pruned bough. "You have labored long here. The trees have not had such good care in years."

Luc strode closer, his brow as dark as thunder. "What do you mean that she was startled?"

Connor met the younger man's gaze. "I saw her eyes and I know my daughter well. She does not love Ruarke, though there were times when I wished heartily that she would."

Luc held Connor's gaze for a long moment. "But she protested long."

Connor scoffed. "And this surprises you?" He let a smile spread over his face and clicked his tongue. "I thought you knew her better than that!"

Luc chuckled and shoved a hand through his hair. Connor watched, liking how that man's resolve dawned anew. "You are certain?"

"She did not intend to laugh," Connor said firmly. "I have no doubt of that. And she is but learning to accept that all cannot go her way." He shrugged. " 'Tis my own fault for indulging her, I suppose, but you already have taught her a great deal. She cares for you, Luc Fitzgavin, and your pledge won you much. Do not blame Brianna for being startled that all happened with such haste."

Luc heaved a sigh and shook his head. "She fooled me," he admitted and Connor chuckled.

" 'Tis the way of women everywhere," he confided easily, the pair sharing a grin. Connor straightened and looked the younger man in the eye. "Pursue her, Luc, pursue Brianna as you intended, and she will be your own." Connor tapped Luc on the shoulder. "I know it well, just as I know that the match will be a good one."

Luc smiled. "I thank you for the encouragement, sir," he said firmly and flicked a glance to the keep. "I shall heed your counsel."

"Good!" Connor wagged a finger. "Leave her this day that she might ponder what has happened. By this eve, I have no doubt that she will receive you."

Luc bowed slightly. "I thank you again, sir."

Connor liked the gleam of determination that lit the younger man's eye. Aye, Luc Fitzgavin was a man Connor could respect, a man who would ensure Brianna's happiness, a man who would protect and cherish her like none other.

And this was a man who deserved to know the truth about the Rose of Tullymullagh. Connor blinked at the realization. 'Twas Brianna's legacy, after all, and that of the children these two would bring to light.

And 'twas time Connor told someone of his secret.

Connor frowned at the household still lingering around the orchard, then bent close to Luc. "Come early to the board this night," he counselled. "There is a tale you deserve to know if you will take my daughter to wife."

"I should be honored to enjoy your confidence, sir." And Luc bowed low.

Connor could not help but smile, all was being resolved so well. Eva would have taken to this man, he was certain of it.

'Twas on his way back to the keep that Connor had a sudden thought. He glanced to the gates, and the despondent Gavin still sat there.

And if Gavin sat outside the gates, then the solar would be vacant.

The chapel could be Connor's alone.

Aye, he would give thanks for all that had come his—and Brianna's—way in this, he would give thanks that his sole child was destined to repeat her parents' happiness. He would whisper to Eva of what had happened, of his hopes for the future, for 'twas there that Connor felt closest to her.

'Twas no small gift to know that Brianna would be secure and happy for all her days. Eva must be told. Connor's steps quickened in anticipation. He must make haste!

But Connor was not the only one seizing the opportunity to be alone in the lord's private chapel.

• • •

BRIANNA RESTLESSLY POKED at the accounts Uther had laid before her. Ruarke's demand on her time had been short-lived, for he had abandoned her to her labor, pleading some errand or another, as soon as they entered the hall. Brianna would have enjoyed a measure of Fenella's cheerful company, but the maid must be back in the kitchens again.

Truly, Brianna would have to have a word with the maid and discourage such unseemly habits. 'Twas well enough for a maid to chatter, but Fenella's sire expected her to learn the decorum of a lady of the manor.

As Brianna should be doing. She sighed and eyed the parchment, unable to shake the image of Luc pledging to win her heart. Just the recollection made her heart pound wildly.

Could he do it?

Could Brianna win *Luc's* heart in return?

Could the love she had long desired truly be so close at hand?

She picked up the quill and examined the ledger before her, wishing she were better with tallies. The accounts had proven to be the greatest challenge of administration and the one Brianna liked least.

This ledger was not likely to distract her on this day. 'Twas part of her education, but Brianna always erred in the addition.

That, indeed, was why Uther insisted she continue doing it. Brianna grimaced at the ledger but the numbers did not tally of their own accord.

She thought once more of Luc, butterflies dancing in her belly at the thought of wedding him. She admitted to herself that the man's kisses were tempting beyond all and indulged herself in wondering what proceeded from there.

'Twas all a secret of the marital bed, Brianna knew well,

though she did not know specifics. Indeed, she had never truly wondered while her mother was alive. She had not wondered until Luc awakened her with his kiss.

And now, there was no one to ask.

"My lady," Uther chided, interrupting her daydreams. "Have you not yet completed this simple task?"

"Nay, Uther, not yet."

The steward clicked his tongue. "You desired to know of this labor, my lady," he reminded her sternly, "and balanced ledgers are a critical ingredient in any well-administered household."

"Aye, Uther." Brianna dutifully bent over the ledger once more. Uther left her at work, but 'twas not to be long before her calculations were interrupted once more.

• • •

THE CHAPEL WAS dark, but Connor knew the way well enough for he had come this way a thousand times. He counted the steps as he climbed the narrow stairs. He lifted his lantern high as he stepped into the chapel proper.

But instead of sighing with pleasure, Connor gasped at the sight before his eyes.

Two figures, masked yet familiar for all of that, spun to confront him. Connor's hand trembled in outrage and the flame of his lantern shook when he saw the damage they had wrought in this sacred place.

"You!" he cried angrily, pointing at one. "And you!" Connor pointed to the other as he stepped into the middle of the chapel and drew himself up to his full height. He glared at them both. "What . . . ?"

'Twas the last word that Connor had the chance to utter. The first blow took him so by surprise that he fell to his knees, dazed. He blinked at the floor but once before a second blow landed across his back and sent him tumbling.

He looked up through the haze of his pain, unable to understand what had gone awry.

And someone, someone whom Connor had long trusted, kicked the old king in the face. He tasted his own blood, then felt the keen edge of a blade as 'twas buried in his side. He caught his breath as the blade was savagely driven deeper and pain flooded through him.

Then Connor of Tullymullagh knew no more.

• • •

"Stubborn fools and blundering asses!" Gavin pronounced from the portal, his booming voice enough to make Brianna forget her sum. Gavin shook his fist when he saw he had caught each and every eye. "I am surrounded on all sides! I have had my fill of the lot of you."

Before anyone troubled to voice similar feelings for his presence, Gavin jabbed a finger toward a scullery lad making his way between the trestle tables. "You! Bring my meal to the solar. *Now*!"

The boy yelped in terror and ran for the kitchens. Uther's lips set in a disapproving line and Brianna frowned, even as she bent over the accounts once more.

She would have to begin this cursed tally again.

'Twas not long before Gavin's outraged bellow carried from far above, interrupting Brianna's addition yet again. Yet 'twas not the anger they had all come to associate from Gavin that made every head in the hall snap up for the second time in close succession.

'Twas the uncharacteristic echo of horror. Gavin roared again and the assembly was on their feet in collective alarm, their gazes fixed at the top of the stairs.

"By the saints above, what has possessed the man now?" Uther muttered. He straightened and headed briskly for the stairs.

Brianna had a sudden foreboding that naught good had

transpired. She slammed the ledger closed and was quick on Uther's heels, wanting to see the truth with her own eyes.

Evidently she was not the only one with such a thought, for the entire household was immediately behind her—their feet pounding on the wooden stairs, their uncertainty tangible.

The door to the solar was unlatched and the party surged through to the next flight of stairs, Uther and Brianna leading the way. To the surprise of all, Gavin was not in the solar proper, but a shuffle from above revealed his presence in the chapel.

"Like as not, he has had an epiphany," Uther commented beneath his breath and headed for those stairs.

Brianna trotted right behind him, her sense of foreboding growing with every step. She could not imagine Gavin in the chapel for any good reason at all.

The man did not strike her as a religious sort.

Gavin stood at the summit, his features oddly smeared with black. He stared fixedly at the midst of the chapel floor, his expression dazed, and seemed unaware of their arrival.

Uther pushed Gavin forcibly aside, and Brianna gasped at the pool of blood spreading across the chapel floor. Then steward and daughter of the house simultaneously saw what had shocked Tullymullagh's conqueror.

The broken body of Connor lay lifeless in the midst of that dark pool.

Brianna took one look and screamed. *"Father!"*

She fell on her knees beside his limp body, cradling his beloved head in her lap, touching his throat.

There was no reassuring murmur of his heart.

Nay! Brianna leaned over her father, desperate for some hint that he yet lived. She strained for the faintest whisper of his breath.

There was none.

Her vision clouded with tears and Brianna shook her head, unable to believe that he was gone, so suddenly and so completely. It could not be true. It could not be so.

'Twas all some cruel jest. It had to be. She could not permit it to be otherwise.

But the truth sprawled in her lap could not be denied. Brianna looked at Uther, still unable to make sense of what she knew to be true.

"He is dead," she whispered unevenly. "Uther, he is dead."

The steward turned on Gavin and fairly shoved that man down the stairs in his outrage. "How dare you commit such a sin in a holy place like this?"

"What is this you say?"

"Do not play the innocent with me!" Uther bellowed in a most uncharacteristic manner. "I have seen well enough the anger between you and my lord Connor! I have seen how deeply you resent his presence! I have seen how you would steal the smallest honor from him!"

Uther inhaled so sharply that his nostrils fairly pinched shut. His disgust was tangible. "But what manner of barbarian takes a man's life in a place consecrated to God?!"

Brianna caught her breath and stared at her father's pallid face in belated understanding. She had not considered the blood, though now she did.

Her father had been murdered.

In his own chapel.

Connor's eyes were yet open, though even now their silvery hue dimmed. His features were frozen in an expression of mingled horror and pain. 'Twas the look of a man betrayed and once she realized it, Brianna could no longer look upon him.

A hard lump rose in her throat at her inevitable conclusion. Her sire had been killed by someone within his own household. Brianna's chest tightened painfully. She looked at the faces of those already in the chapel and yet more crowding the stair.

Dermot, Fenella, Ruarke, Cook, everyone was present, every face was etched with anguish. Brianna heard the rustle of footsteps and knew that yet more lingered below.

Who could have done this thing?

Her gaze landed upon the adamantly protesting Gavin and Brianna knew there was accusation in her own eyes.

Father Padraig pushed his way through the group on the stairs, clucked his tongue in sharp disapproval, then fell to his knees beside Brianna. "The wrath of the Lord is onerous upon us these days," he muttered darkly. "And the price of our sins runs high."

Brianna blinked. "My father was no sinner."

Father Padraig threw a stern glance her way. "We are *all* sinners, my lady, for we are born of sinful union between man and woman."

Brianna bridled at the way this priest referred to her father. "But my sire—"

"Was filled with the deadly sin of pride, my lady," Father Padraig declared with rare savagery. "Why else did he not abandon this solar willingly? Why else did he creep into the chapel that was his no longer? A chapel consecrated to God belongs to Him alone and no other. The Lord saw Connor's sinfulness and smote him for it!"

" 'Twas not the Lord who killed my lord Connor," Uther interjected coldly. He glared at Gavin. "He had a most earthly agent for this wicked deed."

"The hand of the Lord works in wondrous ways," Father Padraig intoned.

As Brianna stared at him, stunned by his harsh words, the priest marked the cross upon Connor's forehead and began to whisper last rites.

Gavin began defending himself vehemently. "I did not kill him! Why would I do such a thing? I have already conquered him and claimed all that was his own!"

"Except the loyalty of those around you," Uther snapped. "Do you think we are witless fools? Who else had any reason to see this man dead?"

"I care naught for your loyalty!" Gavin protested hotly. "I tell you I was attacked when I came into the solar. Someone flung soot from the brazier into my eyes and rushed past me. I believe they were two."

"Did you see their faces?" Uther demanded, taking no trouble to hide his skepticism.

"They were masked," Gavin acknowledged, with no less defiance.

"Indeed!" Uther and Ruarke scoffed in unison and Gavin's ears reddened. He had just opened his mouth to argue anew when a familiar voice carried from below.

"I beg your pardon, I must get through!"

Brianna caught her breath at the low resonance of Luc's voice. There was a rustling on the stairs and suddenly he erupted at the summit, his brow dark with concern.

"My lady, why did you scream?" he demanded, his words fading as he spied Connor's fallen figure. Luc paled, then pushed through the crowd. "How did this happen? Who is responsible?"

Ruarke stepped into his path, his face dark with anger. "Do not sully this place with your presence!" he spat.

Luc straightened and his eyes narrowed. "I thought all were welcome in the house of God," he said with a glance around the chapel.

"Not those with murdering blood in their veins!"

"What is this?"

Uther was more than ready to enlighten Luc. "Your sire has ruthlessly slaughtered my lord Connor."

"I did no such thing!" Gavin protested. "I told you all that he was dead when I arrived here! I told you the truth!"

"Aye, the truth of masked men who assaulted you and cannot be found," Uther snapped and Ruarke rolled his eyes. "A likely tale."

"But that is impossible," Luc argued firmly. "Gavin could only have arrived here moments past." All turned to eye Luc, their expressions confused.

"Aye." Gavin nodded. "I came directly here from the gates, in no mood for the company of others, thanks to your faithless brother."

"But Connor has been dead longer than that." Luc pushed past Ruarke and bent to touch Connor's cheek. He glanced over his shoulder to the others. "Look upon him! His flesh draws chill already. His color is gone."

"You merely defend your own blood!" Ruarke charged angrily.

"Gavin was outside the gates until but moments past," Luc countered. "You must have all seen him enter the hall." A murmur of assent rolled through the group. "And look! There is no blood upon Gavin's tabard, despite the amount scattered here, yet he wears the same garb he has worn all this day. And look upon this place—it has been ruthlessly vandalized."

Brianna glanced around the chapel and belatedly saw the evidence of its attack. The table was dropped to its side, the altar cloth torn, the candles scattered. The crucifix was ripped from the wall and, indeed, it looked as though someone had pried at the planks of the floor.

Luc stood once more, folded his arms across his chest, and met Ruarke's gaze in challenge. "I cannot imagine how Gavin could have been responsible for all of this, remained clean, smeared the soot on his own face, and summoned you all in such short order after his return. Of course, I can judge the timing only by Gavin's return to the hall and the lady's recent scream.''

Luc was right.

The household members began to chatter, agreement with Luc spreading quickly through their ranks. All the same, 'twas not a welcome revelation he brought. Aye, the one person she would have preferred to be guilty in this crime was one of two Brianna knew beyond doubt were innocent.

For Luc himself had only just returned to the keep.

Which meant every other achingly familiar face could be hiding a malice that had seen her own father slaughtered. The realization shook Brianna to the core and indeed, she began to tremble uncontrollably. She looked at her sire and wished he could somehow confide the truth to her, that this crime would not go unavenged.

But 'twas too late for that.

Brianna's tears came to the fore once again. She was suddenly chilled to her very bones. Luc seemed to sense her dismay for he stepped forward. His brilliant blue gaze snared her attention as naught else could have done and Brianna let Luc lift her father from her arms. He lowered him gently to the floor, then closed his strong hands around Brianna's own shoulders, urging her to her feet and toward the stairs.

'Twas good to have his strength to lean upon. Brianna was aware of naught but her heartache and the reassuring warmth of Luc's grip.

"Fenella, take your mistress to the kitchens and have Cook conjure a large cup of mulled wine for her," Luc instructed firmly. "Ensure that she drinks it and if it does not put her to sleep, then see that she has another."

"Most sensible," Uther concurred.

Luc's expression turned doubly grim and his gaze bored

into the maid. "And whatever you do, do not let the lady out of your sight for one single moment this day and night."

Fenella bobbed her head. "Aye, sir."

"Taking us all in hand, are you?" Ruarke demanded mockingly. "Do you mean to force yourself into the lordship, despite the opinion of all around you?"

Luc coldly looked that knight up and down. "The Lordship of Tullymullagh is the last matter of import now."

Ruarke smirked. "Your disregard is touching, though unlikely."

Luc straightened and treated Ruarke to a glare. "When a lady has need of aid," he declared coldly, "a man of any rank should forget himself and bend his knee to her favor." The knight reddened at the chastisement and looked as though he might argue the point, but Brianna did not care.

"Luc is right," she said simply. "I will go." Brianna took Fenella's hand and followed her maid to the stairs, halting at the summit to look back at Luc. His eyes were still a vigorous sapphire and he was watching her with a concern that melted some of the numbness enfolding her.

"What will you do?" she asked.

"I will seek out Brother Thomas before he returns to Endlist," he declared with reassuring authority. "Do not fret, my lady. All shall be set in order. Your father shall be tended immediately and we shall set to finding the one responsible for this travesty."

"Aye," Uther confirmed and Brianna did not miss the considering glance the steward tossed toward Luc. The assembly murmured approvingly of Luc's sentiment and looked at him expectantly.

"Uther, is there a room where we might talk to each member of the household?" Luc asked. " 'Tis possible that someone witnessed something that may aid in solving this puzzle."

"Of course!"

"We shall find the culprit," Gavin declared. Ruarke snorted but Brianna did not care for his skepticism.

She held Luc's gaze for as long as she could, taking strength from the steady blue of his regard. When Fenella tugged on her hand, Brianna turned reluctantly to leave. But she clutched one fist to her chest, as though she would hold a vestige of the warm concern in Luc's eyes close to her heart for the rest of this day.

Ruarke began to argue with someone above, Father Padraig was having his say, and Uther was hotly defending something or other, but Brianna did not care. The assembly parted silently to let her pass, their eyes filled with sympathy, their whispers dying as she drew near. Brianna cared naught for that either.

Aye, Luc would see all set to rights. Brianna could trust him, and him alone, with her very life.

And that, she suddenly realized, was no small thing given the events of this day.

• • •

LUC TRUDGED TOWARD the village, trying desperately to solve the riddle of Connor's death. He had left Uther to the task of clearing a chamber for their questioning and making a tally of all within the hall.

But too late, Luc wished he had asked Ismay what she knew of the Rose of Tullymullagh, what she knew that she was certain all else had forgotten.

What had Connor intended to confide in him?

Luc feared he would never know.

And he sensed that both tales might be critical to solving this crime. He had to find the culprit; he could not let the murder of Brianna's father go unsolved.

For one who would murder once would murder again.

Luc did not permit himself to think of the risk that might

well confront his princess. He would ensure that she was not alone, he would ensure that she was not unprotected. And he would find the killer, before that individual could strike again.

Brother Thomas was at Matthew Miller's home, just as Luc had hoped. A fair and gently rounded woman, Matthew's wife, nodded at Luc's request and ushered him into the kitchen. The room was warm, simply furnished but more than cozy.

And Brother Thomas sat at the board beside a younger, but slightly more careworn version of himself. The monk was in the act of running a piece of bread around his bowl, claiming the last drop of gravy from his midday meal. The smell of a fine rabbit stew was enough to make Luc's own belly protest its emptiness.

Brother Thomas waved his crust of bread in salutation. "Good day to you, master Luc! Come from the keep for a measure of gossip?"

"Master Luc," Matthew's wife echoed, sending a panicked glance her spouse's way. "Would you be the Luc, son of Gavin Fitzgerald?"

"The very one," Brother Thomas crowed before Luc could reply. "He is the one who did not go!"

Matthew now looked as concerned as his wife, his gaze straying guiltily to the pot of rabbit stew.

'Twas clear the miller's wife did not share the monk's enthusiasm. She turned to Luc with stricken eyes. "Sir! You must believe that we did not poach the rabbit from the lord's lands. We did not hunt without permission. The creature beset my cabbages." She wrung her hands together. "If we were to eat this winter, we had to set a trap."

Aye, the old laws granting only the lord the right to hunt upon the lands he held were the root of the woman's anxiety. The penalties were severe, Luc well knew, and typical of the nobles' disregard for those who relied upon their generosity.

"I have not come to enforce my father's claim to Tullymullagh's game," Luc interjected calmly.

The woman fairly melted in her relief. Then her brow puckered in confusion. "Why, then, have you come?"

Luc looked at Brother Thomas. "There has been a death at the keep. I come to ask your aid, once again."

Brother Thomas swallowed his bread awkwardly and frowned in turn. "Who has died?"

"Connor."

The trio gasped simultaneously, the miller rising to his feet. " 'Tis sudden. I did not know my lord was ill. Adelina has skill with herbs, she would have come."

Matthew's wife nodded vigorously. "Anything for Connor of Tullymullagh. He is—" she swallowed and her sudden tears shone "—he *was* a good man."

"Aye, he was," Luc agreed. " 'Tis why his murder is so grievous."

Three pairs of eyes rounded in shock.

"Murder? But who did this deed?"

"We do not know."

Brother Thomas pushed to his feet and stepped away from the board, his gaze startlingly bright. "I will come with you immediately. And I would hear all you know of this matter."

They stepped out of the miller's abode together, leaving confused silence behind them. Brother Thomas burped as they strode through the village and patted his belly. " 'Tis soon after a meal for such a vigorous walk," he muttered, then darted a glance to Luc. "You know more than you tell of this matter."

"I have but suspicions," Luc confirmed quietly. "Though you might be able to aid me in this."

"Me?"

"Aye." Luc flicked a glance to the monk and resolved to ask the question of greatest import first. There was not a moment to waste. "What do you know of the Rose of Tullymullagh?"

The monk's gaze flew to meet Luc's, alarm making his eyes wide. He swallowed visibly, then shook his head. "Not that."

The monk knew something, Luc saw the truth immediately. Yet, he was reluctant to confide the tale. Luc lowered his voice and made his best appeal. "Thomas, there is a tale here, a tale that I suspect you recall, a tale that has much to do with Connor's demise."

Brother Thomas blew out his breath and scowled at the road as he walked. He was clearly considering something and his plump fingers worked together like animated sausages.

He turned his bright gaze abruptly upon Luc once more. "I was told in trust," he confided in a low voice, "and to break that trust is no small thing."

"Whose trust?"

"Connor's own," the monk confirmed and Luc's heart began to pound. Brother Thomas' gaze raked the height of the tall keep rising before them. "I cannot lightly discard a pledge sworn to a man no longer of this earth."

"Even if the tale could see his killer brought to justice?"

Brother Thomas eyed Luc for a long moment, then he clucked his tongue and shook his head. " 'Tis no good thing for a man to be murdered in his own home."

"Still less in a chapel."

Brother Thomas gasped and crossed himself, even as he sought Luc's gaze once more. "Nay!"

"Aye," Luc confirmed grimly. " 'Tis a sight for which you must brace yourself."

Brother Thomas blanched, his brow knotted, then he strode onward with new vigor.

• • •

GAVIN AND FATHER Padraig stood sentinel at the base of the stairs to the chapel, an unlikely pair of comrades, if ever there had been. They exchanged greetings with Brother Thomas and let him pass, though Father Padraig tried to halt Luc's progress.

"I have need of his aid," the monk said sternly, then proceeded up the stairs.

Father Padraig hesitated tellingly.

"Let him pass!" Gavin snapped. "Or I shall see that you pay the price."

The priest's lips thinned and he stepped just sufficiently aside that Luc could brush past him. Luc reached the chapel to find the monk clutching the wall. The older man was trembling slightly. His eyes were closed in dismay, and one hand fingered the rosary hanging from his girdle.

Luc turned his attention to a review of the damage done to the chapel, granting the monk a moment to collect himself. He was surprised to feel the weight of Brother Thomas' hand on his shoulder a short moment later.

Luc looked into that man's avid gaze. "I will tell you," Brother Thomas said heatedly. "But not within these walls." He looked once more upon his old friend, his expression strained. "This evil cannot pass unchallenged."

Luc raised his voice slightly, knowing full well that two pairs of ears below would strive to hear what was said. "Aye, he is not a small man. 'Tis no trouble at all for me to aid you in moving him. I am well used to labor."

"Bless you," Brother Thomas whispered, then crossed the tiny chapel like a man in a dream. He knelt with surprising grace beside the broken body upon the floor and laid a hand upon that man's pale brow.

"And godspeed to you, Connor," he whispered huskily. "Know that I betray your trust only in the hope that a greater justice may be served." He closed Connor's eyes with gentle fingers. "Forgive me, my friend."

And when the monk bowed his head to pray, Luc glimpsed the tears flowing down his cheeks.

Chapter Thirteen

'T WAS LATER THAT EVE WHEN Luc ABANDONED HIS inquiries for the day. The hall was sliding into shadows, he and Uther and Brother Thomas were exhausted. Luc and Uther had talked to half the household while Gavin paced agitatedly behind them, but had learned precious little.

Everyone had evidently been in the hall, the kitchens, or the stables. No one had noted any omissions, but with the household being of such number and spread between three locales, 'twas difficult to ensure anyone was anywhere at any point in time.

Someone, 'twas clear, lied.

But Luc did not know who. And he was too tired to fathom a guess. A night's sleep might set details more clearly in his mind. He bade Uther good evening, confirmed again that Brianna was secure in her chambers, and left the hall.

Luc was stepping into the darkness of the bailey when a whisper caught at his ear yet again.

Immediately, he froze and shrank back against the wall.

"My lady must never know," came the low words.

'Twas a woman, Luc discerned, and he strained his ear. He scanned the bailey, seeking some darker silhouette in the myriad shadows of the rain. Indeed, its incessant patter made the words most difficult to hear.

" 'Tis imperative that she never guess—"

"Shhhh," a man's low tones were fiendishly difficult to hear. "She will never guess the truth until 'tis too late." The man's fervor echoed even in the whisper. "Is this not what you desire?"

Luc straightened silently, a jolt of fear running through him. What was being plotted against Brianna? Were these the same two responsible for Connor's death?

He thought of the two men he had heard in the stables and reasoned that if all were together 'twas two men and a woman involved in this scheme.

"Aye!" the woman affirmed, then the pair dropped their voices, frustrating Luc's attempts to eavesdrop.

It sounded as though the whispered words came from the left, around the corner of the keep. Luc recalled that there was a bare nook between keep and wall on that side, where a rough shed covered a supply of firewood for the kitchen hearth.

The woman gasped at something her companion said. "Oh! We should not! We could not! I could not even think of . . ."

Luc's heart leapt. A thousand foul possibilities of what the man might be proposing flooded his mind.

"*Hush!*" The man's whisper was imperative. "You have come this far—would you not see all resolved to our own satisfaction?"

"All?" The woman gasped again, then her cry of protest was muffled.

'Twas clear the man intended to force her to his will!

"Who lurks there?" Luc leapt into the darkness. "Who is there and what do you do?"

But by the time the shed was in full view, 'twas clear no

one lingered there. Luc heard the patter of running feet, but could not discern their direction. The pair had ducked between the keep and curtain wall.

He cursed and kicked the ground, knowing well enough that beyond was one of those three spots where the wall was incomplete. They could have gone to the river, made their way to the village, or crept back to the keep from the other side.

There was no way of knowing even who they had been.

Luc's lips tightened grimly and he wished he had been quicker. Or had had a torch!

Or heard more of what they schemed. He swore softly under his breath as he turned toward the stables. There had been too many missed opportunities, to his way of thinking, and Luc could not help but fear the import of that.

• • •

'TWAS LATE ON Monday afternoon by the time Brother Thomas and Luc stole a moment away from the keep. Ismay had been buried with suitable ceremony earlier that day, Brother Thomas had prepared Connor to take Ismay's place in the chapel. 'Twas a grey day, which seemed to suit the mood of the keep well.

They sat on the orchard wall to share a flagon of wine, Luc's mind whirling with the testimony he had already heard this day. All remembered precious little, the events of the day overshadowing such small recollections as whom they had seen where and when.

Curse yesterday for being one of such turmoil! In normal circumstance, all would have recalled much more.

Luc could not help but wonder whether Connor's killer had planned as much.

Luc took a draught of wine. He had just seen Brianna and assured himself that she was secure in the company of her maids. The shock that still claimed her lovely features tore at Luc's heart, for he could well understand the difficulty of adjustment. It had been no easy task for him to accept Tyrell's sudden demise.

She had taken more than her measure of the wine again this day and Luc thought it might do the lady good. Sleep would be the best thing for her, and amidst the circle of her handmaids, within her own chamber, Brianna would be safe.

The lady needed time and Luc was content to wait.

At this hour, the bare branches of the apple trees were stark black against the brilliantly streaked sky. The bite of winter was in the wind and Luc drew his cloak higher around his throat. But they two were the only ones outside the warmth of the keep.

None could overhear them here.

Brother Thomas took a hearty swig of the wine, both that and the wind restoring the color to his cheeks. Luc knew the monk was still shaken by the sight of his fallen friend the day before.

Brother Thomas pursed his lips now. " 'Tis a startling thing," he commented softly, "to see a contemporary die." Brother Thomas took another sip of his wine and huddled lower in the folds of his own cloak. "It makes a man taste his own mortality and so much more keenly than when death takes its toll only from the aged and the infirm."

Luc could well imagine that to be so. He sipped his own wine and waited for the monk to compose his thoughts.

Finally, Thomas cleared his throat. "I told you once that Connor had been a young man much infatuated with the allure of battle and the art of swordplay."

"Aye, and I know that he took the cross."

"Aye. He was gone a goodly time, for I had finished my novitiate and taken my vows long before his return. 'Twas years before I saw him again—I came for some funeral or another—by then, Connor was wed and Brianna was a tot making her way into all manner of mischief.'' A smile of recollection briefly played upon the monk's lips before he sobered. '' 'Twas then that I first saw the Rose of Tullymullagh.''

''Brianna,'' Luc affirmed, surprised when the monk looked quickly to him as though he had said something amiss.

He was even more startled when the monk shook his head vigorously. ''Nay, not Brianna. The true Rose of Tullymullagh.''

Luc frowned. ''But I thought she *was* the Rose in question.''

Brother Thomas shook his head again. ''Nay, nay, though later that was what Connor wanted people to believe. Nay, there was another Rose of Tullymullagh and 'tis that I fear which is at the root of this.''

''What was it?''

''Ah, well, Connor had taken trade with a gem merchant in Outremer—''

''Aye, Brianna told me of it. And he was paid for his labor in gems, which he brought home and sold to pay for this keep.''

The monk slanted a glance in Luc's direction. ''She told you much.''

''Inadvertently,'' Luc admitted with a smile of his own. '' 'Twas mixed in the recounting of her parents' love.''

''Ah! There was a rare affection between those two.'' The two men took a draught of wine, as though saluting the departed pair. ''That time I came, Connor was very secretive. He wanted to show me a prize, though I had to swear a pledge that I would tell naught of it before he would unveil it.''

The monk frowned at his chalice. ''It seemed that the merchant had granted Connor a special gift of his esteem, a trinket he had had crafted particularly for him in the design of Connor's own faith."

"Brianna said that pair had treated Connor as their own son."

"Perhaps, for 'twas a princely gift indeed." Brother Thomas flattened his hand and traced a cross across it, from the tip of middle finger to wrist, from thumb to base of smallest finger.

" 'Twas a crucifix, about this size, wrought of gold and infested with gems of rare size and clarity. Two massive rounds of amber made each short arm, four made the longer one. There were several amethysts tucked here and there, but the most striking gem was set dead center. 'Twas an enormous ruby, the like of which I had never seen, the size of a man's thumb and as red as blood."

Luc's mouth went dry. "As red as a rose."

"Aye." Brother Thomas nodded. "So, Connor had named it the Rose of Tullymullagh. He intended it to be the legacy of his holding, an heirloom that would pass through the generations of his spawn. Perhaps 'twas the merchant's thinking behind that."

"But where is it?"

Brother Thomas shrugged. "I do not know. I saw it only the once, so long ago." His gaze rose to meet Luc's and that man saw the monk's concern. "Connor told me then that 'twas secreted where none would think to look, where none would dare to suspect. He told me that the Rose was safe beneath God's own eye."

"The chapel," Luc concluded, the location of Connor's demise making markedly more sense.

"Indeed, I wonder," the monk acknowledged. "For all these years, no one but Connor and Eva and Brianna was permitted to use that chapel. None would dare venture there uninvited, and 'twould be difficult indeed to pass through the lord's own solar unobserved.''

''Uther has a protective eye.''

''Aye. He does indeed.'' The monk nodded solemnly.

But Luc was puzzling the matter through. ''Connor must have surprised someone in the chapel yesterday.''

''It could well have been so.''

''Gavin insists that two masked men cast ashes into his face and shoved past him when he approached the chapel. 'Twas just moments before he found Connor.''

The monk heaved a sigh. ''Then Connor's prize is gone.''

''If 'twas still there.''

''What do you mean?''

Luc's gaze trailed to Tullymullagh's tall keep once more, then ran across the walls with their gaping holes. To leave such a task unfinished spoke of the leisure of an undeserved trust.

Or an empty purse.

''Would Connor have sold the Rose?'' he asked abruptly.

''Nay! 'Twas not his intent.''

''But what if the exchange could bring the completion of Tullymullagh?''

Brother Thomas' mouth opened and closed, then he frowned. ''But Tullymullagh is complete.''

''Three holes there are in the curtain wall.''

''But surely that is damage from the attack?''

''Nay, their incompletion was key to Gavin's victory.'' Luc leaned closer to the monk, his certainty growing. ''To build a keep of stone takes a fierce amount of coin. What if Connor sold all but the Rose, but had to part with his prize or else see his life work incomplete?''

''He would have chosen Tullymullagh,'' Brother Thomas said without hesitation. '' 'Twas all to him. And to see his daughter housed in this keep would mean more to him than to see some trinket, however beautiful, in her posses-sion.''

Luc shook his head. ''And if the Rose was indeed sold, then Connor may have died for naught.''

Brother Thomas' lips thinned. ''Nay, 'twas not for naught. By the expression upon his face, I have no doubt he knew those who besieged him. That was why his attackers deemed he had to die.''

''Whether they had the Rose or not.''

The monk only sighed, the weight of the world's sorrows clearly heavy on his shoulders.

Luc leaned closer to the monk, intent on having the one answer he needed beyond all. ''Brother Thomas, who else knew the truth of the Rose of Tullymullagh?''

The monk's expression turned to one of frustration. ''I do not know! There were tales when Connor first came home that he had brought great wealth. Such rumors even came as far as the priory. And there were whispers of one Rose of Tullymullagh, though I knew not what 'twas before he showed me. 'Twas shortly thereafter that Connor publicly called his daughter the Rose and no doubt deliberately sent rumor in a new direction.''

He sighed and frowned. ''It could have been anyone, any-one about in those days with their ears open.''

''And someone Connor knew,'' Luc frowned. ''This, then, must have been what Ismay knew.''

''Lady Ismay of Claremont?''

''Aye, aye, on the night she died she informed me that she knew something about the Rose of Tullymullagh that all others had forgotten. She was drunk and I thought—''

''You thought she told a tall tale,'' the monk interjected, then patted Luc on the hand. '' 'Twas a reasonable enough conclusion.''

"But she died that very night," Luc repeated, his certainty growing that Ismay had not wandered off the orchard wall by accident.

The monk's eyes went round. "Someone guessed that she knew."

"Or feared that she would tell."

Luc pushed suddenly to his feet, a whispered conversation echoing in his ears. Someone had pledged to make the Rose his own, regardless of the cost! What if they assumed Brianna knew the truth about the Rose? A new sense of urgency clenched Luc's innards. "I must seek Dermot."

"Ah!" Brother Thomas caught his breath. "There is one with a taint upon his name." He lowered his voice. "No one knew who he was or whence he came when he appeared to bid for Ismay's hand."

Luc's lips tightened grimly. "And the lady herself told me that he was not what he seemed." He inhaled sharply, hating that he had not seen the truth in time. "I should have listened to her!"

"You could not have guessed, my son." Brother Thomas lay a reassuring hand upon Luc's shoulder. "Now go, go and set a watch upon this man." He drew himself up proudly. "I shall endeavor to discover where he was, both when Lady Ismay died and yesterday morning."

"I could do that."

"Nay, Luc." Brother Thomas winked. " 'Tis my role, after all, to console the bereaved."

"He does not seem markedly bereaved," Luc commented as he collected flagon and chalice.

"And that, in and of itself, is of interest," the monk murmured. "We had best arrive in the hall separately," he counselled before setting off toward the keep, his robes flying with purpose.

• • •

BRIANNA AWAKENED WHEN the keep was silent. Darkness had flooded her chamber, the warmth of the wine still coursed through her veins. 'Twas her second night of knowing her father lived no more and time had not made the truth easier to bear. She lay there, wishing she could see the stars, and wishing even more strongly that she could see them with Luc.

Brianna had missed him. She smiled sadly at how he would tease her for such an admission and wrapped her arms around herself.

In the darkness, 'twas easy to admit that Luc *was* her favorite.

Brianna stared at the ceiling. Her father's chamber was above her own room. Indeed, the great pillared bed in which she had been conceived now rested directly overhead. When Brianna was young, her dame had virtually held court in that bed, they had played there. Indeed, once, Eva had even had Cook bring the three of them breakfast there. Those days had been happy.

But now, Brianna was all alone.

The truth plunged through her heart with the surety of a knife, a knife as keen as the one that had stolen her sire's life away. She felt alone as never she had before, and the pain of Brianna's loss was greater than she had ever known. She felt the tears begin to flow and did not know how to stop them, did not know how to contain her grief. When her dame died, Brianna and her sire had consoled each other.

This time, though, Brianna was alone with her loss.

But she did not have to be alone. There was one man in this keep who endured similar losses, yet remained strong. There was one man who had pledged to win her heart, who she knew would protect her from harm. It could be no coincidence that he was the only one Brianna knew for certain had not harmed her sire.

Brianna suddenly wanted to be with Luc, her need for his company so strong that it could not be denied.

She was out of bed and on her feet, swinging her cloak over her shoulders and making for the door in the blink of an eye. Fenella, she noted, did not even stir at her departure.

Brianna would have been surprised to learn that Fenella's eyes flew open as soon as the chamber door was closed once again. Indeed, that maid departed not long after Brianna, although she did not follow her lady.

Nay, Fenella had other fires to feed.

• • •

LUC WAS CERTAIN he dreamed.

He laid in the stable loft, staring at the roof. He was frustrated, having learned less than naught these two days. Though at least he had this space to himself once more and would not disturb anyone's sleep with his restlessness. The other stable was sufficiently complete that Denis had dispatched the squires to slumber there, purportedly to guard the steeds.

How annoying that Dermot had spent the entire evening drinking in the hall! He had even bedded down there, so besotted that there could be no mistake that he truly slumbered.

Luc knew he had Brother Thomas to thank for that certainty. The monk had not only "consoled" Dermot, he had ensured the man's chalice was consistently full.

And Dermot was apparently not a man who held his wine well.

But was he a murderer?

Luc had been puzzling and dozing for so long, the stable was filled with such familiar warm sounds, that he could not gauge how much time had passed. He thought he heard the creak of the doorway opening, and sat up suddenly, but only silence carried to his ears.

Until the faintest echo of a footfall sounded on the ladder. Luc eased to his feet and silently donned his chausses, his gaze fixed on the place where the ladder entered the loft.

Did someone think Luc knew more than he did?

His heart pounded at the prospect. Luc poised to attack, sliding against the wall that would be behind the new arrival. Another creak sounded on the ladder. Everything within him tensed in preparation.

He sagged against the wall with relief when a familiar crown of golden hair snared the moonlight. "My lady! What are you doing here?"

Brianna spun to face Luc so quickly that she nearly lost her balance, for she was not yet on the floor of the loft. Luc lunged forward and caught her elbows, moving her away from the ladder with lightning speed.

He felt her tremble against him and gathered her closer.

"You should be in your chambers!" he charged. "Asleep and with your maidens." Anger rolled through Luc as he recalled an important detail. "Indeed, the dark-haired one pledged to keep you in her sight! Where is she?"

"Luc, do not blame Fenella," Brianna murmured in haste. She impaled him with a watery glance. "I left while she slumbered. I—I so wanted to talk to you."

Brianna wrung her hands together as though she feared he would deny her this and Luc's anger faded to naught.

"We can talk on the morrow," he assured her gently, unable to keep himself from pushing a tendril of hair from her cheek with one fingertip. Brianna's vulnerability made him wish he could make this all come right. "You have need of your sleep now."

"I have need of your comfort!" the lady declared, much to Luc's surprise. "Please, I beg of you, let me remain."

There were men aplenty who would have taken advantage of that offer, Luck knew it well. He stared at the woman before him, her eyes bright with unshed tears, her complexion unusually pale. She looked so unlike the strong and defiant woman he had come to admire that Luc wanted only to console her.

And if any took issue with her spending an evening in the stables in his company, Luc would be quick to defend the lady's honor. She was to be his wife, after all, and by dint of her father's approval, Luc already felt the lady was his responsibility.

He would not let either of them down.

"Of course," he said softly and noted how her shoulders sagged. Brianna trembled once more and Luc feared suddenly that she caught a chill. 'Twas too damp after all the rain.

Luc hastily scooped up his cloak and settled it over her own, drawing Brianna away from the draught from below. "Are you cold?"

"To my very bones," she acknowledged, then shook her head with dismay. Her fingers clenched Luc's own. "Luc, I cannot believe he is gone! How did you bear seeing Tyrell die? How did you forget the sight?"

Not for the first time, Luc wished Brianna had been spared the sight of her father's demise. It had not been easy for him to look upon the fallen man and he could well guess how the recollection would haunt Brianna.

"You will never forget," he whispered. Luc brushed a fingertip gently across Brianna's cheek, unable to resist the urge to gather her into the circle of his arms. "But 'twill become easier to remember, in time," he added softly, just as her first tear fell.

It splashed against his wrist. A second followed quickly, then a third, the first evidently having opened the floodgates. Luc's hand rose of its own volition to cup the soft curve of Brianna's jaw. He wrapped his other arm around her shoulders, even as Brianna fought against the flood of her tears.

" 'Tis impossible to believe at this moment," he murmured, hoping his words would reassure her, "but trust me, my lady, trust me in this. The pain will ease."

"I do! I do trust you!" Brianna choked back a sob and shook her head as though she knew not what to do with herself. She looked into Luc's eyes and he glimpsed the fullness of her pain. "Luc, help me, please. I have never felt so alone."

Luc grasped her chin firmly between finger and thumb, compelling the lady to hold his gaze. "First, my lady, do not fight your tears. That was my mistake. It only makes matters worse to trap your sorrow inside."

Brianna's lip trembled dangerously. She caught her breath, and then she closed her eyes. A shuddering sigh broke from the very core of her, and her tears began to stream in a torrent.

Luc folded Brianna against the warmth of his chest, closing his own eyes at the painful sound of her sobs. He stroked her hair and murmured soothingly to her, knowing that there was little he could truly do.

But still he was honored that Brianna turned to him for solace. 'Twas not like this lady to concede any weakness at all and the very fact that she came to him was telling.

Connor, bless his immortal soul, had understood his daughter aright. Luc would not betray that man's trust in any way, nor would he do less than his best for Brianna.

Luc cradled Brianna closer and rubbed her back. He guided her to his pallet and lifted her into his lap, tucking the ends of both cloaks around her feet. She cuddled against him, her arms thrown around his neck with a childish trust that warmed Luc's heart.

Her hair spilled around them and he marvelled at the flaxen hue of it. The scent of her skin and the softness of her curves filled Luc's embrace and there was nowhere else in Christendom he would rather have been.

Luc did not know how long they sat there, indeed, he did not care. His hand moved in an endless caress across her shoulders as the lady wept, the chill of her tears trickling down Luc's flesh.

Finally, though, Brianna laid a tiny hand against his chest and heaved a ragged sigh. "I am sorry, Luc," she whispered unevenly, her head bowed. "You must think me weak." A tremor echoed in her low words. "But I have never been alone."

Luc slid a finger beneath Brianna's chin and tipped her face so that he could look into her eyes. "And you are not alone now," he insisted, noting the ravages of her tears with sympathy.

Brianna frowned. "But . . ."

Luc slipped his fingertip across her lips. "But naught," he chided gently, willing her to understand his commitment to her. "You are not alone, for you have me by your side." Brianna glanced up, a glimmer of hope in her eyes. Luc smiled crookedly. "Not only are you saddled with me in these days, my lady, but for all time."

Brianna bit back a tentative smile. "You sound as though you are going to pledge as much to me."

"I would." Luc nodded. "Without hesitation. You may have my pledge, either now or before the altar, it matters little either way." He smiled at her. "The choice, my lady fair, is yours."

She did smile then, a soft and feminine smile that made

her look young and no less vulnerable. Luc hesitated but a heartbeat before he bent and touched his lips to her brow.

He paused there, uncertain whether he pushed overmuch, but Brianna glanced up, a warmth in her eyes. She reached up and touched his lips with her fingertips, no doubt deliberately echoing his characteristic gesture.

"I like that you pledge to me," Brianna whispered, her gaze flicking to meet Luc's. He could not take a breath beneath her regard, though his heart thundered in his very ears.

"Then I will not cease."

Brianna's smile was fleeting, her lips sobering as her emerald gaze fell once more to her fingertips yet resting against Luc's chin. Luc bent to kiss her temple, her nose, her cheek, her chin, tasting the salt of her tears with every caress.

Then, Luc gently kissed the sweetness of Brianna's lips. He swallowed her sigh and gathered her closer, determined to protect his lady from all the dangers confronting her. His hand slipped over her shoulder and found the ripeness of her breast, though truly Luc had never intended to do any such thing.

When Brianna gasped and arched her back, Luc was loath to abandon the curve he had found. He slipped his thumb across her nipple, feeling it tighten even through the layers of woolen cloaks. Brianna's arms twined around his neck and desire flooded through Luc.

Brianna was to be his wife, his lady fair for all time. She needed the consolation of his touch, she needed to be coaxed to slumber. Brianna needed to forget for a moment the tragedy she had just endured. She needed to be certain that she was not only not alone, but that she was cherished and secure.

Fortunately, Luc had a very good idea how he could achieve all of those aims.

• • •

BRIANNA CAUGHT HER breath when Luc tumbled her to her back and caught her against the heat of his chest. Her heart pounded at the surety of the strong hands cradling her close.

Indeed, Brianna had never felt so safe in all her days. Luc's embrace sheltered her from the chill in the air; the tenderness in his touch made her imagine that the love she sought might indeed be close at hand.

There was a reverence in the way Luc cupped her breast, a gentle affection in the smooth slide of his muscled thigh between her own, both of which made Brianna feel cossetted within his embrace. Luc's eyes fairly glowed, their hue so intense that the sight took Brianna's breath away.

She knew already that she could trust Luc Fitzgavin with her life, with her honor, with anything she held dear. She already knew that Luc was a practical man possessed of good sense, a man who more than once had known better than she.

And Brianna had an inkling that 'twould not take him long to fulfill his pledge to capture her heart. Indeed, the man made decided progress with each passing day.

Given all of that, it seemed perfectly right to welcome the surety of Luc's touch. And truly, Brianna craved the warmth of Luc's caress. She was so cold, had been so chilled since finding her father in the chapel, that she welcomed the heat Luc brought to life beneath her very flesh.

When he claimed her lips once more, Brianna opened her mouth to his caress. Luc's tongue dove between her teeth, the taste of him making her dizzy. Brianna closed her eyes, winding her arms securely around Luc's neck, and surrendered to sensation.

Luc did not disappoint.

Even as he angled his mouth over hers, the pad of his thumb found her nipple once more. His hand had slid beneath her cloak, through the lacings of her kirtle and she could fairly feel the rough edge of his thumb through the sheer linen of her chemise. Brianna gasped as Luc cajoled that nipple to a taut peak and felt her back arch against him. His muscled thigh slid higher between her own, spreading her legs wider. Brianna's breasts were pressed against the hard wall of Luc's chest.

He was so differently wrought from her—his body all heat and muscle, his flesh tanned and of a heavier texture than her own—yet the surety of Luc's touch felt right beyond all.

Luc kissed beneath her chin, nibbling on the softness beneath her ear and Brianna shivered. She grasped fistfuls of Luc's hair, gasping when his hand slid purposefully over the length of her. She froze when his fingers dove beneath the hem of her skirts and slipped through the tangle of hair at the apex of her thighs, her own grip tightening on his broad shoulders.

Luc kissed her earlobe, murmured reassuringly, flicked his tongue across her ear, and Brianna shivered anew. She whispered his name and he brushed his lips across her mouth again, tantalizing her with his touch. Brianna lay back, trusting him, and Luc's strong fingers moved yet higher.

He growled with satisfaction when he found the slick wetness awaiting him there and claimed her lips triumphantly. When his teasing fingertips found the sensitive pearl at the very core of Brianna's heat, she surged against him.

Luc caressed her with gentle persuasiveness, his touch launching a shivering heat through Brianna that left her wanting more and yet more. She writhed beneath him, revelling in his kiss and his touch, wanting something she could not name.

A consuming heat built beneath her very flesh. Brianna found her legs winding around Luc and her hips lifting demandingly toward his touch. She felt the heat of his erection press against her hip; the sign of his own arousal feeding her desire as naught else could have done.

Brianna was aware of naught but Luc, she wanted no one but Luc. Luc touched and teased, Brianna writhed and moaned, Luc slipped a finger into her heat.

Brianna gasped and caught at Luc's shoulders. She looked into the sapphire blaze of his eyes and could not tear her gaze away, even as the tide of her desire broke loose.

"Luc!" She clutched at his shoulder and felt her nails dig into his flesh. "Please! Call me by my name."

His smile was a flash in the darkness, his breath a welcome heat against her ear.

"Brianna!" he murmured, the possessiveness in his low voice bringing Brianna's newfound passion to a crescendo. "My Brianna!"

Luc claimed her lips as the heat surged through her, searing every fiber within her as it passed. Brianna gasped, then cried out, but Luc kissed her deeply, greedily swallowing the sound, as he held her fast against his chest.

His fingers continued to work and Brianna erupted over and over again. Until finally, she sagged spent against his heat. She pressed a kiss to his shoulder, and smiled as Luc kissed her brow and snuggled her close. Brianna's fingers landed in the pelt of hair that graced Luc's chest and she smiled when she felt the erratic pounding of his heart.

Luc was right. She was not alone, after all.

And with that smile yet curving her lips, Brianna closed her eyes and slumbered within the circle of his embrace.

Chapter Fourteen

BRIANNA STRETCHED LUXURIOUSLY AS SHE AWAKened, then reached for Luc's heat.

He was not beside her. Surely he had not abandoned her! Brianna sat up in alarm.

But Luc sat quietly opposite, his gaze steadily blue, his hands upon his knees. He was fully garbed and the first of the night's shadows were being dispelled by the promise of daylight.

Brianna recalled well enough that Luc had held her while she slumbered and was disappointed to be denied the gift of awakening within the circle of his arms.

"My lady," Luc said softly before Brianna could utter a sound. "I would have you make me a promise."

She blinked. "Aye?"

Luc's gaze was solemn beyond all. "Do not suffer yourself to be alone, for even a moment, on this day or any other. Pledge to me that you will *never* be alone."

Brianna frowned, not understanding his concern. "But why?"

"Your sire was murdered, I know not why or by whom." Luc's gaze was steady, his expression stern, his voice low. "Lady Ismay may have been cast to her death, as well. I believe 'tis because of the Rose of Tullymullagh."

Brianna was no less confused by this. "But that is what people call *me!* I had naught to do with this."

"Aye, I know it well." Luc cleared his throat and came to sit beside her. He took her hand within the warmth of his own. "My lady, did your sire ever confide in you of a treasure he kept hidden?"

For a moment, Brianna thought Luc meant her dame's letters, then she dismissed the thought. They were treasures only to a bereaved daughter, a daughter who would hear her dame's beloved voice echo once more in the written words.

She shook her head. "What manner of treasure?"

"A crucifix, a token from that gem merchant in Outremer."

Brianna shook her head once more. "I know naught of it."

" 'Tis important, my lady, for I fear 'twas the pursuit of this gem that led to your sire's death. Perhaps he would not confide its hiding place, perhaps 'tis long gone and the thieves did not believe your sire's claim."

Brianna's heart clenched at the very prospect and she recalled again the expression of betrayal etched upon her sire's features. "Or perhaps he recognized them."

Luc nodded. "Aye. It could well be so."

"But what is this token? Perhaps I know it by another name." Brianna entangled her fingers with Luc's, instinctively liking that they tried to solve this together. "Perhaps I have seen it and never knew its name. Do you know what it looks like?"

"You *are* a woman of good sense." Luc's eyes glowed with approval and Brianna felt herself flush beneath his gaze. " 'Tis said to have been wrought of gold, embellished wit amber and a great ruby. A ruby said to be as big as a man's thumb, and one that once was known as the Rose of

Tullymullagh. Do you think your sire might still have possessed it? Can you guess where he might have secreted it?''

Brianna gasped in sudden understanding and her free hand rose to her lips. "They sought it in the *chapel*!" she declared, horrified. "My sire must have surprised them in the midst of their search! Oh, Luc, this is horrible!"

Luc leaned closer. "Why would they seek it in the chapel?"

Brianna understood to keep her voice low that none anywhere might overhear. "Because there is a place there in the chapel, a hidden place."

Brianna's mind flew like quicksilver and she knew the quartz on the great crucifix had been resolutely locked in place when she had been there the day before.

Perhaps this treasure Luc spoke of had not been found! 'Twould be no small thing to have a token her sire had once held dear, a gift that had been granted to him long ago.

She gripped Luc's arm. "If it still was within my sire's possession, it must be yet there!" Brianna declared. She began to rise to her feet. "Come! I will show you."

But Luc shook his head. "Nay, my lady, 'twill arouse suspicion if you and I ascend there together. Tell me of this place and I will seek your sire's treasure for you."

Brianna knew full well that she could trust Luc with the telling. Without hesitation, she bent and whispered to Luc of the hiding place in the crucifix.

Luc nodded, stood, then gave her shoulders a minute shake. "And you will not be alone in the keep," he reminded her with a stern glance. "Pledge it to me."

"Aye," Brianna said with a smile. "I pledge it to you, Luc Fitzgavin."

"Good." Luc's eyes flashed brilliant blue as he leaned forward to touch his lips to Brianna's. Her heart skipped a beat at his fleeting touch and he smiled, as though he discerned even the pulse of her heart. "Now, we must hasten back to the keep before you are missed."

• • •

THERE WAS A surprising amount of activity in the kitchens for so early in the day. Cook was busy shaping loaves of bread, dozens of scullery boys and maids were scampering to do his bidding. Brother Thomas was nestled in a nook beside the ovens, partaking of a morning mug of ale. Brianna thought a quick glance flashed between the monk and Luc, but could not be certain.

And Ruarke was in the kitchens, much to Brianna's surprise, his golden brows drawing together in disapproval when he spied her.

"Where have you been this morn?" he demanded, his voice loud enough to draw the eye of every soul within the kitchens. Ruarke glared at Luc, as though he longed to do serious damage to him. "What have you done to the princess? Do you dally where you have no right?"

"Nay," Luc said mildly. "The lady merely had need of an escort from the garden."

Ruarke turned his condemning glare upon Brianna. The anger lurking in that knight's usually complacent gaze gave Brianna a start.

She forced a smile. "I wished to pray by my mother's grave," she lied weakly, then passed a hand over her brow in a bid to distract him. "Perhaps I consumed too much mulled wine yesterday, Ruarke, for my head aches this morn."

The knight swept protectively to Brianna's side and captured her elbow in his broad palm. He drew Brianna to his side, even as he glowered at Luc.

"Aye, I knew it well," he declared coldly. "A noblewoman is too fine a creature to drown her sorrows like an alewife." Ruarke arched a fair brow. "Doubtless there are those among us who do not understand the difference."

"I do not doubt that there are those among us who do not know how to treat a lady," Luc retorted coolly. He bowed slightly to Brianna, then strolled toward the hall. Brother Thomas rose and trailed behind him.

Brianna knew as well as any other that it had been Luc's advice to grant her mulled wine, and indeed, the beverage *had* dulled the ache of her sire's loss.

As had Luc's beguiling touch.

Cook shrugged and cast Ruarke a glance. "There is little enough harm done in a fortifying sip from time to time," Cook declared, his girth revealing that he often considered himself due for a consoling sip or a nibble.

Ruarke's expression softened slightly. "Perhaps 'tis harmless enough," he conceded genially. "I was but worried for our princess." Ruarke then granted all a sample of his winning grin, a marked sign that his mood had improved.

Brianna suspected 'twas Luc's departure alone that improved the knight's spirits. Indeed, Ruarke was not nearly so interested in remaining beside Brianna as he had been just a moment before.

"My lady, I must thank you," Cook declared suddenly. " 'Twas a fine treat indeed to have Fenella among us once again yesterday." Cook began to stir some stock and shook his head. "Aye, that girl has a taste for news like no other and we have missed her."

"Missed her?" Brianna halted midway to the portal. "But Fenella is *always* in the kitchens."

Cook glanced up. "Aye, once she was. But not of late." He looked at his staff. "We have seen precious little of her this past week."

" 'Tis true enough, my lady," confirmed one lad, glancing up from the potatoes he peeled. To Brianna's astonishment, all the others nodded in vigorous agreement.

But if Fenella had not been in the kitchens all those times she had been absent from Brianna's side, then where had she been?

Brianna had a feeling she would not like the answer. 'Twas time enough that she knew the truth. Brianna marched with purpose toward the hall.

"But, Brianna, I thought your head ached this morn!" Ruarke called after her. Brianna disregarded him, her pace increasing as she crossed the near vacant hall and made for the stairs.

Moments later, she threw open the door to the lady's chamber and was confronted by dozens of slumbering and awakening noblewomen in various states of dress and undress.

But Fenella was quite absent.

Brianna cast off her cloak and rummaged for a clean chemise, hauling on a different kirtle and stockings with purpose, her annoyance growing with every passing moment. Fenella had been sent to Tullymullagh to be educated for her eventual role of lady of her family estate. And in Connor's absence, the responsibility for ensuring that naught ill befell that maid landed squarely on Brianna's shoulders.

'Twas not an obligation she would ignore.

• • •

LUC WATCHED BRIANNA depart in a noisy assembly of maids and nearly smiled. She had taken his advice with a vengeance—and that could only ensure her safety.

At least for the moment. Luc frowned, fearing anew that Connor's assailants might decide Brianna herself held the key to her father's treasure. 'Twas not so unreasonable that she would know her sire's secrets. Indeed, that was why Luc had asked her counsel.

That thought was far from reassuring. But without knowing who had been responsible, Luc could only strive to ensure Brianna remained unharmed. He hoped fervently that this day would shed some light upon the mystery before them all.

"As I said," Brother Thomas murmured into his mug of ale. "Our quarry was much more squeamish than ever I might have expected."

Luc pushed his errant thoughts aside and turned his attention to the monk without appearing to do so. Although the two sat at the same trestle table, they both strove to appear absorbed in breaking their fast alone.

Brother Thomas was evidently speaking of Dermot, a man Luc had already noted was conspicuously absent from hall or kitchens this morn. "Truly?"

"Truly." Brother Thomas accepted a proffered chunk of bread with a smile to the servant. Luc took one as well. When the boy stepped away, the monk dropped his voice anew. "He was most unsettled by tales that had even the smallest measure of bloodshed. I cannot believe that he could have done a deed of such violence."

Luc considered this as he drank of his own ale. "His response to your words could be due to his own surprise at what he had done. Perhaps he feels guilty."

"Perhaps." Brother Thomas frowned at his bread, as though surprised to find it devoid of honey. "But I think he does not have the fortitude within him to strike such a blow."

"He is reputed to be a knight."

"By his own word alone. He has never ridden to battle, and indeed, was said to have been particularly futile in the assault against Claremont." Brother Thomas waggled his brows. "I gathered that his ineffectiveness was at the root of Lady Ismay's complaints with him. She did not take well to the loss of her holding."

"All the same, he could have panicked and struck a telling blow to Connor."

"Seven times?"

"Seven?" Luc looked up in surprise, but the monk held his gaze steadily, then nodded once before glancing away.

Seven times Connor had been stabbed. Luc swallowed and stared at his ale, no longer having the thirst for it. Brother Thomas had dressed the body—he would know the truth.

Aye, none could strike so viciously without intending that Connor should die, and die without uttering another word that might reveal his assailants. The very prospect sickened Luc.

"Boy!" the monk called. "Have you any honey?"

"The liquid or the comb?"

Brother Thomas rolled his eyes with delight. "A sliver of comb, boy, and you should make me a happy man."

'Twas time Luc checked what Brianna had told him. This matter could not be resolved quickly enough for his taste.

Luc pushed to his feet, murmuring some excuse about meeting his sire, and slipped toward the stairs. No one noted his departure. As near as Luc could discern, most of the hall's occupants were still asleep. And many had gone with Brianna, after all.

The second floor was quiet, its landing vacant. Luc opened the portal to the solar and listened. There was not a sound. He slipped silently through the door and stealthily climbed the stairs, halting at the sound of breathing.

Luc peeked over the lip of the stairs. Gavin slumbered in the pillared bed on the far side of the solar, his hand flung out across the mattress. The braziers had burned down to glowing coals and the room was chill.

There was no one else present but Gavin.

And Luc did not want even that man to know what he did. He crept up the last of the stairs, and Gavin slept on undisturbed. Luc crossed the floor carefully, wincing when a board betrayed his step with a squeak. He stood in frozen posture and eyed his father, certain an explanation would be demanded with a bellow loud enough to wake the dead.

But Gavin rolled over, snorted, and began to steadily snore.

'Twas ironic that the one man Luc knew was capable of such violence was the same one he knew to be innocent. And his sire might well have wanted Connor—the old king to whom Tullymullagh was yet so loyal—safely out of influence's way.

Could Gavin have bidden two of his men to do the deed? Luc could not believe his sire could have feigned such surprise and shock. Gavin was not a subtle man, by any means. And Connor would not likely have recognized two of Gavin's men.

'Twas not reassuring to consider that the killers had been among Connor's own household. Uther? For what reason? He might well have known about the Rose; he might have wanted to protect the gem from Gavin's greed. But could he have killed Connor? Luc could not believe it. The steward's loyalty was unswerving and, no doubt, self-sacrificing.

Could Dermot have wanted the prize of the Rose enough to kill his old neighbor? Was Brother Thomas right about that man's inability to strike a blow?

Had Ismay been killed? And if so, by whom? Luc could not help but recall her certainty that she knew something of the Rose that all others had forgotten. Had that been the claim that ensured her demise? And who else in that crowded hall that eve might have heard her words? Indeed, how often had she proclaimed it?

Luc did not know. He darted for the chapel stairs. They creaked softly as he climbed, but Gavin remained sound asleep.

Then, Luc was finally in the vandalized chapel. 'Twas tragic to see what a shambles had been made of this sacred space, but he dared not linger to look upon it. Quickly, Luc crossed the floor and bent over the crucifix that had been hauled from the wall.

The massive cross lay propped against the exterior wall, the long arm of it splintered and broken. But at the juncture of the arms was the gem that Brianna had told him about. 'Twas a half-sphere of polished quartz so smooth that Luc had never seen the like.

Brianna had said it opened on a hinge. Luc ran his fingertips across the stone and around its setting, but could feel naught even remotely like a hinge.

Much less a clasp. He had best look well, for this might be his only chance alone here. Luc lifted his lantern and leaned closer. To the right, he thought he could see a tiny shadow that should not be cast there. He reached for the shadow and felt a thrill of victory when it clicked.

And the stone moved toward him with a creak. Marvelling at the craftsmanship, Luc eased the little doorway open and touched the secreted hinges. A space the height and width of his fist extended into darkness there. Luc held his breath and reached in to the shadows, but his fingers closed upon naught at all.

Connor's hiding place was empty.

The stairs groaned behind Luc and he knew that someone came. Had his sire awakened? Luc cast a glance over his shoulder, pushed the secret doorway closed, shoved to his feet, and turned.

And managed it just as Father Padraig's tonsured head became visible. The priest's stern glance sharpened as their gazes met. The two men stared at each other, as though challenging each other's right to be in this chapel.

Had the priest come for the same reason as Luc?

Luc took the offensive, folding his arms across his chest to glare sternly at the priest. "Does my sire know you are here?"

Father Padraig cleared his throat. "I had thought to tidy the chapel, in case your sire wished to partake of the Mass upon his awakening."

"Did you knock upon his door?"

"He did not answer."

"Yet even while he slumbers, you hasten to prepare a Mass." Luc eased into the center of the room. "I did not realize Gavin had become so religious."

The priest's eyes flashed. "There is hope for all of God's sinners, that they might repent and learn the error of their ways before 'tis too late."

"Do you oft invade the sleeping chambers of the household?" Luc demanded.

The priest snorted. "I am naught if not vigilant in tending my flock. 'Tis a responsibility which demands my every waking moment."

Before Luc could respond, Father Padraig advanced into the chapel. Space did not permit the two men to stand far apart. "And what brings you to this place so early in the day, master Luc?"

"I thought I had dropped something when we gathered here two days past," Luc lied. "My sire is untroubled by the passing of *family* through his chambers."

Father Padraig lifted his chin. "And what might that have been?" he asked.

"Ah, a buckle I was repairing from a steed's harness," Luc prevaricated. "It did not seem fitting to trouble my sire over such a trinket."

"And you look for it beneath the very cross?"

Luc smiled easily. "One never knows where such things might roll."

But the priest's manner remained decidedly frosty. "Have you found it?"

"Nay." Luc strove to look unconcerned and shrugged. "I must have dropped it somewhere in the stable, after all. Good day, Father."

Luc ducked for the stairs. He glanced back to find the priest's quelling glance fixed upon him. When his gaze danced beyond the man garbed in black, Luc's heart sank to his toes.

For the tiny compartment was yet open. Luc was certain he had securely pressed it closed, but the hinge must have caught.

And now Father Padraig would see what he had found.

There was naught Luc could do about the matter now. He could not dodge past the priest to close the latch without drawing the other man's attention to the tiny treasury.

'Twas too late.

So, Luc forced a smile, hoped for the best, and trotted down the stairs, cursing his own stupidity every step of the way. How could he have been so careless?

Did he dare to hope that Father Padraig would not notice? Or perhaps, Connor's confessor would already know of the hidden compartment. Perhaps Father Padraig would merely close the door, keeping another secret to himself as priests were charged to do.

Luc fervently hoped as much as he slipped from the solar, his sire still snoring in the great bed, and darted down the stairs to the hall.

He reached there just in time to hear the roar of outrage from outside. 'Twas easy enough to blend into the assembly that rolled from the hall into the bailey, murmuring in confusion, as they sought the source of the sound.

Luc blinked and realized that that could have been precisely what Connor's attackers had done on Sunday. They could have descended from the chapel as Gavin bellowed, perhaps to a room on the second floor, perhaps even tucked into a corner in the solar. Then when the assembly surged into the solar, they had simply mingled among them.

As though they had just arrived.

But what of the blood? Someone must have been splashed with Connor's blood or wiped their blade on something. Had any among them changed their garb? Luc could not recall every one who had been there, but between himself, Brother Thomas, Uther, and Brianna, much could likely be concluded.

As he thought, Luc matched his pace to those racing toward the noise coming from the armory. Luc was far from surprised to find the lady Brianna at the very center of matters there.

• • •

'TWAS THE MOAN that gave them away.

Brianna's head snapped up at the unmistakable sound and she felt a flush stain her cheeks. Indeed, it sounded so much like the noises she had made beneath Luc's caressing touch that she feared someone had overheard and mocked her before all.

But the moan came again, and 'twas clear it did not come from the party of maids seeking Fenella.

In fact, it seemed to come from the armory.

'Twas strange, for 'twas far too early for any who labored there to have broken their fast and fired the forge. Could Fenella have fallen?

The moan came again, this time rising so clearly in pleasure that several maids giggled. Several others flushed and Brianna had quite a good idea in that moment which of her handmaidens were innocent and which were not.

There were rather more who understood this particular

sound than Brianna might have preferred. But she forced herself to think of the problem at hand.

No doubt, some scullery maid had tumbled one of the fighting men. All the same, Brianna could not ignore the sound now that all ears had discerned it. And perhaps 'twould make a good example to chastise the girl before those less-than-innocent handmaidens.

Brianna picked up her skirts and headed for the armory with purpose, ducking beneath the portal and blinking in the dim light within.

"Nay, *lower*!" breathed a voice that was very familiar. "Lower and lower again."

"Fenella!" Brianna's call cracked like a whip. The other maids clustered behind their lady with undisguised curiosity.

Far within the armory, there was a rustle of hay, then a gasp. Whispers were exchanged and Brianna's lips tightened as she strode farther into the building.

"Fenella, if that is you—and I know full well that it is—I demand that you show yourself and make an accounting for your behavior." Brianna's voice was cold. "And whoever 'tis you whisper with can step forward as well, that you might answer for your actions together."

The maids giggled excitedly at this, then gasped as one when a decidedly dishevelled Fenella stepped into the ray of light. Her hair was entangled with hay, the neck of her kirtle gaped open, her lips were swollen, and her expression dreamily unrepentant.

Even though she had been caught.

Brianna's heart skipped a beat. This did not bode well for her maid's reputation.

"Good morning, my lady," the maid said with a soft smile. "I do apologize for not being in chambers when you awoke, but I was . . . distracted from my duties this morn.''

Then Fenella turned and offered her hand to someone in the shadows behind.

The women exclaimed as one when Dermot joined Fenella, her hand fast within his own, his garb no less rumpled than that of the maid.

He even bowed slightly to a stunned Brianna. ''Good morning, my lady.''

Brianna inhaled sharply. '' 'Tis far from a good morning. Fenella, you were entrusted to my father's household to learn the duties you must one day take for your own. Surely you know better than to dishonor both your sire's reputation and my sire's hospitality by such behavior?

Fenella stepped out into the wan light and smiled sweetly. She turned that smile upon Dermot who, to Brianna's astonishment, responded in kind.

In truth, the pair of them seemed oblivious to all, including their own predicament.

''I love him,'' Fenella breathed, her eyes filled with stars. Then she looked at Brianna, her expression far from apologetic. ''I cannot explain the feeling to you, my lady, but I care naught for convention and reputation when Dermot holds me in his arms.''

The maids gasped and began to chatter, their consternation masking Brianna's own. People joined their ranks, evidently having heard the commotion and come from the hall to see its source. The maids dutifully recounted what had transpired thus far as more and more souls pressed into the comparatively small armory, craning their necks for a better view.

Brianna looked over the group with some dismay, for she could not imagine how she might salvage Fenella's reputation now. She jumped when she saw Luc leaning against the pillar beside the doorway, and met his gaze.

The glow in his eyes revealed that Brianna was not the only one recalling what had passed between them the night before. 'Twas different from this, however, for Luc had ensured that Brianna's reputation was untainted.

He had given her pleasure but taken naught, denying his own desire. Which left Brianna less than impressed with Dermot's behavior. Why, he should still be in mourning for Ismay!

"And what of you, sir?" Brianna asked. "Can you not even wait for Ismay to grow cold before you lavish your attentions upon another? What manner of faithlessness is this? What manner of husband are you?"

Dermot cleared his throat and frowned. "A poor one, no doubt," he conceded, then raised his strange pale gaze to meet Brianna's own. "And I can make no apology for that. 'Twas true enough that I made undue haste to find myself a wealthy wife when my sire cast me out all those years past. Had I granted more attention to the manner of woman I wed, then I might have been a better spouse than I was."

"I know you will be!" Fenella declared and the pair were lost in each other's eyes once more.

"What is this?" Brianna asked. "You cannot mean to wed this man! Fenella, where are your senses? Your sire will choose you a spouse—and 'twill not be this man who willingly admits he wed Ismay for her dowry!"

"My sire will have no choice," Fenella insisted with rare quietude. She met Brianna's gaze steadily. " 'Twas from you I learned the value of love between man and wife, my lady, and 'twas from you that I learned to ensure I won my own way."

Saints above. Brianna's mouth went dry and she could not find the words to argue with that.

Fenella squeezed Dermot's pale, elegant fingers. " 'Twas to ensure my sire's agreement that I granted Dermot my maidenhead. I love him, as he loves me, and now my father will have no choice."

Brianna exhaled shakily, her gaze dancing between the pair before her. 'Twas clear that Fenella believed she followed Brianna's lead and did not see the pitfalls before her. But, Brianna was far from convinced that Dermot had changed his ways, much less that he loved Fenella in truth.

No doubt he had an eye upon her significant inheritance.

But the decision was not Brianna's to make. She looked Dermot in the eye and hoped her glance was chilling. "What do you intend to do about this matter, sir? You must answer for what you have done."

"Aye." Dermot straightened. "I shall go immediately to Fenella's sire and plead my case. I shall ask him for Fenella's hand in marriage."

The women broke into excited chatter, but Brianna was not satisfied that Fenella's fortune was so very good. "Aye, you will ride and you will ride swiftly, sir. And I shall send a runner to tell Fenella's sire that you come and what you have done."

Dermot looked alarmed. "Do you not trust me?"

"In a word, nay," Brianna retorted.

"And rightly so," Uther contributed. "As I recall, the lady Ismay made a markedly similar prenuptial choice some years past." The older man glowered at the guilty pair. "Your inheritance is a significant one, is it not, Fenella?"

The maid blushed crimson. "My lady, tell them the import of wedding for love!"

Brianna felt the regard of all gathered there, most particularly one steady blue gaze. "Fenella," she said softly, "a man who deserves your love will treat you with respect from the outset. Dermot has not troubled himself with anything more than his own pleasure." She cleared her throat softly. "I am sorry, Fenella, but this is no good sign."

"I love him!" the maid protested hotly.

"And I love her," Dermot argued, clasping the maid's hand in his own.

Brianna felt her expression turn stern. "Then, hasten to her father. But be warned, Dermot, should you not arrive at Fenella's home estate, should you *forget* to make an honest woman of Fenella, you may be certain that word of your deed will be made known to all within the kingdom of Henry II of England."

Brianna took a deep breath, hearing a conviction in her voice that was but an echo of her father's authority. "I pledge it to you, sir, that this woman, left to the care of Tullymullagh, shall not be left sullied and abandoned by you."

Twin spots of color burned in Dermot's cheeks and he held his chin high. "But I love her, my lady Brianna," he declared. "You have naught to fear."

Brianna shrugged. "Then, neither do you."

To Brianna's surprise, Luc's steady words interrupted. "Unless, of course, you know something of how the lady Ismay met her demise."

The assembly gasped as one and pivoted to eye Luc, his own gaze fixed on an increasingly flustered Dermot as he pushed his way through the throng.

"But she fell!" Dermot protested, rare color staining his face. "You all said she fell!"

"Or perhaps she was pushed," Ruarke declared savagely, stepping forward in turn. "How long have you courted this maid, sir? Have you been adulterous?"

The assembly leaned forward with gleaming eyes. Fenella blushed scarlet and Brianna had a horrible feeling of dread. "I loved him long," the maid confessed. "But 'twas only on this visit, when Dermot looked so unhappy, that I sought to console him.''

Dermot hung his head. '' 'Tis true matters proceeded too quickly,'' he admitted gruffly, then looked up with bright eyes. ''But I did not push Ismay! She was drunk, I left her in the hall that Friday eve, disgusted with her behavior yet again. She turned me from her bed years past and mocked me before all since the loss of Claremont.''

''And where did you go?'' Luc asked coldly.

If Fenella's cheeks had seemed red before that was naught compared to this moment. But she stepped forward proudly and laced her fingers tightly with Dermot's own. ''We were here, together, until 'twas nearly morn,'' she declared.

The maids cackled like hens at this revelation and naught else could be heard in the armory. ''We were together!'' Dermot cried. ''We each can speak for the other.''

''And you each had a stake in seeing Lady Ismay gone,'' Luc commented with quiet authority.

The lovers looked at each other in dismay, but Brianna noted a trio of stablehands exchanging sheepish expressions. Luc evidently followed her gaze. ''What do you know?'' he asked the tallest.

The boy stepped forward. ''We saw them, sir, and we heard them, as well,'' he declared. ''Denis bade us sleep in the armory, for the stable was overfull.'' The ostler nodded acknowledgement of this, his single brow bobbing up and down. The boy turned on Fenella and Dermot with a grimace. ''All that moaning,'' he complained. ''We had barely a wink of sleep.''

''Are you certain 'twas them?'' Luc asked.

The boys nodded in unison. ''Oh, Dermot!'' cooed one in obvious mimicry of what they had heard.

''Fenella, my own sweet maid,'' rumbled another, then the trio erupted into giggles.

"You listened!" Fenella cried.

"We could hardly do anything else!"

"Oho, but that was naught to Sunday eve!"

Fenella and Dermot went white, then their faces were suffused with scarlet. "You did not listen to that?" Fenella roared.

"My lord, *take* me!" one boy mimicked. "Take me *now*!"

Fenella gasped and set after the boys in outrage. They scampered into the assembly, their taunting parodies carrying from every corner of the armory as Fenella desperately sought them.

Brianna fought against her smile. Dermot might not be as honorable a man as Luc, but he was no murderer.

"Adulterer!" Father Padraig hissed. "Your sins will not be forgotten."

"We should toss him in the dungeons," Ruarke declared.

Luc shook his head. "We should send Dermot to make his pleas to Fenella's sire," he said firmly with a single glance to Brianna. "The lady's decision is a sage one. 'Twill be Fenella's father's right to mete out any repercussions due."

Dermot grew markedly paler, though he nodded agreement. A murmur of approval slipped through the ranks, but Brianna only had eyes for Luc. The assembly filtered into the bailey, but Luc lingered, a proud smile curving his lips.

"Well done, my lady fair," he murmured. "You have learned quickly to take a keep in hand."

Brianna smiled in return, unable to halt the glow that spread throughout her at Luc's praise. She knew he would not grant it idly, so the words pleased her even more.

Chapter Fifteen

*L*UC SAT AT ONE END OF THE HALL AS THE EVENING shadows drew long, Uther's copious notes spread before him. Somewhere in this stack of vellum lay the answer to Connor's murder. Somewhere, there lurked a lie.

And Luc had but to find it. He frowned as he reviewed the observations of Cook, a flicker of movement distracting him from the task.

Brianna dropped onto the bench opposite and leaned closer. She was yet pale, Luc noted with concern, and there were shadows beneath her bright eyes.

"Did you find anything?" she asked anxiously and Luc knew she referred to the hiding place in the chapel.

He shook his head. " 'Twas empty."

"Oh." Brianna sat back and folded her hands together before herself, her gaze dropping to the sheaves before Luc. "Have you talked to all?"

"Aye." Luc could not keep his frown from deepening. "Yet come no closer to the truth for all of that. Someone must be hiding the truth!"

He glanced up to find Brianna smiling slightly. "Your eyes are very blue," she murmured enigmatically.

Luc studied her for a moment, liking well how a faint

flush stained her cheeks at his perusal. "You seem to find significance in that, my lady," he suggested and she flushed crimson.

"I have noted that they are thus when you find a matter—" she hesitated, licked her lips, then flicked a shy glance to Luc "—*interesting.*"

Her embarrassment only made Luc wonder when else his eyes had been blue.

"Indeed?" There was a prospect of tempting the lady to smile, Luc was certain of it. And that prospect was infinitely more intriguing than that of reading Cook's recollection again. Luc set a sheet of vellum aside and propped his elbows on the trestle table to regard Brianna. "And what matter has prompted them to be so blue before?"

"You tease me again!" Her eyes danced, her gaze falling to Luc's lips, then back to his eyes again. Her cheeks were aflame. "You *know*!"

"Nay, I do not." Luc heaved a mock sigh and shook his head. "There is naught for it. You shall have to confide in me, my lady."

Brianna glanced to the left and to the right, evidently satisfying herself that none was listening, then leaned across the table to whisper. " 'Twas thus when you kissed me," she confided.

"Ah!" Luc let a slow smile ease across his lips. "You speak aright, my lady, that was *most* interesting."

Brianna caught her breath, her lips parted. The hall felt markedly warm as she stared back at Luc.

Luc suddenly recalled an issue that had been forgotten these past days. He deliberately tapped a fingertip on the board. "Do you not still owe me another *four* of those kisses?"

Brianna grinned and tossed her hair, granting him a cocky glance that was more like the woman Luc first had encountered. "I do not know," she said archly. "I must demand an accounting to be certain."

"Ah, but if you demand the accounting of me, I can promise you what the result will be," Luc mused. Brianna's gaze flew to meet his. He winked and she smiled fully.

" 'Tis true enough," she conceded with mock resignation, then wrinkled her nose. "You, sir, only see such matters to your own advantage." Their gazes held for a long moment and Luc dared to hope that the lady would grant his suit serious consideration.

He hoped that Connor had read his daughter aright.

Brianna tapped a fingertip now on the vellum, not glancing downward quickly enough to hide the mischievous gleam in her eye. "Although, Luc, I must wonder that stacks of vellum could be as intriguing to you as a lady's kiss."

Recalled to his task, Luc smiled slightly for her, then shoved a hand through his hair as he regarded the volume of Uther's notes. "Rest assured, 'tis not the vellum," he confided grimly, "but the desire to find your sire's killer that captures my interest in this."

Brianna leaned closer, her eyes wide. "Do you know who did this deed?"

"Nay!" Luc grimaced. "And there are precious few hints of the truth. I overheard whispers on Sunday eve but now can only conclude 'twas Dermot and Fenella."

"What did they say?"

"That the lady must never know, never guess the truth until 'twas too late, that secrecy was imperative."

Brianna straightened. "Do you think they planned to elope?"

"Nay," Luc said grimly. "I think they planned the loss of Fenella's maidenhead. The woman protested, the man insisted that they must finish what they had begun to see matters resolved to their satisfaction."

The lady's eyes widened. "Oh!" Then her brows drew together. "That shameless cur!" She turned an outraged gaze upon Luc. "What if he does not return for Fenella, but merely abandons her in such shame?"

Luc shrugged. "Shame may be easier to bear than a poor spouse."

Brianna's concern for her maid was evident. "Perhaps he truly does love her," she murmured, plainly not convinced. "Perhaps he will change his ways and be a good spouse to her."

There was a hopefulness to her tone that Luc did not have the heart to contest.

"Perhaps," Luc conceded grimly, still not prepared to wager on any such optimistic possibility. "I hope, for Fenella's sake, that he does."

Brianna eyed him carefully. "You are skeptical of love," she charged.

Luc met her gaze without embarrassment. "I have known little of it," he admitted. "Though it seems to be oft used as an excuse for foolishness."

"Like Fenella's."

Luc nodded firmly.

Brianna frowned and leaned across the board once more, her delicate hand coming to rest on Luc's own. As previously, he was transfixed by the contrast between their hands.

"But a man and a woman can have a noble love between them, as my mother and father did. I have seen it." Brianna's gaze clung to Luc's as though she would persuade him of this fact.

She swallowed and when she continued, her words were uncharacteristically tentative. "Do you believe it possible that you could feel such love for a woman?"

Luc could not halt his smile. He captured her hand and

leaned across the board. "*Any* woman?" he teased. "Or one woman in particular?"

"You!" Brianna retorted and made to withdraw but Luc held fast to her hand. "I meant whether you might love your wife."

Luc folded her hand between his palms, interlacing her fingers with his own. He eyed her over their hands. "You meant," he corrected smoothly, "whether I might love *you.*"

Brianna flushed, the only answer Luc needed. She parted her lips, then closed them again, clearly fighting to find something to say.

But Luc knew precisely what she wanted to hear.

"My lady," he rumbled in a low voice, willing her to understand his intent, wanting only to reassure her. *"Brianna."* Her eyes flashed at his use of her name and Luc slid his thumb across her hand in a smooth caress. "I have not a shred of doubt that you will claim my heart as securely as I intend to claim your own."

Her emerald gaze danced over Luc's features, as though she sought some sign that he was not to be believed.

But Luc knew there was none.

"Oh." The acknowledgement was no more than a breath but Luc heard the weight of Brianna's relief within it.

Uther, to Luc's mind, showed markedly poor timing in that moment. The steward appeared by Brianna's elbow and cleared his throat portentously. Brianna jumped at the sound. "My lady? Perhaps you see fit to retire?"

She looked startled by the option and charmingly reluctant to leave. Brianna hesitated and looked again to Luc.

"Perhaps 'tis a sensible idea," he suggested, then subtly reminded her of her pledge to him. "Especially as Uther can accompany you."

Brianna smiled then. "Of course, Uther." To Luc's delight, she squeezed his fingers and cast him a shy smile before easing her hand from his own and rising from the board.

'Twas no accident that Luc's gaze followed the lady's figure as she made for the stairs, nor no coincidence that his heart leapt when she paused at the foot to look back at him.

Nay, Luc was fairly enamored of the lady already, and he knew well that time would only increase her hold over him.

And that suited him well enough.

Luc lingered over his wine until he heard the faint echo of the latch dropping home on Brianna's door. Then and only then did Luc feel assured that Brianna was safe for this night.

Luc quaffed his wine and gathered Uther's notes in a semblance of a pile. He was bone-tired and unlikely to discern any anomaly this night.

Sleep would do him good, as well. When Uther returned, Luc asked him to see the notes made secure, then strode from the hall.

Yet 'twas not the prospect of sleep that claimed Luc's thoughts. 'Twas Brianna's little sigh of acceptance and the accompanying shine of anticipation in her eyes that captured his thoughts. Aye, he would win this lady's heart, if 'twas the last thing he did in this world.

The prize was worth any price.

The moon was full, the bailey quiet. The wine drifted warm in Luc's veins and such was his mood that he did not think anything amiss when a footstep echoed behind him.

It might well be Uther. Luc managed to half turn and almost uttered a greeting before a cloth was cast over his head and someone punched him in the jaw.

But Luc was not so pensive that he did not reciprocate in kind.

• • •

BRIANNA AWAKENED EARLY Wednesday morn, Luc's declaration echoing in her ears once more. Her dreams had been filled with Luc; she could not evict him from her thoughts.

She wanted to see him again.

Brianna dressed in haste as the first light of the morn crept through the shuttered window. Fenella was already awake and, mindful of the pledge she had granted Luc, Brianna indicated for that woman to accompany her.

No matter that the maid sulked and dragged her feet, decidedly unhappy in Dermot's absence.

Luc was not in the hall, nor was he to be found in the awakening kitchens. Fenella fast on her heels, Brianna headed for the stables and the spot in the loft where Luc slumbered. She wondered whether there was some way to be rid of Fenella to have a moment alone with Luc, then knew she should not have such disregard for her own reputation.

'Twas a paltry example to set for those looking to her for guidance. Not to mention that she had granted Luc her pledge to not find herself alone. Brianna climbed the ladder and called softly.

But Luc was not there either. Brianna frowned with new concern. 'Twas not like Luc to simply disappear.

The ostler was yawning in the corridor when Brianna descended. "Denis, where is Luc?"

Denis' brow worked up and down. "He always slumbers in the loft."

"But he is not there. Indeed, his pallet looks undisturbed. Are you certain he returned here last eve?"

The ostler frowned. "I do not know. I did not see him."

"Do you think something has befallen him?" Fenella gave voice to the thought that lurked in every mind.

"Edward!" The ostler bellowed. "Andrew! Cedric!" The three boys came running, stumbling to an attentive halt before Denis. They glanced as one to Fenella, then studied their boots guiltily. "Have you seen Luc this morn? Or last eve?"

The boys shook their heads and exchanged puzzled glances. "Not since the evening meal," claimed one, the others nodding assent.

" 'Tis no good omen," Denis declared. "You and you, check the village and bailey. You and I shall seek him in the stables and addition, then check the other outbuildings. My lady, perhaps you might survey the hall once more. 'Tis easy enough to miss a man in such a large keep."

"Of course." Brianna felt a stubborn thrum of anxiety. "Thank you, Denis."

"We shall find him, my lady." The ostler bowed low, then snapped his fingers at the boys. Brianna summoned Fenella and stepped back into the bailey, just as two of the boys ran past, their footsteps turned toward the gate and village beyond.

What had happened to Luc? Brianna had a terrible sense of foreboding and she could not keep her gaze from trailing to the orchard where first they had met.

And matched words.

Something dark fluttered in the wind and blew against the stone wall of the keep. 'Twas not far from where Luc had demanded his first kiss. 'Twas not far from where Luc had spied Ismay.

On impulse, Brianna strode into the orchard.

"My lady, your kirtle!" Fenella wailed.

Brianna had no concern with the state of her kirtle. She wanted only to find Luc, only to assure herself that naught was amiss.

But 'twas only a piece of cloth that fluttered against the wall. Black cloth. Brianna frowned, noted its frayed edges, and wondered why it was here.

When she picked it up, something clattered to the ground from within its folds. Brianna saw the dark stain in the midst of the cloth almost at the same moment she saw the blood-stained dagger in the turf. Her heart stopped, a lump rose in her throat. She touched the stain, found it yet wet.

And her fingertip was smeared red.

Brianna gasped. She looked wildly over the wall to where Ismay had been found and went cold.

For a man lay on the rough ground that stretched from the wall down to the rushing Darrow. There was blood on his face, his garb was torn, and he did not move.

His matted ebony hair was graced with a white forelock.

"Luc!" Brianna screamed. "Nay, not Luc!"

Not her Luc! Brianna leapt to the top of the low wall, kicking her cursed skirts beyond her, then vaulted to the other side, running to Luc's side as soon as her feet hit the ground.

Brianna fell on her knees beside him and touched the gash upon his cheek. His skin was pale beyond all, the cut ugly and clearly not his only wound. His cheek was cold and when Brianna touched him, he did not move. Her heart clenched with fear.

Brianna whispered Luc's name, barely aware of the tears streaming down her cheeks. There could not be another funeral at Tullymullagh—she could not lose Luc.

But Luc did not move.

Brianna heard Fenella call from behind her, but she had no interest in what the maid might say. She reached beneath Luc's tabard with trembling hands, not balking at the chore even though she feared what she might find.

But her fingertips found the faint drum of Luc's heart.

Brianna cried out in her relief. She leaned over Luc, whispered his name repeatedly, even while she kissed his cheek, his bruised knuckle, his brow. Only when she leaned this close did Brianna hear the whisper of Luc breathing.

Who had done this to him? And why? *Why?*

Just when Brianna was convinced that Luc could not hear her, he cautiously opened one eye. 'Twas bruised and clearly painful to move. The wedge of color that Brianna could see was a wintery silver.

"You are alone," Luc noted, his voice ragged.

The very words brought tears to Brianna's eyes. How could he be concerned first and foremost with her welfare when he lay wounded like this? Truly Luc was a man like none other.

Brianna bit her lip, unable to stem the flow of her grateful tears. She thought suddenly of the night he had consoled her and deliberately chose to misinterpret his concern.

"Nay, I am not alone," she whispered unevenly and touched his shoulder. "I am with you."

Luc closed his eyes, grimacing against his pain. "You pledged it. Not alone."

He could be stubborn when an issue seized his mind, that much was certain!

"Aye, I did. Fear not—Fenella is behind and Denis shall shortly be here." Brianna bent and touched her nose softly to Luc's. "We are alike, Luc, in our determination to keep our pledges."

Luc's lips moved as though he might have smiled, had they not been so cracked. He made a sound suspiciously like a snort and his hand closed tentatively over her own.

His skin was so uncharacteristically cold that Brianna feared anew for his life.

"Careful," Luc urged hoarsely. "Father Padraig. Watch."

The priest? "But why?"

Luc frowned, every word obviously an ordeal for him.

"There when Ismay talked. Behind me in the chapel yesterday."

Brianna gasped. "When you checked the crucifix?"

Luc murmured assent, then frowned. "Not closed, my fault, surprised." He heaved a sigh, no doubt born of disappointment in himself. "Father Padraig came."

Brianna's eyes widened as she understood. The hiding place had not been fully closed because Luc had been surprised by the priest's arrival.

Brianna clutched Luc's hand and leaned yet closer, her other hand stroking the hair away from his brow. "But what happened? You were in the hall when I left last evening."

Luc licked his lips but his eyes did not open again. "You were safe."

Brianna smiled at his gruff protectiveness. "I was and I am," she assured him quietly. "Tell me what happened."

He frowned again. "Could not see."

"But the moon was full."

"Dark cloth." Luc made an exasperated sound in the back of his throat. "Surprised. Again."

The cloth in the orchard. Father Padraig must have ambushed Luc, casting the cloth over his head so that he could not fairly defend himself.

Or identify his assailant.

Father Padraig must have thought that Luc had the Rose. Was it because the gems were shaped into a crucifix that the priest thought the prize should be his own? Or was he as susceptible to greed as any other man?

Despite his frustration, Brianna had no doubt that Luc had fought back when he was attacked. The bruises on his face and hands alone revealed that it had been no short scuffle. She bent and kissed his temple again, hating that he had been lying out here all night long.

No wonder he was so chilled.

"Aid is coming," she whispered. Luc's only response was to tighten his grip upon her hand and Brianna's heart wrenched at the delay.

What kept Fenella? Brianna looked up, surprised to find so many flanking Fenella along the wall. And not a one of them moved! Brianna waved desperately to win their attention, only to realize that they were not even looking at her.

Their gazes were fixed on a point far below. Brianna turned, looking past Luc for the first time.

In the river far below, a man's figure was caught on the rocks. It bobbed lifelessly in the current and Brianna had no doubt that that man drew breath no longer.

There would be another funeral at Tullymullagh, after all.

'Twas but a heartbeat later that Brianna realized the man's sodden dark garb was none other than the robe of a priest.

And she knew that there was naught to fear from Father Padraig any longer.

• • •

LUC AWAKENED IN the midst of unfamiliar softness and warmth, the familiar scent of attar of roses filling his nostrils. He stretched back against the pallet and might have smiled, knowing full well who was close at hand, had the move not sent aches right through him.

Too late, Luc recalled the battering he had taken. There would be evidence aplenty as to whom he had battled, for Luc had not fallen easily.

Aye, he had ensured that his opponent had a blackened eye.

"Not so quickly!" Brianna chided. The heat of her breast pressed against Luc and she dabbed some herbal concoction against the cut upon his cheek. It stung wickedly, both that and his body's enthusiastic response to the lady's presence, assuring Luc that he was not dead yet.

Indeed, he could not be that sorely injured. He forced open his eyes to find Brianna right beside him, her complexion pale, her lovely features drawn with concern.

Apparently for him.

Luc's heart pounded and he scanned the room while he pondered that marvel. He must be an occupant in the men's chamber of the keep. Uther hovered behind the lady with a tray of various ointments. Gavin himself loitered on the far side of the room.

Luc propped himself up on his elbows at the sight of his sire's bruise. "You have a blackened eye!"

"You must rest," Brianna chided, but Luc had no interest in her counsel in this moment.

"At least I look to have won my fight," Gavin snapped.

"What fight?" Luc demanded.

Gavin limped closer, snorting in disdain. " 'Twas that *champion* knight, no less. Filled with the wine of my own cellars, he decided to teach me the price of disciplining a knight."

Gavin snorted. " 'Tis *he* who will have time aplenty to consider his own folly. No one picks a fight with me." Gavin flicked a baleful glance at Brianna. "And no one will be taking him morsels from the kitchens this time."

Brianna did not even look inclined to challenge that statement. Luc was relieved that she appeared to have learned not to press his sire.

He had more than enough cause for concern on her account without Gavin angered as well.

Luc leaned back against the pallet, wincing slightly at the move, and decided to be less direct with the others than he had been with Brianna. "Are there any others in the keep with a blackened eye this morn?"

"Nay," Uther said crisply. "Except, of course, Father Padraig."

Luc's eyes flew open. "And what news of Father Padraig? How did he come by his bruise?"

"Presumably from you, though he will never tell the tale," Gavin said harshly.

Luc felt his eyes narrow. "What is this?"

"He is dead, drowned in the Darrow."

"Dead?" All nodded in unison and Luc feared their suspicions. "I did not kill him," he said quickly, for he knew he had not.

"Nay, you did not," Brother Thomas confirmed from the portal. He wiped his hands as he strolled into the room, his assessing gaze slipping over Luc's bruises.

"You understand my expertise is more with the dead than the living," he rumbled with a wink, "but I do not imagine that you will be joining their ranks soon." He took a sniff of the concoction Brianna was using and nodded approval, pointing at another gash on Luc's jaw. "Put some more of it on that one."

The princess did as she was bidden and Luc stifled his response to the twinge the ointment sent through him. Brother Thomas smothered a smile, clearly well aware of that effect.

"What of Father Padraig?" Uther asked.

"He drowned," Brother Thomas declared. "Nearly on the other side of the river and facing away from the keep. I believe Father Padraig was fleeing Tullymullagh in the wake of his battle with Luc." He nodded to Brianna. "The dagger he dropped in the orchard could easily have been the one that spelled your sire's demise."

Luc looked at Brianna in confusion. "I found a blood-stained black cloth in the orchard," she supplied.

Luc nodded grimly. "The one used to blindfold me."

"Aye," Brianna agreed. "But a dagger was wrapped within it."

Luc straightened at that, only to find Brother Thomas nodding agreement. "Aye, a dagger that matches Connor's wounds well. It would seem that Father Padraig was responsible for the deaths of both Lady Ismay and Connor."

Brother Thomas frowned. "The cloth looks to have been torn from a tunic and there is old blood upon it as well as Luc's own."

The occupants of the room exchanged a glance. "My lord Connor's blood," Uther murmured and Brother Thomas nodded.

"Aye. I would guess that Father Padraig wore a black tabard that day as well."

The sense of relief that flooded through the small chamber was tangible. Father Padraig had been the guilty party, after all. Luc leaned back and closed his eyes while Brianna tormented him.

"You are certain that he drowned?" Gavin questioned.

"Aye, 'tis easily done." The monk gathered two handfuls of his ample habit. "These robes are cursedly heavy, thick wool, though that is naught compared to when they are wet. I have nearly lost my footing in fording quite a shallow stream when they wound about my legs. Father Padraig likely fell, perhaps he hit his head then, perhaps when the river cast him across the rocks."

"But why would he kill Connor?" Gavin demanded.

Brother Thomas looked at Luc. "It would seem that Connor had a treasure yet remaining from his travels in the East, or at least, many believed he did. 'Twas called the Rose of Tullymullagh."

Gavin looked at Brianna and frowned in confusion, but

Uther's eyes rounded. "I never truly believed it existed," he admitted quietly.

"Apparently, Father Padraig believed it did," Luc said.

"And he wanted it for his own," Gavin breathed, obviously understanding that manner of motivation. "It should have been *mine*!"

"I believe 'tis long gone," Luc insisted and his father's face fell. "But Ismay told me she recalled something of the Rose of Tullymullagh that all others had forgotten, that last night in the hall. Father Padraig was there when she said as much."

"He did not want any others seeking his prize," Uther guessed.

"Aye, 'tis easier to hunt alone," Gavin concurred.

"My father had a hiding place in the chapel," Brianna contributed.

"But Father Padraig did not know where it was within the chapel," Uther breathed in understanding. "And Connor surprised him when he sought it there. My lord must have recognized him!"

"So, he could not be left to live," Gavin concluded. He jabbed a finger through the air at his son. "But why did he attack you?"

"Brianna told me of the hiding place in the chapel, and when I checked it yesterday, 'twas empty." Luc shook his head. "Father Padraig surprised me there, but I did not manage to close the tiny door completely before his arrival."

"So, he thought *you* had the Rose that he desired," Uther concluded.

"And ambushed you in the bailey," Gavin nodded.

"But why did he flee?" Luc asked softly. All eyes turned on him. "If Father Padraig wanted only the Rose of Tullymullagh, he did not win it by attacking me. He could not flee with the prize he sought, for I did not have it!''

"Perhaps he thought you dead, but his actions observed," Brother Thomas speculated. "Perhaps another came along and saw what he did."

"But no one raised a hue about Luc being injured," Brianna observed. " 'Twas this morn when he was found and thence by fortune alone."

The monk frowned. "Perhaps he realized Luc knew his identity and dared not remain here any longer."

"Aye. Or perhaps there is yet another piece to the puzzle we have yet to find," Luc concluded grimly. He looked to his father. "Did you not say there were *two* in the chapel?"

Gavin nodded and scowled anew. "An accomplice!"

And Luc had heard two men conspiring in the stables. Father Padraig could have been but one.

The other could have been anyone at all.

The other might have been the one so determined to make the Rose of Tullymullagh his own. Luc's heart clenched.

Uther flicked a cold glance Gavin's way. "You could have been mistaken. Are you certain 'twas two?"

Gavin's frown deepened. "At the time, I was certain. . . ." His voice trailed away and Uther snorted disdain.

Brother Thomas shrugged. "Or perhaps 'twas Dermot who aided Father Padraig."

Luc watched his father. Perhaps it had been Gavin behind the foul deed, after all.

"I suggest we call the matter resolved," Uther said tightly. " 'Tis clear there is no certainty that Father Padraig did not labor in this alone."

"Aye, we know he killed Connor." Gavin declared. "We

know he killed Ismay. Surely it matters little if he coerced another to aid him in his quest to the chapel."

Luc was not nearly convinced of that, but Uther and Gavin clearly considered all issues of import resolved.

"I agree," declared the steward.

"To be sure, 'tis no loss to have such a man gone from this keep and this world," Gavin declared with a frown. "And indeed, 'tis good to know the truth." He nodded approval toward Luc and Brother Thomas, then commented gruffly to Luc. "I should see you well soon."

Luc blinked in surprise, but his sire was gone.

Brother Thomas moved closer, his lips twisting as he examined the cut upon Luc's cheek. "It has need of a stitch," he declared, then turned a quelling eye on Uther and Brianna. "Off with you both. 'Twill not be easy and my charge must have the privacy to roar."

Brianna smiled, then bent suddenly to brush the softness of her lips across Luc's temple. A heat flooded through Luc at her unexpected touch and the lady flushed.

"I shall come and see you later," she said hastily, then hooked her arm through Uther's elbow.

"And I shall have Cook bring you soup," the steward declared. " 'Tis the best thing for you, soup and slumber. 'Twill see you healed in no time." He bowed low, then actually smiled stiffly for Luc. "I thank you, sir, for seeing my lord Connor's murderer brought to justice, in one manner or another."

Luc nodded, but he was markedly less than convinced that all was resolved. The only thing he knew for certain was that his princess was far from safe as yet. He made to rise but Brother Thomas laid a large hand on Luc's chest and pushed him back against the pallet.

"You have nowhere to go, my friend," the man counselled firmly. "And you will be fortunate indeed if I permit you to leave this bed in time for Connor's funeral two days hence."

"But, matters are unresolved!"

"The killer is found, Luc. The accomplice, if indeed there is one, will wait."

Luc heaved a sigh and frowned as he reluctantly lay back, not in the least bit persuaded of that.

"Aye, prepare for the worst," Brother Thomas advised. Luc closed his eyes as the needle bit into his skin and fought his grimace, frustrated beyond all.

• • •

BY FRIDAY MORN, Brianna was tired beyond belief. She was certain there had never been a keep in the throes of a second funeral while needing to plan the third to fall within a week. Another priest had come with haste from the priory to ensure the Masses were said for Connor. The prior himself had arrived thin-lipped to decide where Father Padraig should be laid to rest.

But 'twas not the activity that left her feeling drained. Indeed, such duties had occupied her thoughts when idleness might have left her weeping.

'Twas the knowledge that on this day, her father would be laid to his final rest.

And Brianna was not quite prepared to say farewell.

The gentle patter of rain echoed against the shutters and Brianna listened for a long time, half certain that if she did not rise, there could be no funeral.

'Twas whimsy, of course, and she knew it, but still she delayed the ordeal before her.

'Twas Fenella's touch on her elbow that compelled Brianna to compose herself. Brianna knew that the people of Tullymullagh were waiting for her. They relied upon her for an example of strength and 'twas her duty to be gracious in her bereavement.

Brianna did not know how she would do it. Indeed, she nearly turned back on the threshold of her chamber, uncertain how she could manage even the procession when grief so crumbled her defenses from the inside.

But a man stepped forward from the shadows of the landing, a man in sombre garb with a steady blue gaze. Brianna halted, Luc offered his hand.

"I did not want you to walk alone," he said simply.

Brianna caught her breath and blinked back unexpected tears. "I thought Brother Thomas consigned you to bed."

Luc rolled his eyes and she knew he tried to conjure her smile. "Two days there gave me enough strength to wrestle him and win," he jested.

Now that she truly looked, Brianna noted that the cut on Luc's cheek was less angry, the bruise around his eye vastly diminished. Even the crack in his lip seemed to be healing.

Her heart swelled beneath his steady gaze and she felt herself straighten. Brianna liked that Luc had guessed that she would need him and had made the effort to rise.

She took Luc's hand, savoring his gentle strength as his fingers closed over the chill of her own. "He was a wise king," she said softly.

"Aye," Luc agreed. " 'Tis the mark of a good administrator to put selfishness aside to serve his responsibilities, to weigh the testimony of those around him, and make decisions for the good of all. Your sire left you an uncommon example of such ability. I have no doubt that his memory will long burn bright in every heart in Tullymullagh."

The very reminder that her father would live on in her own heart, as well as the hearts of all those on this estate, made the rite of this day seem a little less final. Others had said as much, but Brianna believed Luc when the declarations of others had seemed no more than words.

Luc arched his brow ever so slightly as he held Brianna's gaze. "You will do Connor's memory proud as Lady of Tullymullagh."

Luc's thumb moved across her palm and Brianna knew he was telling her that she could survive this day with aplomb.

And he spoke aright, the ladyship of this keep would be hers. 'Twas no small responsibility, as she had already glimpsed in laboring beside Uther. And to serve the good of all beneath the lord and lady's hand, 'twas necessary to consider matters beyond oneself.

Brianna realized suddenly that it had been willfulness alone that prompted her refusal of Luc—no more than a selfish desire to see all dance to her tune. It seemed a childish choice to have made and she felt suddenly that she learned much in recent days.

Ayc, Luc was a man whom her sire had thought a fitting choice for Brianna. That much was clear from Connor's defense of Luc in the orchard when Brianna laughed. Luc was a man who challenged her and made her smile, a man who protected her, a man well accustomed to administering a holding, a man who had seen Connor's killer named.

Luc would be a good lord of Tullymullagh.

And Luc had pledged to win her heart. Brianna straightened and met his gaze, knowing the time for willfulness was past. She tightened her fingers over Luc's hand.

"Would you walk with me this day, Luc Fitzgavin?" she asked softly, holding his gaze all the while. " 'Twould be the only fitting place for the man I mean to wed."

Luc's eyes widened ever so slightly, their vivid hue evident even in the shadows, then his firm lips curved in a smile. Brianna's heart leapt for she saw the evidence of his pleasure and knew that could only be a good portent for their years together.

"I should be honored," he declared with a conviction that left no doubt of his feelings. Luc kissed Brianna's knuckles, then fitted her hand in his elbow. "Indeed, my lady, by your side is the only place I desire to be."

And Brianna knew the satisfaction of having made the right choice.

• • •

'TWAS A FOUL day for a funeral, not only cursed with driving, cold rain, but plagued by a wind that tormented the mourners. 'Twas as though the environs of Tullymullagh itself protested the loss of its lord. Luc remained steadfast beside Brianna, striving to keep her dry despite the elements, ensuring he was there when she faltered.

The funeral itself was solemn and elegant, no expense spared in the burning of candles or incense. Uther's eulogy was long and left not a dry eye in the tiny chapel. The villagers clustered through the doors to mourn their overlord.

Brianna did her father's memory proud, but then, Luc had expected as much. Only he knew when she clutched his fingers tightly. Only he and Uther could discern her tears during Uther's emotional farewell to his liege lord.

The lady's kirtle was indigo, dyed so dark as to be almost black, and the color made her look as fragile as a rare flower. Though Brianna was veiled, the wondrous golden gleam of her hair could not be disguised through the sheer fabric, nor could the fair perfection of her features be marred. Her full lips were ruddy, though Luc guessed 'twas no carmine that granted their color. Brianna's only ornament was the gold circlet that held her veil resolutely in place.

There was no arguing that she was a rare beauty, and Luc

was humbled that she had chosen to accept his offer of marriage. He would do her proud, he solemnly vowed, unable to shake the sense that Connor lingered in their midst.

Luc would treat this woman with the honor she deserved. No less would do.

In the windswept cemetery, Brianna cast the first handful of dirt upon her father's casket. It echoed hollowly and she winced when the gravediggers began to shovel the wet soil into the grave. She turned away, leaning more on Luc than she had thus far, and he led her, without apology, from the churchyard.

'Twas time the lady had a hot drink within her. Aye, he would have Cook conjure more of that mulled wine and again, sleep would soothe the lady's hurt.

On the morrow, they two would plan their nuptials. Aye, 'twould be time enough for such merriment.

Chapter Sixteen

ALL WITHIN TULLYMULLAGH WERE SEIZED WITH DE-
light upon the prospect of a wedding. By the afternoon of the Monday following Connor's funeral, the hall was decked with greenery, the chapel filled
with beeswax candles, and Brianna smiled once again.
Gavin growled at all and sundry when duties were not done
with acceptable haste. Cook filled the hall and bailey with
tempting aromas. Uther hastened to and fro like a busy bird.

All was so cheerful that Luc was nearly convinced that
Uther and Gavin had spoken aright, that everything of import had truly been settled.

But still a kernal of doubt lodged within him, still he
ensured his princess was not left alone. Indeed, he found
excuses to find himself in the lady's company, much to her
amusement.

That Monday morn, the sun shone with rare fervor for so
late in the year. Luc found himself whistling as he strode to
the River Darrow to wash in its icy waters. He took a deep
breath of the morning air, glad he had spurned the crowded
quarters of the kitchens, this morn. All would be clamoring
for a bath, but Luc would have these few moments alone.

Uther had conjured a tabard of deep green for Luc and a
crisp white chemise of finely woven linen, more fitting for

events of this day than his simpler garb. His boots had been polished, his hair trimmed.

Aye, on this perfect day, he would make Brianna his wife.

And Luc wanted to look his best. He eyed his reflection in the water skeptically and confirmed that the bulk of his bruising had healed. Then, refusing to glance to the rock that had claimed Father Padraigh's life, Luc set to the labor of scraping the whiskers from his jaw.

A shout from the bailey made his head snap up, the jingle of a thousand bells made Luc's eyes narrow. He straightened and stood, a chanting that could only come from minstrels granting him sudden understanding of what he heard.

Minstrels arrived, which could be no coincidence. It must be that Rowan was returned. It made perfect sense that Rowan would have found such a company of entertainers, having been raised among their kind, and Luc could only smile at the fortuitous timing.

'Twould be fitting to have entertainment on this day of days.

Luc hauled on his new chemise, his anticipation rising as he climbed to the orchard wall. He reached the summit of the wall just in time to see the last of a gaily garbed troupe of troubadours be swallowed by the shadows of the portal. Luc retrieved the new tunic he had laid aside and donned it, knotting his belt overtop, then strode in the company's wake.

Luc started when Ruarke lunged out of the shadows just inside the doorway. The bruise Gavin had granted him was still a glaring yellow. Indeed, the knight had been trapped so long in the dungeons that Luc had nigh forgotten him.

Or tried to do so. Luc felt a curious satisfaction that the other knight had not healed as quickly as he, then chastised himself silently for a lack of compassion.

"What travesty is this?" Ruarke demanded. "I have just heard that you intend to wed Brianna!"

" 'Tis old news, Ruarke," Luc retorted calmly. "Indeed, you were in the garden yourself when she laughed."

"She will not wed you," Ruarke growled. "She *cannot* wed you." He jabbed himself in the chest. "Connor intended that Brianna should wed *me*."

Luc moved to step past the other man, not interested in his insistence. "How odd that Connor forgot that detail when his daughter laughed."

"He did not!"

"Aye, he did," Luc said firmly. "Connor endorsed my suit that day in the garden and you know it well."

To Luc's surprise, his agreement made Ruarke grin coldly. "I am surprised you do not recall the rest of that day's events," he declared. "Connor also conceded that Brianna should wed the brother who made her laugh loudest and longest."

Luc waited, for 'twas clear the other man would continue.

" 'Tis doubly odd," Ruarke mused as he folded his arms across his chest, his eyes glinting with antagonism, "but I cannot help thinking of the last time we had troubadours at Tullymullagh."

"Aye?"

"Aye." Ruarke's smile broadened. "The lady Brianna laughed so hard she wept. Indeed, she was yet giggling the following day."

Luc's blood ran suddenly cold. 'Twas only too easy to recall that Brianna had laughed only slightly that day in the garden. Indeed, she had not even loosed a guffaw. 'Twould not take much to best that!

But Luc could not lose her now!

Ruarke leaned forward and poked Luc in the chest, his

eyes gleaming. "Do not be so certain, humble Luc, that this bride truly will be yours."

Luc bit down hard on his response, not wanting to grant this man more of a response than he already had. "I thank you for your concern," he said frostily. " 'Tis *good* of you to take an interest when there is naught you might win this day." When the knight's eyes flashed in anger, Luc pivoted and strode to the hall.

Ruarke, he was quick to note, followed immediately behind.

• • •

EVEN HAVING BRACED himself for a display, Luc found the giddiness of Rowan's entourage startling. There was a drumroll just as Luc entered and fanfare of horns, then a jongleur garbed in bright green and gold tumbled head over heels across the hall. He bounced to his feet and grinned outright at the assembly.

A trio of minstrels trotted fast behind him, their clothing no less merry. Their faces were painted and bells jingled around their knees. The foursome squared up quickly and began a dance, chanting infectiously as they cavorted in the hall.

One jongleur encouraged the assembly to clap in unison. The few minstrels still resident at Tullymullagh began to pluck their own lutes and dulcimers in time.

The assembly applauded and exchanged smiles; the troupe's arrival clearly considered a timely one. Luc quickly spied Brianna, looking startled at her place on the dais. Garbed in emerald and gold, she was bewitchingly beautiful. He pushed his way through the crowd, anxious to be by her side.

"Rowan!" Gavin roared as he came from the kitchens. He held a chalice high, darting a significant glance to Luc.

"My son Rowan de Montvieux returns from the bride quest!"

No doubt Gavin did not intend to defend Luc's status. He wondered what advantage his father hoped to gain and could not help but think of Margaux's significant influence.

But Luc knew 'twas Brianna who held the outcome of the day in her delicate hands. And as much as Luc might have preferred otherwise, Ruarke was right.

The lady must stand by her own dictate.

Chatter erupted and rolled through the assembly at Gavin's words, those gathered taking a more avid interest in the arrivals.

"But—but this cannot be!" Brianna protested. "There is no longer a bride quest, for I am to be wed this very day!"

"My lady!" Luc strode to her side and all eyes turned upon him. He was aware only of Brianna's alarmed gaze, his heart beginning to pound when she looked to him. Luc hated to argue with her, but there was no question of the right course in this matter.

'Twas a matter of principle.

As much as Luc chafed at the knowledge of that.

"You granted a quest," he reminded her solemnly, "and you must stand by your own terms."

"Aye," Ruarke bellowed. "Victory belongs to the brother who makes the princess laugh longest and loudest!"

The assembly held their breath as one—all eyes fixed on their princess. Brianna swore under her breath. Her grimace might have been humorous under other circumstances, but Luc felt no less frustration than she.

"Curse duty," she muttered, then flicked a mutinous glance at Luc. "This lesson of putting aside selfish desire does not come readily," she complained.

Luc shook his head, as he came to stand behind her. She

would take the right course, he knew it well. "You know what must be done," he said softly.

Brianna heaved a sigh and straightened her shoulders, leaning slightly against Luc as though she had need of his support. She raised her voice and addressed the crowd. "Luc speaks aright," she conceded graciously. "I stand by my duty and the terms of my own quest. Let the troubadours begin."

And her fingers closed over his with a vengeance. "Oh, Luc," Brianna murmured for his ears alone. "Why *troubadours*? Any other circumstance would have been easier."

"Do *not* laugh," Luc counselled grimly.

"I shall try." Brianna took a deep breath, and they faced the assembly together.

Only now did Luc spy Rowan, leaning against the far wall of the hall. Rowan lifted a hand and the foursome of jongleurs danced out onto the floor once more. One encouraged the assembly to clap in unison, another stood precariously on his hands. The rest of the troupe danced, clapped, and whistled.

The assembly leaned forward with curiosity. Several whispered their certainty that the jongleur would fall. A woman gasped when he not only balanced on his hands, but a second jongleur climbed atop the first. That one balanced his elbows on the knees of the first, then rolled to the same inverted position as the first.

The assembly was captivated.

Brianna gripped Luc's fingers more tightly.

When the third jongleur climbed atop the other two, and made to echo the pose of the second, the assembly gasped as one. A good third of those gathered rose to their feet, certain the performers would tumble. The clapping grew louder and faster; the minstrels hastened the beat of their music. More than one stamped their feet and whistles echoed through the hall.

Brianna did not even seem to breathe.

The crowd roared as one when the third jongleur found his balance. They gasped as the human tower wavered, no doubt deliberately, then righted itself again.

And the fourth began to climb. He made a show of being the least talented of the lot, grimacing as though indecisive of where to step. The others contorted as he evidently chose wrong, those in the assembly shouted directions. He stepped on the groin of the second man, that jongleur's exaggerated expression of pain launching more than one chuckle.

Luc did not dare to look at his princess. She caught her breath, his heart stopped as her shoulders shook, and then she was silent once more.

The dismay of the climbing jongleur coaxed yet more laughs from the others, though. He mocked losing his balance and noisily fell, grimaced and scratched his head. He ran around the tower, apparently frantic to see his goal achieved, then seized an aide from the assembly.

He chose Ruarke.

"Nay!" Brianna whispered unevenly. Luc held her hand firmly.

The knight smiled tolerantly, bowing low to Brianna as he allowed himself to be tugged on to the floor. The jongleur made a great show of acting out how Ruarke, being so much taller, could readily place him at the summit. Ruarke laughed easily. Then he plucked up the much smaller performer and made to bodily set him upon the stacked acrobats.

In the blink of an eye, the bottommost jongleur "stepped" a few feet away, those above him swaying slightly at the movement but holding their ground. 'Twas clear they anticipated the move. Luc leaned forward himself, amazed at how easily the jongleurs had managed the feat.

In that very moment, the last jongleur mocked Ruarke's blackened eye, mimicking a great battle with his fists flying so quickly that 'twas hard to discern precisely where they were.

And Luc gasped along with the rest of the assembly as Ruarke, apparently distracted by the jongleur he held, put that smaller man down in the wrong place.

The jongleur wailed and snatched at the air. He kicked and apparently knocked at a critical shin in the human tower. The others shouted in mock dismay. The assembly cried out.

But Luc saw the last jongleur tug very hard on a string that seemed linked to Ruarke.

The entire group fell, tumbled bonelessly across the floor, and bounced to their feet in four opposing corners. They held their arms up for applause, then turned as one to salute Ruarke.

Ruarke blinked, obviously not certain what he had done to merit such a salute, just as his chausses fell around his boots.

The assembly roared with laughter, as much at Ruarke's astonishment as his abruptly bare buttocks. Luc choked back his own and felt Brianna's shoulders quake. She made a suspicious sound in her throat as though she fought against wayward laughter. Luc did not dare look at her face lest they take one look at each other and laugh aloud.

For the jongleurs had chosen their victim well. Ruarke, who clearly took great pride in his appearance, turned beet red and struggled for his chausses with such dismay that Luc could not keep a single chuckle from escaping his lips.

Brianna dug an elbow hard into his ribs and Luc fought to control his response.

'Twas clear enough what that string had been. Somehow,

the crafty jongleur had untied Ruarke's chausses while the knight was distracted.

Ruarke had retreated to one corner, his chausses safely over his buttocks again, but he had apparently just realized that the string was missing. He looked around himself most comically, obviously unaware that the entire hall watched his response.

Then Ruarke looked up and his lips drew to a thin line to find every eye upon him.

The bold jongleur taunted the knight from across the hall, flicking the string, much as one would tease a cat with a length of wool. He danced and cavorted, casting the cord at the knight as though daring him to lend pursuit.

His good humor spent, Ruarke roared in frustration and dove after the tormenting jongleur.

His chausses, of course, fell to his knees again. Ruarke stumbled, swore vehemently, tore off the offending garment, and lent chase in the buff.

"Saints above!" Brianna whispered unevenly. She bit her lip hard as though 'twas the only way to restrain herself. The very corners of her lips quirked and she clutched Luc's fingers nigh tightly enough to break them.

The assembly howled as knight and jongleur toppled chairs and jumped across trestle tables. The rest of the troupe encouraged all to clap again. Women shouted lewd comments when they spied what lurked beneath Ruarke's tabard and the man's face grew yet more ruddy. He swore angrily and snatched at the man who made him look a fool.

The din in the hall was deafening as all of Tullymullagh laughed and laughed.

Except for one princess.

And the man behind her.

Finally, Ruarke laid claim to the tie from his chausses, though Luc suspected that only the presence of so many around him kept the knight from retaliating for his embarrassment. 'Twas clear Ruarke was angered beyond all.

The jongleur wiped his brow as though vastly relieved, then danced away unrepentant. Ruarke glowered and retreated from the hall, no doubt to see himself more suitably garbed. Luc braced himself for another humorous assault.

But Rowan stepped forward and bowed low before the dais. "Lady Brianna, I have tried to prompt your smile and clearly failed," he declared gallantly. "May you yet find a man to prompt your laughter."

'Twas only then that Luc realized whose wedding Ruarke would be attending.

For the lady had not laughed.

"But I already have," Brianna declared with a smile for Luc alone. " 'Twas Luc Fitzgavin who made me laugh both first and most." Brianna held Luc's gaze, her wondrous eyes blazing with triumph.

They had done it!

Luc hooted with laughter at their success, then swept his bride into his arms. He swung her high; the assembly clapped with delight. Brianna giggled as she wrapped her arms around his neck. Luc held her tightly against his chest, savoring the pound of her heart against his own.

He had won the lady's hand in truth!

Luc turned to confront the delighted occupants of the hall. "Thus ends the bride quest," he declared proudly. " 'Tis time enough that Tullymullagh witnessed a wedding."

And the entire household cheered as one at the prospect of that.

• • •

RED WINE HAD flowed with abandon since they returned from the chapel, and the dancing had been vigorous. Rowan's troubadours had been persuaded to remain. The lady Brianna's eyes sparkled with delight.

Luc had seized every opportunity to kiss his bride soundly. 'Twas still a most satisfactory means of surprising her and Luc heartily anticipated the prospect of surprising her yet more this night.

However, Brianna would surprise him once herself. Evidently her shyness was overcome by the wine, for when he kissed her yet again, she mimicked one of his moves and slid her tongue tentatively between his teeth.

Luc gasped, Brianna giggled against his lips. Desire coursed through Luc in a wave.

He lifted his head with a snap, knowing that if he continued their kiss all would have more entertainment than they deserved. Indeed, Luc thought he might burst his chausses.

Brianna flushed slightly when their kiss ended so abruptly, as though surprised by her own boldness, then playfully tapped the end of his nose.

"Blue eyes," she teased.

Luc snorted. "Aye, and you know the import of that well enough," he mused, glancing pointedly her way. Luc cleared his throat deliberately. "Tell me, do you not feel the need to retire as yet, my lady?"

Brianna's eyes widened, her lips parted, and she leaned against him, her voice low. "Luc! We cannot leave yet! What will people *think*?"

"Only that all is right between us." Luc grinned as he securely captured her hand in his own. Brianna smiled into his eyes and Luc nearly urged her again to consider the timing of their departure.

'Twas then that Gavin rose to his feet and clapped his hands for the assembly's attention. Clearly, he did not win silence quickly enough for his taste, for Gavin let out a bellow that Luc knew was long perfected on the fields of battle.

The assembly fell restlessly quiet.

"And now," roared Gavin as though he still called over the din of celebration. "And now comes the moment for which we have all waited. My son has wedded the princess of Tullymullagh—" there were cheers all around "—and 'tis time enough he earns the fruit of that match."

Luc's eyes narrowed, for he was suspicious of his father's intent. To what fruit did Gavin refer?

Gavin, though, turned to Luc with a smile and beckoned. "Come, Luc of Llanvelyn, come and swear yourself to me. The seal of Tullymullagh must be granted to the spouse of Brianna, as pledged to her sire and King Henry of England."

The seal of Tullymullagh? Luc blinked. He had never thought beyond making Brianna his wife, though now he felt a fool for forgetting such pertinent details. Indeed, lordship of such a grand estate was a step closer to the life Luc had left behind, and that, combined with the necessity of swearing fealty to Gavin, gave Luc pause.

"Luc! He means to grant you the seal already!" Brianna's excitement with the prospect was more than clear.

His reservations were as naught in comparison to erasing Brianna's concerns for Tullymullagh.

Luc squeezed Brianna's fingers and rose to his feet with purpose. He crossed the floor, the assembly parting before him as they had done for all three brothers just a few weeks past. Luc dropped to one knee before his sire, as Gavin gestured to Uther. The steward hastened to Gavin's side, a bulging pouch within his grip.

Luc folded his hands together and raised them to his father, the pose not unlike an attitude of prayer. Gavin's toughened palms closed over those of his son. The two men's gazes met and held, and the assembly was silent as Luc's fealty was solemnly sworn.

Then Gavin bent, as was expected, and kissed his son on

either cheek, grasping Luc's hands and raising him to his feet once more. Gavin took the bundle from Uther and bestowed it with unexpected grace. 'Twas more bulky than Luc had expected and he fingered the contents in absent curiosity.

He realized there was not one but two seals within the bag.

Luc's gaze flew to his father's, that man's smug smile telling Luc all he needed to know about the second seal.

"My word," Gavin said silkily, "is not worth so little as some might believe."

'Twas the seal of Llanvelyn Luc held in his grip! He did not need to look within the bag to know the truth. 'Twas exactly what he had come to Tullymullagh to make his own.

But, oddly enough, Luc felt no satisfaction in seeing his goal achieved. He realized that he had little interest in returning to Wales, though certainly he would see to his responsibilities.

But all Luc had ever desired was here, his entire future was here, within the walls of Tullymullagh.

Garbed in gold and green like a fairy queen.

Luc glanced back to Brianna's shining eyes, his heart clenched, and he understood that the greater prize had been one he had never anticipated.

But the greatest prize of all would be the lady Brianna's heart. Luc would waste no time in courting the lady's affection.

Gavin snatched up his chalice in that very moment. "A drink!" he bellowed. "A drink to the health of the new Lord of Tullymullagh!"

A page offered a chalice for Luc and he lifted it high, deliberately holding Brianna's regard. "Nay, we drink to the health of the Lady of Tullymullagh!" he cried and the assembly roared approval as their chalices rose high.

• • •

THE SOLAR WAS shrouded in mysterious shadows, the only light cast by a trio of flickering oil lanterns. The room seemed hushed in anticipation when the merrymakers abandoned the new couple with naught but their chemises and each other.

The pillared bed brooded in the corner, its linens freshly folded, its pillows plumped, its curtains tied back. Brianna eyed the bed, half certain it knew more of what would transpire here than she.

"Are you frightened?" Luc asked softly.

Brianna glanced back to find his arms folded across his chest, his eyes brilliant blue, his expression thoughtful. She forced a smile. "A little."

Luc closed the distance between them with a single step. Just the heat of him so close beside her was reassuring. He lifted her hand in his, standing close but not touching her, ensuring that Brianna did not feel cornered by him.

"There is naught to fear," he whispered and pressed a kiss into her palm. "We shall proceed slowly and you have but to say that we must stop." Brianna watched him, breathless, and caught her breath when he glanced up suddenly. "Did your dame tell you of this?"

Brianna shook her head hastily.

Luc's easy smile was soothing. "Then, I shall have to do so," he said easily, nodding to the bed before Brianna could think of what to ask him. " 'Twas your parents' bed?"

"My mother's pride." Brianna smiled in recollection. "A nuptial gift from her sire. And oh, how the servants cursed it!"

"Why?"

"As the keep was constructed, it had to be moved. My mother would sleep nowhere else, my father would only sleep with her and he insisted upon sleeping in the finest chamber of the keep.''

Brianna's smile widened. "First 'twas in the old hall, then in what is now the hall of this keep. Then onto the first floor, then finally, here.''

She met Luc's gaze and her lips twisted. '' 'Twas said there was a merry celebration in the kitchens on the night my mother deemed its location in this room precisely right.''

"I can well imagine.'' Luc chuckled and lifted strong hands to the pins in Brianna's hair. He released her braid more gently than Fenella oft did and set to untying the lace. Brianna watched him as he worked, taking advantage of the moment to study his features etched golden in the light of the lantern.

"Your hair is long,'' he mused. "You must not cut it often.''

"Nay.'' Brianna shook her head. "Fenella trims the ends once in a while.'' She watched Luc set the lace aside, his strong fingers making quick work of unfurling her braid. He spread her hair across his fingers and shook his head.

"The color of it is a marvel,'' he whispered, flicking a glance her way. The admiration in his eyes stole Brianna's breath away. "Look how it snares the light!'' Luc spread her hair across his hands and Brianna looked in turn at the golden glints dancing within it. "I have never seen the like of it.''

"My mother's was the same hue.''

A smile pulled the corner of Luc's mouth and his steady gaze met Brianna's own. "Then 'tis no wonder your sire was allured by first sight of her. Your hair looks to have snared the sunlight.''

Brianna blinked and felt herself flush. "Were you so allured?''

Luc grinned. "Aye," he admitted, then sobered. "I had never seen the like of you, though 'twas the unexpectedness of your terms that caught my attention, not merely your flaxen tresses."

Brianna's heart pounded at this admission, her breath catching when Luc combed his fingers gently through her hair. " 'Tis so very soft," he whispered, his gaze falling suddenly to her lips. They tingled in recollection of his kisses, the heat simmering in his eyes making Brianna's knees weak. "Is all of you so very soft, my lady?"

"I do not know," she confessed breathlessly.

Luc bent and brushed his lips across her own. He paused a fingerspan away and arched his brow. "Soft," he concluded, then kissed the tip of her nose. "Definitely soft."

Brianna giggled at his whimsy, his lips moving across her cheek. "Very soft," he murmured and she closed her eyes when his breath fanned her temple. "Ah! Perfectly soft."

Luc's hands fell on Brianna's waist, his chest was before her. She took a deep breath, liking well the clean masculine scent of Luc's skin. He nibbled on her ear and she gasped at the murmur of his words.

"Too soft to be wrought of flesh," he whispered, then looked to her eyes again. "Could you truly be a fairy queen?"

Brianna laughed aloud, liking well that he took pains to reassure her. "Not I!"

"Good." Luc feigned relief. "I would not want to awaken trapped in a barrow or some such dire fate."

Brianna frowned, wanting to know more of what would transpire this night. She pleated the linen of Luc's chemise with unsteady fingers, knowing that if she but asked the question, he would answer her honestly.

He waited in silent stillness, his heat close beside her, demanding naught.

"One hears whispers in chambers, Luc," Brianna began, then her words faltered and she looked to his eyes, unable to hide her fear. "Will this hurt?"

Luc's gaze was sombre. "Perhaps this once, perhaps twice or thrice." He shook his head and ran fingertips along her jaw. " 'Tis impossible to know in advance." Brianna felt a shiver slide over her skin.

"But know this, my lady," Luc continued, tipping her chin with gentle resolve. He bent toward her, his eyes gleaming, as though he would persuade her of all he said. "I shall endeavor that it does not hurt at all."

Brianna managed a tremulous smile. "Do you pledge it to me?"

Luc grinned, but his eyes shone. "Aye! 'Tis pleasure we can give each other here and pleasure alone that has a place in this bed." He leaned down to gently kiss her lips, his caress as light as a butterfly. "Trust me," he whispered. "Brianna."

Because she did trust him, because his very certainty was reassuring, Brianna did not hesitate. She slipped her arms around his neck and flicked a glance through her lashes to her husband. "I like when you say my name," she confessed.

Luc grinned, his hands bracketing the back of her waist. "Who am I to decline your will?" he teased, then winked. "Brianna," he whispered, his breath launching an army of tingles across her skin. Luc trailed kisses along Brianna's jaw, punctuating each with her name.

He kissed her temple, her forehead, the tip of her nose, her very eyelids, as though he could not get enough of the taste of her flesh. Each kiss was marked with Luc's murmur of her name. He was so gentle, so tender, his every touch awakened those tingles that Brianna had come to associate with him.

"But Luc, I do not know what to do," Brianna protested.

"You have naught to do," Luc whispered into her ear. He teased her lobe with the tip of his tongue and Brianna shivered in delight. "Naught to do, my Brianna, but enjoy."

'Twould clearly be an easy task to fill. Luc traced circles on the back of her waist with his thumbs, he tormented her with tiny kisses everywhere but upon her lips. She ached to taste him again. She found her hands winding into the thickness of his hair, her nipples tightened when his breath fanned into her ear.

He eased her chemise from her shoulder, his path of kisses meandering along her shoulder, her collar bone, the hollow at the base of her throat. Brianna leaned back in the strength of his embrace as heat coursed through her. Luc's hand rose from her waist to cup the fullness of her breast.

Brianna gasped, instinctively loving the sensation of his strength against her softness. He bent lower and kissed the curve of that breast, the heat of his mouth closing over her taut nipple. Brianna cried out at the passion that simple touch unfurled. She clutched the corded strength of Luc's neck, she pressed kisses to his shoulder.

Just when she thought she could bear no more, Luc straightened. He merely uttered the words "soft indeed," before claiming her lips.

Brianna surged against him, opening her mouth to his caress and surrendering all to his glorious touch. She was not certain precisely what 'twas she desired, but she knew that this man would grant it to her. Brianna kissed Luc as deeply as he kissed her. She deliberately copied the way he teased her with his tongue and was delighted when his embrace became more urgent.

Luc swept Brianna into his arms, never lifting his lips from hers and carried her to the bed. No sooner was Brianna stretched across the mattress, Luc long and lean beside her, than his fingers began to work the lace from her chemise. When her breasts were bare to the chill of the room, he lifted his lips from hers, his gaze smouldering as he glanced over her nudity.

Brianna raised her hand shyly to cover herself, but Luc captured it within his. He kissed her palm, his sapphire gaze meeting hers. "You are beautiful, my lady," he whispered, his tone leaving no doubt of his sincerity. "More beautiful than any mere fairy queen."

As she watched, Luc cupped her breast in the strength of his hand, sliding his thumb deliberately across the nipple. "Still fearful?" he asked, his gaze insistent.

Brianna shook her head. "I have never felt this way," she admitted breathlessly.

Luc arched a brow, his eyes twinkling. "Dare I hope that is good?"

Brianna smiled. "Aye!"

Luc's crooked grin warmed her to her toes. "Good."

Then he bent and kissed her nipple again.

When his tongue began to work its magic there, Brianna was nigh certain she would swoon with delight. She arched with pleasure and cried out as Luc suckled and teased. He leisurely turned his attention to the other breast, lavishing his touch upon it in turn. Brianna had never felt aware of ever fiber of her being before.

Luc's hand slipped below the hem of her chemise, as he lifted his head to taste her lips once more. The heat of his fingers rose, dancing along Brianna's inner thighs with tantalizing slowness. She guessed his intent, remembering well how he had pleasured her thus before and parted her legs willingly.

And he touched her there once again, his teasing fingers awakening the heat within Brianna. He caressed and cajoled,

he teased and toyed, he tempted her until she thought she
could bear no more.

Brianna writhed beneath his embrace, but Luc granted her
no quarter, driving the heat beneath her flesh to a crescendo,
then demanding she climb yet more. Brianna twisted and
turned and arched her back. She was certain she could bear
no more.

But Luc persisted and the heat rose yet further. Brianna
twisted anew, she writhed against the great bed. She knew
she could not escape his teasing touch.

'Twas that certainty that drove her over the edge. Brianna
cried out as the tide surged through her. She shouted Luc's
name and could not stop herself from trembling from head
to toe.

Brianna opened her eyes to find her husband watching
her, his strong arm wrapped beneath her shoulders as he
leaned over her. Luc unable to hide his smile of satisfaction.
"You were pleased?"

"You!" Brianna gasped, not even trying to disguise her
pleasure. " 'Twas even more than before!"

Luc chuckled. "Is that so?" he mused playfully. "Then,
we must ensure you climb even higher the next time."

Brianna giggled at his determination, then fell silent when
he abruptly sat up. Luc doffed his chemise and cast it aside,
the lantern light making the golden hue of his tan gleam.

She swallowed, unable to halt her curious survey. Luc
seemed amused and Brianna felt herself flush. "I have never
seen a man nude."

"Then, look." Luc paused, granting Brianna the opportunity to satisfy her curiosity, then slowly stretched out beside
her again.

The sight of his lean strength sent a feminine thrill
through Brianna. Luc was so differently wrought than she,
all sinew and strength. She ran a hand over his shoulder and

down to his elbow, intrigued that his flesh was so different from her own. Even the hair that graced his forearm was stiffer.

Emboldened by his patience, Brianna let her fingertips pass over his flat nipple and slide into the wiry pelt of dark hair upon his chest. She found his heartbeat, noted its accelerated pace, and looked to his eyes. Luc smiled encouragement, as though acknowledging her effect upon him.

Brianna found that most pleasing. She nibbled her lip and traced a path to Luc's navel, where the hair tapered to a point, then looked beyond.

Her gaze danced back to meet the humor in Luc's blue eyes. "Is it always like that?"

Luc shook his head solemnly. "Only when a certain princess kisses me," he teased. He took her fingertips and placed them over his heartbeat once more. "This, too, quickens in her very presence."

Brianna held his gaze for a long moment, vastly reassured that she was not the only one whose body reacted so strongly to another's presence.

Then, still curious, she reached down and touched Luc's erection tentatively. It rose beneath her touch and Brianna hastily drew her hand away.

Luc chuckled.

" 'Tis not amusing. I have never seen the like before!" she protested, her cheeks flaming.

Luc grinned wickedly and rolled her to her back. "Ah," he breathed, "the words every man longs to hear on his wedding night."

And he captured Brianna's lips with a kiss that swallowed her laughter. His erection nudged against her thigh and Brianna caught her breath in understanding of where that strength must go.

Aye, she had walked the pastures in the spring and had seen animals about their business.

But she trusted her spouse. Luc laced their fingers together and stretched Brianna's arms over her head. He propped his weight up on his elbows, his chest a finger's breadth from her own.

Then, Luc looked directly into Brianna's eyes.

"Tell me if it hurts," he counselled so solemnly that Brianna knew he would stop if she made the barest sound.

"I will." Brianna felt Luc's strength nudge against her. She held her breath, she braced for the worst.

But no more than a heartbeat later, she felt only a faint twinge. Luc's heat slipped into her as though she was wrought for him alone. Brianna sighed with satisfaction as he surged to fill her completely.

"Brianna?"

Brianna smiled as she met the concern in Luc's blue, blue eyes and stretched to press a kiss to his tightened jaw. "I am yours," she whispered, unable to look away from his bright gaze. "All yours."

Aye, there was nowhere else she wanted to be. Brianna was cosseted within the circle of her husband's embrace. She was secure, she was safe, she was warm.

A shudder rippled through Luc's muscles at her words, then he began to move with a powerful grace. The feeling was like no other, yet 'twas exhilarating beyond all. Brianna immediately sensed that this was the completion for which she had yearned.

Luc's scent inundated her, his strength surrounded her, his hardness rubbed against the pearl he had awakened earlier. With surprising speed, Brianna felt her passion rising again. She lifted herself against Luc in silent demand and clutched his broad shoulders.

They moved together in perfect harmony, the heat rising

between and within them. Yet again, Luc pushed Brianna further, yet again the heat fired through her veins.

Yet again, she tasted the very stars. Brianna called out just as Luc bellowed her name.

The heat of Luc's seed spilled within her. She smiled at the featherlight kiss he bestowed upon her ear. And then, Brianna drifted to sleep as she had once before.

• • •

BRIANNA AWAKENED WITH the strength of Luc pressed against her back. The chamber was darker, two of the lanterns gutted. She felt Luc's erection against her buttocks and stretched languidly when his hand cupped her breast. Brianna could not help but arch against Luc's strength when his hands roved over her and he chuckled against her ear.

"Tired?"

"Nay."

Luc's hand drifted lower and Brianna sighed with delight. "Sore?"

She smiled over her shoulder at him. "Nay."

Luc's slow smile melted her heart. "You are so tiny," he mused. "I feared you would be hurt."

Brianna lifted a hand to his jaw, wanting only to reassure him. "You were gentle, indeed."

Their gazes met and held for a breathless moment, then Luc's fingers danced down the length of Brianna once more. "You are overdressed," he observed and Brianna could not help but chuckle at the tangle left of her chemise. She sat up, well aware of her husband's appreciative gaze, pulled it over her head and cast it aside.

"Better?"

A gleam lit Luc's eye and his brows rose in comic alarm. "Why, you still wear your stockings!" He clicked his tongue in a mimicry of Uther's disapproval. "They will be ruined, my lady, if you wear them to bed."

Brianna had but a moment to guess Luc's intent before he dove for the foot of the bed. She gasped at the heat of his breath upon her thighs, then felt the brush of his teeth against her knees. Luc lifted her leg and took care to kiss the back of her knees most thoroughly.

"Luc!" His touch tickled mercilessly, even as it heated her flesh anew. When he untied her garters with his teeth, his eyes glinting dangerously all the while, Brianna shivered. Luc's strong fingers eased down her stockings. The warmth of his palm slid over her skin in the wake of each stocking removed.

And those deliberate kisses heated Brianna once again. Luc sampled her calves, tasted her ankles, kissed each toe in turn. He caressed her instep, the firm sweep of his thumb there enough to make Brianna's bones melt.

His hands lay claim to her knees, kisses and hands easing over her thighs, as he crawled back toward the pillows. Luc ran his tongue over Brianna, his teeth, his lips, and his fingertips, changing from one to the next so quickly and persuasively that Brianna was aware of naught but his touch.

She reached for him as Luc drew near the pillows but only caught the flash of his smile as he evaded her touch. Brianna frowned in confusion. She eyed the broad strength of Luc's shoulders, the snow and ebony of his hair, and the deep sapphire of his eyes, then felt his hands lay claim to her buttocks.

Then, the wet heat of Luc's tongue slipped through the nest at the apex of her thighs and laved the secret spot he had caressed once before.

Brianna lay back against the linens with a gasp, realizing she had much to learn of the pleasures they might share within this bed. She smiled, even as Luc awakened her passion, loving that her new spouse was so intent on ensuring she learned with all haste.

Chapter Seventeen

THE MORNING LIGHT WAS FALLING INTO THE SOLAR, cast into bands of light and shadow by the shutters, when Luc awakened again. He watched the marvel slumbering in his arms and felt himself smile. Indeed, the lady embraced every facet of life with the same unbridled passion.

And Luc liked that trait well indeed. His gaze traced the gracious sweep of Brianna's jaw, the ripe curve of her lip, the golden splay of her lashes upon her ivory cheek.

A single unwelcome thought dismissed Luc's sense of well-being. He leaned back and frowned at the canopy, irritated anew by the uncertainty of who had been Father Padraig's accomplice. Whose voice had he heard in the stables?

Luc's determination to protect Brianna redoubled in the wake of the night they had shared and he feared anew that this unknown accomplice might see fit to harm her. But he had made no progress in solving the puzzle any further these past days and was loathe to linger at Tullymullagh where danger could lurk at any turn.

There was but one course to follow. They must leave Tullymullagh, Luc and Brianna alone, in order to ensure her safety. They might well leave trouble behind or trouble might abandon the keep in their absence.

But in each other's company alone, Luc could be certain of the lady's security without trying to watch hundreds of souls he did not truly know.

But Brianna must know naught of Luc's fears. He did not want to frighten her with a threat that might not materialize.

Ah! Luc smiled as the perfect solution slid into his thoughts. He would take Brianna to Llanvelyn with all haste. There were matters to be resolved there, at any rate, and Luc knew full well that there would be no danger to the lady at the remote estate. And there he knew every man, woman, and child.

'Twas perfect.

• • •

BRIANNA AWAKENED, NESTLED against Luc, the length of his legs entangled with her own. He lay on his back, his arm held her against his side. Brianna stretched and opened her eyes to find Luc watching her. He smiled when he saw she had awakened, but Brianna had already noted his fleeting frown.

"Is something amiss?"

Luc pursed his lips. "Not truly. I was but thinking."

"Of what?"

His blue gaze slid to meet hers. "Of Llanvelyn."

Brianna sat up abruptly, her hair spilling over her shoulders. A lump of dread rose in her throat, for she knew that Luc himself had confessed he had only come to Tullymullagh to win that estate in full. "What of Llanvelyn?"

Luc shrugged. "There is no steward there. I did not appoint one after Pyrs died, but merely filled the task myself." He eyed her carefully, as though choosing his words, his hand caressing the small of her back. "What would you think if we went there?"

Brianna swallowed and fought against her impulsive response. "To live?"

Luc shook his head so quickly that she was relieved.
"Nay!" He flicked a playful fingertip across the tip of her
nose and smiled with affection. "You look dismayed at the
very prospect."

Brianna flushed slightly. "I thought perhaps you did not
want to administer Tullymullagh." She traced the outline of
his hand lying against the linens between them. "I thought it
might not suit your conviction to leave the noble life behind."

"Ah, well, 'twas eleven long years ago I made that
choice."

"Then, you are pleased to hold Tullymullagh?"

Luc nodded solemnly. "Aye, 'tis a fine holding."

Brianna smiled. "You hesitated when your father summoned you. I thought perhaps you would decline."

Luc rolled his eyes. "I but considered the wisdom of
pledging fealty to him."

"Did you not before?"

"Nay. Though effectively, I was his vassal, for I adminis-
tered Llanvelyn in his stead. In truth, the responsibility is
not much different, though Tullymullagh is certainly larger
and more complex." He lifted a hand to her cheek and
smiled. "I can well understand that you would want your
father's holding free of Gavin's immediate grip."

"He must think you will obey his bidding."

Luc grimaced, then grinned ruefully. "Gavin must know
better than that, after all these years."

Brianna had to have all clear between them. She leaned
closer and tapped a finger on the mattress. "But you told me
that you made a pledge when Tyrell died."

"A pledge that accepting this seal does not challenge,"
Luc argued with resolve. "A man with his wits about him
can learn much in eleven years and should have the grace to
admit when he has erred. I cannot flee what I am, I cannot

hide from my own ambitions. I admired Tullymullagh from first sight and since coming here, I have learned that there is another role of leadership beyond that of both my father and Tyrell's father.''

Brianna dared to meet Luc's eyes, only to find sincerity gleaming there.

''Your own father,'' he said firmly, ''was a shining example of how a nobleman might lead his life with honor and treat his villeins justly. I would follow his example alone. 'Tis a grand legacy he has left Tullymullagh and one I would see continue.''

Brianna smiled in her reassurance. ''Then why go to Llanvelyn at all?''

Luc shrugged, his gaze flicking away from her own. ''I simply must see matters in order if we are to make Tullymullagh our residence,'' he said stiffly and Brianna sensed that this was not all of the tale. ''Llanvelyn has need of a steward, at least.''

''Will Gavin not see to such concerns?''

Luc snorted. ''Not he!'' He caught her hand and kissed her fingertips. ''Brianna, I am not one to leave a task half finished.'' Luc's voice dropped low, his eyes were solemn. ''I but ask you to indulge me in this one detail, my lady fair.''

Brianna's breath caught. How could she refuse him when he had already done so much to assure her happiness?

But still she would tease him, much as he teased her. ''Perhaps!'' she said archly. ''But what reward shall be mine for such indulgence?''

She liked how her words put that wicked twinkle in his eyes. ''Fear not, Brianna, I shall make the concession worth your while,'' Luc growled, then tickled her until she squealed. Brianna squirmed and tried to tickle him in turn, but without success. She laughed, she struggled, and they rolled back and forth across the great bed.

Until finally, Luc had her cornered against one of the heavy posts. Brianna tossed her hair and folded her arms across her chest, keeping a wary eye on his mischievous fingers. "How long shall we be gone?" she asked with a defiant tilt of her chin.

Luc shrugged. "With all likelihood, for the winter's duration. The foul weather draws near, after all." He regarded her with a slow smile that heated her very blood. "But how, my lady, will we ensure we keep warm?" Luc arched a dark brow and Brianna thought of a dozen ways before more immediate concerns stilled her smile.

Brianna gripped Luc's arm. "But what of Fenella?" Luc's eyes narrowed in consideration as she voiced her worries. "If Dermot spurns Fenella and her father casts her out, she might be round with child by the spring." She raised her gaze to Luc's. "What if her father comes while we are gone? Luc, he might beat her!"

Luc's lips set grimly. "No woman shall be beaten within this hall." He grasped Brianna's shoulders and looked into her eyes with determination. "Fenella is entrusted to the care of Tullymullagh, leaving her as our responsibility. If Dermot spurns her and her father casts her out, we shall ensure her welfare. I promise you as much."

"Then we will not go?"

Luc frowned, then rolled quickly from the bed. He restlessly paced the width of the room and back. Brianna's heart sank at the evidence of how desperately Luc wanted to return to his Llanvelyn. Would he ever be truly content at Tullymullagh?

"How far is it to Fenella's father's holding?"

Brianna struggled to recall. "A week's ride, perhaps a day or two longer."

"And what manner of man is Fenella's sire?"

Brianna shrugged. "I do not know him well enough to say. He is a distant cousin—I daresay my father knew his character better than I."

Luc frowned out the window for a long moment, then flicked a piercing glance her way. His words were terse. "We shall await his arrival, to see your concerns set at ease. I would not have you worry for her all the winter long." Luc nodded quickly. "Indeed, 'twill grant us time to see all set to rights here at Tullymullagh before we leave."

There was a rap at the door and Luc dove back for the warmth of the bed. "They come for the linens." Brianna gasped, sneaking a glance to ensure all was in order.

The dark stain of her maidenhead was more than clear.

"Ah, but *who* comes to gather the evidence?" Luc jested, his playful manner restored as he cuddled Brianna against his side. His protectiveness made her feel less self-conscious about this necessary rite and she was glad he ensured they faced the scrutiny of the household together.

"Gavin," Brianna whispered with certainty, pulling the linens over her bare breasts. "He wants to ensure your prize is truly won."

"Nay, 'tis Uther," Luc argued with conviction. "He wants to see with his own eyes that his lord's daughter is not shamed." He scooped his chemise from the floor and eased it over her shoulders, fastening the tie with quick fingers. His hand paused against her jaw, and their gazes clung in recollection of the night they had shared.

It truly had been a wedding night worthy of a bard's tale, to Brianna's thinking.

"I do not think she is," Brianna said breathlessly.

Luc smiled slowly, then bent closer. "Good," he whispered against her lips, then kissed her once again.

Another rap sounded and Luc lifted his lips reluctantly,

then arched a brow. His sapphire eyes glinted dangerously. "Shall we make a wager, my lady, on who crosses the threshold first?"

Brianna laughed in delight at this unexpected suggestion. She guessed well enough that even losing would be no loss. "Aye!" she agreed and poked a finger in Luc's chest. "Winner names the terms."

Luc's eyes widened, his grin flashed, then he turned to face the portal. "Enter!" he bellowed and the door was opened immediately.

Both men were there, both clearly anxious to see the truth. Uther would have stepped across the threshold, but Gavin dug his elbow into the other man's ribs with resolve and forced his way into the solar first. His expression was triumphant, but his rough manner launched a tremor of fear within Brianna.

For she recalled well enough that Luc's long-ago pledge was to never take a blade within his grip again. What if another like Gavin came to Tullymullagh's gates in the years ahead? Would Tullymullagh be captured anew?

And would all be resolved so satisfactorily as it had this time? Brianna could not believe the fates would smile so benevolently upon her again.

She swallowed and realized she could only hope that Luc would come to change his thinking. Perhaps he would come to take not only the peaceful life of the nobility once more, but resume the responsibility of war.

But then, Brianna knew well enough what pride the man put in keeping his pledge.

• • •

THE DAYS PASSED quickly at Tullymullagh, despite Luc's impatience to be gone. Indeed, there was much to do. Brother Thomas, his priest, and the prior returned to Endlist in short order, and Luc ensured they went with an endowment for the monk's aid in recent matters. The prior murmured that he would ensure Father Padraig was buried quietly in unconsecrated ground. A new priest arrived, a markedly more cheerful sort than Father Padraig, and Luc was pleased that the villagers accepted him so readily.

Ruarke sank into a corner of the hall and settled to making a considerable dint in the wine stores of Tullymullagh. He played the jilted and dissatisfied suitor to the extreme, but Luc noted that Brianna had no time for the knight at all.

He rather liked that.

Rowan went on his way on the same day his jongleurs moved on, the two brothers sharing a moment before they parted again. Gavin returned to France and, no doubt, Margaux's demands.

In truth, Luc breathed a sigh of relief when his father departed, for he could not completely shake his suspicion that Gavin knew more of Connor's death than he told. 'Twas no doubt only the brutality of the murder that made Luc's thoughts run in that direction, but he waved a hearty farewell to both Gavin and his troupe of mercenaries.

Brianna set to her duties as lady of the keep with diligence. Indeed, she had laid claim to many of the keys and those in the kitchens had developed a hearty respect for her inventories. The woman forgot little and Luc could see the admiration all within Tullymullagh's environs had for Connor's daughter.

Indeed, he felt no small measure of it himself. With each day that passed, Luc found himself seeking the lady's company more and more, and he savored each of her victories as his own. He showed Brianna a trick with the addition of the accounts that vastly increased her speed with sums and earned him a sound kiss for his aid.

Aye, though Brianna came late to the duties of administration, she had a keen intellect and learned at fearsome speed.

Luc teased Brianna one night that she would soon have no need of him at all. When the sparkle of her laughter filled the air, Luc scooped her up and carted her to the solar, much to the amusement of all in the hall.

And then, he had made her moan with delight, taking great pleasure in proving to her one deed for which he could not be replaced.

Luc and Uther set a court for Tuesdays, the issues of short gallons and stolen pigs and missing measures of flour not unlike the disputes Luc regularly settled at Llanvelyn. Brianna sat beside Luc, at his request, for she knew better than he what the custom of Tullymullagh had been. Luc appointed Matthew Miller as reeve, for that man seemed to have the respect of many in the village and Brianna thought well of him.

Luc and Brianna took alms to the poor together twice weekly and visited the sick and weakened midweek. Luc knew that another from the keep could have accompanied his wife on these duties long considered the domain of womenfolk, but he enjoyed watching her. Indeed, 'twas a good opportunity to meet his tenants, as well.

And Luc took time to visit a certain destrier, to brush that steed's coat until it gleamed and to ride Raphael several times a week. Aye, were it not for a threat he feared yet lingered within Tullymullagh's walls, Luc would have been content to remain there for all time.

• • •

ON FIRST ADVENT, Fenella's sire came riding out of the hills and Brianna feared the worst.

"Daughter!" he roared before he even had dismounted. "Show yourself, Fenella, and make an accounting of your deeds!"

Brianna fled the kitchens only to find Luc already striding across the bailey, his expression grim. The entire household spilled into the bailey, their eyes wide at the spectacle. Indeed, Brianna was glad of Luc's early arrival, for her cousin's entry made her fear for Fenella's hide.

But Fenella held up her chin, though her features were pale. "I am here!"

"Is it true that you have granted your maidenhead before the grace of nuptials?"

"Aye!" The maid blushed fearsomely at her own admission.

Fenella's sire snorted. "And are you with child?" he shouted. He was a portly man, more aged than Connor had been, his hair as white as snow and his face ruddy.

Fenella tossed her hair. "Nay."

"Praise be for small mercies." Her father dismounted and cast aside his reins, a squire hastening to catch them. "At least there is naught for the gossips to gnaw upon." Fenella's face fell.

Luc stepped forward. "Are you Fenella's sire?"

"Aye."

"What do you intend to do?"

Fenella's father glowered at Luc. "Who are you to question my intent? She is my daughter alone and her future is mine to assure."

Luc folded his arms across his chest. "I am Lord of Tullymullagh, and this maid is consigned to my protection. She will not be beaten within these walls and she will not leave them before I am certain her safety is assured."

Fenella's father harumphed. "So, 'tis you who wed Connor's daughter."

"Aye," Luc said smoothly. "I am Luc, now of Tullymullagh."

The older man eyed the occupants of the bailey and seemed to swallow his anger.

" 'Tis good," Luc continued with a politeness that was

doubtless deliberate, "to make the acquaintance of my wife's cousin."

"Likewise, I am certain." Fenella's father looked sternly to his daughter. "Would that it had been under less dire circumstance. Have you a draught of ale in this place for a man who has ridden long and hard?"

"Of course. Perhaps we might discuss your daughter's prospects in the hall?" Luc gestured to the portal and Brianna sent servants scattering to make all ready.

Fenella's father harumphed and stomped into the hall behind Luc, a wave of chatter erupting behind them. The pair finally sat opposite each other in the hall, Fenella lingering fearfully behind her father.

Brianna hovered behind Luc, hoping he would see her fears assured. She doubted that Fenella would see her way in this and hoped heartily that all would be well resolved.

Her cousin nodded acknowledgement of her presence, then lifted his chalice. The men saluted each other's health with formality and drank of the ale.

"Dermot came to you, then," Luc commented.

Brianna caught her breath as the older man glared at Luc. "Aye, that he did."

"And he told you all?"

Fenella's father snorted. "Aye, I know his sordid history well enough." He drummed a heavy fingertip on the board and his color deepened. "When first he rode beneath my portcullis, I must tell you that I was not inclined to welcome him. Nay, I remember well enough Ismay of Claremont's determination to wed this man and the ploy they two used to see their will achieved, despite her guardian's objection."

He harumphed and took another drink of the ale. " 'Twas no surprise when he confessed Fenella's circumstance, though truly I thought the girl a bit more keen of wit than that."

Fenella stiffened, but Brianna signalled her to silence. 'Twould serve naught if she angered her father now.

"I am surprised he is not with you," Luc said.

"Ha!" Fenella's father inhaled another measure of ale. "He had no such chance! 'Twas what took me so long," he declared. "I thought to test the lad."

"Test him?" Luc straightened slightly at this.

"Aye." The older man nodded vigorously. "I told him I would grant my holding to no man who could neither manage nor defend it. I cast him to my knights."

Fenella's eyes went round. "Father, you did not!"

"I most certainly did. And to his credit, he not only survived but learned much." Fenella sagged in relief, but her father shook a finger in her direction. "You may be assured that the man you sent me is not the one who awaits you."

"But—"

"But *naught*! I will make a man of honor of him, if 'tis the last deed I do on this earth."

"But Father, you cannot treat him so poorly! 'Tis unfair!"

The older man turned smoothly to regard his outraged daughter. "Unfair? How is it unfair that I would see you well-wed, well-matched, and with a man by your side upon whom you may depend? God willing, you will have many years without me, Fenella, and 'tis my duty to see you secure." He scowled, taking in the entire hall with his disapproving glare. "And what have you told this new lord of me, that he assumes I shall beat you for your folly?"

Fenella flushed. "Naught, Father."

He poked a finger through the air to his daughter. "Have I ever laid a hand upon you?"

Fenella shook her head. "Nay, Father." She winced. "Though you oft bellow most fearsomely."

"Ha." Her father took another swallow of ale, his gaze

turning upon Luc once more. "And can a man be blamed for that when women addle his wits all the day long?"

Fenella took a hesitant step closer.

Luc cleared his throat, evidently noting her uncertainty and guessing the question she would ask. "What of Dermot?"

"He will make a fitting enough groom," her father conceded gruffly.

Fenella caught her breath. "Truly?"

"Truly. The priest makes ready for the exchange of your vows and your mother—" he rolled his eyes "—nigh drives me mad with her fussing about. Dermot is not the man I might have picked, but you have chosen him and he will have to do."

"Oh, Father!"

That man eyed his daughter when she hesitated a half dozen steps away from him. "You have grown to a woman within Tullymullagh's walls," he said unevenly. "And now you are to be a bride." He opened his arms. "Come here, Fenella, and let me look upon you."

Fenella burst into tears in her relief. She ran into her father's embrace. He held her close and closed his eyes as he laid his cheek against hers. "Fear not, child of mine, I have no intent of dying before I deem Dermot a fitting heir to me and suitable husband for you."

Luc cleared his throat pointedly and Fenella's father looked to him over his daughter's dark hair. "You have naught to fear, Luc of Tullymullagh," he declared somberly. "You have my pledge that this woman shall not be bruised, however foolish she has been. She is my daughter and my pride, and this we shall see resolved together."

And he offered Luc his hand.

The men shook hands solemnly, sealing an agreement between men of honor, and the entire household sagged with relief.

Brianna bit her lip, her own tears rising that all had been resolved in the end. Dermot must truly love Fenella to have endured her father's testing. It could only be a good prospect for their future.

Luc rose from the board, leaving the two to their reunion and came to Brianna's side. "Tears?" He eased one away with a fingertip and smiled. "Do not tell me you wanted a different resolution than this one?"

"You!" Brianna took a deep breath and leaned against him, looking up into his eyes. "I thank you for this."

Luc's crooked smile warmed Brianna's heart and she loved the weight of his arm around her waist. "I am not a man to shirk a responsibility," he declared, then flicked a fingertip across the tip of her nose. "Nor one to miss an opportunity to make my lady smile."

Brianna did smile, knowing 'twas her turn to ease Luc's concerns. "There is naught keeping us from Llanvelyn now," she reminded softly and Luc nodded.

"Shall we leave on the morrow?"

"Aye." Brianna nodded agreement. "But there is something I must retrieve in the morn before we depart." Luc looked puzzled, but Brianna squeezed his fingertips. "Letters from my mother, written to my father before they were wed."

Luc smiled down at her. "And a precious legacy they must be to you. Of course, we shall not leave without them."

• • •

IN THE MORNING, Brianna led Luc to the side of her dame's sarcophagus with hasty steps. She checked that none was about, then dropped quickly to one knee. Luc followed suit, his brow furrowed in a frown, though he said naught.

Brianna scrabbled with her fingers to remove the one loose stone—the one that did not appear loose—and as soon as Luc saw what she did, he finished the deed. His gloved hands were so much stronger than her own that the stone was quickly removed.

And the metal box was securely in Brianna's grip once more. She bit her lip with her relief, then handed it to her spouse. "Will you carry it for me?"

"If you prefer." Brianna nodded at his inquiring glance, not trusting herself to ensure the safety of the treasure. Luc smiled, accepted the box, and slipped it into the pouch secured beneath his tabard.

'Twas there he had secreted all their coin for the voyage and Brianna liked very much that Luc considered her mother's letters as much of a valuable. He shifted his tabard and cloak, then arched a dark brow at Brianna.

"It cannot be discerned," she confirmed and Luc captured her hand securely within his own.

A sound carried from the stables and Brianna caught her breath, feigning that she prayed while with shaking fingers she tried to replace the stone.

Luc covered her hand with his own and smoothly managed the deed, his low voice murmuring the paternoster beside her ear. Their gazes met and held for a charged moment, then Brianna folded her hands around Luc's own.

When they finished, Luc helped her to her feet, then led her toward the stables. Denis was there, his squires busily tending a pair of palfreys while the ostler murmured to none other than the destrier Raphael.

Brianna looked to her spouse in surprise, but Luc strode to the steed's side and took a brush in hand. "He looks anxious to run, Denis."

"As always, my lord. He seems to sense when you mean to ride him."

Brianna blinked. "You have ridden him since the day you went to Endlist?"

Luc grinned. "Aye, a man must occupy himself while his wife tallies the accounts."

"You! I labored while you played!"

Luc chuckled and winked at Denis. "The lady clearly has not brushed down a steed so large nor cleaned his hooves of mire."

The ostler nodded approvingly. "A solid few hours of labor, my lady, of that you may be certain." He beamed at the destrier. "But such attention has made all the difference to this one."

Raphael, apparently knowing he was being discussed, snorted and stamped his foot. He fixed Luc with an expectant glance and tossed his head. When Denis reached for his bridle, though, the stallion danced away from the ostler with a disdainful flick of his tail.

Luc chuckled and grasped those reins, urging the steed to his side. "Always one to challenge expectation, are you not?" he murmured to the beast. Luc rubbed Raphael's ears and the horse nuzzled his neck with obvious affection. "But when it matters, such a noble creature can be relied upon. I have missed his ilk, Denis."

Raphael tossed his head as though he would agree with the sentiment. Dozens of tiny silver bells fastened to his harness rang at his move. 'Twas clear the beast was delighted with his appearance, for there was a gleam in his eye.

Brianna watched Luc check the steed's harness, gentleness in his every move, and listened as he murmured to the beast. And as she stood in the sun-flecked interior of the stables, a simple truth echoed in her heart.

She loved this man. She loved his gentleness and his strength, she loved his concern and his protectiveness. Indeed, she knew she could rely upon his integrity, just as she knew he would occasionally challenge her expectation.

Luc Fitzgavin had sworn a pledge, after all, to win Brianna's heart, and she smiled with the certainty that once again, he had kept his word.

Luc's eyes were deeply blue as he turned to Brianna and lifted his gloved hand to her. Not for the first time, she had the sense that he could read the secrets of her very heart.

But this time, Brianna did not care. She held his gaze and smiled.

"My lady, shall we ride together?"

Brianna accepted Luc's aid, liking how his hands fitted securely around her waist. "Perhaps," he murmured against her temple, "you might be so kind as to remind me to fetch my spurs while we are at Llanvelyn."

Brianna pulled back to meet his eyes. "You yet have them?"

"Of course!" He glanced significantly to the destrier. "And I shall have need of them to ride this feisty steed."

Brianna tapped his shoulder with resolve. "If your spurs are there, then we shall retrieve your mail, as well. I do not like you travelling without such protection."

But Luc chuckled easily at her concern. "I think, Denis, the lady means to keep me."

The ostler chortled in turn. Luc kissed Brianna's brow, as though unable to resist the opportunity, then lifted her to the fore of his saddle. "Luc, I am most serious."

"I know." But a moment later, Luc's warmth was fast behind her, his arm around her waist, his muscled thigh against her own, his breath in her hair. "Fear not," he whispered against her hood, "you will have the leisure of ensuring all you desire from Llanvelyn comes to Tullymullagh for our return."

And Brianna had to be satisfied with that.

The destrier was exultant and clearly impatient to be on his way. Luc and Denis made short work of looping the reins of the two palfreys to Raphael's saddle, then the trio of steeds pranced into the chill of the bailey. Brianna was delighted to find so many roused so early, all evidently intent on waving farewell.

"I shall ensure all runs smoothly," Uther declared.

"I have no doubt," Luc countered, a thread of humor in his tone. His arm tightened around Brianna and he gave Raphael his heels. The first few flakes of snow tumbled from the pearly morning sky as Brianna left Tullymullagh for the first time in all her days.

But she was with Luc, and the love burning in her heart meant that her home was wherever that man might be. Brianna had found her one true love, where she had least expected he might be, precisely as she had always dreamed.

And now, all Brianna had to do was win Luc's heart for her own.

Though truly, the man treated her with such consideration that she dared to hope the deed was already well begun.

• • •

Two days later Brianna awoke when the first pink of the dawn stained the horizon. The light fanned through the shutters, painting the humble tavern chamber in rosy hues.

Brianna smiled as she nestled deeper against her husband's warmth. Luc breathed deeply and evenly, the rhythm of his heart steady beneath Brianna's ear. These days of each other's company had been a delight, the intimacy between the two growing by leaps and bounds without the distraction of obligations.

Brianna smiled, as she admitted once more that her husband had decided aright.

Knowing that they must be on their way to the ship soon, she eyed the confusion of their belongings and decided to surprise him. Brianna rolled from the heat of the bed with reluctance. She packed her few things quickly, then scanned the comparative order of Luc's possessions.

A church bell rang in the distance, surely for Matins.

But Luc only nuzzled the spot Brianna had vacated, sighed, and slumbered on. She resolved immediately to let him sleep yet longer, for the man had labored heroically the night before. Brianna bit back her grin and folded his chemise, laying aside the chausses Luc would surely wear on the ship that day.

Beneath the chausses was the satchel Luc wore beneath his tabard. Brianna could not resist the urge to check upon her dame's precious box. 'Twas there, as she had known it would be, but beside it lurked the sack Gavin had granted Luc at his investiture.

Curious, for she had never handled the seal of Tullymullagh, Brianna pulled out the sack. She slanted a glance to the sleeping Luc, then resolved it could harm little to look. She loosened the lace, dumped out the contents, and was stunned to find not one seal falling into her hand, but two.

One bore the familiar crest of Tullymullagh.

The other made Brianna's heart stop cold. She could not be certain, so she kneaded the red sealing wax also in the sack and pressed the seal deep into its softness. When Brianna regarded the imprint, she felt the blood drain from her face.

'Twas the seal of Llanvelyn Manor she held in her hand.

'Twas the very seal Luc swore he had come to Tullymullagh to make his own that he carried in his satchel, the seal that Gavin had denied him.

The seal Gavin had promised to grant Luc if he but went on Brianna's quest.

Win or lose.

Luc had refused that offer, Brianna had not wed Burke, yet now Luc had the seal.

Brianna's mouth went dry. Was her wedding the result of some wager between father and son? She could not believe it!

But she had to know the truth. Brianna launched herself across the room and shook Luc bodily awake. Surely the man would reassure her?

"When were you granted the seal of Llanvelyn?" she asked breathlessly when first Luc's eye opened.

"What?" Luc frowned, ran a hand through his hair, and regarded her as though she spoke in tongues. Brianna wagged the seal beneath his very nose until his eyes widened in recognition.

"You said your sire would not give it to you—you said he had broken his word," Brianna choked out the words, her tears rising in fear. "Gavin said he would grant it to you when Burke took my hand or when you went upon the quest. Luc! Is that why you took me to wife?"

Luc gave himself a visible shake. "Brianna, 'twas not like that. You have concluded wrongly." He reached for her shoulders, but Brianna danced away.

"Then why did he grant it to you?"

"I do not know! Why does the man do *anything*?" Luc frowned impatiently and sat up on the side of the bed. "Brianna! You make much of little. If you but grant me a chance to explain—"

"You have but one thing to explain," Brianna declared, her back against the most distant wall of the chamber. 'Twas clear she had her spouse's full attention for his eyes were deadly blue. "Did your sire grant you the seal of Llanvelyn in exchange for wedding me?"

Luc looked away. His lips drew thin, he swore softly, then

he turned his gaze upon Brianna. "I cannot guess his thinking."

A lump rose in Brianna's throat, for this was far from the reassurance she desired. "When did he grant it to you?"

Luc swore softly. "You must not make overmuch of this," he urged with a shake of his finger. "But when he granted me the seal of Tullymullagh, the seal of Llanvelyn was also enclosed."

"On the very day of our nuptials?"

"Aye."

Brianna frowned. "But you said naught to me. Why be secretive if you truly have naught to hide?"

Luc grimaced and shook his head. "I did not think it of import."

"Not of import!" Brianna was outraged by these words. "But, Luc, you said 'twas all you wanted!"

"I was wrong." Luc shrugged. "I felt naught when Gavin entrusted it to me." His sapphire gaze blazed into her own and his voice dropped low. "It did not matter. Brianna, I swear it to you, I did not wed you for Llanvelyn."

Brianna came within a hair's breadth of believing him. In truth, Luc had never lied to her and there was a sincerity shining in his gaze.

But there was one confession she needed to hear and it could wait no longer. But three words would make all come aright.

Brianna caught her breath and leaned closer, never breaking Luc's gaze, her grip tight on the seal. "Why *did* you wed me?" she asked unevenly. "You told me yourself that marriage was not for you. What compelled you to change your thinking?"

And for the first time since Brianna had known him, Luc Fitzgavin seemed at a loss for words. He stared at her, though not a word fell from his lips.

He was completely flummoxed by her question.

But Brianna knew full well what that meant. She felt her very heart rend in two. Luc could not pledge his love for her because he felt none.

And Luc told her no lies.

"Knave!" Brianna cried and flung Llanvelyn's seal in his very face. "I *loved* you! I granted you my all! I even believed that there was some tenderness lurking within your heart for me!"

Luc cast the seal he had instinctively caught aside. He came after her, nude, his eyes bright with determination. "Brianna, you must let me explain. . . ."

But she already knew he could not tell her what she wanted to hear. Brianna snatched up her small satchel, hating the weak tears that blurred her vision, and felt the anger drain from her voice.

"You and my father were right," she confessed softly. " 'Twas folly indeed to believe in the merit of love."

And Brianna pivoted toward the door.

"Brianna!" Luc roared, but Brianna was not going to stop. She darted from the chamber, slamming the door forcefully behind herself despite the hour. Hot tears plummeted down her cheeks, blurring her vision, but she clung to the wall and raced down the steps as quickly as she was able.

She had been such a fool!

Love was not to be hers, 'twas clear. She would return to Tullymullagh, for she had nowhere else to go, and there she would weep until she could weep no more.

Brianna heard Luc call from behind her and stumbled in haste down the last of the stairs. She knew she fled the traitorous yearning of her heart to return to Luc.

How could he care naught for her?

Brianna reached the street and nearly fell on the frosted

cobblestones. She righted herself and fled toward the shadows of the tavern's stable, intending to steal one of her own steeds.

But Brianna did not get that far. She barely rounded the corner of the house when someone snatched at her from a doorway.

Thieves!

A man's hand clamped over her mouth, another hand pinned her arms to her waist. Brianna struggled, to no avail, and belatedly wished she had been more cautious.

"And good morning to you, Lady Brianna," an appallingly familiar voice droned in her ear.

Brianna jumped and twisted—her captor was perfectly content to let her look. Her eyes widened in horror when that person smiled with cold malice.

And Brianna knew with dreadful certainty precisely who her father had met in the private chapel of Tullymullagh.

Just as she knew she would shortly share her sire's fate.

Chapter Eighteen

*L*UC SWORE WITH ENTHUSIASM. HE STRUGGLED TO get into his chausses and boots, but every article of clothing seemed to fight his intent. His mind was yet fogged with sleep; his chemise was completely unhelpful.

And his wife was gone.

Luc fought to get the satchel around his neck and sling his tabard over all. Knowing that to leave anything in the chamber was to invite theft, he cast his cloak over his shoulders, grabbed up the remaining saddlebags, scanned the chamber, and set after his infuriated lady.

Not that he could blame Brianna for her response. Her guess was all wrong but Luc had not aided matters in the least.

Luc cursed himself up, down, and sideways as he slammed the door in his turn and stormed down the stairs. The lady had granted him a chance to pledge his love and he, he had been too much of a fool to give his feelings voice.

He had been so startled by Brianna's own confession of love that it had taken a trio of heartbeats to realize he loved her in turn.

But by then, the lady had been gone.

Luc kicked open the door to the street. If anything happened to Brianna, Luc would never forgive himself. 'Twas no consolation that the lady had a talent for casting caution to the winds and oft at her own expense.

Luc scanned the silent street to the left, the empty yard to the right. There was no sign of an enraged princess or even any echo of her passing.

But Brianna was a woman of good sense. She would head home to Tullymullagh, Luc was certain, and for that journey, she would need a steed. Luc strode for the stables in poor temper, never guessing what he would find when he flung open the door.

Ruarke de Rossiers stood behind Raphael, his hand clamped over Brianna's mouth and a wicked blade held to her throat. Her satchel had fallen at her feet.

Luc froze and stared. The lady's eyes were wide with terror but she appeared unhurt.

At least, as yet.

It seemed they had not fled the threat lurking at Tullymullagh, after all. And Luc had only himself to blame.

Ruarke smiled. "At last," he purred. "I had feared you might not deign to join us, Lord of Tullymullagh."

Luc stepped into the stables with a confidence he was far from feeling. He cast his saddlebags aside to have his hands free, should any opportunity to aid Brianna arise. When the door swung closed, there was naught but the glow of the dawn filtering through the boards to illuminate the space.

"You followed us," Luc charged.

"Aye, but I could not be certain where you slumbered. At least," Ruarke gave Brianna a shake and she glared at him, "not until this morn."

"What do you want?" Luc asked silkily. He took a step forward, but Ruarke retreated, the knife moving too enthusiastically against Brianna's throat for Luc's taste.

He halted and waited, hoping Brianna did naught to provoke her captor.

"I want the Rose of Tullymullagh," Ruarke declared boldly. "It should be mine. Connor had chosen me as his heir."

"Brianna made her own choice of spouse," Luc said softly, deliberately misunderstanding the other knight. "And our match is duly made."

Ruarke snorted. "I care naught for the woman!" He dug the blade into the soft flesh of Brianna's throat and could not completely muffle Brianna's cry of pain. Luc dove forward, but Ruarke shook his head and drew the princess to her very toes. Luc could see that Brianna was trembling with fear.

He had to aid her!

"Make no mistake," Ruarke purred. "She is a pretty enough prize, but the Rose is a finer one. And markedly less trouble. Give it to me, Luc, give to me my due and your bride *may* live."

"The Rose of Tullymullagh is naught but a legend," Luc argued, keeping his voice deliberately low and persuasive. " 'Tis long gone." He did not have the gem Ruarke claimed, yet somehow he had to see Brianna safe.

It seemed that Luc had few decent options.

"A lie!" Ruarke declared. "I know the Rose of Tullymullagh exists, just as I know it should be mine!"

"How can you be so certain?" Luc deliberately kept Ruarke talking in the hope that some path would become clear.

"I heard tell of it before Connor sent me abroad and then found an old compatriot who told me of it truly. He swore the old man would not be parted from the gem and that it must be hidden in the solar's private chapel itself."

Luc sauntered closer as he dared to speculate. "It must have been you I overheard in the stables."

"Ah!" Ruarke's eyes flashed. "You! You were the one who troubled this cursedly skittish beast?" Ruarke did not try to hide his scorn. " 'Tis no marvel that misfits like you and he should find each other." Raphael snorted and stamped, no less pleased to find this knight so close behind him again.

"But how could you have even been in the stables that night?" Luc asked calmly, determined to have all finally answered. " 'Twas days before you arrived again at Tullymullagh."

Ruarke laughed harshly. "I was there that night and several times before. Surely you do not imagine that I would sully myself with a deed as barbarous as warfare? I have my own good looks to assure, my steed's health to care for, my new caparisons to preserve."

He chuckled. "Nay, 'twas *perfect* when Connor sent me for aid, for I had the ideal excuse to remain abroad. In fact, I believe I may have given him the idea." Ruarke's eyes shone. "Yet I lingered nearby once I knew the prize I coveted was yet within those walls."

Brianna took a deep breath, her eyes flashing with indignation. 'Twas clear she thought little of the performance of Tullymullagh's pledged champion and Luc well recalled that there were many who had died in Gavin's assault.

He deliberately played the simpleton, fighting for time to find some solution to his conundrum. "But how could you return unobserved?"

"Three unfinished sections of the wall are there, and wilderness on three sides of Tullymullagh." Ruarke scoffed. " 'Twas easy for a man with something between his ears."

Luc arched a brow. "A man deserving of Connor's prize?"

"Aye! The Rose of Tullymullagh is no mere pretty wench, but a gem that would see a man's wealth assured for a lifetime. I wanted it, I *deserved* it, as Connor's chosen heir 'twas mine as much as Tullymullagh or his daughter.'' Ruarke chuckled. ''Though indeed, 'twas the only one of the lot I truly desired.''

Brianna gasped in outrage and struggled anew. Luc stepped forward, uncertain what Ruarke would do when his lips drew to such a cruel line.

But Brianna surprised them both.

Her eyes flashed, she abruptly lifted her heel and jammed it upward into the knight's crotch. Ruarke's eyes boggled, he staggered, Brianna jabbed an elbow in his ribs. Her wince revealed that Ruarke wore his chain mail, but in the same moment, Brianna slammed the top of her head against the underside of the knight's jaw.

Ruarke bellowed in pain. ''I bit my tongue!'' he roared as Brianna broke free. Luc lunged forward, cursing the distance he had to cover in short time.

''Luc!'' Brianna ran for Luc, but Ruarke snatched at her hair. He caught the end of Brianna's braid, and she gasped. Luc was halfway across the stable, but Ruarke had plenty of time to backhand Brianna and send her sprawling into a stall.

The stable echoed with the sickening crack of Brianna's head against the wood. Ruarke spat in the hay toward her limp form, then turned with a coldly confident smile that stopped Luc in his tracks.

''I will have the Rose now,'' Ruarke invited.

Luc halted and blinked. ''I do not have it.''

''You must!''

''I have never seen it nor laid a hand upon it.''

Brianna, to Luc's relief, stirred slightly. He flicked an intent glance her way when her eyes fluttered open and she froze in understanding. Then, she lay back against the wall, her face a mask of pain, and touched her fingertips to her head.

But she watched their exchange avidly.

Ruarke did not notice her awakening.

"You lie!" Ruarke's eyes flashed. " 'Twas in the chapel, I knew it well, but I knew not where." He advanced upon Luc, gesticulating wildly. " 'Twas bad fortune that Connor found us there, and poorer fortune that Father Padraig found *you* making off with the treasure. I know full well you hid it because you did not have it upon your person that night."

"So, 'twas you who attacked me, not Father Padraig?"

Ruarke grinned. "Though you surprised me, I must admit. I had to insult Gavin to provide a tale for your blackening of my eye."

"You killed the priest?"

"Father Padraig had outlived his usefulness." Ruarke scowled.

"And you killed Ismay?"

"Of course! That fool woman would have told all she knew, to the detriment of my plans." Ruarke's eyes narrowed in assessment. "Yet still I could not fathom where you had hidden the Rose."

"Such a prize must be kept safe," Luc countered evenly.

Ruarke smiled. "Trust me, I shall treasure it for all my days." He squared his shoulders and extended his hand. "And I saw you gather it when you left Tullymullagh. Give to me what you took from beside Eva's grave. Give to me what is rightfully mine."

Luc blinked.

Brianna's box.

The box of letters her sire had given her, letters purportedly written by Brianna's dame. If the Rose of Tullymullagh was indeed there, then that prize hung around Luc's very neck.

Brianna must never have seen the contents, for he knew she would not have lied to him.

But Luc would not surrender anything Brianna held so precious. Whether it held letters from her mother or a gem from her father mattered little.

'Twas her legacy and hers alone.

In that moment, Luc knew that he would break an old pledge to see matters come right. Aye, to see Brianna safe and her prize protected was worth abandoning a vow made in haste. 'Twas true enough that villains terrorized with their blades, but equally true that an honorable man could only defend the course of right with his own.

As Luc would defend his lady's claim to the box her father granted to her.

"I will not surrender it to you," he declared grimly.

"Then, you do have it!" Ruarke's eyes flashed victoriously.

"But still you cannot have it." Luc fingered the short dagger he carried at his belt and eyed the knight with resolve. "Though I have only a small blade, you will not win your prize easily from me."

Ruarke snorted laughter. "Another lie!" He reached into a saddlebag Luc only now noted resting on the floor. There was a flash as a blade was withdrawn and another as 'twas cast toward him. The sword buried its point in the wooden floor and quivered, the sunlight catching its wickedly sharp edge.

'Twas a good blade, if not a great one.

'Twould have to do.

"Take a blade and welcome to it," Ruarke declared with a cold grin. "Your sire shared the tale of your pledge to never take the hilt of a sword in your hand again." His lip curled. "Coward!"

Luc glanced to a watchful Brianna, then stepped forward

with purpose. He pulled the blade from the floor in one smooth move. Luc savored the weight of the weapon in his grip and deliberately met the startled gaze of his opponent.

"My sire oft misunderstands what is of import to me," he confided coolly.

Ruarke's eyes flashed, then he gripped his own blade. "I do not fear a rusty knight! Your skills will be as naught compared to mine!" Ruarke's sword flashed dangerously as he lifted it high. "To the death, Luc Fitzgavin, to the death for the Rose of Tullymullagh."

"To the death," Luc agreed coldly and adjusted his stance. "But for the honor of the lady, not the gem."

"Fool!" Ruarke lunged forward with sudden speed.

• • •

'TWAS NOT A fair fight!

Brianna struggled to rise as the knights' swords clashed heavily. Not only was she certain that Ruarke had not offered his better blade to his competitor—for Ruarke clearly had not a drop of chivalrous intent within his veins—but the former champion of Tullymullagh wore his mail.

Luc had none. And Luc had not raised a sword in over a decade. Brianna feared the lack of practice would not serve him well.

Even if his noble gesture had stolen her very breath away. She only wished she would have the chance to tell Luc as much.

Brianna clung to the edge of the stall and had to concede that Luc fought markedly well. His eyes flashed with determination, he parried and thrust with a vigor unexpected. His blade caught Ruarke on the elbow and that knight bellowed, no doubt more out of annoyance than pain. He dove after Luc once more and as they circled, Brianna had a dreadful glimpse of the fury burning in Ruarke's eyes.

How could she ever have imagined there was any kindness in his heart?

Luc's eyes, by contrast, were cold. He prodded Ruarke again and again, driving that man to retaliate with increasing vigor. Ruarke's color rose hotly on his neck, but Luc repeatedly danced from the path of his sword with agile grace.

'Twas as though he deliberately provoked the better-armed man. Brianna glimpsed the shine of perspiration on Ruarke's brow and recalled her sire's complaints about the cursed weight of mail.

Luc was tiring his opponent apurpose. And Ruarke, with every passing moment, struck more vigorously yet with less accuracy.

Brianna clasped her hands together and prayed fervently for Luc's success.

"I had expected you to be vastly more skilled," Luc commented in an undertone that revealed no strain.

Ruarke's nostrils flared. "I am a far finer knight than ever you might have been!" he retorted angrily. "For I am no coward!" And Ruarke punctuated his accusation with a savage slice at Luc's knees.

The sweep of the blade came dangerously close before Luc stepped nimbly out of its path. He arched a brow at Ruarke, taunting him to repeat the deed.

Ruarke cursed and attacked with renewed vigor. They battled endlessly back and forth across the stable, and Brianna caught her breath when Luc faltered.

'Twas not her imagination that he parried Ruarke's last thrust with less resolve. Was he more tired than she had guessed?

Ruarke clearly saw the same weakness. Brianna bit her knuckle in fear. Ruarke pounced upon Luc and, with a triumphant roar, drove his blade directly at Luc's very heart.

"Nay!" Brianna cried as Luc not only took the blow, but

fell to his back. He sprawled in the hay and, despite Brianna's fervent prayer, her spouse did not move again.

Luc's very stillness made Brianna's blood run cold.

Then she heard the scrape of Ruarke's dagger upon its sheath.

"Do not touch him!" she cried, but that knight only spared her a mocking glance.

" 'Twas to the death we fought, princess." Ruarke chuckled as he stepped over Luc. "Be patient but a moment until I finish the deed."

"Nay!" Brianna cried. She flung herself across the stable, uncertain how she would aid Luc but knowing she had to do something.

But in truth she did not.

No sooner had Ruarke bent over the inert Luc than that man made a marked recovery. Luc's sword flashed like lightning. Brianna saw his eyes flash with determination, and he drove his blade into his opponent's chest with sudden vigor.

Brianna gasped.

Ruarke stumbled backward, his fingertips touching the hilt of his own blade. "My blade," he murmured unevenly. "Mine own blade betrays me."

"As you have betrayed so many others," Luc said flatly. He rose to his own feet and watched the other knight falter, a decided chill in his eyes.

"You, you have the Rose of Tullymullagh," Ruarke muttered and clenched a shaking fist. " 'Tis unfair, 'tis wrong, it should have been *mine*!"

Luc raised his brilliant sapphire gaze to meet Brianna's own and her breath caught in her throat. "The Rose of Tullymullagh that was the greater prize could readily have been your own," he said with deliberation. "Had you had the wits to pursue it."

"Sentimental fool!" Ruarke looked at Luc in disbelief, then stumbled to his knees. He coughed, then gasped in pain as the blood coursed between his fingers. He paled, then fell bonelessly into a stall. The steed stabled there took but one look at the wounded knight beneath his own feet.

Then Raphael snorted and kicked Ruarke savagely in the head.

And the former champion of Tullymullagh was no more.

"Nay, 'twas you who was the fool, Ruarke de Rossiers," Luc stated with quiet resolve. He shook his head, then strode to Brianna's side.

"Are you injured?" Before Brianna could answer, Luc's fingers were quick and gentle in her hair.

She caught her breath when he found the sore spot on her head. " 'Tis but a small bump, Luc, and naught worthy of concern."

" 'Twas a fearsome crack," he insisted, his gaze bright with worry.

Brianna smiled up at him. "It has been said that my head is wondrously hard."

Luc smiled crookedly in turn. "Not by me."

"And what of you?" Brianna asked, her concern no less. "I thought that blow a telling one."

"Ah, but my lady wife ensured my survival." Luc's eyes twinkled, though Brianna could not imagine why. He reached beneath his tabard and tapped the spot with his fingertip where he had taken the blow.

The ring of metal was unmistakable.

Brianna felt her eyes go round. "The box with my dame's letters!"

"Aye, though, there may well be no letters within its sanctuary," Luc advised. He touched Brianna's cheek as though marvelling that she stood before him. "I hope I am wrong, for 'twas clear you looked forward to reading what she had written.''

Brianna ran her hands over his chest, still incredulous that he was not more sorely wounded. "The box took all of the strike? You are certain?''

Luc's smile turned rueful. "No doubt there is a dint in it like the bruise that will blossom on my chest. The blow took the wind from me, that much is certain.''

"But no more than that,'' Brianna breathed in relief.

"Nay.'' Luc smiled down into her eyes. "No more than that.'' The passion that suddenly shone in his eyes made Brianna's heart pound. "You left before I could find the words,'' he charged softly. "I should have never forgiven myself if you had paid a toll for that.''

Brianna did not dare to breathe. "What words?''

"I will have no doubt lingering in your mind, Brianna,'' he said in a low voice. "Know this and know it well, for naught but love could have persuaded me to take your hand. I did not know its name so soon as that, but from the first moment we met, you intrigued me as never a woman had before.''

Luc smiled. " 'Twas but a portent that you would seize my heart and make it your own.''

As Brianna watched, Luc dipped his head and brushed his lips across her knuckles, his bright blue gaze boring into her own. "I love you, Brianna. I swear it to you.''

His words rang with a conviction that could not be denied.

Before Brianna could catch her breath, Luc's smile turned teasing. "Though, truly, I should not have been surprised that you would lay claim to my heart while I was so diligently seeking yours. You have a way of confounding expectation, my lady.''

Brianna could not halt her delighted smile. "As do you, sir!''

"Ah, then perhaps we should confound each other for a good many years."

" 'Twould only be fitting!" Brianna retorted with a grin and Luc gathered her close.

The door of the stable creaked open in that inopportune moment. "Why in the name of God are you folk making such a noise so early in the morn?" complained the tavern proprietor. "I know well enough that you have a ship to meet that sails with the tide, but is it too much to ask for a little consideration . . ."

The man's words faltered as he evidently took in the sight before him.

Luc turned, Brianna's hand clasped firmly in his own, and his voice rang with authority. "This man, one Ruarke de Rossiers, killed Connor of Tullymullagh, Ismay of Claremont, and a priest known as Father Padraig."

"Mother of God!" the innkeeper whispered and crossed himself.

"He was once the champion of Tullymullagh and must have followed us here. He declared his intent to steal my wife and my steed out of some misbegotten conviction that they rightly belonged to him. There was naught I could do, of course, but defend my wife's honor."

Luc glanced at Raphael, then to the mark of his hoof upon Ruarke's brow. "The steed, like many of his ilk, is somewhat temperamental."

"Of course, my lord." The innkeeper's eyes went round. "What shall be done with him?"

"See that his body is sent to my steward Uther at Tullymullagh, complete with this tale. Uther shall see you duly compensated for your trouble."

The innkeeper bowed low. "Aye, my lord! But what of you?"

"My ship leaves this morn, with the very tide, as you

say." Luc turned and offered Brianna his hand. "Shall we, my lady?"

Brianna smiled and clasped Luc's hand within her own. "Of course."

• • •

BRIANNA DID NOT take well to the sea. Indeed, she turned pale as soon as they left the port and Luc spent the better part of the day holding her tightly while she vomited over the ship's rails.

He was not about to lose his bride now.

By nightfall, Brianna was weak but claimed she felt better. Luc carried her to the hold below, where one end had been left for them, the only paying passengers on this late season journey. The two palfreys and Raphael were tethered in makeshift stalls at midship and the captain had gruffly provided a curtain of sorts across the nook Luc and Brianna made their own.

Luc did as well as he was able to see to his lady's comfort. One lantern hung from the beam overhead, a veritable nest of cloaks surrounded her. The lady had charmed the ship's cook, even in her state, for that man brought her a hot cup of broth.

Once 'twas clear Brianna would hold the soup in her belly, Luc doffed his own clothes and curled his heat around her. Brianna cuddled against him as Luc reached for his satchel. He dug out a particular metal box and laid it in his wife's tiny hands.

She cradled it and slanted a glance his way. Brianna wrinkled her nose. "I am almost afraid to open it."

" 'Tis yours alone," Luc assured her quietly. "Whatever it contains."

Brianna ran her fingers over the new mark on its lid and smiled up at Luc. "My dame wanted you alive, make no mistake," she teased.

They exchanged a warm smile, then Brianna pried open the box. Luc hoped against hope that she would find some missive from her mother there.

But the pair caught their breath as one at the treasure revealed. 'Twas marvelous, far more beautiful than Luc could ever have expected.

The Rose of Tullymullagh.

'Twas a crucifix wrought of amber and set in gold, of a size that would nestle easily in Luc's flattened hand. Two rounded golden stones made each short arm, four equally large formed the long. Amethysts and pearls shone throughout the setting, and at the juncture where the arms met lay a ruby.

A blood red ruby the size of a man's thumb. 'Twas wondrously made, the craftsmanship superb, and Luc was awed that any man could be granted such a gift of kings.

Brianna touched the gem with trembling fingers and Luc heard her tears. "My sire was killed for this," she whispered unevenly.

"Nay!" He closed his hands over hers, his tone prompting her to meet his gaze. "Your sire was granted this," Luc corrected firmly. "As a token of esteem from an elderly couple who loved him as their very own. That is how and only how you must think of this prize."

Brianna smiled through the mist of her tears and ran her hand over the amber. "I do like that tale better." She traced the setting around the ruby with a fingertip. "They must have cared for him deeply."

"As he cared for you." Luc assured his lady. "Your sire wanted to ensure you had it as your own, no doubt that 'twould become an heirloom to be prized." Brianna glanced up at him once more and Luc smiled. "Though indeed, its symbolism of that love is the more powerful legacy."

Brianna held Luc's gaze long and slowly her sadness

eased. Luc glanced to the box, yet within her hands, and frowned at a glimpse of parchment. "Look! There is something else beneath it."

Brianna looked in turn, her tiny fingers trembling as she unfolded not one, but two sheets of vellum. The ink was faded, but still the script stretched from edge to edge, and 'twas clearly from an educated hand. She turned the fragile pieces in her hands, scanning them with evident anticipation.

And Brianna crowed with delight when she found what she sought.

"Luc! 'Tis signed by my dame!" She turned shining eyes upon him, and he smiled at her delight. "These are letters in her hand to my father!" Brianna shook her head and surveyed the contents of the box once again. "I never would have expected to have such a treasure, let alone the Rose of Tullymullagh itself."

"Nay," Luc corrected quietly. When Brianna looked at him in confusion, Luc grinned. "The Rose of Tullymullagh," he murmured with intent, "is mine alone." Brianna giggled as Luc bent and kissed that very rose so thoroughly that she could giggle no more.

'Twas no laughing matter for a man to claim his lady's heart for his very own.

No less to grant her the custody of his heart in exchange.

Epilogue

Tullymullagh
April 1172

'T WAS EASTER SUNDAY AT TULLYMULLAGH, THE promise of spring in the air and the first hint of green tinting the ground. The sun shone with vigor, the birds had begun to sing. 'Twas a season of rebirth and renewal, a time of reaffirming bonds betwixt lord and tenant.

Brianna and Luc, recently returned from Llanvelyn, strolled from the village chapel through the throngs of villagers. The walls had been completed beneath Uther's supervision this winter, much to Brianna's relief. Now all followed the pair to the hall, bearing customary gifts of eggs, chattering merrily, all eagerly anticipating the hearty feast the Lord and Lady of Tullymullagh would grant their tenants.

Indeed, the most tempting scents carried from the kitchens into the bailey. All of the villagers had a word of welcome upon their lips, all lips curved in smiles. More than one pressed a first flower into their lady's hands and she flushed beneath her husband's proud glance. 'Twould be a week of great festivity and Brianna was glad to be home.

She had liked Llanvelyn's pastoral beauty well enough and its tenants had been charming as well. But Brianna had seen quickly that Luc did not intend to tarry there. She accompanied him to Pyrs' grave and knew she did not imagine that Luc said farewell. She understood they would return to Llanvelyn at intervals to ensure that all went well, but Tullymullagh would be their home.

Brianna hugged the secret lodged in her belly and thought perhaps Llanvelyn would be a good gift for their son.

If indeed, 'twas a son she bore. A daughter would be just as welcome, she decided with a smile.

They had nearly reached the portal of the hall when the echo of hoofbeats made all turn to the gates. A black destrier trotted proudly under the portcullis, tossing his mane when the knight astride him pulled him to a halt before the company.

" 'Tis Burke," Luc murmured in evident astonishment, then strode to welcome his brother.

Brianna wondered why Luc's brother had returned here. Surely he could not bear some summons from Gavin? Surely Burke had not surrendered anew to his father's authority?

The brothers shook hands, Burke saying something to Luc before they turned as one to Brianna. What was this? They matched steps, looking more similar than Brianna had realized before. Not only were they of similar height and build, but there was a steadiness in both knights' eyes that was compelling.

Though only one man's sapphire gaze could make her heart leap.

To Brianna's astonishment, Burke dropped to one knee before her. "My Lady of Tullymullagh, 'tis the season for atonement and I do owe to you an apology."

Brianna blinked, uncertain what to make of this confession. She looked to Luc, but he appeared as bewildered as she. "An apology?" she echoed.

Burke nodded but once. "Though I see all has ended well enough, I must confess that I did not take wholeheartedly to your quest. I did you grave disservice, my lady, in not truly endeavoring to win your hand."

Brianna gasped in surprise. "So, Gavin was right!"

Burke grimaced. "Aye, he knows me well enough." He flicked a glance to Luc and thence to Brianna, inclining his head once more. "I grant you belated congratulations on your nuptials and trust you found what you sought."

Brianna looked to Luc in turn and felt herself flush as she smiled. "Aye, that and more." Luc lifted a brow, and she turned her attention back on the repentant knight before her. "But why did you not truly pursue the quest? Did you not desire a bride?"

Burke sighed and frowned. "I could not in good conscience court the esteem of a lady when my own heart is securely held by another."

"Who is she?" Brianna asked with delight. "When are you to be wed?"

But Burke's eyes were filled with sadness. "It matters little. Alys spurned me, seven years past, though still she holds my heart in thrall."

"Oh! She did not return your regard?"

"She did not know of it," Burke declared grimly. "I never told her, to my own regret."

"If you love her, she must be told!" Burke looked uncertain, so Brianna put her hand on his shoulder, wanting only to persuade him. "Burke, do not repeat an error I nearly made! I thought to spurn Luc when I doubted his heart," she confessed softly. "But I was wrong. 'Twould have been most grievous, if he had not told me the truth, for we would have sacrificed the happiness we now share."

Burke shook his head in defeat. "But I do not know where Alys has gone. She fled her family home." He frowned anew and cleared his throat. "My lady, this is not for you to resolve. I came here only to apologize, for my behavior was unchivalrous."

Brianna straightened as an impulsive thought came to her. "I will not forgive you," she declared pertly, enjoying how quickly both brothers' heads snapped up.

"Brianna!"

"My lady!"

Brianna lifted her chin. "I will *only* forgive you if you seek this Alys and tell her of your love." The men blinked. "I will only forgive you, Burke de Montvieux, if you depart upon your own quest for a bride. And without delay."

Burke looked dumbfounded by this condition, but Luc began to chuckle. Brianna met her husband's sparkling gaze and smiled beneath his proud regard. "The lady makes good sense in this as much else," he counselled his brother. "Indeed, Brianna holds love in such great esteem that she has persuaded me to her cause."

Burke looked between the two of them, though truly Brianna was aware of little but the love shining in her husband's eyes.

"I will do it!" Burke declared suddenly. The assembly, listening carefully to every word, erupted anew in a cheer. "I will find Alys and tell her the truth!" The knight rose from his knees with purpose. "I will go this very moment."

"Nay, stay for the midday meal at least, brother of mine," Luc teased, then winked at Brianna. "If Alys proves as much of a challenge to your convictions as Brianna did to mine, you shall need your strength."

"Oh!" Brianna launched herself at her husband and he scooped her up in his arms as he laughed. She tapped his chest with her fingertip, more than happy to be nestled against him as he strolled toward the hall once more, Burke trailing a discreet distance behind. "I am not so troublesome as that, sir!"

"Nay, but you are most beguiling when your eyes flash." Luc punctuated his declaration with a kiss. Unable to wait a moment longer, Brianna whispered to Luc the news she had been saving. She was not disappointed by his response.

"A child? You bear a child?"

"I bear your child."

Luc scanned the bailey anxiously. "Is there a midwife at Tullymullagh?"

Brianna laughed. "Luc! Such aid will not be needed for another six months."

"One cannot prepare overmuch," he said grimly.

Brianna grasped his hand and laid it firmly on her still-flat belly. "We shall have ample warning, Luc, that such time is upon us."

He exhaled and grinned, bouncing her lightly in his arms. "Aye, you speak aright." Then he caught her against his chest, his sapphire gaze sobering. "I would not lose you in this, Brianna. There is no choice between you and a babe."

She kissed his cheek, easing the furrows of concern from his brow. Indeed, she was humbled by the depth of love shining in his eyes. "There is no choice to make, Luc."

"But you are so tiny!"

"My dame was tinier than I and was said to have managed the deed with ease."

Luc's eyes narrowed assessingly. "Then why do you have no brothers and sisters?"

Brianna lifted a brow. "My father would not hear of her conceiving again." She felt her lips curve in a smile. " 'Twas the only thing they argued about, to my recollection."

Luc harumphed and ducked beneath the portal without

putting her on her feet. "Yet again, I can only conclude that Connor of Tullymullagh was a man of rare good sense," he declared with resolve. "Time 'tis, Brianna, that you were warm in the hall."

"Luc, I can yet walk!"

"You should not strain yourself."

Brianna laughed aloud at his protectiveness, even as she kicked her feet playfully. "One day," she scolded lightly, "you will realize that I am not wrought of gossamer like a fairy queen."

"And do you imagine, Brianna," Luc asked, his voice so low that it awakened all the tingles within her, "that 'twill make any difference at all?"

Just one look into the intense blue of Luc's eyes told Brianna the truth. She caught her breath and shook her head beneath his steady regard, transfixed as Luc slowly smiled.

For the certainty of Luc's love suited Brianna of Tullymullagh very well indeed.

If you enjoyed the romantic tale of Luc and Brianna in THE PRINCESS, you will absolutely fall in love with Burke de Montvieux as he goes on his quest for a bride in Claire Delacroix's, THE DAMSEL, the second book in the Bride Quest Trilogy.

This is a Cinderella story unlike any you've ever read. Turn the page and you'll get a preview that will no doubt leave you breathless and waiting for this next book.

Chapter One

BURKE DE MONTVIEUX CRESTED A RISE, REINED IN his destrier, and stared at the scene spread before him. He had ridden hard for three days, pushing his steed to the limits of the beast's endurance. Burke's heart was pounding, and he felt a rare impatience flood through his veins.

For his objective lay directly before his eyes.

Castle Kiltorren clung to the craggy west coast of Ireland, its moss-encrusted stone walls rising from the rock as if they always had been thus. Clouds swept in from the west to blanket the sky in pearly silver as the air turned chill.

With the fey moodiness of early spring, the sun had been hot this day before secreting itself away. Indeed, a trickle of sweat ran down the midst of Burke's back beneath his mail, the cool salt wind that assaulted him on this rise prompting a shiver.

The shadows were drawing long as mist rose from the dark water to shroud Kiltorren's tower. Burke could hear the waves pounding beneath its farthest walls. The sun hung low over the horizon, an angry red glow that pierced the clouds and painted the sea with a ribbon of light.

It had been two years since Burke had last seen the spire

of Kiltorren, three years since a maid's sparkling eyes had captivated his heart beneath that tower's long shadow. Twice he had been there, twice he had found naught but heartache at Castle Kiltorren.

Yet the love he had so fleetingly tasted brought Burke back yet again. And as he paused on the high rise of the road, the familiar keep before him, Burke de Montvieux was deluged by memories.

• • •

THE SUMMONS TO tournament could not have come at a better moment, for as a young knight, Burke's spurs were fresh on his heels, his newly earned blade a welcome weight in his hand. Like his fellows, he was eager to prove himself upon the field, and he was not alone in answering the Lord of Kiltorren's call.

Burke was, however, alone in noting that lord's niece, Alys of Kiltorren.

The lord Cedric and his lady wife, Dierdre, were arrayed in their finest to meet the arriving party of knights, jewels flashing on every finger in the summer sunlight. The way they pushed their two daughters forward made their true objectives more than clear, although those two young women were scarcely worthy of note.

One had been spared no indulgence in her garb and was ornamented far beyond her family's station, her tiny eyes taking greedy note of the caliber of each knight's steed and entourage. The second seemed terrified to be singled out thus, and spent the better part of the ceremonies staring at her hands.

But one lady there was, standing to the back of the party, not part of the servants, yet not of the family proper either. Her expression and pose were of resignation; the very fact that she was not considered to be worthy of note had caught Burke's eye.

And once he drew near and looked upon her, the lady's gentle beauty snared Burke's interest fully. Her heart-shaped face was as sweet as that in any bard's tale; her full ruddy lips looked in dire need of a smile. The unadorned indigo of her fitted kirtle showed her slender curves to advantage, for she was as tall and slender as a keen blade. An errant curl of her wavy blond hair had escaped her veil and danced against her cheek in the breeze, as though beckoning to Burke.

But a single glimpse and Burke knew he must learn more of this lady. Impatient with introductions, he nodded hastily to Lady Dierdre, her daughters Malvina and Brigid, then turned his finest smile upon Lord Cedric when that man appeared to have said all he intended.

"Is this lady also of your family?" Burke asked smoothly, and gestured to the beauty behind.

The lady in question flushed in a most beguiling way. Lady Dierdre's eyes flashed. Malvina—the spoiled one—grimaced, and Lord Cedric coughed into his hand.

"She is but a niece," he declared with a curl of his lip. "But a ward of the family, devoid of dowry and scarce worthy of note."

Burke thought precisely the opposite and did not take pains to hide his conclusion. "Surely, 'tis not too much to ask the honor of making her acquaintance?"

Lord Cedric scowled, then turned a fierce glare upon his niece. Her eyes widened slightly and, too late, Burke saw that she would be the one to bear the burden of his curiosity.

Then she stepped forward and Burke cared for naught else.

"My niece," Lord Cedric supplied testily. "Alys of Kiltorren." His wife sniffed in ill-concealed disdain.

Clearly unused to such attention, Alys flushed and shyly smiled when Burke kissed her knuckles. Her hand trembled slightly within his, and Burke resolved at that very moment to pursue this lady. He would know more of her, he would prompt her laughter, he would discover why her family thought her worthy only of disregard.

• • •

BURKE SIGHED AND rubbed a hand across his brow, wishing he had not been so young, so trusting, so certain that naught could stand between him and the course of love.

For he had sought Alys in every corner of the hall, each exchange convincing him yet further that she was a woman of merit. Burke had coaxed her laughter early and had felt a thrill of victory beyond that won on any field when her brown eyes sparkled. Those eyes were of the most wondrous shade, a marvelous golden brown flecked with specks of sunlight that seemed to dance when Alys laughed.

And her eyes had glowed when Burke had claimed his first kiss from his lady fair. But Alys had kissed the ardent knight back, and it took no more than that encouragement to see Burke smitten.

There had been more sweet kisses and more laughter, more tales of dreams and desires, more stolen moments than Burke could name, each one putting him more securely beneath the lady's spell. For the first time in all his days, Burke had fallen in love.

And it seemed his regard was returned.

Until that ill-fated day in the stables. Burke scowled at the distant keep, knowing he would never forget the fleeting moment that had changed all.

• • •

BURKE FOUND ALYS in the stables that warm afternoon. 'Twas not by accident, for he had been seeking her, though he feigned that he but stumbled upon her. Alys, of course, saw through his artifice. Burke laughed at her teasing accusation.

For Alys was consigned to some ignoble labor, no doubt to keep her out of his sight, but even in such circumstance the lady shone like a beacon. She smiled at Burke, but would hear naught of him taking the labor upon himself. Burke lingered; indeed, he could not tear himself away from her presence. Just to know she was near made Burke's heart pound; the barest glimpse of a smile made him long for another of her sweet kisses.

On this day Alys's hair was tied up and her kirtle worn thin. It gaped around the fullness of her breasts in a most intriguing way, her ankles flashing beneath the hem. 'Twas clear the gown was a remnant from years before the lady's figure bloomed to perfection. Burke hated that she must bear such indignity, and knew there must be some way he could see matters set to rights.

When she made to heft a full bucket of slops, Burke could bear the injustice no longer. He strode to her side and swept the full bucket out of her grip. "Where do you take this?"

Alys's eyes widened. "Burke, you cannot! 'Tis unfitting!"

"'Tis more unfitting that you perform such labor," he said grimly. "You have but to tell me where."

"But you are a guest!"

"And you are a lady." His determination must have shown, for Alys shook her head and smiled.

She folded her arms across her chest and regarded him, a teasing glint in those golden eyes. "You, sir, are most stubborn."

Burke grinned and put down the bucket, taking a step closer. The lady's eyes gleamed as she evidently guessed his intent, and she took a playful step back.

'Twas clear she had no objections, and Burke grinned as he easily backed her into the wooden wall of the stall. "And you, my lady fair, are most fetching." He lifted one hand to the soft curve of her jaw, but Alys laughed aloud.

"In this?" She gestured to her tattered kirtle and wrinkled her nose in a most fetching way, then laughed anew. *"Burke, is it your wits you have lost or your sight?"*

"It is my heart that I have lost," he confided, trapping Alys within the circle of his arms. 'Twas not the first time he had cornered her thus, and Burke saw anticipation light her eyes.

"Incorrigible," she charged, a dimple appearing in one cheek. Her eyes sparkled merrily and Burke could see the flutter of her heartbeat at her throat. He touched her creamy flesh with a fingertip, liking well how she caught her breath, and let it wander along the edge of the ill-fitting kirtle.

"Tempted," he acknowledged, and ran that fingertip across the ripe curve of her breast when it tried to escape her kirtle. Alys gasped. Burke let his palm graze her nipple, and when she whispered his name, he could not resist her any longer.

Burke bent his head and captured the lady's lips beneath his own even as his hand slid beneath her gown to caress her bare breast. She surged against him, her hands slid into his hair, and Burke had caught her fully against him for the first time. She was all sweetness and softness, both strong and supple, and Burke wanted naught but to make this woman his own.

• • •

THAT SINGLE KISS had been their undoing. Burke could taste Alys still, he could feel his heart hammering, he could smell the straw heated in a summer's sunlight. He could see the shine of wonder in Alys's marvelous eyes.

And he could feel the curve of her breast beneath his hand once more, the taut nipple jutting against his palm.

But at that very moment the stable door had been kicked open to hue and cry, lord and lady and half the household pouring in to demand an accounting. Burke closed his eyes against the recollection of their din; he hated the memory of his own failure to conjure some manner of suitable explanation.

He felt again his anguish when Alys flushed scarlet and—to Dierdre's muttered accusation *"whore!"*—fled the stables, clutching the front of her kirtle.

Little did Burke know that he would never see Alys again.

Aye, he had tried to pursue her, but without success, for the family had barricaded him in that stall. Burke scowled with recollection. It had been nigh half a day before he broke free of their incessant questions, and that only because he roared he would wed the woman, if only to silence them.

His declaration had both silenced them and sent them away to consult among themselves. Alys, it seemed, was not interested in any such match, for the word came that evening that she would have none of his proposal. Indeed, 'twas said she refused even to see him again. Burke was sent from Kiltorren's gates, caught in an unfamiliar maelstrom of emotion.

An older knight had informed Burke he would grow to be glad that all had finished as it had. In his youth and uncertainty, Burke had dared to hope that Alys's choice might all be truly for the best.

A mere year away from Castle Kiltorren had only proved the strength of Alys's grip upon Burke's heart. She haunted him, she occupied his dreams, he fancied he heard her laughter in the thousand murmurings of any crowded hall. Finally, Burke had returned to Kiltorren, newly determined to see the lady, determined to either destroy her hold over him of hear rejection from her own lips.

But Lady Dierdre and Lord Cedric had confessed that Alys was gone, they knew not where. The magnitude of Burke's disappointment had nearly taken him to his knees, and he had left this place yet again with a heavy heart.

He eyed the village and the fields from the crest of the road, all those old feelings coursing through him, and noted that the holding had changed little. Burke could not help but wonder whether all would be the same within its walls.

Could Alys have returned?

Would a confession of love have earned a different response from Alys than three years past? Would such words make a difference to her now?

There was but one way to find out.

Suddenly Burke heard the gatekeeper's cry of warning and realized the twilight fell across the land. His heart leapt and he gave Moonshadow his spurs, determined to pass beneath Kiltorren's gates before they closed this night.

Indeed, the sun already dipped dangerously low.